The Asymptote's Tail

ONYXIS STONE PRESS, First Print Edition, May 2015
ONYXIS STONE PRESS, Firstish Print Edition, August 2015

Copyright © 2015 by Bryan Perkins
Print ISBN: 978-0-9963953-1-1
eBook ISBN: 978-0-9963953-0-4

www.bryanperkinsauthor.com

The Asymptote's Tail

Bryan Perkins

ONYXIS STONE PRESS

For you.

Table of Contents

nulla. Shoveler

The black coal burned bright and hot. Each load he piled onto the Furnace's fire brought it that little bit closer to white in his impossible pursuit of the asymptote's end.

His limbs moved unconsciously. Shadows cut across his stomach and chest. The towering fire danced all over his skin.

With his rhythm, there was no way the Creator could be ignorant of the roar of his flame, not even with Her fingers stuck in Her ears. His muscles moved in perfect lock-step with one another, bringing his fire closer to white hot than it had ever been before.

He inhaled a deep breath of the dark smoke, savoring the taste of his labor, picturing the black mountain behind him—too tall to see the peak of even in the light of the Furnace itself—as the coal supply continued to grow despite his every effort to deplete it. He dug deeper into himself, shoveling harder and faster to match the speed of the pourer who replenished his mound, when the cough of a watcher sent his shovel off target, breaking him away from his spiritual connection to the Furnace.

"*Hoooooot!*" he whistled, trying to get back into his rhythm. "*Hoooooot!*"

That tiny thing didn't belong anywhere near the Furnace. He never understood why the Creator saw need for such a frail being in the first place. It and the other watchers, each one an equally useless battery for him to recharge with his personal labor. Their lungs weren't even capable of recycling carbon fumes!

He shook his head at the thought of their ineptitude, shoveling more and larger piles of coal into the fury of productivity, driving the fire ever closer to white hot, and imagining the watcher's skin melting under the heat he produced.

He smiled. What irony it was. The watcher was sent to him as some punishment, he was sure—they always seemed to hate their every second near the Furnace—but what sort of punishment could it be? To witness the miracle of production at its most basic level. To become a part of the Furnace itself.

He nodded in rhythm with his shoveling. That must have been it. It was in their name. Their punishment was that of watching without being able to do. He couldn't think of anything more torturous than to be forced to sit idly by as another reaped the glory of production which he was made to forego. No wonder watchers were such wretched little beasts. They—

The thought stopped. He blacked out into nothingness for what seemed like a split second.

—lived wretched little lives.

When his senses returned, flames licked and spit against his heat resistant skin. He couldn't tell how long he had been out for, but it was more than a second. The fire had escaped from the Furnace which was all but gone, covered in cement rubble. Above the debris, dim rays peeked through the black clouds. The entire plant must have come down on top of him.

The watcher. Where was it? He tore through the remains of the plant, shoveling through cement debris like any other pile of coal, looking for the mutilated body of the watcher so he could destroy it further. *It* was responsible for this. It and the others like it. They had to be. Who else could it be? They were trying to shirk their punishment.

"*Hoooooot!*" he screamed, forcing recycled oxygen through his vocal organ. "*Hoooooot!*"

He dug through the rubble around him, frantic to reconnect with the Creator, still finding no sign of the watcher. "*Hoooooot!*" he whistled, tearing his way up the black coal mountain, crawling on hands and knees, hooting all the way, to stand atop the summit and cry at the top of his whistle, "*Hoooooot!*" Hurry up builders! "*Hoooooot!*"

For as far as his eyes could see, in every direction, there were identical mountains of coal, crumbling cement at their feet, each with their own shoveler, standing on the peak, whistling for the return of the Furnace.

ༀ ✳ ༀ

I. Haley

In her spartan grey kitchen, it was a pleasure to cook second breakfast. The smell of bacon sizzling gave Haley a hunger no protein smoothie could ever cure. The only way it could be better was if she could taste the bacon, but Lord Walker would punish her for even the tiniest missing crumb. She shuddered for a moment at the thought of it, then went back to the joy of cooking.

The kitchen was efficient. Counters lined three walls of the room with not two steps between parallel sides. The 3D printer and trash chute were set flush with the counter on the third wall, and Haley stood at the stove on one side of the room, cooking four pieces of bacon and four eggs in two separate pans.

She thought about the cyclical nature of mealtime as she watched the meat sizzle and waited for the coffee to percolate. Two eggs, two strips of bacon, and two pieces of toast for first breakfast. Four eggs, four strips of bacon, and four pieces of toast for second breakfast. Eight eggs, eight strips of bacon, and eight pieces of toast for third breakfast. And so on and so on until fifth breakfast. Then the bust and back to one hamburger, one french fried potato, and one loaf of bread pudding for first lunch. Two hamburgers, two french fried potatoes, and two loaves of bread pudding for second lunch. Over and over again every single day. It reminded her of the numbers she ran for Lord Walker at the Market, the way they went up and up and up, and you had to try to guess exactly when they'd shoot back down. She almost laughed thinking about it.

The toaster popped, and she ordered a jar of jam, a tray, a plate, a mug, and some platinumware from the printer then set to spreading the toast with jam. Her movements were so well-rehearsed they took on the fluid motion of dance as she laid each egg on a piece of toast, crossed the room on her toes to toss the pan in the trash chute—Lord Walker preferred the taste when she used a fresh pan every time—then twirled back around to stack the bacon on top of that. She pirouetted to throw out the next pan, tip-toed to pour a cup of coffee, then curtsied deep as she set the mug on the tray, laying the finishing touches on second breakfast.

With the tray propped up over her shoulder, she pushed her way through the only door in the kitchen—on the fourth wall of the small room—out into an elaborately decorated hallway. Though "hallway" may not be the right word for it. It was about as long as it was wide and larger even than the kitchen. The walls were covered in colorful silken tapestries and gold-framed paintings depicting tuxedoed owners climbing piles of money, the ceiling and floor were lined with ornate platinum filigree, and the carpet was the softest surface that Haley had ever touched. To her right was the door to the garage, and to her left was the door to Lord Walker's room which she entered without knocking.

Lord Walker's room was decorated with the same filigree as the hall. The bed was an ornate four-poster, covered in silk sheets and a velvet bedspread, which took up most of the space in the bedroom. Lord Walker's gargantuan, lumpy body was propped up with a stack of pillows behind his back, so he could watch the television which hung across the room as it spat out stock numbers and made predictions as to what should be bought and what should be sold. Their suggestions were always so wrong, Haley wondered why Lord Walker listened to them—especially since she was the one who ran the numbers at the Market anyway.

"Haley, sweetheart," Lord Walker said through a mass of egg and bacon. A little half-chewed glob of something dribbled out onto his beard as he spoke, and Haley shuddered at the thought of cleaning it out later. "Just in time, my dear," he went on, not noticing a thing. "As I finish my final morsel of first breakfast, here comes you, carrying breakfast two. *Ho ho ho.*" His whole body jiggled with his laughter, and Haley had to hurry to catch the empty coffee cup it sent tumbling off his tray. "And again you save me," he said. "Twice in ten seconds. *Ho ho ho.*"

Haley waited until his jiggling was done before setting the newly filled tray on his lap. She didn't need a similar accident with hot coffee.

"Sweetheart," Lord Walker said, pointing at the TV. "Would you be so kind as to change the channel for your Lord? Put the reality network on, would you? I've had enough of work this morning. *Ho ho ho.*"

Haley changed the channel for him. It wouldn't have taken

Lord Walker more than the effort to think it and it would have happened, but Haley didn't question it. He probably had more important things on his mind. He couldn't waste his brain power with such base work. On the screen now—instead of endless stock numbers—were several tiny children working in a factory. Haley tried to imagine what it would feel like to be so small, to be a child, but Lord Walker interrupted her thought.

"Speaking of enough work," he said. "I think I'll stop with third breakfast this morning. We have Christmas Feast today, so I want to be at the top of my game. Three breakfasts should be a healthy warm-up, wouldn't you agree?" He chuckled, patting his stomach which folded and flopped dangerously close to the still steaming cup of coffee.

"Yes, sir," Haley said with a curtsy, though she couldn't take her eyes off the children on the screen. The way their bodies fit into the tiny crevices to clean the places no one else could reach left her in awe of their ability, like they were perfectly molded parts of the machine itself.

"Very good," Lord Walker said. "Thank you, dear." He waved his fork at her. "Run along then."

"Yes, sir." Haley broke away from the screen and carried the empty dishes back to the trash chute. As the bedroom door swung closed behind her, she thought she heard the sound of tiny voices screaming, but she tried to ignore it.

She set to cooking the eight eggs, eight strips of bacon, and eight pieces of toast for third breakfast and wondered why the Creator would let those children feel pain, why She would give them the ability to scream. She touched the pan with the bacon cooking in it. How would it have to feel to make her want to scream like that? Could she even scream like that? Could she get louder than a polite, "Yes, sir"?

She almost found out when she heard a meow behind her. She stifled a scream and turned to find a black cat licking itself on the counter. When it saw that it had her attention, the cat rubbed its face on the faucet.

"Hello," Haley said with a smile, after she had gotten over the initial shock. She had no idea how the cat always got in so quietly and had never once seen where it leaves to. "Are you thirsty?" She turned the faucet on a dribble and the cat lapped up the water. "There you are," she said, patting it once and noticing its collar was red instead of the yellow it had been for some time. Then she remembered Lord Walker's breakfast. She finished up the bacon and eggs, and when she turned around to get a new set of dishes, the cat was gone.

Haley carried third breakfast to Lord Walker's room, and he jiggled in his bed at the sight of her, knocking an entire tray onto the floor with a clatter. At first she thought he was choking and rushed to his side to help, but when she set the tray on the side table, he finally got it out of his mouth, "Look!" he said. "The screen! You'll miss it!"

Relieved, Haley turned to see Lord Walker—his upper body rolling and folding over the pneumatic pants that held his weight up for him—on the screen in a tuxedo and top-hat with monocle in eye and cane in hand. He was prancing up and down a red carpet with celebrities, musicians, and sports stars all trying to shake his hand, take his picture, or get his autograph. In a deep, bodiless voice a narrator spoke over the video. "Lord Walker, your Christmas Feast Head. Not only the richest man in the world, he's the celebrity's celebrity." Then it cut to graphs and numbers depicting his net worth.

"So," he said with a proud grin. "What do you think? Perfect, isn't it."

"Yes, sir." Haley nodded.

"You're right it is," Lord Walker said, trying to slap his knee but hitting a fold of fat instead. "And that'll be in every owner's home with a right to be at the Feast. That *was* in every owner's home with a right to be at the Feast. And you know what they're all thinking right now?" He grinned from ear to ear.

"No, sir." Haley shook her head, lowering her eyes.

"*I guess I'll have to listen to that Lord Walker lord it over us again*," he said. "That's what! *Ho ho ho.*" Haley thought the bed might break from all his shaking. "Oh, yes," he went on. "And that they will, dear. That they will." He shook his head, composing himself. "I only need you to be a sweetheart and go make some trades for me first. Can you do that, dear?"

"Yes, sir." Haley curtsied.

"Of course you can," Lord Walker said. "This is what I need from you: First, drop some textiles. That's a dangerous industry if you ask me. *Ho ho ho*."

"Yes, sir."

"And pick up some more policing. I know we own most of the stocks in Outland 1 already but we need more. You got that? You can never have enough protection."

"Yes, sir."

"Then there's this Russ Logo." Lord Walker smiled. "He's an actor. Have you heard of him?"

"No, sir."

"Of course not, dear," Lord Walker said with a chuckle. "But he's the next big thing in propaganda. I *guar-an-tee* it. Pick up as much ownership in him as you can. You got that?"

"Yes, sir."

"Ok. Good. Now repeat it back to me." Lord Walker went back to eating as she did.

"Drop textiles," Haley said. "Pick up protectors and Logo."

"Bingo," Lord Walker said, flinging some eggs around in his excitement. "*Perfecto*. And be bold, darling. I have a Feast to Lord over."

"Yes, sir," Haley said with a curtsy and a smile. She picked up the empty tray and carried it to the kitchen.

Why did he always make her repeat it? As if she couldn't remember simple instructions or didn't know how to trade stocks. *She* did all the trading. The only time he ever set foot near the Market was to ring the New Year bell or film a commercial. He wouldn't be the richest owner in the world if it weren't for her. But at least she got to go to the Market for a while. She tidied up the kitchen one last time and headed the other way down the hall to the garage.

The garage was a vast cave lined with cars and trucks and buses and RVs. The floors were shiny, and the walls and ceiling looked like a hangar made out of platinum. There were vehicles of every make and model imaginable, but only two that ever got used: the giant white stretch Hummer—which was the only thing big enough to fit Lord Walker comfortably—and the tiny silver Tesla coupe that he allowed Haley to use. She got inside the one-seater and said, "Market."

The engine started without a sound. She felt like she was gliding as it rolled out through the garage door and into the Market employee parking garage. The employee parking garage was smaller than the owner's garage—smaller even than Lord Walker's private garage—and instead of entering onto the Wall Street photo-op set, the employee garage entered onto the Market proper where the trading actually occurred.

The Market itself wasn't much: a few folding tables and office chairs, with a touchscreen on one of the gray brick walls, that was about it. There were never more than thirty or forty secretaries there at one time—most owners chose to do their trading remotely—but much like he preferred to have his food printed fresh and prepared on-site, Lord Walker preferred doing his trading the old-fashioned way—or at least he preferred that Haley did it the old-fashioned way for him.

Today there were only three other secretaries at the Market, two who Haley didn't know by name—she had never traded with them—only by their model number and the net worth of their employers, and Rosalind, Mr. Douglas's secretary—Mr. Douglas being the second richest owner in Inland. As soon as Haley walked in, Rosalind initiated a conversation with her.

"Hello," Rosalind said, looking so awkward in her funny pantsuit. She never wore the black and white laced uniform shared by all the other secretaries.

"Hello," Haley replied with a slight nod.

"You're Lord Walker's secretary."

Haley couldn't tell if it was a question or a statement. "Yes," she said.

"Mr. Douglas is creeping up on him." Rosalind smiled.

Haley smiled back. "Not if I can help it," she said with a wink.

"What are you looking for today?"

"Oh, dropping some textiles, picking up some protectors."

"Was it the accident?" Rosalind frowned.

"Accident?"

"Lord Walker didn't say why?" Rosalind shook her head.

Haley shook hers, too. She was surprised to feel her cheeks flush. Usually only Lord Walker could make her feel that way.

"I can do that," Rosalind said. "Protectors for textiles."

"Oh—*uh*—deal," Haley said, absently, still trying to control her blushing.

"Deal," Rosalind repeated, extending her hand.

Haley shook it and nodded, then started towards the touchscreen on the far wall to set up the order for Logo shares, but Rosalind put her hand on Haley's shoulder to stop her before she could get very far.

"Yes?" Haley said, turning and trying to smile.

"Lord Walker," Rosalind said. "How does he treat you?"

Haley thought about it for a second. She didn't know how to answer. Lord Walker treated her like she had always been treated. "I'm sorry. I don't understand."

"You know," Rosalind said. "Is he bossy? Is he nice? Does he try to touch you? How does he treat you?"

Haley thought about it again. How could a secretary use such unproductive words? "He treats me like his secretary," she said.

Rosalind dropped her hand from Haley's shoulder. She half smiled but her eyes didn't look the part. "Good luck with your purchases," she said, and she walked out to the owner's garage.

Haley stood there in a daze. Rosalind was like no other secretary she had ever met before. And she was right, too. Mr. Douglas *was* creeping up on Lord Walker. If Haley wasn't careful, Lord Walker might not be Lord for long and then where would she be? Maybe she should start taking more interest in why he was making the trades he was making. Then she might know what Rosalind meant by "the accident". She resolved herself, put in the orders for Russ Logo, and set off home to start on first lunch.

🙢   ✶   ♉

By the time seventh lunch came around, Haley wondered if it would have been less work for Lord Walker to eat five breakfasts in the first place. Still, she didn't complain. She knew that seventh lunch had to be the last lunch because there was no way he could eat more and be on time for the Feast—and there was no way he was going to be late for this one. After he had eaten the one-hundred-and-twenty-eight burgers and fries and bread puddings, Haley's real work set in. She had to strap him into his pneumatic pants. He would always wiggle and try to help, but more often than not, his "help" only made her job more difficult.

She found the best method was to start by grabbing his feet

and twisting him around so they were sticking off the bed. Luckily it was a kingdom size bed, as long as it was wide, so it fit him facing either way—he was as tall as he was wide, anyway, so it really had to be. Once his legs were dangling off the bed, she forced the pneumatic booties onto his sausage feet and slowly inched him further and further off while carefully inching the pants up over the folds of his legs. He always slept in a nightshirt—"to let his legs breath"—preventing the need for her to take his previous pair off, which helped her more than anything else he could do. She got the pants all the way up around his waist and said, "Are you ready, Lord?"

"Yes, dear," he replied. His voice sounded restricted in the pneumatic pants, even when they weren't activated. "Hop to it. We mustn't be late."

"Yes, sir." Haley pressed the little button on the ankle of the pants and they hissed into action. All of a sudden Lord Walker's legs stiffened, sending his mushroom cap upper body shooting into the air with the appearance that he would be flung right off the bed face-first into the floor, but just before he was, the pants caught his weight and sent him tottering up again to rock back and forth into a standing position, like a flabby, slow motion version of the doorstop she flicked to pass the time in her closet at night.

"Very good, dear," Lord Walker said when the fluids in his ears had settled down. "Now, a little grooming, please."

"Yes, sir." Haley brushed the hamburger, bread pudding, and—even still—egg crumbs out of his beard. She wiped the liquids off his face with a damp cloth, then brushed his shaggy white facial hair straight with a tiny comb. When she was done, Lord Walker lifted his hands as far above his head as he could reach them—which wasn't far—so she could pull off his nightshirt. She slipped a white undershirt over his arms as fast as she could, then buttoned the rest of the layers of his tuxedo on over that.

"There we are, dear," Lord Walker said with a huff when she was done. "I'll get my monocle and top hat in the car. Could you fetch a black and gold bow tie, too? Thank you, sweetheart." He winked.

"Yes, sir." Haley curtsied.

The ground shook as Lord Walker's pants carried his mushroom frame toward the garage.

Haley took his night shirt, the rag, and comb to the trash chute to dispose of them. She ordered a top hat, monocle, cane, and bow tie out of the printer and went to meet Lord Walker in the Hummer. The pants had already carried him into the huge backseat, thank the Creator—with the old pneumatic pants she had to lift him up into it herself—so she only had left to climb into the backseat with him, tie his bow tie on over his beard—"Otherwise how will anyone know I'm wearing it, sweetheart?"—and place his monocle in his right eye.

"Thank you, dear," he said, waving her away before she finished. "Let's go, then. Front seat."

"Yes, sir." Even though the car drove itself, Lord Walker preferred the appearance of having a driver in the front seat, so he made her sit up there apart from him, like a chauffeur, as the stretch Hummer drove them out of the garage and into the Feast Hall parking garage.

"Alright now, sweetheart," Lord Walker said before the car had stopped moving. "The door please."

As soon as the car did stop, Haley stepped out and opened his door for him. His pants carried him out of the Hummer and toward the Feast Hall. He only had time to swipe his monocle and cane before crying, "My hat, dear! Don't forget my hat!"

Haley snatched the hat and slammed the door closed. Lord Walker would be furious to be seen in public without the tallest hat in the building, who knows how he would react to being seen with no hat on at all. She ran towards the door he was about to pass through and tumbled to the ground, tangled up with some other secretary. She hurried to her knees, searching for the hat she had dropped, when she heard Rosalind's voice.

"Here you are," Rosalind said, holding the hat out to to her, still wearing the same funny pantsuit, even at the Christmas Feast.

Haley stood and took it. "Thank you."

"You're welcome." Rosalind bowed her head. "Now hurry up. You don't want to be late."

Haley stared at her for a second, wanting to say something, to ask her about the way she talks or dresses, or how Mr. Douglas treats her, but she knew she didn't have time for that, so she left it at thank you and hurried off to catch Lord Walker.

She burst through the door into the Feast Hall's great

entryway, relieved to see its cavernous decadence empty except for Lord Walker. As soon as she ran up to him and plopped the hat on his head, her relief was replaced with a sense of dread deep in her stomach. Mr. Douglas was standing there, talking to Lord Walker, hidden from her first sight by Lord Walker's Hummer-sized girth.

"Haley," Lord Walker said, obviously trying to stifle his anger. "There you are, dear. Perhaps in the future you won't forget to bring my hat. Mr. Douglas and I were just discussing errors in textile production and commending the advancements we've made in the service industry when you come and prove us exactly wrong. Isn't that so, Mr. Douglas?"

Mr. Douglas didn't react, not even a smile or nod.

"Anyway," Lord Walker went on. "I hate to see good food go to waste. And I *must* kiss those hands. You know how it is being the Lord of the Feast and all. Or...no. You don't. Do you?" He winked. "Well, anyway. If you'll excuse me, Mr. Douglas." He tipped his hat.

"Yes, Lord Walker," Mr. Douglas said with a deep bow, taking off his own top hat as he did. "And you *will* consider my offer, won't you?"

"*Ho ho ho*. Always the shrewd businessman, Mr. Douglas." Lord Walker chuckled. "Always! But let us concentrate on the Christmas Feast for tonight and leave our business for the Market. *Ho ho ho*." He set off toward the Feast Hall.

Haley made to follow him when Mr. Douglas mumbled something she couldn't quite make out. "Excuse me, sir," she said, turning to him.

"Nothing, ma'am," Mr. Douglas said, tipping his hat, which was almost as tall as Lord Walker's.

Haley marveled at his form. He was so small relative to the other owners—he probably didn't need help putting on his pants—and had such darker skin. He seemed like a foreigner compared to them. Not to mention the way he treated her was so different from the way the other owners treated her. It was like he saw her as more than a secretary.

"Your Lord Walker gets to me with his calcified ways," Mr. Douglas said. "If only he weren't so conservative, we'd get the economy running better in no time."

"Yes, sir." Haley curtsied.

Mr. Douglas smiled. "*Yes, sir,*" he said. "That's exactly what I mean, Haley. That is your name, isn't it?"

Haley nodded, feeling a blush coming but trying to fight it.

"Haley, do you mind if I ask you a question?"

"No, sir." Haley curtsied. "Anything, sir."

"How does your Lord Walker treat you?"

Haley was less surprised with this being the second time in one day that she was asked the same question, but she still couldn't help wondering why Mr. Douglas and his secretary were both so interested in how Lord Walker treated her all of a sudden. This time, at least, she had a prepared response. "He treats me like a secretary, sir," she said with a curtsy.

"Ah, yes," Mr. Douglas said with a smile. "As I suspected, dear. Like a secretary. Well, in that case, Haley dear, you better hurry and get him a drink. It's what a good secretary would do." He bowed low to her.

"Yes, sir, Mr. Douglas, sir," Haley said with a curtsy, blushing and skipping away as fast as she could. What was with people today?

The Feast Hall itself was a cavern identical to the entryway, only filled with long rows of tables that were big enough to fit five-hundred owners. Diamond chandeliers hung from the ceiling, and the walls were platinum-trimmed and covered in similar tapestries and classical paintings to those that covered Lord Walker's walls. Owners of various shapes and sizes—mostly mushroom shaped and giant—filed around the room, talking to each other and drinking, and at the head table—big enough for the five richest owners—Lord Walker talked with Mr. Smörgåsbord and Mr. Loch, his closest confidants in the Fortune 5. Haley hurried through the Hall into the kitchen. She knew that Lord Walker wouldn't want to see her without a drink in hand.

The kitchen was the same gray as Haley's, but it was much longer and a bit wider—wide enough for two secretaries to cook and two carts of food to pass by at the same time. It was lined with counters, stoves, and printers, and filled with secretaries that had about as much variance in appearance as the owners in the Feast Hall. They were almost exclusively women, and they were all lean and sleek and just the opposite of the owners, each one dressed in a similar black mini skirt with white lace frills.

Haley hurried to her printer—closest to the door—to get an old fashioned for Lord Walker, and Rosalind was at her own printer, across the kitchen from Haley's, smiling and trying to catch her attention. Rosalind even went so far as to say her name, but Haley pretended she didn't hear, rushing the drink out to Lord Walker.

"Haley, dear," he said when she got it out there. "*Finally*. I think everyone else is drunk already. Imagine that. Everyone drunk but me. *Ho ho ho*. What a strange place." He elbowed Mr. Loch next to him who laughed along, probably drunk already as Lord Walker had said. "And turkey for the feast tonight," he added. "Lots and lots of turkey. And potatoes. And gravy over everything. You got that, sweetheart?"

"Yes, sir," Haley said with a curtsy.

"Very well, then," Lord Walker said, waving her away. "Off and get it started. I have business to attend to."

"Yes, sir." She curtsied again and made her way back to the kitchen.

There wasn't much to do, but what little there was she busied herself with to try to avoid the gaze of Rosalind. She got a pot of water from the printer and set it to boiling on the stove. The turkey would have to be printed fully-cooked or it would take too long and Lord Walker would complain that he was starving. With nothing left to do, she set to printing and mixing the ingredients for a pumpkin pie, Lord Walker always asked for one on Christmas. All the while she was all too aware of Rosalind trying to attract her attention.

"So, Haley," Rosalind said, walking over to watch her pour the filling into the crust. "How is your Feast so far?"

"I'm sorry," Haley said, nothing left to distract her. "I don't understand."

"Your feast," Rosalind said. "Are you enjoying it?"

Haley thought about it. It was no different than any other day. She cooked for Lord Walker every feast, but here the kitchen was bigger, and there was company, and speeches and music. But what was it to enjoy a Feast?

"Well," Rosalind said. "How is it?"

"It's—"

"And don't say it's like a Feast." Rosalind chuckled. "I already know that much."

"It's like a—well..." Haley wanted to say exactly what

Rosalind had told her not to say. She had to come up with something else, though. Anything. "Yes," she said, nodding. "I am enjoying it."

Rosalind smiled wider than Haley had ever seen her smile. "Good," she said. "You don't know how happy I am to hear that. I've got some fish to deliver now. If you'll excuse me."

Haley found herself staring at the door even after Rosalind had passed through it. She had never used such unproductive words in her life. What did she mean when she said she was enjoying the feast? What did it mean to enjoy something? And why would Rosalind care either way? It was getting to be too much when the potato water boiled over and distracted her with her duty to Lord Walker.

Potatoes mashed and pie cooled, she printed a whole turkey and put it on the cart with them. She wasn't the first out of the kitchen—and not the last, either—so she added another pair of old fashioneds to ease Lord Walker's inevitable ire. Haley could see his eyes widen and hear his stomach groan from across the Feast Hall as she rolled the food toward him.

"Haley! Haley, sweetheart," he called while she was still halfway across the room. Half the owners looked up from their food at the sound of his voice. "I'm so hungry I was going to eat Mr. Douglas over here. I thought he might be food because he eats what my food eats. *Ho ho ho*!"

The room erupted in laughter with him. Mr. Douglas put his fork on his plate, staring at Lord Walker while Lord Walker stared at the turkey rolling his way. Haley placed the food in front of Lord Walker and wondered if Mr. Douglas was enjoying his feast. She wondered why she cared. When Lord Walker didn't notice the old fashioneds she had made and asked for another, she didn't respond. Not even with a, "Yes, sir." And when she stepped into the kitchen, she didn't stop to think about her answer when Rosalind asked if she could ask her a question.

"Go ahead," Haley said.

"What do you think your life would be like if you didn't work for Lord Walker?"

"Is that even possible?"

"That depends on you."

II. Ansel

Ansel jumped out of bed at the first sight of light and ran to the balcony to watch the sun rise over the Green Belt. In all her years on this planet she had never seen such a beautiful sight. Never before had the sky been so big and blue or the world around her so green and alive. Not even her first day of school could ruin it.

School. Ugh. She shuddered at the thought of it. Maybe school *could* ruin it.

She heard a creak behind her and turned to find her dad—dark eyes puffy from sleep and still in his pajamas—standing in the balcony door.

"*Yyyyuuuuuaaaahhh*—Isn't it beautiful?" he said through a yawn, stretching his arms way up over his head.

"It's the most beautiful thing I've ever seen," Ansel said, not taking her eyes off the shimmering blue and green.

"Just wait until recess," her dad said, smiling and nodding. "Then you'll get to run and play in it with the other children."

She shuddered at the thought of them, too. "Do I have to, Dad? I could just go play in it now."

"No, no, Ansel. The schooling is one of the main benefits of living here. Life is more than blue skies and green trees. You should know that as well as anyone coming from where we come from."

"I know, Dad. But there *are* blue skies and green trees here. Why can't I take advantage of that now?"

"Because you need an education. How do you think your mother and I got to where we are now? Hard work and learning everything we could to make ourselves more valuable."

"*And stealing printers,*" Ansel mumbled under her breath.

"Excuse me, ma'am."

"I said what can they teach me that I don't already know?"

"And just what is it that you think you know?" Her dad smiled.

"Well, I can count... And add. Read most things. And I trap a mean rat. Not to mention I can hit a pigeon from a mile away with my slingshot." She patted it in her back pocket.

"And I guess that's everything there is to know."

"It's served me just fine." Ansel crossed her arms.

Ansel's mom poked her puffy-haired head out of the balcony door. "What's all the racket out here so early?" she said, coming outside. She looked like she had been up for a while because she was already wearing a purple, flowery dress which Ansel had never seen before.

"Your daughter was just explaining to me how she knows everything there is to know," her dad said with a smile. "She doesn't think she needs to go to school because they can't teach her anything."

"Is that right?" Her mom looked at Ansel for confirmation.

"Well, not everything," Ansel said, kicking nothing with her feet. "But I still don't need school."

"I beg to differ, ma'am," her mom said. "Now go put on that new dress of yours, and I'll walk you down there myself. You should meet some of the kids in the neighborhood, anyway. You'll need some new friends"

"*I want my old friends*," Ansel mumbled.

"Excuse me, ma'am," her mom said.

"I don't want to wear a stupid dress!" Ansel stomped her foot. "I want to play in the grass and climb trees."

"You *will* wear that dress," her mom said. "You don't know the trouble it cost us to get you something so clean and new."

"But it doesn't even have pockets," Ansel complained. "How am I supposed to carry my slingshot without pockets?"

"You aren't, dear," her mom said. "You won't be needing your slingshot at school. I'll ask you to leave it in your room, please."

"Bu—"

"Go!" Her mom stomped her foot.

Ansel looked to her dad for help, but he avoided eye contact with her by pretending to be enjoying the view of the Belt. With no more lines of defense, she stomped to her room to get dressed.

Her new bedroom was smaller than her bedroom back home, but it didn't make a difference, it still fit her bed and dresser with the mirror on top. She looked at herself in the mirror. She was from the Green Belt now, but she didn't feel any different. A pencil drawing of two girls holding hands was stuck in the corner of the frame. Looking at it made her miss Katie back home. Katie would probably wake up today and go out trapping rats or hunting pigeons. She definitely wouldn't be going to any stupid school. But at least there was the Green Belt to look forward to. There was no green grass or blue sky in Katie's future. Not anytime soon, at least. Just the concrete, tar, and steel of completely streets and the oppressive skyline of rows and rows of skyscrapers.

Ansel's mom called in to see if she was ready, and Ansel called back to say almost. She got the dress out of her dresser and rubbed the blue floral cloth between her fingers. It was soft and clean and new, she had to give her mom that much. Ansel wasn't sure if she had ever seen clothes made from anything but recycled rags, and now she was holding just that in her hands. But it was still a dress, and a dress was no good for playing in an open field or climbing trees. She had never played in an open field or climbed a tree in her life, and even she knew that. She also knew that she wouldn't get out of the house without the dress on, though, so she relented. When she slipped it on over her head, it was so soft and smooth, she felt like she wasn't wearing anything at all, a second skin. She almost blushed when she walked out to show her parents.

"Now *that* is the most beautiful thing I've ever seen," her dad said.

Her mom said nothing. She just stared with a little moisture in her eyes.

"Are you alright mom?" Ansel asked when she noticed.

"Yes, dear," she said. "I—You're lovely, dear. Just lovely." She smiled.

"Thanks, ma," Ansel said, although she thought she would look just as good with a new pair of pants and t-shirt on, it was just the fact that the dress was new that made them like it.

"Alright," her mom said. "Let's go on then. Say goodbye to your father."

Her dad squatted down and gave her a big hug. "Remember that you always have something to learn, Ansel," he said. "And everyone knows something you don't know. But most of all remember to have fun out there. Okay."

Ansel nodded.

He kissed her on the head. "I love you, sweetheart," he said.

"See you after class. You'll have to tell me all about it."

"I will."

He gave her one last hug and let her go.

"Alright, sweetheart. Let's go." Her mom held out a hand and Ansel grabbed it.

Their apartment was on the fifth floor of a nine floor walk up. The sound of their steps echoed through the stairwell as they made their descent. Walking out the front door of the building was like walking into Ansel's old neighborhood. The apartment opened up onto the Street side of the building and all they could see were the lines and lines of skyscrapers towering over either side of them. It felt like a comforting embrace to Ansel.

They walked around their apartment building toward the Green Belt which was called that because it was exactly a green belt: a long skinny strip of green grass and trees in the middle of a sea of tall balconied buildings. It was two blocks wide and as long as the eye could see. For all Ansel knew it went on forever and ever without end. The school was right on the edge of the Belt, and only families who lived right on the edge themselves could send their children there. Graduates of the Green Belt Day School went on to hold top positions in all the most important families.

"Ansel, dear," her mom said as they walked along the grass, holding hands. "There's something I need to say to you."

But Ansel couldn't keep her eyes off the trees and the bugs and the sky. She wanted to study and understand all of it. If only she didn't have to go to stupid school.

"Are you listening to me, Ansel?" her mom said.

"Yeah, ma," Ansel said, not listening.

"Ansel." Her mom stopped dead in her tracks. Ansel's arm yanked back and she stopped, too. "Ansel. I'm serious."

"Yes, mother," she said. "I'm listening." And she really was this time. She stared at the silver necklace her mom was wearing so she wouldn't be distracted from her words.

"Ansel," her mom said. "I know you don't want to go to school—and I don't blame you, really, because, honestly, they won't be able to teach you much you don't already know—but you have to understand that school is about more than that. You have to put up with the teachers while you teach yourself how to interact with your classmates. Do you understand?"

Ansel nodded. "I think so."

Her mom looked deep into her eyes and smiled. "Of course you don't, kiddo," she said, shaking her head. "Its nonsense. To tell you the truth, *I* don't really know what I'm saying. But let me say something else. We do nothing alone. You got that? Can you repeat it for me?"

"We do nothing alone," Ansel said with a nod.

"That's right, sweetheart," her mom said with a smile. "Now, there's one more thing that's even more important for you to remember, more important than anything in the whole entire world. Do you want to know what it is?"

Ansel nodded.

"I love you, Ansel. I always will." She kissed Ansel on the top of the head.

"I love you too, mom."

Her mom brought her in for a hug. She was wiping her eyes when she let go, but Ansel didn't notice because a bug with big colorful wings fluttered by and distracted her.

"What's that, ma?" she asked, running to catch it.

"A butterfly, dear," her mom said. "Like my necklace."

"I thought your necklace was silver," Ansel said, getting further into the grass. "That thing was colorful."

"My necklace is silver but butterflies aren't," her mom said. "Now let's get going."

The school was on the first floor of a squat grey building. There were two women standing at the doorway, and Ansel's mom had to literally drag her away from the grass to meet them.

"Ah, this must be Ansel," the older of the two—with white hair—said. "We were expecting you."

Ansel tried one last time to run off to the grass but her mom held strong.

"You'd rather be playing in the field," the other woman said. She was younger and had darker hair.

Ansel didn't respond. She kicked dust at her feet.

"Me, too," the younger woman said with a smile. "That's why I'm having class outside today."

Ansel beamed.

"Did you hear that?" her mom said.

"Am I in your class?" Ansel asked.

The younger woman looked over at the white-haired woman who nodded with a solemn face. "It seems you are."

Ansel dropped her mom's hand and grabbed the younger woman's. "Alright. Come on, then. Let's go," she said, trying to pull the woman out to the Belt.

"Slow down, child. You have to meet the rest of the class, first. Go on inside. Room two. I'd like to have a word with your mother before I follow."

"Oh, alright," Ansel said with a sigh, dropping the woman's hand and stomping inside. Her mom called out that she loved her as she did.

Behind the glass door of the school was a long hall with speckled vinyl floors and faded teal walls. The rooms were numbered with signs that had foreign dots under them. Ansel studied the little formation of dots under the one sign, wondering what they meant, then she remembered that she was supposed to go to room two and walked that way. She held her breath for a second, trying to imagine the worst thing that could be on the other side of the door before she opened it, and what she found was so much worse.

There was a chalkboard with a name written on it: Mrs. Lerner. Ansel assumed it was the teacher's name. There were also rows of desks, each with kids, mostly light-skinned, sitting behind them, and all in shiny, new, clean clothes. She felt for a second like she was standing naked in front of them, then she remembered her own shiny new dress and felt even more embarrassed than she would have been if she actually was naked. She felt her face flush, making her mad at herself for being embarrassed, and clenched her fists, not sure if she should sit down or wait for Mrs. Lerner since they were going outside anyway.

"Don't you know how to sit, girl?" came a mocking voice from a back corner of the room.

The class erupted in laughter.

"I can teach you if that's what you're asking," Ansel yelled back at the room in general.

"*Ooooh!*" came a lonely voice from the other corner of the room. Everyone in the class turned to see who it was.

"Shut up, Pidgeon!" a large boy yelled, chucking a wadded up piece of paper at the boy who had *Ooooh!*ed.

"You shut up!" Pidgeon yelled back just as Mrs. Lerner

walked in the door.

"Richard Maid. You apologize right now," she said before the door closed. "We do not tell people to shut up in this class. Do you understand me? You're setting a bad example for our new student."

"But Mrs. Lerner," Pidgeon said. "I—"

"No, sir," Mrs. Lerner said. "I don't want to hear it. Apologize."

The class *Ooooh*!ed together.

"Class!" Mrs. Lerner quieted them.

"It wasn't his fault, ma'am," Ansel said, looking at the floor.

"I'm sorry, child?" Mrs. Lerner said. "You'll have to speak up."

Ansel looked over at Pidgeon. He waved his hands and shook his head, trying to communicate something Ansel couldn't understand. "Don't blame Pidgeon, ma'am," she said. "I started it. It's my fault."

"Oh...Well." Mrs. Lerner looked from Ansel to Pidgeon and back again. "If that's so, you're not making a very productive start to your first day here, Miss Server."

"Yes, ma'am," Ansel said, shaking her head and still looking at the floor. "I'm sorry, ma'am."

"I'll let it slide this once," Mrs. Lerner said. "Now, class, this is our new student Ansel."

"Good morning, Ansel," the class sang in unison.

"Please take a seat so we can get started, Miss Server."

"I—but—" Ansel protested. "I thought you said we were going outside."

The class laughed.

"We will, child," Mrs. Lerner said. "But first we have to take care of business. All play and no work. You know. Now please, Miss Server, take a seat. There's one…"

"There's one right here, Mrs. Lerner," Pidgeon said.

The class *Ooooh*!ed again.

"Mr. Maid," Mrs. Lerner said. "That's strike two. If you act out one more time today, I'm reporting you to the principal."

"Strike two?" Pidgeon complained. "But I—"

"*Richard*." Mrs. Lerner said.

"Yes, ma'am." Pidgeon put his head down on his desk.

"Now, Miss Server," Mrs. Lerner said. "Please take your seat and we'll get started."

Ansel hesitated but knew protesting was futile. She was under Mrs. Lerner's control now, she had no say in the matter. She took as long as she could to walk back to her seat, though, her small act of defiance.

"Okay," Mrs. Lerner said. "Where did we leave off yesterday? Ah yes. I remember. The history of the ownership of the Green Belt. Now, no one knows the history of the entire Belt. That would be impossible. No, let us not concern ourselves with that big of a picture for now. What concerns us is the local familial relationships in our immediate area of the Belt. If we start here with the Concierge sector—owned, of course, by the Concierge family and subsidiaries..."

Ansel lost all power of concentration at that. She couldn't get her mind over one little speed bump, one sentence that Mrs. Lerner stated as a matter of fact then breezed right over. *No one knows the history of the entire Belt.* How could that be? Someone had to know. Didn't they? Or could it go on for ever and ever like everyone always said it did? Before she realized it, Ansel blurted out, "But how?"

"Excuse me, Ansel," Mrs. Lerner said. "Please raise your hand the next time you would like to speak. But how did the McCannick's usurp the original Union? That's a good question, and the explanation goes back to before the—"

"No," Ansel said, shaking her head. "How does no one know the history of the entire Belt?"

"Again, Miss Server," Mrs. Lerner said. "Raise your hand if you would like to speak."

Ansel raised her hand.

"Yes, Ansel?"

"How does no one know the history of the entire Belt?"

"Well, that, too, is a very good question, child," Mrs. Lerner said. "I would say that it's a result of the fact that—"

A loud, metallic, clanging bell drowned out her voice. Ansel jumped in her seat—knocking her desk over—at the sound of it. The class laughed at her reaction as they filed out of the room.

"The cafeteria's just down the hall, miss Server," Mrs. Lerner said after everyone else had left the room. "Would you like me to show you the way?"

"I can find it myself," Ansel said, setting her desk up again.

"Very good," Mrs. Lerner said. "Just see to it that you're back in your seat promptly after the bell."

The door to room two clicked closed behind her. Ansel ignored the growling in her stomach, and instead of dealing with the inevitable insults from the class—and possibly other classes—in the cafeteria, she decided to take this time to explore the Belt. She hadn't had a chance to play in the green grass since they moved there and it didn't look like any sort of outside time was actually on Mrs. Lerner's agenda.

Ansel opened the door and glared out into the sunlight. The sun was exactly overhead, so the belt was spotted with patches of inviting shade under each tree. Ansel couldn't help herself but to run over to one of them and try to climb it. First she did a few circles around the trunk, looking for a good place to grip it, and when she thought she had planned a course, she went to work, hand over hand, one step at a time, up the tree. She was ten feet off the ground when she heard a familiar voice from above say, "Hey! What are you doing in my tree?"

She looked up to see who it was but couldn't make the person out through the thick foliage. "I don't see your name on it!" she called up anyway. Her time in the Streets had taught her that letting too many insults slide was dangerous, and one was too many.

"Technically, my name *is* on it," the voice came back. "I've carved it in all over the place."

"Pidgeon, is that you?" Ansel said, starting up the tree again.

"Who'd you think it was?" he called back down.

"You know," she said, she could see him now, petting a little, black, furry creature on the branch next to him. "You didn't have to let me take *all* the heat this morning."

"I didn't ask you to take *any* of it," he said.

"Well, part of it *was* mine, wasn't it?" She sat on a branch a little higher than his in case he tried anything funny. He still didn't have to look up to see her, though. Ansel thought he looked a few years older than her, but she couldn't tell how many. "And I wasn't going to let the class think I was a snitch and tell her it was really that asshole's fault," she added.

"Jimmy?" Pidgeon chuckled. "He is a—an *ass hole* isn't he?"

The way he said it, it looked like it tasted about how it sounded.

"If that's his name," Ansel said. "Then yes."

"It is," Pidgeon said. "And mine's Richard."

"I like Pidgeon."

"I don't." He shook his head, petting the cat.

"Pidgeon," Ansel said. "Who's your friend?"

Pidgeon grimaced. He pet the furry little beast a few times before deciding the battle wasn't worth fighting, exposing a fatal weakness. One was too many.

"This is Mr. Kitty," he said.

"Mr. Kitty?"

"Yeah. He's always hanging out in this tree at lunch. That's why I came up here. I wanted to see if he would be here again."

Ansel didn't know why someone would skip lunch just to pet a cat, but she did want to touch it. It sat there licking itself, letting Pidgeon scratch its back as it did.

"You can pet him if he'll let you," Pidgeon said. "He won't bite."

"I know!" she yelled, which caused the cat jump.

"You scared him!" Pidgeon yelled back, scaring it more.

"Now you did!" Ansel said, and the cat jumped off the branch and down the tree where it seemed to disappear.

"Look what you did now," Pidgeon said. "Now I have to wait until tomorrow to try again."

"Try what?" Ansel asked, but Pidgeon wasn't paying any attention. His ears were perked up and he was listening to a far off sound that Ansel couldn't hear.

"That's the bell, anyway," he said. "We better go. Come on." He started his quick, monkey-like descent down the tree.

"Wait," Ansel called after him. "Try what?" But it was too late, he was gone. She hurried down the tree after him, but by the time she caught up, they were both sitting in their desks and Mrs. Lerner had already gone on talking about which families controlled which local sectors of the Green Belt and how they got that way.

"What were you trying to do up there?" Ansel whispered to Pidgeon who pretended to be listening to Mrs. Lerner so he could ignore her.

"*Psst.* Pidgeon," Ansel said. "Listen to me."

"*Shhh,*" he shushed her.

"Mr. Maid," Mrs. Lerner said. "Quiet down please."

"But—"

"No, sir," she said. "I said quiet. Now, where was I..."

After she went on for a while Ansel whispered, "Pidgeon. Tell me."

"Tomorrow, okay," he whispered back. "Or after class."

"Now!" she said too loudly.

"Miss Server," Mrs. Lerner said. "You, too, child. Do I have to separate you two on your first day of class?"

The class *Ooooh*!ed, and Ansel decided she could wait until Mrs. Lerner was done droning on. It seemed like an eternity. When the final bell rang and everyone scrambled out of their seats, Ansel was ready and up as fast as anyone, but Mrs. Lerner had them all sit down again before they could leave.

"Alright, children," she said. "You did very well today. Your parents would be proud. Now, I want you all to look forward to tomorrow because we'll be holding class outside." She paused for a reaction but no one responded. "For homework tonight," she went on. "I want you all to think about how your family got to where they are today and to compare that to what we've learned about the families who came to own the Green Belt throughout its history. Very good now, children. Have a nice day. See you tomorrow."

By the time she said "history" half the class had already left. Pidgeon got up and out before Ansel, but she ran to catch up with him outside and grabbed him by the arm to stop him.

"What were you doing up there?" she demanded.

"I told you already," he said, shrugging her off. "What do you want?"

"You were just petting a cat? That's it?"

"Is there something wrong with that?"

"I just—" Ansel looked out at the sprawling green of the Belt, at the tree they had climbed and the blue sky above. "No. I just thought there had to be more to it than that. Where'd that cat come from, anyway?"

"That's exactly what I was trying to find out!" He smiled.

"Is that why they call you Pidgeon? Because you spend your lunch in the tree?"

The smile faded. He looked at the ground and shook his head. "No. No one even knows I come out here for lunch. We're not supposed to. If they knew I did, there would be no way I could."

Ansel wanted to know more about how he got his name, but she could tell it was a sore subject, and she didn't want their already rocky start to get any worse. *We do nothing alone.*

"So what's with that teacher?" she asked to change the subject. "I thought we were supposed to have class outside today. And what about recess? I was told there would be recess."

"*Ha!*" Pidgeon chuckled. "Recess is a lie. Mrs. Lerner's a liar. The sooner you learn that the better."

"And that cat..." Ansel said.

"Mr. Kitty?"

"Mr. Kitty, yeah. You only see it when—"

"Him," Pidgeon said, cutting her off. "He's not an it."

"Okay," Ansel said. "You only see *him* at lunch. Have you ever seen *him* any other time?"

"Nope," Pidgeon said, shaking his head. "Just in the tree at lunch. It was pure luck I found him the first time, too. I was out here, playing with some bugs in the grass, when Mrs. Lerner and Mrs. Grover came out and walked right up to the tree I was sitting under. I had no choice but to climb up it, and I found him sitting up there all alone." He smiled and shrugged.

"Do you see a lot of cats around the Belt?" Ansel asked.

"Well, it's the first cat I've ever seen. I haven't lived here all that long, but that's why I wanted to find him. Have you ever seen one before?"

Ansel shook her head. "Heard of em. And I've eaten some— so I've been told—but I've never seen a live one."

"Where do you think it came from?" Pidgeon asked.

"I don't know." Ansel shrugged. "But I know how to find out."

She didn't wait for a response, setting out for the tree at full speed. Pidgeon did his best to keep up, but even with his climbing ability, Ansel was sitting on the same branch she sat on for lunch, with her breath back, before he got there.

"What—" Pidgeon tried to say through his huffing and puffing. "Way—is—that?"

"Well, this way," Ansel said.

Pidgeon clearly didn't understand, but he was too out of breath to argue.

"You've only ever seen the cat here, right?"

He nodded.

"Then we have to wait here until it—until *he* comes back. Once we see him again, we follow him. Simple as that."

"That's what I was trying to do when you interrupted me at lunch," Pidgeon said.

"Then why'd it take you so long to understand the plan?"

"Besides, I already know when he's coming back. Lunchtime tomorrow. Like always."

"Yeah, but do you know he doesn't come around at other times?"

"I know he comes at lunch and leaves after,"

"Have you ever sat out here any other time? Does he come every lunch?"

Pidgeon didn't answer. He looked down at his feet and played with the hem of his shirt.

"I thought so," she said. "Now I'm gonna stay out here and wait for him. You can do whatever you want." She turned away from Pidgeon to look up at the branches of the tree.

After a long silence he said, "Why are you interested in this cat, anyway?"

Ansel shrugged. "I dunno," she said. "I haven't thought about it. I just like to hunt, I guess."

"I don't know," Pidgeon said. He broke a twig off of the branch next to him and tore it to tiny pieces. "I think its more than that."

"You don't even know me."

Pidgeon shrugged. "I guess." He tossed the little bits of branch down into the foliage where they disappeared into the tree, indistinguishable. "Have you ever heard of the legend of the Curious Cat?"

"Of course I have," Ansel said. "So what?"

"I don't know." He shrugged. "Do you—Do you think it's real?"

Ansel turned slowly to look at him. She couldn't tell if he was being sincere or looking for a weakness. His eyes were averted, like he was a little embarrassed to even bring it up. He either wasn't looking for a weakness, or he was a really good actor. "Why do you ask?"

"Do you think—" he said. "I mean—I don't know. Do you think *this* could be him?"

Ansel laughed. Pidgeon didn't, though. "You're saying to me that you think *this* is the mythical Curious Cat who knows the way to Prosperity."

"I—I don't know," Pidgeon said. "I'm sayin—I'm saying that I think he *could* be."

"And you're trying to find out where it comes from so you can follow it there?"

"I mean—Well, yeah. Wouldn't you? Don't you believe it's true?"

She looked him up and down, sizing him up. She still wasn't sure if she trusted what she saw. Finally she said, "We should take the tree in shifts if we want to cover the most time."

෪   ✖   ௯

III. Russ

Slip, snap, click.
　　Slip, snap, click.
　　A bead of sweat rolled down his nose. He blinked and squinted, trying to get it to drop from his face, but he couldn't take attention away from the task at hand to wipe it away.
　　Slip, snap, click.
　　Slip, snap, click.
　　He was a producer, not a consumer. He put in the hard work it took for everyone else to have their precious entertainment.
　　Slip, snap, click.
　　Slip, snap, click.
　　The repetition of it was already getting to him. He hadn't put together ten pieces on the day and he had already had enough. He could feel the weight of all the pieces still to come bearing down on him.
　　Slip, snap, click.
　　Slip, snap, click.
　　Pieces? Pieces of what? They didn't even look real. Just a bit of wire and two little metal things that snapped together and clicked into place.
　　Slip, snap, click.
　　Slip, snap, click.
　　It could be a part of anything. It could be a part of nothing. It was probably nothing. Just another way to make them look busy.
　　Slip, snap, click.
　　Slip, snap, click.
　　He looked up and down the line of people working beside him, repeating the same task he repeated, over and over and over.
　　Slip, snap, click.
　　Slip, snap, click.
　　How could they need so many? Why would they have to do this for so long in silence?
　　Slip, snap, click.

Slip, snap, click.

He turned to get the attention of the worker next to him, but she was focused intently on her own work. There wasn't time to communicate with one another on the assembly line. You were expected to keep up a certain pace, and it was impossible to do that while socializing.

Slip, snap, click.

Slip, snap, click.

He tried to remember how many pieces he was supposed to put together. Was it the same as yesterday? More? Why did they need so many?

Slip, snap, click.

Slip, snap, click.

All he could think about was the lunch bell, the lunch bell and putting together endless pieces of nothing.

Slip, snap, click.

Slip, snap, click.

Just when he felt like he couldn't take it any longer, relief came in the form of a loud, metallic clanging. He dropped the half-finished piece in his hand, stood up, and rushed off toward the food cart.

"Cut!" came an inhumanly loud voice—amplified by a megaphone. "Russ! You put down a half-finished piece," the voice said. "We need to run the whole scene again."

Russ looked up from the food cart, his mouth full of cheese. With his tattered costume and made-up face—made to look dirty—he looked every bit the down-and-out assembly line worker who hadn't eaten in days. "What?" he said, a crumb of half-chewed cheese falling to his shirt to complete the assembly line worker effect. "You've got to be kidding me. Again?"

"That's what happens when you get the scene wrong, Russ," Wes, the director who was yelling through the megaphone, said. "You have to do it again."

"C'mon, Wes," Russ complained. "I put pieces together just like you said, just like the script said. *Slip, snap, click, slip, snap, click* until the bell rings. I did that!"

"That's right, Russ," Wes said. "Then when the bell rings what do you do?"

"I put the work down and go to lunch a happy employee.

That's what I did!"

"No, Russ." Wes frowned. "You finish two more pieces, *then* you go to lunch a happy employee. If you don't finish two more pieces, you might be behind quota. If you're behind quota, the boss will dock your pay. If the boss docks your pay, you won't have enough money to feed your son and daughter back home. Your wife is sick, and though she normally works, you're the only breadwinner in the household right now. You wouldn't want to leave the job without knowing that their future is safe. You wouldn't leave without finishing those two extra pieces to ensure you reached your quota. You couldn't be a happy employee with the thought that your children may not have breakfast in the morning and your wife may not have the medicine she needs. Do you understand why you did the scene wrong now, Russ? Do you get it?"

Russ swallowed the last bit of cheese in his mouth. He nodded without a word.

"So are you ready to try again, then? And to put those last two pieces together this time. Maybe even three?"

"Yeah, sure," Russ said, shrugging and taking another bite of cheese. "Whatever."

"Alright, then," Wes said, clapping his hands. "Places everyone!"

Russ sat back on the hard, cold stool. All the pieces he had put together were long gone down the assembly line, probably to be disassembled and put back through the cycle again. Now the constituent parts were all that was left in front of him. The other actors filed in and sat at their places around him. None of them ever got publicly called out by the director, but then again they weren't stars. With great fame came great responsibility.

"Lights!"

The world faded into darkness around him, all except for his work area which was lit so brightly it had a shining aura that looked like a halo.

"Cue the belts."

The constituent parts started moving down the conveyor belt in front of him. He had a Pavlovian urge to pick them up and start piecing them together, but he wanted to wait for the official start of the scene. This time he was going to make sure to do it up to the director's exacting standards, the exacting standards of the audience.

"*Aaaaannnd...action!*"
Slip, snap, click.
Slip, snap, click.
All he could think about was why they needed so much footage of him putting together pieces of nothing.
Slip, snap, click.
Slip, snap, click.
Slip, snap, click...

☚   ✂   ℈

The solitude of his dressing room was a welcome repose to the cold hard assembly line. The seats were softer, and the colors were softer, and the floor was softer under his feet. Not only that, he had a 3D printer, the seed of all life, the technology which made assembly line work obsolete for humans. Everything was done by robot and printer now. Everything, that is, except for acting, which a robot could never do nearly as well as a human. And so a small few producers still had to make the sacrifice of assembly line work for the entertainment and edification of the hungry audience. That was the burden of being a star.

Russ sat at the brightly lit vanity and stared at himself in the mirror. The makeup he was wearing really did do magic. He wouldn't be able to recognize himself if he didn't know it was a mirror he was looking at. And his clothes? *Disgusting.* Obscenely retro. Ragged beyond trendiness. No sane person would be caught dead looking like he did just then. No, Russ Logo didn't look back at him from his battle station mirror, a poor, hungry assembly line worker did.

His stomach groaned at the thought of it. He sat and stared at himself for a minute longer, trying to decide between eating first or changing out of his ghastly costume, when hunger got the best of him. "Alright, alright," he said in response to another growl. "I hear you. Give me a second."

He walked over to the printer and stood staring at it in a daze with his hand hovering over the voice activation button. This was the fatal flaw with 3D printer technology: With every possible meal imaginable at the tip of your fingers, how were you supposed decide what to eat next? His stomach growled again imagining the possibilities.

"I'm trying," he said to it. "Maybe you could be a little more specific."

His stomach rumbled in response.

"That helps me none," he said as the door to his dressing room swung open. "*Ugh*, have you ever heard of knocking?" he snapped before he saw who it was. "Jorah Baldwin," he said when he did, shaking his head. "I should have known." He laughed.

"Who else would visit your appalling self," Jorah said. "Speaking of which, who picked your outfit?" He grinned with his white teeth standing out starkly against his painted red lips and dark skin.

"I'll have you know that this is all the rage in Paris." Russ struck a pose with one hand behind his head and the other on his hip. "The latest in assembly line chic couture."

They both burst into laughter and leaned in for a hug.

"For real, though, Russ," Jorah said when their laughing was under control. "You have got to change out of that hideous dress and put on some makeup. I'm about to gag just looking at you."

"Alright, alright," Russ said, waving his arms. "Give me a second."

He sat back at the battle station and pressed the little red button at the base of the mirror. A mechanical arm with a cloth wiped his face clean of the dirty assembly line worker makeup, leaving a fresh base. It poked him in the eye while it was doing it, and he let out a shrill yelp. "Fortuna!" he complained. "Will they ever get these things working properly?"

Jorah shrugged on the couch, flipping through a gossip magazine. "I hear they're coming out with a new model next month," he said.

"They come out with a new model *every* month," Russ said. "And more often than not they make it worse."

Jorah shrugged again. "What are you gonna do?"

Russ flipped through the shades of lipstick on the battle station's touchscreen, choosing purple to go with the suit he had already picked out in his mind. He added a winged eyeliner design and set the station to work. Putting the makeup on was nothing compared to taking it off, the little mechanical arms were deft and their sensors sensitive to his every subtle movement. He still had to try to sit still, of course, but it was nothing like before when your eyeliner would be on your lips if you even breathed. He felt like a new person when he looked at the result in the mirror.

"There," he said, standing from the vanity. Jorah glanced up from his magazine, nodded, and went on reading. "Now, something to wear." Russ had no trouble making that decision. He had been eyeing a purple paisley suit and alligator cowboy boots for days now. Finally, with Jorah there, he had someone famous enough to show the outfit off to.

Russ slipped out of his assembly line worker clothes and threw them down the trash chute. He called up a pair of silk boxers, a soft cotton undershirt, and a pair of argyle socks on the 3D printer's voice activation system and put them on under the suit and boots. When he was all dressed and had himself straightened out, he struck a pose in front of Jorah, who was still reading, and said, "What do you think?"

Jorah glanced up from his magazine, did a double take, then set the rag on the table. "You look absolutely stunning," he said, standing to get a closer look. "And like nothing I've ever seen before."

Russ blushed. "I thought it would be good for the show tonight. You really like it?"

"Of course, darling. Would I lie to you?" Jorah held Russ's hands out so he could get another look. "Beautiful."

Russ's stomach groaned in response.

Jorah jumped back in surprise then laughed. "I think your stomach likes it, too."

"*Ugh.* I forgot how hungry I was. I haven't eaten anything but stale food cart cheese all day. And I can never decide what I want with this stupid printer. Too many options."

"Fortuna! I know exactly what you mean," Jorah said, shaking his head. "I have the same problem picking out what I want to wear in the morning. Who can decide? Well, besides *you*, of course. It's like you have a sixth sense for fashion."

Russ blushed again. Only Jorah could get him to respond so humbly to compliments. But his stomach rumbled again, too, ruining the mood.

"Well, dear," Jorah said. "Why don't we get something in that stomach of yours and take your new suit out for a spin? What do you say?"

"Anything's better than sitting here, trying to figure out what to order from that stupid printer," Russ said. "Where do you want to go?"

"*Hmmm*." Jorah tapped his chin with one finger. "I don't know." He smiled. "I can't decide."

They both burst into laughter.

"What's at the top of the chart today?" Russ asked. "Did you look it up yet?"

"*Duh*." Jorah scoffed. "We have Alinea in Chicago at three, Kitch in Tokyo at two, and...drum roll please...at the number one position we *haaave*...the Plantation in New Orleans!"

"The Plantation?" Russ said. "I've never heard of it."

"*Ooooh*." Jorah's eyes grew wide. "It's brand new. And all the biggest celebs are going there."

Russ scoffed.

"Well, not *all*, of course," Jorah said, backtracking. "Obviously *you* haven't been there yet. But some big directors and producers have been seen there, and you know how crucial it is to get buddy buddy with them."

Russ nodded. That was true, though not as important for him these days—it was more important for writers and directors to try to get buddy buddy with him—but it was certainly still true for Jorah. "I haven't been to New Orleans in a while," he said.

"It's such a party atmosphere," Jorah said, clapping his hands. "It's so artistic down there, I just love it."

"And you're sure this is a definite trend?" Russ tapped his foot. "Not just a bubble fad? I don't want my name anywhere near another burst bubble, Jorah."

"No no no," Jorah said, shaking his head. "Nothing like that, Russ. This is the first day it's been at number three, but its been in the top five for a while now. Anyway, if *you* go you know it'll be a definite trend in no time."

"That is true." Russ smiled, winking. "Let's do it, then."

The elevator port was directly across the hall from Russ's dressing room. He peeked out to make sure the coast was clear before exiting, not wanting to be forced to sit through another lecture from Wes. Russ didn't have to listen to anyone try to tell *him* how to act, especially a lowly documentary director. As if Wes knew better than the all time highest viewed actor in the history of entertainment. *Ha*!

Russ's elevator was a ten foot cube lined with mirrors and a soft carpet. A velvet couch sat against the back mirror, and automated pop music trickled from the speakers overhead as they plopped down into the nest of a sofa.

"Where are we going again?" Russ asked.

"*Uh*, the Plantation," Jorah said. "New Orleans," he added for the elevator.

The elevator fell into action with an almost imperceptible jolt of inertia.

"Street entrance, please," Russ added.

Jorah gave him a look. "Buoy, do you want to get mugged by the papos?"

"C'mon, man. I haven't been to New Orleans in forever. I wanna see the city." Russ smiled.

"You can see the city from a balcony. They have a lot of them in New Orleans, you know."

"It's not the same." Russ shook his head. The elevator stopped with the same small jolt. "And we're here anyway. Come on. It's just a little walk down the block."

"Oh, alright," Jorah huffed. He stood to check himself in the mirrors. "Let me straighten myself out first. How shall we present ourselves?"

"*Hmmm*." Russ stood to look at himself, too. His suit *did* look good on him. Whatever pose they decided on had to accentuate that. "What do you think?" he asked.

"Well, we could go for the classic *we didn't think you'd be there* pose," Jorah said, putting on a surprised face.

"*Ugh*." Russ groaned. "Not that. It's so cliché. As if *we* wouldn't expect papos at *our* elevator door."

"Then what about the *don't take my picture* pose?" Jorah crossed his hands in front of his face and looked away from Russ.

"No," Russ said with a chuckle, shaking his head. "Too far the other way. If we didn't want our pictures taken, we'd just take the restaurant entrance."

"*Oooh*," Jorah said, wide eyed. "Wait wait wait, I know, let's do a *fake don't take to the ooh we gotchu*. How about that?" He smiled wide.

"Well...It *is* the Christmas season."

"*Yes!*" Jorah clapped his hands together. "We'll get jolly with it. *Perfect*. Let's do it. Doors open."

The elevator doors slid open to reveal an oppressive humidity with the sun high overhead. They were hit with a barrage of flashing lights and clicking cameras while holding their *don't take my picture* pose, with their hands covering their faces, until the papos started complaining behind their cameras, then they laughed, smiled, hugged, and posed for a few pictures, ensuring everyone knew they were only joking in the Christmas spirit. Jorah kept laughing with a fake jolly, "*Ho ho ho!*" which sent Russ into bursts of uncontrollable genuine laughter. They had to push their way through the mass of papos with him still hunched over and giggling.

"I don't know why they use the flash during the day," Jorah said as they walked up the street toward the restaurant. "Seems bright enough to take pictures without it to me."

Russ shrugged, finally getting his giggles under control. He eyed the ancient architecture around him which seemed to hold a history he could see but never know, a history he felt like he had lived. He thought he remembered these very buildings from a past life. "Jorah," he said, tugging Jorah's arm. "Did this used to be something else?"

Jorah scrunched up his nose to indicate he was thinking. "*Hmm*," he said. "Yeah, you know, I think you're right. A casino or something."

A casino. Of course. Now Russ remembered. The casino where he had first gotten discovered. How could he forget? "But the building looked completely different back then," he said. "What happened?"

"They moved the whole thing so some producer could live in it," Jorah said. "Least that's what I heard. They put the Plantation in its place instead."

"The things they do these days," Russ said, shaking his head as they stepped into the restaurant.

An android with jerky, robotic movements greeted them at the door, and Russ was a little appalled at the sight of it. His stomach gurgled with something other than hunger at seeing a robot that was so subtly not human trying to pass off as one.

"Misters Logo and Baldwin," the android said in a barely

mechanical voice. "So nice of you to join us. Can I take your coats?"

"No, I'm fine," Russ said, cringing.

"No coat," Jorah said, shrugging.

"Will anyone else be joining you today?"

"Just us," Jorah said.

"Follow me."

The restaurant looked like the set of an old southern drama, one of the ancient classics like *Interview With the Vampire*. Everything was made of wood and the floor creaked as you walked along it. Russ wanted less and less to be there the closer they got to the table. "Are you sure about this place?" he asked when they had been seated with menus in hand. "I mean, is that fungus on the wall?"

"I'm telling you, Russ," Jorah said. "Give it a shot. The food is supposed to be great, and the atmosphere is half the charm. It's gonna be big, sweetheart. Like 60's diner big."

"I don't know." Russ perused the menu. It was all oysters and crawfish and alligator—and some things he didn't even know how to pronounce. "Are these even foods? I mean, I don't see kale anywhere."

"Just order the special like you always do, dear. I'm sure it'll be to die for." Jorah placed his menu on the table without reading it. He always got the special, too. You had to get the special every time you went anywhere or you might miss that one time when it was given the most delicious meal on the planet award.

A little pole on wheels with a screen attached to it rolled up to the table. The screen showed a yellow frowning face. "I'm sorry," it said in a wholly mechanical voice. "Our normal service staff is out of service. I'll be taking your order today. How can I help you?" The frown turned into a smile.

Russ gave Jorah a look. Jorah shrugged, smiled, and waved it off. "We'll take two specials," he said.

"Your order will be right up." The screen on a stick rolled away.

"Fortuna," Russ said. "I don't know what's worse, that jerky, almost-human host or the screen on a stick they have taking orders tonight. I can't believe I let you talk me into this."

"Calm down, Russ," Jorah said. "You'll make a scene. Just relax and enjoy the ambiance."

"Ambiance?" Russ scoffed. "This isn't ambiance. I don't want mold growing in the restaurant I'm eating at unless they're making cheese. Do you—*Fortuna*! Did you see that?" A black furry blur ran past them and into the kitchen as the screen on a stick rolled out to take another table's order.

"What? What is it?" Jorah looked around to see what he was screaming about, but the thing was already gone. "Fortuna," he said. "That *is* a hideous dress. But it's nothing to scream about, Russ. That's too dramatic even for me."

"No, Jorah," Russ said. "I just saw an animal run into the kitchen. I'm not—"

"A what?"

"—gonna stay and eat—*yes*, Jorah. An animal. A—uh—a cat, or something. I don't know. But I saw it run through the dining room and I'm not eating at any restaurant with a cat-infested kitchen. I'm sorry. I'm leaving." He stood from the table and let his chair fall to the floor to punctuate his ire. He remembered doing it in an old movie he had acted in and thought it would serve to drive his performance home, to convince Jorah to leave with him, or—at the very least—to make some of the other guests look around and see his new suit. He didn't want to leave yet because too few people had seen how good he looked, but a little bit of a scene ought to remedy that.

"And I suggest that all of you leave here, too!" he said, looking around at the other diners, some of whom he was glad to see were already staring and whispering. "If you want to know why, then tune in to my show tonight at primetime. *Me* being Russ Logo for anyone who's been living under a rock their entire life." He looked over at Jorah who was already eating the food that had been delivered while Russ was distracted plugging his show.

"You sure you don't want some of this?" Jorah asked through a full mouth. "It's good."

Russ's stomach grumbled in longing. He shifted his feet as if to pick the chair up and sit down, then thought better of it. "*Ugh.* No," he said. "I can't. Not after that performance."

"*Bravo*," Jorah said with a smile, still chewing his food.

"Look," Russ said, his stomach growling. "I'll see you after the show tonight. Right? *Last day of partying before the big speech.*"

"Of course, girl." Jorah said, waving a hand. "Go break a

leg."

Russ decided to get one last look at the old neighborhood and take his elevator at the street entrance. The sky was the same bright blue, and if it weren't for the papos shuffling around, taking his picture, and asking why he had left the restaurant so soon, it might have reminded him of when he used to work at the casino on this same lot. He turned to look up at the Plantation which, unsurprisingly, was in a building that looked like an old plantation. It had big white columns holding the porch roof up, and the walkway to the entrance was lined with oak trees whose branches were hung with moss. He wondered what would stand in its place the next time he was here and where the Plantation would stand in the future. It was a historic relic and he knew how much they loved their history. They were exacting about every last piece of it. *Slip, snap, click.*

Russ felt a tug on his arm and turned to see a dirty-faced assembly line worker in among the crowd of papos. She looked like she had just walked off the set he was on earlier but had forgotten to change and do her makeup before she left her dressing room.

"Russ?" the dirty assembly line worker asked in a pleading, urgent voice. "Russ Logo?"

"Do I know you, ma'am?" Russ said. "You don't look like one of these dirty papos," he added for the cameras, and the faces behind them laughed.

"No. You don't. But I know you."

"Well, who doesn't?" He shot another big smile at the cameras and more laughter came from behind them.

"That's the point, sir. I have something important to tell you."

"Well, then, why don't we do lunch? But not here, please. For reasons why check out my show tonight at primetime." Russ winked at the cameras. "But maybe you'd like to change into something more—uh—let's say...*presentable* before we go." He looked her up and down. The cameras panned to her and back to him again.

"I don't have much time. I just wanted to tell you that we're not robots. We're living, breathing human beings. And we won't be working for you much longer."

The camera snaps quickened. More and more papos swarmed onto the scene as if attracted by the scent of a newsworthy story.

Russ didn't know how to respond. What was she talking about? No humans worked for him. She must have been trying out some publicity stunt. "Woah there, little lady," he said. "I'm not sure I understand. You say you work for me?"

She nodded. "On an assembly line."

Humans on an assembly line? "And you committed no crime?"

"I was born into my family."

"And your contacts," Russ said with a smile, putting his face close to hers to look into her eyes. "They're not hidden cameras?"

"What?" She looked confused. "I don't understand."

"Come on. You're pulling my leg, right? This is a hidden camera show or something. Bruce, you got a camera out here somewhere? Or is this something new?" He looked around the crowd to see if any of the "papos" would fess up to the job, but no one was giving in just yet.

A peal of sirens rang out from down the street near the elevator bay. The "assembly line worker" looked toward the sound then back at Russ, and said, "We're humans. We're humans and you have to know. You have to tell everyone." Then she disappeared into the still thickening crowd of papos.

Russ thought about chasing after her, but his stomach groaned in protest. He still hadn't eaten anything but stale food cart cheese. Instead of waiting for the protectors to finish with the elevator—and in the process getting trapped with the need to file a report—he slipped back into the Plantation and used their elevator port. The protectors could learn all about what had happened from the papos if they really wanted to know, and if they wanted more they could watch his show that night when he would undoubtedly discuss the occurrence. For now, though, it was better to head back to his dressing room unseen, fill up on something from the printer, and relax in preparation for the impending show.

ჩ   ✖   ♋

The hip hop beat of the *Logo Show*'s theme song played on low in the background. Russ sat at an "R" shaped desk in the dark. A live audience of B and C list celebrities held their breath, waiting to hear him speak. Behind a camera, the director counted down from ten with his fingers. Russ stared into the black mirror of the camera lens, trying to see himself as the world saw him, see himself through the eyes of the lens. At a specific time signature change in the theme he knew to start smiling, any later and the smile looked faked or forced for the rest of the show no matter how genuinely he was actually doing it. He took a deep breath at the upbeat, the director pointed at him, the lights flashed on, and the cameras took focus.

"Hello world," he went into his opening monologue as if he were programmed to do it. "I'm Russ Logo, and *this* is *Logo's Show.* For anyone out there who's been living under a rock since they were born, the *show* I'm talking about is life. And...let me tell you—let me tell you world—never before in the history of existence was I more convinced that this is in fact Logo's show than I am on this very day. Not to get into too much detail—because we have some guests to talk to and electioneering to get through"—he winked at the camera—"but let me just say that someone approached me today and wanted to talk about—wait—you'll never guess...robots."

The crowd *Ooooh!*ed in response.

"Now, a lot of you watch this show religiously, and you often hear me complaining about shoddy robot technology—especially in the home beauty and food service industries—but I know how hard they work on our assembly lines at least. Am I right people?"

The crowd cheered and clapped on cue.

"That's right they do. But this woman today—now this woman said that *she* worked on an assembly line. Can you believe that?"

The crowd booed.

"She said that humans worked on the front lines, not robots. Now can you believe that?"

A chorus of "no"s echoed through the studio.

"Well, on tonight's show we're going to discuss just that and so much more. So if you want to know what's hot and happening in the world today, stick around. Because *this* is *Logo's Show.*"

The hip hop theme came on again and the lights dropped. Russ stretched his legs a bit, wriggling in his seat, congratulating himself on another great opening segment. He could feel the crowd yearning for more, not just in front of him but all around the world. This, he knew, was going to be a great show. Maybe the best one he had ever put on.

Out of the corner of his eye, he saw two protectors in their big white boots and white cargo pants—*cargo pants!*—with chunky white plated vests—and all of this long after Owner Day which every respectable person knew was a fashion *faux pas*. They were wearing white helmets with facemasks that looked like something out of a samurai movie with deep, black, pointed eyes and misshapen mouths that flashed electronic green, red, and yellow as the protectors spoke in their unnatural modulated voices.

One of them tapped the director on the shoulder, and after a short, neon conversation, the director pointed in Russ's direction. Russ's body tensed up. The hairs on the back of his neck stood on end. He tried to calm himself, to breath deeply. He had no reason to feel like this. He had done nothing wrong. But he couldn't help it. It was an instinctual reaction. His knees started to shake under the desk as the protectors approached.

"Russ Logo," one of them said, hand on his holster, voice modulated somewhere between human and robot. The same sinking feeling knotted Russ's stomach as when he saw the jerky server at the Plantation.

"Yes?" Russ said in a squeaky voice. He coughed and overcompensated in the deep range with another, "Yes?"

"We have a few questions. Come with us."

"Can't this wait?" Russ said, regaining his normal voice. "I have a show to do."

"Now citizen!"

℞   ✳   ℞

IV. Mr. Kitty

The bed was soft and it smelled like home, that's why Mr. Kitty kept going back to it. It was soft because it was a bed. It smelled like home because it was in the house he lived in.

While he was drifting off to sleep, he liked to think about who's bed it was. Mr. Kitty slept in the thing. He undoubtedly got the most use out of it compared to anyone besides a few short-lived fleas. Yet still, he couldn't help but imagine that one of those humans would say that they owned it. They always had to own everything.

He also like to eavesdrop on the humans around him. Sometimes he would pretend to be asleep and listen to what they said when they thought they were alone. Humans were always more honest when they thought they were alone. One of them was in the room with him now and he thought he was alone. Mr. Kitty stretched his back, climbed out of the bed, and jumped up onto the desk the human was sitting behind. Still the human thought he was alone. Mr. Kitty could see everything he was doing and the human didn't care one bit. That was another thing about humans. They always underestimated the power of what they didn't understand.

The human sat in front of a long desk with four computer screens stacked up on top of each other like a window pane. For most of the day he watched as numbers on the screens rose and fell and changed color, and he listened to the beeps and blips the computer made. Each different combination of bleeps and hues and digits elicited a slightly different response from the human. Each time he would hit a few keys on the keyboard or move the mouse— Mr. Kitty thought they were talking about a live mouse when he was younger—and click a few times. It all seemed repetitive and boring to Mr. Kitty. Though the colors were pretty. And the sounds were strange.

While the human watched the numbers, a phone rang. Mr Kitty jumped at the sound of it. The human laughed and pat him once on the head. "It's just the phone, cat," he said.

Mr. Kitty went back to licking himself like nothing had happened while the human answered the phone.

"Hello," the human said.

"Yeah, well, I saw the numbers drop. I transferred production to 05437."

"Really? That many? I swear the old models had less problems."

"Uh...Yeah. Putting in the order right now."

"Alright. See you tonight."

"Yeah, you know it, because you already voted for me."

"*Ha ha ha*. Alright. Have a good one."

The human hung up the phone and pet Mr. Kitty on the back a few times before typing in another set of keystrokes. He groaned and leaned back in his chair.

"You know, cat," he said. "You have got the life. Even better than one of those actors or musicians in the advertising department. You don't do any work at all. Not that they do, either. *Heh heh*."

Mr. Kitty stretched out on the desk and yawned. If the human only knew the work that he did, the places he had been. As if looking at numbers and hitting keystrokes was any more important than Mr. Kitty's chores. Why, if he stopped hunting mice for one week, they would probably overrun the entire house. Well, maybe he didn't hunt mice that often these days.

"But what do you know of work?" the human went on. "You're just an animal. It takes a human to work, to earn their keep. Cats are nothing but pets. You're as much property as a robot."

And there it was again, the curious human notion of ownership. As if anything could be yours beyond what you consumed and made a part of yourself—or whatever you were willing to fight to defend. This human here thought he could own Mr. Kitty. *Ha*! Mr. Kitty traveled the worlds while the human sat in his house all day like a caged animal. If anything, the human was the pet.

"No," the human said. "It takes a human brain and a little bit of responsibility to truly be able to enjoy life. Something your cat brain will never understand."

Mr. Kitty had heard about enough. He stood to stretch, and was about to leave, when the phone range again. This time he didn't jump.

"Tillie, dear," the human answered.

"Oh, no. Of course. Holiday traffic."

"Yeah, I'll be here. I'm just giving the numbers one last—"

"No, no, no. As soon as you get here all work dropped, just like I promised."

"Okay. No. Okay. I love you, too."

He hung up the phone and patted Mr. Kitty on the head. "You hear that? Tillie's gonna be late."

Mr. Kitty had almost forgotten that she would be coming home today. He decided against leaving, and laid back down on the desk. Tillie was the one who really loved Mr. Kitty. In fact, he expected that her dad—the human at the computer screens—only kept him around as a reason for her to visit. If she was out of the picture, the supply of cat food and his welcome would wear out fast. But Tillie was always a joy to see.

Numbers flipped, noises beeped, and colors changed while the human moaned and groaned and clicked and typed. It was so boring Mr. Kitty didn't have to pretend to be asleep. Sleep came naturally. He didn't wake again until he heard the doorbell, the human cursing a few times, then the sound of him walking out of the room. Mr. Kitty followed behind, trudging along on the soft puffy carpet. That was another reason he kept coming back. The carpet felt so good under his paws, he loved to tear it up.

The human took a few deep breaths before opening the door and smiling. "Tillie!" he said. "So nice to see you. How are you?"

Tillie hugged him but it was awkward with the big backpack on her back. "Fine, fine," she said. "It was a ridiculous line, though. You wouldn't believe."

"I'm sure," her dad said. "Traveling during the holidays and all."

"Yeah," Tillie said. "Yeah, the Christmas Election. But could I put this stuff down?" she added, adjusting her obviously heavy backpack. "It's really heavy."

"Oh, yes, dear," her dad said. "Of course. I fixed up a room for you. Follow me. Though I don't know why you brought so much stuff. We do still have a printer, you know."

"Yeah, well," Tillie said. "I have some library books I thought I might get a chance to read. And the pajamas I like to sleep in. You know."

"Ah. Of course of course," her dad said. "Well, let's go."

They started down the hall, but Tillie saw Mr. Kitty and dropped her backpack to scoop him up in her arms. "*Hey there Mr. Kitty*," she said in a babying voice. Normally Mr. Kitty found that offensive, but coming from her it was almost endearing. "I missed you *so much*. Yes I did. *Has daddy been taking good care of you?*"

Her dad laughed. "*Heh heh*. Yeah, we're great pals," he said. "Mr. Kitty here loves to watch me work. Don't you buddy?" He scratched Mr. Kitty's ear.

"*Awww*," Tillie said. "You love computers, don't you Mr. Kitty? *Yes you do.*" She set him down and scratched his stomach. "I'll give you some wet food in a minute, okay Mr. Kitty."

"The room's right this way," her dad said

"I really love this new house, dad," Tillie said, following him through the halls, lugging her heavy backpack, as Mr. Kitty slunk along behind them. "Where'd you import this one from?"

"Got it from New Orleans," her dad said. "I was lucky to pick it up when I did, too. They were putting a restaurant there, or something, and the buyer who was gonna take it fell through. I got it for a steal. Not to mention I made a profit on selling the old one. Not bad, wouldn't you say?"

"It's just beautiful," Tillie said.

They dropped her bag in a spare bedroom, then Mr. Kitty followed them to the kitchen where Tillie pressed the voice activation button on the 3D printer.

"Cat food, please," she said.

"*Please?*" Her dad scoffed. "You don't have to say please, dear. It's a robot you're talking to."

"Well, *my parents* taught me to be polite," she said, getting the bowl of wet food out of the printer and setting it on the counter for Mr. Kitty to jump up and eat.

"Yes," her dad said. "To be polite when necessary. In this instance it's not, however. But could you get me a beer, *please*, dear." He chuckled.

She pressed the button again. "Beer, pl—" She stopped herself.

Her dad laughed as she handed him the frosty pint glass. "So, how are your classes going?" he asked, taking a sip. "Still doing well?"

"Yeah, well," Tillie said. "I have some difficult professors this semester, but I'm learning a lot about statistical analysis. I think I might want to go into operations programming."

"Coding?" her dad said, shaking his head. "Are you sure about that, sweetheart? Computer programs will never outwit the human brain."

"Sure," Tillie said, nodding and giving a thumbs up. "And not too long ago robots would *never* match human physical precision, either. Now they're working in every factory that still turns a profit. So we know what never looks like, don't we?"

"But creative work is something completely different, sweetheart. I mean, imagine a robot that could think like a human. How would it be any different from anyone else?"

"It'd be immortal for starters," Tillie said.

"It'd be impossible for starters," her dad said. "No. Leave physical labor to the robots and the creative labor to the only ones who can do it: us humans."

Mr. Kitty finished licking the juices off the wet food and started licking himself. There were those strange human tendencies again. As if they were somehow unique, somehow different from every other natural phenomenon. As if the processes in their brains were fundamentally different than those in his brain, or the inner workings of a robot, or the processes that made the computer screens change color and beep. Always the humans tried to put themselves above nature so they could justify their own need for ownership over everything.

After throwing his mostly full bowl of food into the trash chute, Tillie carried Mr. Kitty into the living room with her where her dad was already sitting in a big, comfy rocking chair, flipping through the channels on the TV until a football game came on. He only partly listened to Tillie after that.

"Speaking of robots, dad," she said. "Have you watched the news lately?"

"Huh? What?" her dad said. "Oh, no. I try to stay away from it. What happened?"

"Well, you know that Russ Logo? He's like—well, I guess he's like *the* it star right now, or whatever. Anyway, he's the most viewed ever, and he does this daily talk show, right. Dad, are you listening?"

"Huh?" her dad said, still looking at the TV. "Yeah. Russ Logo. Go ahead." He waved her on.

"Anyway," Tillie said. "He has this show—*Logo's Show*—where he talks about, just life and movies and restaurants and stuff. But they're like, these restaurants that don't exist—right—or only exist in the show or something—I don't know. It's hard to explain unless you've watched a few episodes and researched it, and it would be really helpful if you were actually listening to me right now and not watching this stupid game. Because, honestly, I'm pregnant and it's quadruplets."

"Right," her dad said. "Logo's show. I'm listening. Go on."

"Well," Tillie said. "The father's literally a dog, and the babies might come out with four legs. *Soooo*, you're a grandpa of puppy centaurs. Congratulations!"

"That's nice, dear," her dad said, nodding.

"Dad!" Tillie slapped his arm, rustling Mr. Kitty in her lap. "You're not listening."

"I am, dear," he said, rubbing his arm and staring at the screen. "I am. Let me just...watch...this...one…more...play...*ohhhh!* And commercial. What were you saying, honey?" He turned to her and smiled.

"This guy Russ Logo does a talk show, and he said that someone came up to him on his way home from a restaurant claiming to be a factory—or—er—an assembly line worker, or something."

Her dad laughed. "That's rich!" he said. "Was he dressed up in silver and doing the robot? *Ha ha!*"

"First of all," Tillie said. "*She* had dirt all over *her* face, and *she* was wearing rags. Dad, she said that there weren't robots on the assembly lines at all. She said they were humans."

"*Ha ha ha!*" her dad laughed. "Humans on an assembly line!" he said, slapping his hand on his knee. "Next you'll tell me we have robots inventing new technology, or managing corporations even! *Ha ha ha!*"

"Dad. But what if it's true?"

Her dad scoffed. "What if Santa Claus is real? Then we'd all get what we want for Christmas. But he's not, so what's the point in asking?"

"But why would someone do that?" Tillie said. "Why would

they show it on TV?"

"I think you answered your own question, dear," her dad said.

"How's that?"

"Well, it was on TV," he said. "You can't believe everything you see on TV, sweetheart. People will say anything to get you to watch."

"Yeah," Tillie said. "Then why did the Protectors interrupt his show?"

"How's that?"

"Right after the intro, the show got cut off," she said. "He never got to say what happened, but the papos are supposed to have it all on film."

"Then what's the point in not letting him talk about it?" her dad said, sighing and looking back at the TV.

"You tell me."

"I will," he said. "At the next commercial, dear. Could you get me another beer?"

"*Ugh*. Fine, dad." She stood, forcing Mr. Kitty off her lap onto the couch, and went to the kitchen.

If only those humans knew what was going on around them. But no. They were stuck in their animal cages like his pets. The worst part about it was that they couldn't even see their chains.

Tillie sat back on the couch and handed her dad the beer. "You know..." She paused, thought about stopping, and went on. "I've been thinking about going into lobbying, too."

The sound of the word flipped some switch in her dad's brain. It was enough to draw his attention away from the game.

"Tillie," he said, raising his eyebrows. "Lobbying? You can't be serious. I'd believe that wacko nut-job who was talking about human factory workers before I would believe that *my* daughter would be a lobbyist. It's out of the question. Impossible. I won't hear it." He shook his head, gesturing with his hands as he spoke.

"That's exactly why the lobbyists are necessary, dad. Because *you* won't hear it. You never listen."

"I'm listening right now, aren't I? And I'm saying no. Lobbyists aren't necessary. Far from it. I tell you, if you just got rid of all the lobbyists, my job would be all that much easier."

"Then how would you know what people want?" Tillie

asked. "How would you know what they need?"

"The same way we have forever," her dad said. "The same way we always will. The market. They can buy whatever their heart desires, and anyone can sell it."

"And what about those who can't afford it?"

"Those who can't afford what?" Her dad scoffed. "Look around you, dear. Everyone has everything they need. You're asking about humans on an assembly line again. You're asking about Santa's elves. Why waste your time worrying about things that don't exist?"

"That's not entirely true, dad," Tillie said. "There are—"

"There are what?" her dad said. "3D printers in every corner store. Homelessness eradicated. A longer life expectancy than any time in history. All thanks to the market, no lobbyists needed."

"But lobbyist have been there guiding it along the whole time."

"Lobbyists have been there holding it back," her dad said through gritted teeth. "The less they do, the more we get done. Come on, honey. We're Managers. You should know that. Who would you lobby anyway? Lobby yourself for yourself? It's silly. What's good for you is what's good for production, and the market knows that best."

"But dad," Tillie said. "I don't think it's—"

"*Shh.*" Her dad looked back at the TV. "Now that's enough politics," he said. "You didn't come home just to argue with your father, did you? This is the holiday season, Tillie. A time for family."

"And there's no coincidence that the election is during the holiday?" she asked.

"What's that, dear?" her dad said, lost again in the game.

"Nothing, dad," Tillie said, shaking her head. "Nothing. Go ahead back to your game. I'm gonna go put my things up, okay. I'll be right back."

"Alright, honey," he said. "I love you."

"C'mon, Mr. Kitty," Tillie said. "Let's go unpack."

They walked back to the spare bedroom where Mr. Kitty jumped up onto the bed. Tillie sat down next to him and patted him on the head.

"You don't think I'm crazy," she said. "Do you Mr. Kitty?"

Mr. Kitty meowed. If she knew his language anywhere near as well as he knew hers, she would know that he meant to say that she was as far away from crazy as humans got these days. Instead she only heard a meow.

"You know, humans did used to work on the assembly lines," Tillie said. "I learned about it in history class. So its not that outlandish. They were phased out for robot labor to make management that much easier. But there's one thing I wonder..." She shook her head. "No."

Mr. Kitty meowed again. "Go on," he said.

"I mean, I know my dad says its impossible, but what if the robots *did* have the capability to think like humans? What if, in order to work in our factories and serve our food, they *had to* be able to think like humans? Well then, who will speak for the robots if there's no one to lobby for them?"

"Well, you could let them speak for themselves," Mr. Kitty meowed.

"Yes. Exactly," Tillie said, standing up and pacing the room. "I should look into this. I should speak for them if no one else will. But first, but first... But first, what? What, what, what?"

"That's not what I said," Mr. Kitty meowed. "You're not listening. Just like your father."

"Great idea, Mr. Kitty," Tillie said. "I'll see if I can... I'll see if I can contact Russ Logo somehow. I'll ask him about what really happened and about what the protectors had to say to him. That's the perfect place to start. You're so smart, Mr. Kitty."

"I give up," Mr. Kitty meowed one last time. "Do what you want and learn from it." He stretched out and laid on the bed, pretending to be asleep while Tillie made the call.

"Hello," she said. "Is this Russ Logo?"

"Oh. Well, is there any way I would be able to speak to him?"

She walked around, unpacking her pajamas into the drawers and her books onto the dresser, while she talked.

"No. Does this have anything to do with why his show was cut short?"

"No, sir. No no no. I'm sorry. Thank you. B—" She hung up the phone. "*Bye*."

"*Ugh*, Mr. Kitty," she said, plopping onto the bed next to

him. "Some people are so rude. He said I'll just have to watch the show to find out."

"Tillie!" her dad called from the other room. "Tillie! Turn on the TV!"

"What?" she called back.

"The TV! Turn it on!"

"What channel?"

"All of them!"

She stood and flicked the TV on by hand. Mr. Kitty yawned and stretched to get a closer look at what was so important to her dad. On the screen was a human face with lots of makeup painted on, clearly being used to cover up bruises and other injuries. Tillie gasped when she saw it. She must have noticed what the makeup was hiding, too.

"I repeat," the human face repeated. "It has been verified that the woman who spoke to me outside the Plantation today was an independent filmmaker working on a yet unreleased prank reality show where historical figures interact with modern celebrities. In no way do I believe that humans are working on assembly lines, and I do not wish to promote such an *absurd* idea with my unknowing participation in a work of art that may or may not promote that idea. That's all there is left to say on the matter, and I would appreciate it if we could lay this to rest. Thank you."

The picture of the bruised and painted human gave way to a barrage of prediction numbers. Tillie turned off the TV and threw the remote down on the bed, almost hitting Mr. Kitty who jumped out of the way just in time.

"Oh, I'm sorry, Mr. Kitty," she said, sitting on the bed next to him. "I didn't mean to scare you."

Mr. Kitty rubbed his head on her hand.

"Something's going on here, Mr. Kitty," she said. "Did you see Russ? His delivery was so dry and monotone. And he didn't even plug his show. He always plugs his show. Something happened to him, and I think it's because of what he said on TV."

Mr. Kitty meowed in agreement. He followed Tillie out of the room, and stood behind her in the door of the living room where her dad was still watching the game. "Did you see that?" he said without looking away from the screen.

"Yes, I did," Tillie said. "You didn't—"

"And what did he say?" her dad said. "*Just a publicity stunt. Some independent artist putting on a reality show.* I told you it was for TV. Was I right or was I right, dear?"

"That *is* what he said," Tillie said. "But you didn't—"

"But, but, but," her dad said. "I told you not to believe it because it was on TV, and now that the TV tells you it was a prank, you don't want to believe that. I don't understand your insistence on believing in fairy tales, honey."

"You didn't notice anything strange about him, dad?" Tillie said. "Like maybe the bruises under his makeup, or the way he had none of his usual inflection in his voice. No. You wouldn't, would you? Because its all numbers on a computer screen for you. There aren't real people behind them."

"I wouldn't notice because I don't have time to watch every clown with a camera who wants to rant at the world," her dad said, getting red faced and loud. "I'm busy doing the work it takes to keep everything running the way it does. For me to do that effectively it requires that I stay grounded in reality. I don't have time for *La La Land* like you students do. When you get older, you'll grow out of this phase just like everyone else."

"Unseen Hand, you're impossible," Tillie said. "I'm leaving. I'm gonna go see Shelley or something. I'll be back for dinner." She grabbed her coat and left before the play was over and her dad could break away to stop her.

Mr. Kitty stretched. Football was boring and the human could be staring at it for a long time. As he jumped down from the couch, though, the human stood up, mumbling to himself, and went back into his office to sit in front of the pane of computer screens. Mr. Kitty followed him and sat on the desk, cleaning himself from a good vantage point to see what was going on.

"Show's how much she loves us," the human said, his eyes flicking across the screen.

Mr. Kitty wanted to mention that Tillie was mad at her father—not at Mr. Kitty—but he decided to keep his mouth shut and busy cleaning his coat.

"Just numbers," the human said. "*Just* numbers. As if that's all I care about."

Mr. Kitty thought that there were also colors and noises—not just numbers—but he kept that to himself, too.

"She simply doesn't understand what I really do. Sure, there are a lot of numbers. But that's not *all* I do. Why, take this right here." He made a few keystrokes and clicked something. Mr. Kitty tried to bat at the mouse as he did.

"You see. They don't just show me numbers. Right here they had some cleaner bots malfunction, or a textile machine malfunctioned, I don't know. But look." He moved the mouse on the screen as if the cat would know what to look at, and Mr. Kitty did. "They give us the production numbers here, of course, but this here"—he pointed to a tiny camera icon—"also gives me video evidence of the accident so I can prevent the same occurrence in the future. You get it?"

He looked at Mr. Kitty then shook his head. "Of course not," he said. "Why am I telling all this to a cat?"

"You should tell it to Tillie," Mr. Kitty meowed.

"*Ha ha*. Maybe you do understand," the human said. "Well, don't tell our Tillie this, but I rarely ever look at the photos. There's never really anything there to see. *Ha ha!*"

"Click this one," Mr. Kitty meowed.

Almost as if he understood, the human clicked it and a photo came up. A bunch of children were all trying to pull three or four others—it was hard to tell how many exactly because only parts of them were still visible—out of the bloody jaws of the machine. The blood looked black like oil spread all over everything. Mr. Kitty could see the horror on the children's faces as they pulled the pieces of their friends out of the cold metal jaws of death. He wondered what the human could see, and the human told him.

"You see. Robots cleaning up the mess they made. That's all it is. That's what they do, they're cleaner bots. You know, maybe if I show Tillie this—show her that it's not all numbers…"

"Do it," Mr. Kitty meowed.

"You're right, cat. That's against policy. And I've had about enough of work for today. Back to the game." He pet Mr. Kitty on the head and left.

Mr. Kitty curled up into a ball on the desk to get some sleep. He just had to wait for Tillie to get home and hope that her dad would show her. Otherwise he'd have to find a way to show her himself. She would see it one way or another, the terror on those kids' faces, the humanity. Maybe then she'd find what she was looking for.

He woke an indeterminate time later to the sound of Tillie sitting at the desk and clicking around on the computer. She was searching through a law database for any signs of "human" and "factory" or "assembly line" in the same file, but all that came up were stories about how the "Logo stunt" was a hoax and how the video footage would be coming out soon. She clicked and typed and clicked, then slunk back into the soft, leather chair with a huff.

"He didn't close it," Mr. Kitty meowed. "You're so close."

"*Awww*. Mr. Kitty." She pet his head. "I know *you* care. You never let me down."

"Look. It's still open." He walked across the keyboard, trying to bring the picture back up.

"Mr. Kitty, stop it!" She scooped him up and sat him on her lap. "I'm trying to find out more about the assembly line workers," she said, scratching his ear and squinting at the screen.

Mr. Kitty wasn't able to pull the picture up when he walked across the keyboard, but he did pull up the production numbers. Colors changed on the screen, and numbers flipped, but there were no beeps.

"What's this?" She clicked around on a few icons.

"Click the camera," Mr. Kitty meowed.

"I knew it," Tillie said. "Numbers, numbers, numbers. That's all he sees."

She clicked back through the historical data. There was so much to see it took a few pages to get even to that morning.

"What's the point in looking at all these stupid numbers?" Tillie said.

She was about to give up when Mr. Kitty bit her wrist. She flinched, clicking something, and yelled, "*Ouch!*"

"Are you alright, sweetheart?" her dad called from the other room.

"Shoo, Mr. Kitty." She pushed him off her lap. He jumped up onto the desk and started licking himself. "Don't do that, Mister."

"Tillie!" her dad called again. "Do I need to come in there?"

Tillie looked at the screen. The picture her dad had been looking at was on top now. She gasped at the sight of it. She stared in shock at the faces of pain and anguish on the children, at the blood on the floor and the machinery and their clothes—which had clearly been retouched to look black instead of red—at the mold on the walls and the youth in their eyes, caught just as it disappeared.

Her dad walked in and said, "Tillie, what are you doing?"

"I was just trying to look up information about the scene with Russ today," she said. "But I accidentally found this. Why were you looking at historical photos of factory accidents?"

"Historical photos?" Her dad looked at the screen, frowning. "Oh, dear," he said, shaking his head. "You should not have seen that. It's against policy. You should not have seen that."

"Against policy?" Tillie frowned.

"Yes," her dad said. "You shouldn't be looking at it. It's a photo of an accident that happened this morning. We lost three cleaner bots. You see, I told you it's not all numbers with me."

"Three cleaner bots, dad?" Tillie scoffed.

"Yes, dear," her dad said, pointing at the screen. "Right there. You're looking at it."

"Dad," she said. "Those aren't robots."

"Sure they are, honey. What else would they be? Humans that bleed oil? *Ha ha ha!*"

"Look at their faces, dad. Why would they look so terrified if they were robots?"

He squinted at the screen. "I don't know," he said. "My eyes are going again. The hazards of work, you know. I didn't notice. But those robots are getting more and more realistic every day. Who am I to ask why they design them the way they do?"

"But, dad—"

"No more buts," her dad said. "It's almost time for dinner, and I have some people coming over who I'd like you to meet. They'll tell you all about lobbying, dear. Now come on."

He left, but Tillie stayed seated and pet Mr. Kitty. "Those aren't robots, Mr. Kitty," she said. "And I'm going to get to the bottom of this."

Mr. Kitty purred in response.

☙ ✳ ৶

V. Ellie

There was a time in her life when Ellie thought that no job could be more boring than slip, snap, clicking. That was a long time ago, before the accident that took her son. They *took care* of an employee after an accident in the family like that. That was how she got her pity promotion.

She went from production to quality assurance. Where production was repetitive and tedious, quality assurance was random and exhausting. There would be long stretches in which she could only stare at an empty conveyor belt, sitting alone in her ten by ten cube, just one door and the conveyor belt spanning between dark metal hoods on either side of the room. Then, during the rushes, there would be a flurry of work as items sped in from one side of the conveyor belt, stopped for a moment, then sped out the other: four eggs, *check*, four strips of bacon, *check*, four pieces of bread, *check*, blueberry jam, *check*, tray with plate, platinumware—not silver apparently—and coffee mug, *check*, *check*, and *check*. Then a slight rest. Then eight eggs, *check*, eight strips of bacon, *check*, eight pieces of bread, *check*, and so on and so on. She felt as if she were feeding a beast that got hungrier and hungrier the more that it ate until it couldn't hold anymore and its stomach exploded. Then the thing woke up and ate its own insides, which only served to make it hungrier and hungrier again until it went through the same process over and over.

There she sat in her tiny gray room, counting the time away, ensuring that each item on the conveyor belt matched the words on the little screen in front of her. They always matched. There was a little red button next to the screen that she was supposed to press if there was ever a mistake, but she had never had the opportunity to press it. There was never a mistake.

She spent a lot of time wondering what would happen if she did press it. Not out of the blue, of course—she would probably be fired for that, and there was no good reason to test the hypothesis— but what if it didn't match for once? What if the screen said "pan" and out came a fully cooked chicken? She'd press the button, of course, but then what? Would the conveyor belt stop? Would an alarm sound and lights flash? Would whoever needed the pan go waiting? Where was the pan going anyway?

That was another thing she spent her time thinking about. Where did the conveyor belt go to and where did it come from?

A bell rang. The screen read sixteen hamburgers. Sixteen hamburgers came out with barely enough time for Ellie to count them before they zoomed on down the line and out of sight. Sixteen buns, *check*, sixteen potatoes, *check*...

When the flood of work subsided she cleared her mind. She wondered again what the red button would do. Would it set off lights and sirens? Then she remembered she was on to wondering about the conveyor belt and went back to that.

It was strange, the conveyor belt. Impossible really. The "out" end went through the wall that Ellie had never seen the other side of, but the "in" end went straight through the same wall the door was on. Ellie had been on the other side of that wall, and she knew there was nowhere for anything to come from. The conveyor belt didn't continue out into the hallway. It stopped right there at the wall. And there was no way it was coming from above, either. There were metal hoods covering the "in" and "out" ports, so no matter where she stood in the room she was unable to see where the things came from or where they went to, but when she stood up as tall as she could, she could see over the hoods to the other wall and knew that nothing was coming from up there.

The bell rang. Thirty two hamburgers, *check*, thirty two buns, *check*, thirty two potatoes, *check*. And so on and so on.

When it had all gone by and the work died down again, she wondered if the monster on the other side of the wall had finally burst. She squirmed in her chair, trying to lean over to see where the things came from, where they went to, but there was nothing, only darkness under the hoods. They came from nothing and went to nothing, stopping on the way so Ellie could make sure the correct goods got from here to nowhere.

She knew better than that, though. She might not know where they went—that much stuff all at once never ended up in the hands of anyone she knew—but she knew all too well where they came from. She had spent her time on the assembly line slip, snap, clicking away at who knows what, and everyone else she knew had spent their time on their own lines producing something else for someone none of them knew. Hell, she had paid the ultimate price for production, more expensive even than her own worn-out weary life, she had lost the new, endless life of her son, and as a reward, she got to sit in QA instead of work on the assembly line. Some reward!

Her heart beat faster at the injustice of it all. She wanted to break something, to take something, to get revenge somehow. She wanted to press the red button and see the look on their faces, see if they even had faces. She wanted to shut everything down, go out to the bar, and get stone cold drunk until she forgot who she was and thought the bar and the beer were all the world that existed, get drunk until she forgot the cost. But that wasn't an option, that was death, and death wasn't a choice. Her death wouldn't bring her son back. It would only prevent her from getting revenge. The only recourse she had left was to wait, to bide her time until she could find an effective way to exact that revenge.

She checked the conveyor belt again. Still she couldn't see anything. Right about then she would normally have another string of hamburgers and potatoes, but nothing came. The bubble must have burst early. The monster was full and her shift was almost over.

The time ticked by slower when the work didn't come. She sat staring at the conveyor belt, going through the same cycle of thoughts over and over again: Nothing on the screen. Where does the stuff go anyway? Where does it come from? Oh, I know all too well where it comes from. How could I let them know that I know? I need this job to exist, though. Nothing on the screen. Where does the stuff go anyway? Where does it come from? Oh, I know all too well where it comes from...

Sometimes she'd linger on one bit a little longer than the others, but most of her time was spent thinking about her son and how nothing could ever make up for losing him. The seconds ticked by at a glacial pace whatever she had on her mind.

A bell rang. This one was slightly different in tone. She still looked to the screen first to see what was supposed to come through, but when she saw that it was empty, she jumped from her seat and rushed to the door.

Her hurried footsteps echoed through the concrete hall. She

kept her eyes forward, intent on the destination in front of her. She could hear some small conversations going on around her, and she had to fight through clumps of traffic because of it, but she tried to ignore it all. She was leaving. It was about to be a long weekend. She didn't have to hear their stupid gossiping for a full three days, and she was overjoyed at that fact. She couldn't believe that she was feeling as much Christmas joy as she was without her son there to bring it out of her.

She choked back tears at the thought of him and set her mind again on the bar. The sun was low when she burst out of the glass doors of the factory lobby. Shadows from the tall buildings all around cut across her face as the air started to cool. She shook her body a little to warm it up, and was about to set off toward the elevator terminal when, from behind, she heard a gravelly old voice that grated at her insides. "Ellie! Ellie, dear!" it called. Ellie shuddered more at the sound of it than she did at the cold air.

"Ellie, wait up, dear," the voice said. "Please. My old legs aren't what they used to be."

Ellie relented, stopping in her tracks but not turning to greet the woman. She knew who it was. She knew the old lady had gotten the same pity promotion that Ellie had gotten, only for Gertrude it had been many years since. Gertrude was promoted for losing a son and a husband. She, too, knew the real cost of production. That was a big part of the reason Ellie didn't like her. Gertrude had been put through the same torture at the hands of production—more, considering it took her husband, too—and here she was with nothing to show for it but a prolonged lonely life. Deep down Ellie feared that Gertrude was some kind of omen revealing her own future self.

"Oh, dear," Gertrude said, finally having caught up to Ellie who still wasn't moving. "I'm sorry, honey. You'll have to let me catch my breath."

"Hello, Gertrude," Ellie said with no inflection. She looked the old woman up and down, studying her crow's-feet and sagging cheeks, her sagging everything. More than even behind the conveyor belt, Ellie wished that she was at the bar, deep in drink, instead of on this busy sidewalk.

"You know, dear—You know..." Gertrude looked suspiciously at the people walking around them, as if they might be eavesdropping on their conversation. She lowered her voice so none of them could hear. "You know, I heard a juicy little morsel of information today. Juicy juicy, sweetheart. You wouldn't believe."

Ellie rolled her mind's eyes. "Oh yeah, Gertrude? Did Maci finally find out who the father of her baby is?"

"Trudy, dear. My friends call me Trudy. And, in fact—now that you mention it—there has been another possible father added to the list. He's a nice young man, it seems—much nicer than any of the current frontrunners, that's for sure—from what I've heard at least. My fingers are crossed for her that it's this one and not one of those other two deviants. That's all I know."

"Well, Gertrude—er—Trudy," Ellie said. "You'll have to tell me all about it after the long weekend, huh? Right now I'm off to celebrate. Merry Christmas to you." She started again toward the public elevator.

"Ellie, dear. Wait!" Gertrude grabbed her arm.

Ellie almost gasped in surprise. It wasn't like Gertrude to be so forceful.

"*Ahem*. Excuse me, dear," Gertrude said. "I apologize. It's just—I…" She looked around again at the people leaving work or going to it.

"What is it Ger—Trudy? Is something wrong?"

"I—uh—" Gertrude shrunk back into her old self. She seemed to age ten years with the bad posture. She looked frail and weak. Ellie almost pitied her. "Perhaps we could talk somewhere more…personal," she said, looking around again, but still no one was paying attention to them.

Ellie didn't know what to do. She didn't want to sit and listen to some pointless anecdote about the social life of someone she didn't know or care the least bit about, and that was probably exactly the "juicy morsel" of information that Gertrude was so excited to share. But then there was something in the shrillness of her voice when she called for Ellie to wait, and it *was* strange to see her being so secretive with her gossip. Yes, usually she asked everyone she told not to tell a soul, but that was because she wanted the honor of telling as many people as she could herself. If anyone ever asked her about any piece of gossip, Gertrude would jump at the opportunity to share even the most personal of secrets, as long as it was her doing the sharing. This time, though, it was almost as if she was afraid that someone would find out what she knew. As if the secret was more important than the latest social gossip.

"I hear there's an okay bar just down the street," Ellie said. "Do you drink?"

Gertrude laughed a scratchy laugh. "The Water Cooler, dear?" she said, shaking her head. "Too many co-workers. I was thinking of something a little more...private."

It must have been more than gossip if she didn't want co-workers to hear it. Ellie was more curious than ever, but at the same time she was torn. She knew the perfect place to talk, where no co-worker would ever overhear them, a bar that no co-worker knew about, but that was exactly why she liked it. Everyone at the production plant and in a five mile radius would learn about it if Gertrude knew. But was that worth it for finding out what made the old lady so nervous to know and share?

"I might know a place," Ellie said.

"Great, sweetheart," Gertrude said with a smile. "It's not too far is it?" She started toward the public elevator without waiting for an answer. "I'm not sure my old dogs can take it."

"I said I *might* know," Ellie said without moving. Gertrude stopped and turned back to her with a puppy dog look on her face. "But I wouldn't want it getting around about this place. If you know what I mean."

"Oh, sweetheart," Gertrude said. "You can trust dear old Trudy with that, you can." She crossed her heart and spat on the ground. "If not me, then who can you trust? Huh?" She smiled wide as if she meant it.

"Like Maci and her potential fathers could trust you?" Ellie said. "Or Merl when he had his ED problems? Or Sally with her miscarriage? Maybe I can trust you like—"

"Now, now, child. Hold your tongue. None of those were secrets entrusted to me. They were all gossip floating in the air for anyone to catch and pass along. Secrets are different. Secrets I can keep." She had a stern, serious look on her face as she said it, a look Ellie had never seen from her.

"But this will be a secret I entrust to you and you alone," Ellie said.

"And I'll keep it as well as I expect you to keep the secret I'm entrusting to you."

Ellie looked her up and down one more time and nodded.

"Let's go, then," she said. "I need a drink."

The public elevator was crowded. It was always crowded. As they waited, the sun went further down, producing a cold breeze through the skyscrapers that towered over them. Gertrude took the chance to go over the finer points of Maci's new baby daddy possibility while they waited. He loved reality TV and hated sports, which was so strange in a guy. He had a job in food production, so he made a good amount of tokens, but apparently he wasn't very good looking. Although Gertrude thought that part shouldn't matter. Then she admitted that it did matter. "Of course it does," she said, winking at Ellie. "You're lying if you say it doesn't. But he's an honest, productive worker, and that's more important."

When they were finally at the head of the line and the elevator doors slid open, Ellie was hit by the stale odor of urine. They stepped onto the elevator without acknowledging it, and Ellie said, "Elysian Fields."

"So," Gertrude said, as the elevator fell into motion. "Elysian Fields." She tapped her nose with a finger.

"A secret you're entrusted to keep," Ellie reminded her.

Gertrude nodded and mimed a key locking her lips. Ellie suspected it might not have been a mistake to bring her along when Gertrude didn't add another word for the entire walk from the elevator to the bar, down an alley a half a block away.

The air inside was stale with the scent of burnt tobacco and rank with the sour aroma of still fermenting yeast. Ellie took in a deep breath of it and her muscles relaxed. She walked straight up to the bar, sat at her regular seat on the far end, and ordered a beer, forgetting Gertrude who paused at the door to look at the place before walking cautiously over and taking the seat next to her. It didn't take long because there was nothing more than a jukebox, pool table, dartboard, and a few booths to see.

"I'll have what she's having," Gertrude said when the bartender brought Ellie's drink.

"On my tab," Ellie added, feeling guilty for not ordering one for her already.

Gertrude took in the place one more time. There was one other customer sitting at the opposite end of the bar, staring at the football game on the TV in front of him. "This is a nice place," she said. "What did you say it was called again?"

"I didn't." Ellie took a drink of her beer. She remembered the long weekend and felt the Christmas spirit again, adding, "I mean, it doesn't have a name. I just call it *the bar* because it's the only one I ever go to. That's why I wanted to keep it a secret."

Gertrude nodded and locked her lips again. The bartender brought her beer, still frosty and wet from where the head had overflowed, and Gertrude looked at the glass as if it wasn't clean. She picked it up anyway and took a tiny sip, then smiled and raised it when she saw that Ellie was watching.

"So," Ellie said, taking a drink from her own glass. "You had something you wanted to tell me."

Gertrude looked over at the other patron, still enraptured by the game on the TV, then leaned in close to Ellie. "Something you want to hear, dear," she whispered. "This is one piece of information I'm not sure I want to share." The door opened as she said it, and she jumped at the sound, looking around to see a few regulars who Ellie knew always came in to play pool. "Wanna take a booth?" Gertrude asked when she had gathered herself. "It should provide more privacy."

Ellie nodded and led Gertrude to the back booth. She had to know what it was that made the old lady so jumpy. "So..." she said when they had both sat down.

"So," Gertrude said. She looked behind Ellie at the people playing pool, the door, and the lone drinker, watching the game, before she continued. "How's your new job treating you?"

"It's paying for these drinks." Ellie took a sip to drive the point home.

"Yes. It does pay, doesn't it. If only it paid better." Gertrude laughed.

"It can always pay better."

"How true." Gertrude nodded. "How true. I wonder, dear. Do you know where this bar gets their beer?"

Ellie shrugged. "Out of the tap. As long as I can drink it, what do I care where they get it?"

"*Hmmm.* I guess you're right." Gertrude took a thoughtful sip of beer. "But you know where it *comes from*, don't you?"

Ellie thought about her son, tightened her lips into a line, and nodded.

"Well, dear," Gertrude said. "Do you ever wonder where it

all goes?"

Ellie took a big gulp of beer. Getrude couldn't have found that out. Could she? It did seem like a piece of knowledge that she would put more discretion into sharing. "Every day I sit behind the conveyor belt and ask myself that same question," Ellie said.

"Yes, dear," Gertrude said, nodding. "Yes. I think we all do. And not just in QA, either. Every one of us down here slip, snap, clicking, and growing food, and shipping this and that here, there, and everywhere. But still, with all these advancements in production, all these jumps in productivity, still not even the slightest percent of what we make ends up in our hands. No, it all just seems to...seems to...*disappear. Poof!*" She waved her hands as she said it and laughed, then perked up in silence and looked around the bar to see if her outburst had drawn the attention of any curious onlookers. When she was satisfied that it hadn't, she leaned over the table close to Ellie and whispered, "I'm sorry, dear. I've been gossiping a long *loooong* time to get this piece of information." She sipped her beer.

There was no doubt left in Ellie's mind that this was actually something worth knowing, something beyond Gertrude's usual workplace gossip. She took a big gulp of beer in anticipation and emptied her cup with it. "Wait," she said, holding up a finger. "Wait. I know what this means, but wait. I need a beer to take it with. You want another one?"

"Of course, sweetheart." Gertrude smiled. "Thank you. And, ַyes. I think a beer would help grease the gears, so to speak."

Ellie went to order two more. She sat in the booth, handed Gertrude her beer, and took a swig of her own. "You said you know where it goes."

"Oh, *ho ho*. No, sweetheart," Gertrude said, shaking her head. "No no no." She looked around the bar and leaned in close. "If I knew that I wouldn't be here to tell you. No. It's not me. But...You work in QA. You know we're on the last line of defense, we're the last thing that each commodity sees before it goes on its way out into the wide world. You know all that already, right?"

Ellie nodded.

"Of course you do, dear," Gertrude said. "We all know that down in QA. It's our job to know it. But none of us knows where the commodities go. None of us who can talk about it, at least." She grinned and took a sip of her beer. Here was the Gertrude Ellie knew: happy to lord her knowledge over the ignorant.

"How?" Ellie asked. She didn't want to give Gertrude the satisfaction of asking what was already implied.

"How else, dear?" Gertrude said. "She went right down the conveyor belt like a Christmas turkey!" She had a big smile on her face when she said it.

Ellie almost choked on the beer she was drinking. She set it down and said, "No." So many times she had thought that going through herself would be the only way to find out where everything went, but she never thought that anyone would be stupid enough to actually try it. She wondered what it felt like, what she—Ellie didn't even care who *she* was—saw, what Gertrude knew about it and how.

"Yes," Gertrude said with a smug grin, taking a sip of her beer.

Ellie waited a full minute, staring at the delight on Gertrude's face from dangling the information in front of her, before she said, "Well..."

"Well, dear?" Gertrude said, prolonging her joy for as long as she could.

"What did she see?"

"Sweetheart," Gertrude said, shaking her head. "I told you I wouldn't be sitting here if I knew what she saw. You're asking the wrong questions, dear." She sounded like Ellie's school teacher lecturing her on proper slip, snap, clicking technique and timing. They both used the same patronizing voice and had the same pompous look on their faces when they spoke.

Ellie thought about what to say next, about what the right question might be. Gertrude didn't mind waiting. She was happy to hold out on her information for as long as she could. She was relishing it. "How did you find out?" Ellie finally asked, satisfied it was a pointed enough question.

"Ah, dear," Gertrude said. "Now that's a question worth asking. And for the first line of evidence I present to you the fact that she didn't leave her hall with the rest of us at the end of shift on the day in question."

Ellie knew there was more to come, but she humored the pause in Gertrude's explanation with the hope that cooperating would speed the process along. "But that doesn't mean anything," she said. "She could have been sick and gone home early. That doesn't prove she went through the conveyor belt."

"True, dear," Gertrude said, nodding solemnly. "True. But she also told me about her plans to go through."

Ellie had more questions about that point, but she knew if she went off on a tangent now, they would never make it to the end of the explanation, so she held them for later. "Still," she said instead. "She could have lied."

"Also true," Gertrude said, raising a finger. "But then why would the protectors have come and questioned everyone on our hall about her whereabouts?"

How was Ellie supposed to know that they did? She took a big gulp of beer. But that did seem to point to it being real. "But why'd she do it? What was her plan when she got through?"

"That, dear, I'm not entirely sure of," Gertrude said. "She did mention to me that she planned on doing it, but that information came at great cost. As to what she planned on doing once she was through, that was too expensive to bear, even for me."

"What's on the other side?"

"Again. I couldn't tell you if I knew."

"Okay," Ellie said, sighing. "So you're telling me that she went through the conveyor belt and never came back, then the protectors came and questioned you about it."

"I don't know if she came back or not," Gertrude said.

"What did the protectors say to you?"

"Like I said, they asked general questions. If we noticed any suspicious behavior, if we knew where she might be, things like that."

"Just like that?" Ellie said. "Nothing else?"

"Just like that." Gertrude nodded.

Ellie took a swig of beer, started her question, then took another drink. "What would it cost to know what she planned on doing?"

"Now that's the question I've been waiting for all along, dear," Gertrude said with a smile. "Are you sure you want to know the answer?"

Ellie nodded.

"She told me I'd have to commit to going through myself. Or at least, to doing something equally insane. She wasn't specific, and she didn't want to tell me about it at all, but that was the gist of it."

Ellie thought about whether she would do it, about going through the unknown into a dark abyss. She wondered how it would

feel, what she would find, and if she could bear to try. "You thought that was too expensive?" she said.

"We've seen what it did to our poor friend—well, sort of," Gertrude said, shrugging. "It cost her everything for all we know."

"We haven't seen, though," Ellie said. "We've only assumed."

"Well, I guess that's true, dear," Gertrude said, nodding. "But do you think the presence of the protectors indicates any other outcome?"

"Maybe they took her for what she did."

"Then why would they ask if we knew where she might be? And what would they do with her if they did take her?"

"I—well…" Ellie didn't know how to answer that.

Gertrude smiled and sipped up the last bit of her beer. "Would you like another, dear?"

Ellie nodded. She could use one to help process all this new information. Gertrude went off to order them.

What would she actually be risking by going through? She could die. It could be something impossible to live through. She had never seen a living thing come down the conveyor belt. But what cost was that? She had lost everything worth living for except her need to avenge that fact, and Gertrude was offering the only real piece of information concerning where the things that her son had died making went.

But then again this was really nothing. It was all hearsay and rumors and all from Gertrude the Gossip Queen. So some woman Ellie had never met said that she might want to go through the conveyor belt. Ellie herself had thought the same thing on many occasions but never mentioned it. If she had mentioned it to someone and happened to miss work for a couple of days, they would be saying the exact same things about her.

But then there were the protectors. They lent credence to the theory that this mystery woman had attempted to go through. But they also added an element of danger if Ellie decided to go through herself. She knew good and well that there were things worse than death—worse even than the helpless, alienated life she already lived—and if anyone could make those things a reality, it was the protectors.

Gertrude set the beer in front of Ellie before she sat down. She looked around the bar one more time for good measure, took a sip of

her beer, smiled, and said, "So, dear. Do you think you'd be willing to
pay the price?"

                   ❧   ✺   ❧

VI. Officer Pardy

Officer Pardy checked himself in his locker mirror one last time. He wanted his uniform to be perfectly up to code for his first day on the job. Assured that it was, he brushed his finger across the picture of his wife and son on the inside of his locker door, decided he would take it with him after all, stuffed it in his cargo pants, and slammed the locker shut.

Another Officer, putting socks on beside him, jumped at the sound of it. "Amaru above, Tom!" Rabbit said. "As if I didn't have enough going on to destroy my nerves already."

"Settle down, Rabbit," Officer Pardy said, picking up his helmet from the bench. "You'll have nothing to be afraid of out there. I'll protect you."

A couple of others getting dressed in the locker room laughed. Everyone knew Rabbit was meant to do housework. He didn't have anything that a protector needed in him except for the blood of his hero mother. Rabbit was a liability to the entire operation, and that was a secret to no one.

"Yeah. Right, Tom," Rabbit said absently, putting on his boots. "Thanks."

"Hey, Rabbit," Officer Pardy called as he walked out of the locker room. "Rabbit!"

"Huh? Yeah, Tom?" Rabbit said. "What is it?"

"You gotta put your pants on before your boots, boy. I know it's not regulation, but it is common sense."

The locker room burst into another bout of laughter. Rabbit looked down at his feet, realized what he had done, then got to untying his boots and getting redressed properly. Officer Pardy—the first dressed because he was the first there—marched out to the sound of Rabbit jokes.

The stark white briefing room was empty. Rows and rows of stadium chairs sat facing a tall podium on a stage in front of a screen that covered the entire wall behind it. Officer Pardy marched to the front center seat and sat with perfect regulation posture. He had to make a good impression, to set an example for the other rookies to follow. He wanted to show everyone that he was the epitome of a protector. He slipped his helmet on, and his vision shifted into darkness for a split second before the goggles measured the exact location of his pupils and projected the image of the world around him onto his eyes with far more detail—and a much wider range of vision, a full 360°—than he could ever pick up helmetless.

Slowly, the other rookies filed into the briefing room, taking their seats around him. They talked to each other, and joked to relieve their nerves, but—unlike in the locker room—Officer Pardy was all business. There was a time for play, and there was a time for work, and when your helmet was on, you knew you were working. The aura of officiality he put off was so dense that no one sat in the seats next to him. At least until Rabbit came in and plopped himself into the chair to his left.

"How do I look?" Rabbit asked, sounding out of breath.

Officer Pardy looked over at him. His helmet saw through Rabbit's, and he could see that Rabbit was pale and frightened underneath. The helmet scanned Rabbit's heart rate and temperature. There was nothing there but housekeeper. His chest plates were off balance and his helmet too large, but it was too late for Officer Pardy to help him with that now, so he stared straight ahead again and said, "Regulation, Officer."

"*Amaru*," Rabbit said, shaking his head. "I don't know. Why am I here, Tom? Why am I here?"

Officer Pardy wouldn't have answered if he could. The Captain marched in with her mustached helmet and took the podium anyway, so he didn't have the option. The entire room stood to attention. The entire room, that is, except for Rabbit who first made a ruckus getting to his feet—almost knocking the entire line of protectors to his left down as he did. When Rabbit had finally gathered himself, the Captain said, "At ease." and the room sat in one fluid motion, even Rabbit. Officer Pardy couldn't help but think that the error would have been made an example of if it was made by any other Officer, but he wasn't about to question the judgment of his superiors on his first day as a member of the force.

"Protectors of Outland," the Captain said in a modulated voice, the mouth of her facemask flashing red, yellow, and green under her bristly, dark mustache. "Let me repeat that, *Protectors* of

Outland. From this day forward, that includes you. You have sworn to uphold the sacred duties of Protectorship, and you *will* uphold those virtues or perish in embarrassment. Now, don't get me wrong, children—because, truly, you are all still babies when it comes to the force—the worlds out there are much different than the worlds you've seen on TV. Life out there is real. It's nothing like the fairy tales you learned about in school. We're here for one reason and one reason alone: To protect the ideals of Outland. Protectors, what are those ideals?"

"Property. Liberty. Life," the room said in unison.

"I said, *protectors*! What. Are. Those. Ideals?"

"Property! Liberty! Life! Sir!" the room sang.

"And without these basic freedoms what are we? We are not civilization. We are not human. We are nothing."

"Hoo-ra!" a lone voice called.

"Hoo-ra," the Captain repeated. "That's right. Hoo-ra! Are you ready protectors?"

"Hoo-ra!" the room sang in unison.

"Today you are tried by fire. Every protector is baptized into the force the same way. If you cannot make it in Outland 6, then you are not strong enough, you are not fit enough, you *are not enough* to protect any of the Outlands. Do you understand me? This work is dangerous, protectors. You know what you signed up for. You've heard the stories of your ancestors. You've been trained. You know as well as you can what awaits you out those doors. So I'm going to ask you one more time. Protectors, are you ready?"

"*Hoo-ra!*"

"We're sweeping the Neutral Ground, today, rookies." A map of Outland 6 with the section of the Neutral Ground that they would be focusing on came up on the screen behind the Captain. "We have one hundred rookies here in this room. We have countless rooms like this around Outland 1, all with the same mission. You've been through the drills. You know your vows. You'll be paired with another rookie and led by a Sergeant. I suggest you listen to your Sergeant if you want to make it through this alive."

Rabbit swallowed loud enough for Officer Pardy to hear it.

"You'll find your partner and Sergeant assignments on your comm link and in your viewscreens. Go meet your Sergeants and do your jobs, protectors. Hoo-ra!"

"Hoo-ra!"

Before Rabbit could check his assignment, Officer Pardy pulled him up by his collar and dragged him to stand in front of the Captain.

"Tom, what are you—" Rabbit pleaded as he did.

"Captain Mondragon, sir," Officer Pardy said, standing to attention in front of the Captain and saluting. "Officer Pardy, reporting for duty."

Rabbit looked at him then at the captain and half saluted. "Er—Ra—No—*uh*—Officer Jefferson, *uh*—sir, or—Captain."

"At ease, Officers," the Captain said, ticking off a salute herself, her arm brushing against the dark mustache adorning her facemask with the motion. Rabbit was already at ease. Officer Pardy followed orders. "I selected the two of you for a special operation." The mouth of her facemask flashed as she spoke, but the voice modulator was off. "I'll be joining you because I want to see how you do with my own two eyes. Do you understand?"

"Sir, yes, sir," Officer Pardy said, looking through the black mirrors of the Captain's eyes.

Rabbit nodded.

"Then load up and let's go," the Captain said.

They got into the transport bay with three other teams, twelve protectors in formation waiting for the doors to open. When they did, the sun came in bright through the skyline and oak trees, and Officer Pardy's helmet had to adjust his viewscreen to compensate. The trees reminded him of a park back home in Outland 1, one tree in particular he used to climb. He was caught off guard when Rabbit marched out with the rest of the troop, leaving Tom to play catch up.

"Alright," the Captain said. The Sixers around were starting to clear out of the area, but Officer Pardy noticed a little boy going up the tree he wanted to climb. "Beta team, Sector G," the Captain said, pointing. "Gamma team, Sector D. Delta team, Sector E. Go, go, go."

The other teams moved out into the city, away from the Neutral Ground.

"Pardy, Jefferson," the Captain said. "Follow me."

They followed along the park. As they went, word of their coming passed in front of them, and the crowds dispersed like flies when swatted at. Officer Pardy was beginning to wonder how they would catch anyone doing anything if everyone knew they were coming when the Captain veered off into an alleyway.

"Alright, boys," she said, unlocking a padlock on a door halfway down the alley. "While they're out there, stirring up the population, we're going to do some real protector work. You hear me?"

"Sir, yes, sir," Officer Pardy responded automatically.

"Um. Where are we, sir?" Rabbit asked, stumbling through the dark doorway.

The Captain flipped on the lights. "You just walked here, Jefferson," she said. "You should know where you are."

"Sector F, sir," Officer Pardy said. "An alley two blocks east of the transport bay, sir."

"Okay, Pardy," the Captain replied, giving a thumbs up and nodding. "No need to show off. Just get out of your gear like a good little Officer and put on some of these plain clothes."

The room looked like a giant costume closet for a theater company in Outland 3. There were shirts, shoes, and dresses piled everywhere, on top of cupboards and cubbies and hanger racks, and there were carpet-covered benches in between piles of clothes. Officer Pardy thought that there was no way that what they were doing was regulation, but he couldn't rightly ignore a direct order from a superior officer, either, so he set to picking out a costume and changing into it.

"Um. Right here, sir?" Rabbit asked, appalled by the idea. "Right in front of—but there's no—"

Pardy laughed as he slipped on a pair of sneakers. He wanted to remind Rabbit to put his pants on before his shoes, but he wasn't sure if it was appropriate while on duty, even without a helmet on. When the Captain started redressing herself, Rabbit relented, too.

"We'll be posing as your typical Sixer scumbag," the Captain said as she got dressed. "The type of person who's too lazy, stoned, or stupid to work, so they resort to stealing from those of us who have the common decency to earn our own living. We have intel that says there's illegal printer activity on this very block. Jefferson and I will enter the establishment—posing as a family looking for food. Pardy will enter five minutes later as back up. Jefferson and I will procure an illegally printed commodity and arrest the operators of the stolen device. When Pardy comes in, we'll confiscate all the printers on the premises and make arrests as needed. Now, are there any questions?"

"I—I'm supposed to be your husband?" Rabbit said.

"Yes, Jefferson," the Captain said with a grin. "Can you handle that?"

"I—uh—yes, sir." Rabbit blushed.

"You got any problems, Pardy?" the Captain asked.

"Sir, no, sir," Pardy said. Not on his first day he didn't.

"Good," the Captain said. "Jefferson and I are heading out. You tail us and enter on your cue. Do you understand?"

"Sir, yes, sir," Pardy said.

"Let's go protectors," the Captain said, slapping Rabbit on the back and leading him out of the closet.

Pardy walked as far behind them as he could without losing sight. The sidewalk was full now that they were out of protector gear, so he had to stay close. The Captain and Rabbit entered a nondescript door in between two apartment buildings, and Pardy walked past it, bending down to tie his shoe and count away the seconds in his head. He whistled the Protector's Alma Mater to keep time as he observed the area around him. He was closer now to the tree that reminded him of his favorite one to climb as a kid, and he looked up to see two little forms sitting high up in the branches. He had almost lost track of his whistling while watching them when someone bumped into him from behind and he did lose track of it.

"Watch out," the person said, pushing Pardy away.

"Stand down, citizen," Pardy said, standing and holding his fists up in a defensive stance.

"What was that?" The person looked at him like he was speaking a foreign language.

"I said—uh—excuse me, sir," Pardy said, dropping his hands.

"Right," the person said, walking away and shaking his head.

Pardy tried to calculate how much time he had lost to find out where he should be in the tune, but his eyes kept going back to the kids in the tree and he couldn't think. He decided it had been long enough and went for the door. He turned the rusty knob and pushed, but it didn't budge. He looked around, and a little girl smiled at him then ran away to her mom. He turned the knob again and pulled this time, almost falling over backwards when the door swung open.

The hall was dark and short. It led to a steep staircase. Pardy wondered why no one else had come in or gone out since Rabbit and the Captain had. He tried to quiet his steps but the staircase echoed everything back at him. He was at the top of the third flight, reaching out for the doorknob in front of him, when the gunshots rang out. One. Then two. Then one more.

His heart skipped a beat. He shoved the door open and swung out his gun. The Captain's gun was pointed at a man who had his hands on his head. Rabbit was bleeding on the floor, maybe groaning, maybe not moving. A flutter of motion disappeared out a back door.

"Follow her!" the Captain ordered, cuffing the man and calling for backup.

Pardy's legs moved before his mind did. He didn't have to be quiet anymore, and his presence stormed through the back staircase. He was at the last flight of stairs before the purple flower pattern of her dress disappeared around the corner of the door. He scanned left and right when he emerged from the building, then followed her wake into the still busy sidewalk. He slid to a halt, almost passing the alley she went down, before following her, his footsteps echoing like a war cry. She got to the end of the alley and tried to escape into another door, but it wouldn't budge.

"No!" she screamed, beating her fists against the door. "Damn you! Let me in! No!" She started to cry.

Pardy pointed his gun at her heart. "Freeze."

"Fuck you." She didn't turn around. She just kept banging on the door.

"Put your hands in the air and turn around." Sweat started to pool on his forehead.

"Fuck off!" the woman yelled, not looking at him.

"Please, ma'am. I don't want to have to hurt you. Turn around slowly and put your hands on your head."

She turned fast. Pardy took a step back, his heart skipping a beat. "Oh yeah?" she said. "I'm sure *she* didn't, either. Is that right?"

"I don't know what you're talking about, ma'am. Just put your hands on your head, and we'll get this all sorted out. If you've done nothing wrong, you have no reason to worry."

"*Her!*" the woman yelled. "That—that—*that fucking woman*! She was a protector. And you—you are, too. Aren't you? You fucking pig!"

"Please, ma'am," he said, adjusting his grip on his gun. "Put your hands up."

"No." She shook her head, stepping closer. "*You*. You put your hands up. Do you hear me? You!"

"Please, ma'am."

"We didn't have any guns," the woman said, chuckling or sobbing, Pardy couldn't tell anymore. "None of us. Just think about that, *protector*. Think about my daughter who won't see her parents ever again because you were *protecting* us."

"Ma'am," Pardy said.

"You heard me," the woman said. "Fuck off!" She took a step toward him, or reached for something in her dress, or—something—Pardy didn't know.

But his finger reacted before his brain did. The gun blast went off and she fell. He caught his breath for a second, his gun poised, and reeled at what he had done. The world spun around him and he wanted to pass out. He fell to his knees at the woman's side, pressing on her chest to stop the bleeding.

She coughed. "H—How—"

"No, I'm..." He pressed harder. What had he done? As she took her last spluttering breaths, he tore the silver butterfly off her neck and shoved it in his pocket.

A group of protectors in full gear swarmed into the alley around him. They asked him questions he didn't remember answering. They didn't seem to matter. They said that the Captain would be waiting for him at headquarters for debriefing. They said he was a hero, that they had found a stockpile of illegal printers waiting to be distributed. They patted him on his back for that, and no one asked him where his gear was or who the woman dying in the alley was. No one asked why he had shot her. No one told him how Rabbit was doing. He probably wouldn't have heard them even if they did.

He made his way through the crowd of protectors, bunched up in the alley, out to the main drag that ran along the Neutral Ground. The sidewalks were empty again and he could finally breathe. He took a few deep breaths and sprawled out on his back in the grass, staring up at the trees, at the clouds that passed through the holes in their canopy. He laid there and stared at nothing, asking himself if this was what the job was. Was this protecting? Was this what he had signed up for? Why would anyone agree to this?

He stood and brushed himself off, taking a few more deep breaths. This wasn't the reaction of a protector. He knew that much. He had followed direct orders. He did nothing wrong. He had nothing to worry about. The rest would have to wait.

But still. He wasn't ordered to kill her. *She reached for something*, he told himself. She had said that they didn't have guns, but that's what a Sixer would say to catch you off guard. She was raving. What was she saying besides that? She must have been in shock from finally getting caught. That's what it was.

She said she had a daughter.

Pardy wanted to sit down again, but he fought the urge. He pictured his son living in an orphanage because he and his wife were killed in the line of duty. He pictured the look on his son's face when he heard the news, the tears and the crying. He swallowed hard, shoved it all back down into his subconscious, and marched to the costume closet to change out of those dirty rags of clothes and put back on his clean, white, regulation protector gear.

The transport bay was empty when Pardy got there. Everyone was either cleaning up the crime scene or still parading around their designated sector, putting on a show. He stared at the doors as they closed, imagining the Captain's response to his actions, wondering where Rabbit was and if he was alright, and generally trying not to picture that woman's daughter or his own son's crying face. The transporter stopped, the doors opened, and Pardy realized he was facing the wrong direction.

"Rabbit. Is that you?" a modulated voice came from behind him, followed by eerie laughter. "No, eh. It's Pardy," the voice said. "But he looks like he's seen the ghost of Rabbit, doesn't he? *Ha ha ha.*"

More laughter. Pardy clenched his fists, marched between the two laughers, bumping their shoulders with his, and stomped down the hall to the debriefing room. They would have to wait until he was off duty before real justice could be served.

The debriefing room was smaller than the briefing room. It was more intimate. There was one long table with chairs all around it so the protectors could sit facing each other. It was empty when Pardy went in, so he took the middle seat to wait, straight-backed and full regulation. He had a long time to continue his cycle of thoughts concerning the Captain's reaction, Rabbit's health, and the woman's son before an Officer came in and told him the Captain would speak to him in her office.

Her office was bigger than the debriefing room, and her desk was almost the size of that table. The Captain was sitting in a big, leather chair with her mustached helmet on the desk. Two low, soft stools sat on the floor in front of Pardy, and there were no pictures or decorations on the walls besides her Captain's diploma and a copy of the *Protector's Manifesto: Property. Liberty. Life.* framed on one wall. The Captain had her back turned, staring out a window that made up the entire back wall of the room, overlooking a beautiful snowy-white mountain view. Pardy closed the door, marched up to the desk, and said, "Pardy, sir."

"Yes, Pardy," the Captain said. "I know." She didn't turn around when she spoke. "Take a seat, please. And take your helmet off."

Pardy struggled down onto one of the stools, his knees bending up to his chest. He slipped off his helmet and breathed a deep breath of air tinged with stale liquor. He had nowhere else to put his helmet but the floor next to his low seat, so he did just that.

"You did good out there, Pardy," the Captain said after a long silence. "I'll start with that. You did good." She nodded, still looking out the window.

Pardy took another deep breath and nodded himself. That was one less stop on the cycle of worries.

"And no, Pardy," the Captain went on. "I don't mean you did *well*, either." She turned around as she said it. "I know my grammar. You did good and you did it well. You understand?"

"Yes, sir."

"Good," the Captain said, smiling. "Very good. Pardy... Now—before we get on with this debriefing, I need to ask you a question."

"Yes, sir. Of course, sir. Whatever you say, sir."

"Good, Pardy. Good, good, good. I get it. You do it by the book. Chain of command. Follow every regulation to the dot. Do what you're told not what you want. *I get it.* That's why I chose you today, Pardy. You know that, right? You're top of your class, a physical specimen, the perfect candidate for promotion through the ranks. Do you agree, Pardy?"

"Sir, yes, sir."

"*Haha.* Of course you do, Pardy. I knew you would. Now, how much are you willing to do to get that promotion?"

"Whatever it takes, sir," he answered without hesitation.

"You need to think about this, Pardy," the Captain said, shaking her head. "*Whatever it takes* leaves open a lot of possibilities. What if it takes breaking regulations? What if it takes ignoring your superior officers?"

"I don't follow, sir."

"I didn't expect you to, Pardy. That's why you're so perfect for the position. It doesn't matter anyway. I just needed to plant the seed, see how you'd respond. Regulation response if I've ever heard one, Officer. Regulation response."

"Thank you, sir."

The Captain laughed. "Pardy," she said. "You'll have my job yet. *Hahaha.* Now, let's get down to it."

"Yes, sir."

"Why don't you start by telling me what happened after you left the room in pursuit of the suspect."

"Yes, sir." Pardy nodded. "I followed the suspect down the back staircase and caught up to her in an alley a block and half west of the back exit. She was attempting to enter a domicile through a door in the alley, but the door was locked. She yelled at me, reached for something in her dress, and I dispensed justice. At that time backup arrived and I left the scene to come here for debriefing."

"In her dress, Pardy?" the Captain said, frowning.

"Yes, sir."

"Let me ask you, Pardy." The Captain grinned. "Have you ever worn a dress?"

"Excuse me, sir."

"Have you ever worn a dress?"

"No, sir." He shook his head.

"Did you see me wearing a dress out there?"

"No, sir."

"Do you know why?" the Captain said, raising her eyebrows.

"No, sir."

"Because it's not easy to hide a gun in a dress, Pardy. Especially the kind she was wearing."

"I didn't know, sir."

"I know you didn't know, Pardy. But *I* know. And *now* you know. And, another thing. She yelled at you?"

"Yes, sir." He nodded.

"What did she say?"

"She cursed, sir."

"*Haha*. Oh, sweetheart," the Captain said, smiling and shaking her head. "She cursed? That's adorable. But we're both adults here. What did she say?"

"She told me to fuck off, sir. She said you killed her husband, sir. She said they didn't have guns and that she had a—"

"Alright, Pardy," the Captain said, waving her hands. "Alright, I get it. But I'll tell you this: If you ever want a chance of getting that promotion, you have to leave out the part where she said she didn't have a gun. She had the gun out already. You can't hide anything that'll get through protector gear in a dress. You got that?"

"No, sir," Pardy said, shaking his head.

"Pardy," the Captain said, sighing. "She didn't have a gun. We didn't find a gun on her. She was telling the truth. You leave that part out in the official report and you come out better for it. You got it?"

"Uh—er—Yes, sir," Pardy said.

"*Uh—er—Yes, sir*," the Captain mocked him. "You sound like Rabbit, Pardy. Get it together."

"Yes, sir." He nodded.

"That's better. And about Jefferson...That was a necessary casualty in the war on injustice. You understand that, right?"

"Yes, sir," Pardy said. He didn't understand, but he didn't know how to say no again.

"Then you might survive yet, Pardy," the Captain said, smiling. "If you stick with me you certainly will. You got that?"

"Yes, sir."

"Good. Now remember what I said and go fill out your reports. You'll have your choice of patrol for the coming week if you play your cards right. And that's the first step in a long line of them to your promotion, Pardy. By that time I'll have a goatee and I'll remember what you did here for me today. Are we clear?"

"Yes, sir," Pardy said. They weren't clear, but again.

"And do close the door behind you on the way out," the

Captain said, turning back to the view and waving him away. "So many people forget to do that it's ridiculous."

"Yes, sir." Pardy struggled up out of the stool, grabbing his helmet and slipping it on, then took extra care to close the door as quietly as he could behind him.

The report form was already up on his computer when he sat down. He stared at it, not wanting to fill it out, not sure if following the Captain's orders was up to regulation, and groaned. Of course he knew that following her orders was regulation, but was it still regulation if she was ordering him to break regulations? Never before had he been faced with such a paradox. All through school his education was simple: Follow the rule of law and protect the essence of society: Property, liberty, life. His teachers ordered him to complete assignments, and he followed through. That was how simple the job was supposed to be. But this, this was different. The Captain said that the woman he had killed wasn't lying. She said they didn't find a gun. Did that mean that none of them had guns? Who fired the shots? Who shot Rabbit?

He realized he didn't even know if Rabbit was still alive and called down the room to another Officer who was doing busy work at her desk.

"Didn't make it," she said, happy to take a break. "Ironic almost, dying in action just like his mother. A hero's bloodline, I guess."

"Yeah," Pardy said. "A hero."

"It's just a shame it had to happen on his first day, though, you know. We all ribbed him, but he was a good guy. No protector deserves that. Not even the least of us. But you and the Captain showed them, didn't you?"

Pardy didn't answer. He stared blankly at the forms on his computer until the other Officer went back to her's.

If they didn't have a gun between them, then the Captain killed Rabbit and they didn't show anyone anything but that it was okay to kill protectors. But why would she do that? Why would she want Rabbit dead? She was a protector.

They *did* have a 3D printer. A whole stack of them, apparently. A printer was as good as a gun. A printer was an unlimited supply of guns, bombs, and any other weapon your heart could desire. If they had even one printer, then at least one of them would have a gun to protect it. The denizens of Outland 6 would do anything to get their hands on a printer, including perpetrating violence against one another, and they wouldn't stop at violence against protectors. Pardy had learned that through his studies of the historical arrest records.

But *she* didn't have a gun. That woman didn't. She was unarmed, and he shot her. He killed her. He heard her yell at him, telling him to fuck off. He heard her crying and pleading to whoever was behind the locked door to let her in. And he pictured her daughter. He pictured his son. He was a protector. It was his duty to uphold justice and what did he do? He killed a mother, created an orphan, and had been praised as a hero for doing so, not only by his fellow Officers, but by a Captain who said that he had what it took to climb the ranks to his dream job. So why was he having such a hard time accepting it all?

He knew he had only one option he could live with, that there was only one regulation course of action he could take. He set to filling out the report. The orphan girl would have to wait just a little bit longer for justice.

ଓ   ✳   ✆

VII. The Scientist

Every day the same. Every day different. The only constant is change. Reality was filled with just such contradictions.

She stood in front of the printer—as she did every meal—and imagined the people who grew, reared, and harvested, built the things to make possible, and sent along the food she was about to consume. She always ordered her meals as raw as they came so those people were forced to do as little of her work as possible. Her personal thrift was only a drop of water on the face of the sun, and she knew it, but it made her feel a little less responsible, a little less complicit, and it wasn't anywhere near the end of her actions.

One egg, one piece of bread, two strips of bacon. She placed the same order she placed most mornings and it took no more than seconds before each item was in her hands and ready to be prepared. She had done this so many times before that her movements were instinctual. There was no thought in cracking the eggs, cooking everything all at once, and spreading the jam on the pan-fried toast just as the bacon was crisp to perfection. She woke up, and before she knew it, it was done. Just like that. As if she hadn't woken up until breakfast was cooked and ready even though she was the one who prepared it herself. She was sleepcooking.

With the smell of bacon following her from the kitchen, she brought her breakfast back into her office to start on the day's security checks. She set the plate in front of the keyboard and bank of monitors on the big oak desk—overlooked by a wall-sized window with a view of a functioning assembly line—and slid into the fluffy, leather chair. She hit the spacebar to wake the computer, picked up her plate, leaned back in the chair, and started on breakfast while the machine warmed up.

The screen flashed "Good Morning" in pale green on a black background before it hummed away, getting down to business. She chewed her toast as the various checks were performed. First the top tier printers of Inland, those which were owned by the owners. They were the most important printers according to company protocol. Of course, being the property of the owners themselves, they were the newest model printers, and as such, the least likely to malfunction. Still, they were the "most important", and they were to be fixed before any others. The computer went down the list marking every unit green for fully functional as expected.

Then came the printers in Outland 1. Being the center of the defense of property, liberty, and life, Outland 1's printers were on a tier with the owners' own. A few were slightly older models in comparison, but even those were from the previous year at the earliest, and all were highly unlikely to malfunction. The computer ran through these, and there was a minor plug in one of the printer streams, but a mechanic bot was already working on clearing it out, and the bot looked to have everything under control.

Then came the Walker-Haley fields. She always suggested that they run this check first, as it was the basis of the entire system and making changes here could affect the printers she had already inspected, but she wasn't in charge, the owners were. They had the money. They owned the property. They decided that their printers, and their soldiers' printers, were more important than their walls or her time. She had no choice but to comply, so she did. The computer went down every single Walker-Haley line, checking every square inch of field for proper wave function. There were more miles of Walker-Haley field lines to check than there were miles of roads at the height of the automobile era, and every morning she sat and watched the computer check every single one, inch by square inch.

The holes came next. You couldn't separate the worlds like that without leaving connections. What would be the point? No, that's where the holes came in. So many of them. Transport bays, elevator ports, printers, communication portals, heat transfer—to prevent weather aberrations which plagued early attempts—repair hatches, you name it. Those and the holes that formed from the natural wear and tear of the system, holes like the one that was flashing red on the screen to her left.

"Woah now," she said, spinning in her chair to get a closer look. "Where are you?" She tapped off a few keystrokes. "Outland 2? That's odd. Let me just..." She typed a few more strokes and touched the screen with her hand then clicked on the mouse. "Ah," she said. "Well is that so?"

A video came up on her center monitor, surveillance footage

from the area where the hole was. A college-aged woman in a black hoodie was talking to someone in the shadows, maybe an assembly line worker who had found a hole, they had been getting more restless in Outland 5. More than likely it was a Sixer, though, left there to rot in a sea of skyscrapers, fighting over the only strip of green. It was brilliant really how the owners handled that problem, and equally disgusting. Made all the worse by the fact that the Scientist was the one who mended the walls that propped their entire system up, by the fact that she had invented those walls without knowing how they would be used.

She let them talk a minute more, finishing her breakfast and cleaning the dishes, before she called the mechanic bot to fix the hole and set the emergency lights to flashing—which sent the conversants running in opposite directions. She watched the video until the bot got there and set to work, then she switched back to the maintenance scan and leaned back in her chair.

The computer started its check over again from the beginning. Exactly the inefficiency she had warned about, but money didn't care. There was always more. Nothing had changed, so the computer skipped from Outland 1 to Outland 2 and on down the line. There were less and less printers to check as it went, but more and more of them had problems. She sent bots to those she could afford to, but it wasn't many, and they were mostly in Outlands 3 and 4. Five would have to wait and 6 wasn't supposed to have any printers. It was a complex job, managing which bots went where, but she had a sixth sense for the triage needs of the system, which was why they still had her doing it instead of a computer.

As she set to deciding who in Outland 3 would be least likely to complain about a short delay in delivery so she could send a few bots to 5, a black cat jumped onto her lap and meowed.

"Mr. Kitty," she said, clicking a few more times before she looked down at him "Still in yellow I see. Are you sure you don't want a change?"

He meowed again and jumped onto the keyboard to lick himself.

She scooped him up and brought him into the kitchen. "I know," she said. "But I have work to do." She scratched his head and put him on the counter, then thanked the people behind the printer for the cat food. Mr. Kitty ate it greedily as she went back into the office to work.

She really didn't have much to do but watch the mechanic bots and computer do their jobs, so she leaned back in her chair to get comfortable. It was almost serene watching them fix her creation. Until she remembered how things used to be. She used to spend all her time working with her hands and her mind, creating new inventions that the world had never experienced before, putting machinery into configurations which had never been attempted. She was herself then. Even though she still worked for *Wally World Llc*, she felt as if she worked for herself. If she had an idea she could follow it and see where it led her. She was free to work on the projects *she* thought were worth her time.

Then she had made the discovery. She created the Walker-Haley fields. The Walker-Haley fields led to "printers"—a masterstroke of advertising if there ever was one. Printers led to the creation of the Outlands. But still, even with all the work it took to build and maintain such a massive and complex system, still she found time to invent, she found time to create, and she came up with her third great invention, her masterpiece, the customizable, almost-human android with full AI capabilities. And when for the third time Lord Walker ripped her creation from her hands and claimed it as his own, she vowed that she would never invent for him again. But still he needed her to maintain his system, to keep up the status quo, and she needed his printers to reproduce herself. So there she sat, building up his walls for him, biding her time until she could finally tear them all down again.

She flipped the center monitor to a television station and let the repairs run on autopilot for a while. She cycled through the channels. She had access to all of them with her clearance level, and she liked to guess which Outland each show was broadcast to based on what it depicted and who was acting in it.

Protector dramas were almost exclusively for Outland 1. She wondered how many different departments and cities they could plaster onto the names of the "different" shows before the people there realized that they were all the same thing.

There were a few different stock analyzers—all giving mutually exclusive advice—and a few political journalists—all arguing for one of two mutually exclusive positions—obviously directed at Outland 2, but they broadcast all the way to Outland 4 and in between.

Outland 4 was bombarded with documentaries and scientific programming of various levels and branches of study.

Outland 3 had everything because they made everything, but she knew that they only watched the self-indulgent, talking head, who's who in celebrity culture programming. That was the one thing that talked about what they all loved the most, themselves.

Outland 5's programming was all about the glory of toil and working hard for the common good in the hopes that you would make it big and become a middle manager. She thought that some of those shows actually carried good messages, but the creators didn't put any effort into entertaining, just educating. Then again, they didn't have to entertain. That's all there was to watch in Outland 5. The Fivers didn't know any better, so they didn't ask for any better, and no one was about to tell them otherwise. Well, almost no one.

She stopped flicking through the channels and checked on the repair work. Everything seemed to be in good order. It was about time for her lunch meeting so she set a few bots on standby for emergencies with the owners' printers and left the rest running on autopilot. She went into the kitchen and Mr. Kitty was gone. She washed his dish, staring out the window above her sink at the line of assembly line workers slip, snap, clicking, and collected herself. She sighed, then went out through the small hall to the elevator and said, "Outland 5, please. Frenchmen entrance."

She came out of the elevator into the sun between classic New Orleans buildings, the kind with short stoops, sweeping porches, and lots of balconies. She was surprised they were left in Outland 5 but assumed they were too structurally damaged to be worth repairing enough for transport. They were good enough for the Fivers, though.

She walked down a sidewalk that was ravaged by tree roots, climbing up and down the concrete hills. This elevator exit wasn't the closest to where here meeting was, but she had some time to kill, and she enjoyed the walk. She went through Washington Square Park, down St. Claude, to St. Roch to find the sign she was looking for. It just said "Bar" on it. Nothing else.

The bar was so dark she couldn't see until her eyes had adjusted. She took in the stale smoke and the sound of pool balls clacking before she saw anything that was going on. She went straight for the bar when she could see, ordered a beer without asking—the bartender knew what she wanted already—and went to the back corner booth to wait.

There were three people at the pool table, two at darts, the bartender, and her. A song she liked came on the jukebox, and she couldn't help but think that she'd enjoy a game of pool herself, but there wasn't time for that now. Maybe after everything was under way. That and maybe all the worlds would be put back together in one fell swoop.

She laughed out loud at herself, and no one even glanced in her direction. She laughed again because she could, and while she did, the door opened. A dirty-haired, ragged-clothed worker with dark skin walked in, her chest pushed out for everyone to see. The worker caught the Scientist's eye and went to the bar to get a beer before sitting at the corner booth with her.

There was a silence. They sat studying each others faces, sipping their beers. The Scientist found it was best to let them talk first. Usually they'd tell her exactly what they were there for with the first words that came out of their mouth. So she learned to wait and to watch, and she already knew what to answer before the worker said, "Are you the—"

"The Scientist," she said. "Yes, Ellie."

They drank some more. She knew that Ellie wanted to say the right thing, and she was willing to give her the time she needed to figure out what that was.

"I heard you know what's on the other side," Ellie decided on.

"That's true," the Scientist said, nodding. "I could tell you how many other sides there are, too. But I don't think that's what you really want."

"I'll decide what I want. *Thanks*." Ellie sipped her beer.

"That's fair." The Scientist sipped hers, all part of the game.

"What I mean is…You know where everything goes, right. You know who we make it for."

"I do."

"Who then?"

"It's people who aren't you," the Scientist said, with a shrug.

"Tell me something I don't know." Ellie scoffed.

"What could I tell you about them that would satisfy you?

They do less work than you do. Their work is easier, less soul crushing. They have better houses, bigger beds. Many of them own their own 3D printers, their own endless source of anything. And none of their children ever die in factory accidents. You can be sure of that." She could tell she hit a nerve with that last one from the look on Ellie's face.

"No," Ellie said, shaking her head. "They wouldn't. Would they?"

"No, Ellie. They wouldn't. And they have property so they don't have to. So what are you going to do about it now that you know?"

Ellie slammed her fist on the table. "Something, God dammit!" she yelled and still no one turned to look at them.

"I apologize." The Scientist waved her hands. "I didn't mean to imply that there was nothing you could do. I literally meant to ask what *you* specifically would do about it? I know what you want, Ellie. I want what you want. My interests are your interests. I have the privilege to live a life of pampered luxury with access to everything you would ever need to get what you want, to everything that keeps our society running. Don't get me wrong, I too labor—nothing like you of course, but more than others—but you... I want to do everything I can to help *you* get what *you* want. So—if you will—tell me Ellie. You came here. You had no idea who I was. You have no idea who I am beyond *the Scientist* which means nothing to you. You took a risk coming because you wanted something. I want to know: What do you want?"

"I want to punish them," Ellie said through gritted teeth. "The people who killed my son."

"I'm not sure we can find one person and say that they were the one who killed your son."

"Then I want to punish all of them."

"It's not just the people, though." The Scientist shook her head. "The people are but the heads of a hydra. If you punish one, three will take their place, and those three will be worse than the first. Your son wasn't killed by people, Ellie, he was killed by the system that puts those people in power. He was killed because he was forced to work in that factory, and he was forced to work in that factory because he lives in Outland 5."

"I want it all to stop, then," Ellie said, slamming her fist on the table.

"Do you know what that means, though? Do you know how big they are?"

"I don't care how big they are! Do you know how big—how important to me—how huge my son wa—*is*?"

"Good, Ellie," the Scientist said, nodding. "Good. I didn't mean to rile you up, but I need you to know that this isn't something you should undertake lightly. You'll have to break the law to get what you want, and in doing so, you'll be risking death or worse as punishment."

Ellie nodded with a stern face. The Scientist smiled and took a sip of beer. Ellie looked surprised at the change in her demeanor and took a sip to cover it up.

"One more thing," the Scientist said, still smiling and looking Ellie in the eyes. "Trudy. She's the one who told you how to find me, right?"

Ellie had to think for a second before she connected Trudy to Gertrude and nodded. There was a hint of fear in her eyes, as if she thought she had done something wrong by giving Trudy away. Or maybe it was shame for revealing a secret.

"That one is a terrific judge of character," the Scientist said. "And a dear friend of mine. We've been working together now ever since she got her promotion. She found me faster than any other, and she's proven more valuable to our cause than anyone I've ever known. Do you understand what I'm saying?"

Ellie nodded.

The Scientist laughed. "Oh, I'm sure you don't. I'm sure I don't understand what I'm saying half the time. But in time, it always reveals itself. Remember that and you'll be just fine." She took a big gulp of beer and finished her glass. "Let me get us a refill and we'll talk about what you really want to talk about. After all, this *is* about you. Not me." She swept off to the bar, leaving Ellie to think about what she had said while she ordered another round. When she sat back down, Ellie looked like she had something to say, so the Scientist took a sip and let her go ahead.

"Did you send that woman through the conveyor belt?" she asked.

"I don't send anyone anywhere," the Scientist said. "I force no one. I only give them the information they need to do what they want."

"But you did talk to her."

"I gave her some information. Yes. She wanted to meet a celebrity."

"And you helped her do *that*?" Ellie scoffed

"Like I said," the Scientist said, shrugging. "I'm privileged. I want to give back in any small way I can. I want what you want."

Ellie took a drink of her beer. She didn't seem to believe what the Scientist was saying.

"She came to me because she wanted to meet an actor," the Scientist said. "I told her his name, and I directed her conveyor belt to where he was."

"And that's it? That was worth risking someone discovering that you had helped her."

The Scientist chuckled. "Trudy is a *fantastic* judge of character. Did I mention that? No. I also told her that Russ—the actor she wanted to meet—thought that his clothes were created by androids. Having worked in costume construction before she got her promotion, she was devastated to know that he had no idea she had sewn most of his wardrobe while she was a tailor."

"He really didn't know?"

The Scientist shook her head.

"How? How could robots do what we do?"

"That's the thing. Androids *could* do all the work that humans do, but humans are cheaper."

"Then someone knows. They're not all oblivious."

"Yes," the Scientist said, nodding. "But it's such a small minority who benefits so much from it that they don't care. In fact, they work as hard as they can to maintain the system as it stands."

"And that's why you helped her." Ellie shook her head. "He's a celebrity. He could—"

The Scientist nodded.

"What happened to her?"

The Scientist shook her head.

"What?" Ellie said. "Dead?"

"We think not. We hope not. Maybe. Maybe worse. You should know what you're getting into. She would have stood a better chance if she could have waited, but she grew impatient. Now she's nowhere to be found. In the end, though, it was her decision, and I can't blame her for making it the way she did."

"So if I wanted to go back right now and slip through the conveyor belt to meet a celebrity, you would let me."

"I would advise against it." The Scientist shook her head.

"But you would let me anyway," Ellie said, pushing the point

"Whatever I could do to help you get what you want." The Scientist shrugged.

"And why would you advise against it?"

"Well, in the near future we will be crossing *en masse*, and crossing for you would be safer because of it. The more people who go through at the same time, the less likely it is for each one to get caught."

"Not a bad reason." Ellie nodded, sipping her beer.

"We don't know exactly when the operation will occur, though. Mary didn't want to wait."

"That was all she was supposed to do, though? Talk to an actor."

"And tell him she created his clothes, not androids. If he knew, he might spread the word. He has the platform to spread it. He's privileged in ways that even I am not."

"Nothing else?" Ellie looked suspicious. Trudy knew how to pick the smart ones.

"A little something else. But its different for everyone, and there's no requirement that the thing is done for you to get what you want."

Ellie took a big gulp of her beer. She thought about what she had just heard, shook her head, and said, "And if I want to be put in a room alone with some of these people who know what they're doing and do nothing to stop it?"

"I can get you close to them, but I can't promise you'll be alone. Not to mention I'm not sure that anything you could do alone with them would be of any use to getting real revenge."

Ellie clenched her fists. She made as if to slam them on the table again but stopped herself. "Dammit. It's so easy for them. Isn't it?"

The Scientist nodded. She sipped her beer.

"What can I do, then?"

"What *can* you do?" the Scientist said. "You're not personable. You're no Trudy."

Ellie laughed, shaking her head. "No. I'm not that."

"You want to go across, don't you? You want to see it."

Ellie looked into her beer and nodded.

"You know, it's not too different from here," the Scientist said. "Though they do have all the great natural beauties. Oh, you should see the mountains."

"Can I?"

"Yes. But you'd be doing them a favor. If you drop out, that's one less person who knows what they're doing wrong and wants to fight against it."

Ellie shook her head, sipped her beer, and stared at it for a while. After a moment of silence she said, "You weren't lying then."

"I try not to."

"Do you think there's a way I can help? A way that I can get revenge?"

"I don't think it will be easy, and I don't know how long it will take, but I have a plan, and I know there's a place for you in it."

"I'll do whatever it takes."

"You're in a position like our friend who wanted to meet Russ was," the Scientist said. "Quality Assurance is the front line, it's the perfect position for a revolutionary. I'm sure I can find something for you."

"Revolutionary?" Ellie scoffed.

"You didn't think it would take anything less to get what you want, did you? To get the revenge you deserve. To prevent them—or anyone for that matter—from doing to someone else what they've done to you and your family. You still have time to walk away if you're not ready for this."

Ellie took a long drink to resolve herself. "I said whatever it takes."

"Good." The Scientist smiled. "Then how do you feel about losing your job?"

Ellie had to think some more at that point. The Scientist knew it. That was the ultimate test of a worker's commitment to the revolution, the threat of losing their livelihood. She liked to believe that she knew exactly what was going through Ellie's mind at that moment. Ellie would be wondering how she would eat without her job, where she would live. Once a person got fired from a pity position they never got hired by anyone ever again. By that time they were too old, not valuable enough, their model was dated. But then she would remember why it was that she had come to this meeting in the first place, what she wanted. She'd remember the day they told her that her son had been killed. How they had waited until the shift was over when the accident had happened in the morning, and all because they didn't want to risk losing productivity. How they had given her two days off then sent her to QA to do robot's work. Then she'd remember her son, and the days her stomach roared with hunger because she only made enough to feed him. She'd remember all the blood, sweat, tears, and love she had invested in him, that she has nothing left to lose, that she had already lost everything a long time ago. And then she'd answer, imagining all the people who could lose everything just like her, lose everything for the same reasons, lose everything to the same people, and she'd know that they're people she could help.

"Anything," Ellie said.

"Good." The Scientist smiled. "Very good. Well, dear. This is what you do."

℘   ✄   ℘

VIII. Haley

Rosalind disappeared out of the kitchen and into the sea of owners in the Feast Hall before Haley had time to respond. Haley had nothing to do, so she stood again watching the door Rosalind had long passed through.

What would her life be like if she didn't work for Lord Walker? It probably wouldn't be much different. She'd still be doing the same work—she didn't know how to do anything else. Maybe she'd be doing it for someone different, but who? Who would need her skills who didn't already have a secretary to do it for them? The answer, of course, was no one.

So how would she get her protein smoothies? Where would she spend her time if not in the kitchen, tending to Lord Walker's every need? She could try to find some way to taste bacon, or discover where that cat always came from—*ooooh*—she could try to meet a child and ask them what it was like to be so small.

But how could she do any of that without a car? Where does bacon come from without a printer? How would she ever find a child to talk to? No. She needed Lord Walker's printer, house, and car for everything she did. What would life be like if she didn't work for him? It would be miserable. That's what.

Haley set to making Lord Walker's favorite dessert, a strawberry cheesecake with graham cracker crust, piled high with whipped cream. She felt that even thinking about life without him was a betrayal on her part, and she wanted to make up for it even if he never knew what she had done. She thought about all he had given her: A way to produce something for this world, three square smoothies a week, a roomy closet to sit in while there was no work to do. And what a joy that work was, to cook, clean, and labor in general. It made her feel like a productive member of society. Almost like the owners themselves.

The cake was mixed and set to cooking so she made another old fashioned and ordered up another round of potatoes, rolls, and gravy from the printer. She set it all on her cart and made one more old fashioned to add to the pile before pushing her way into the Feast Hall.

The meal was well under way for all the owners in attendance. Their chewing was so loud Haley could barely hear the symphony behind her, playing patriotic Christmas carols. Add to that their raucous loud drunkenness, and it was all but impossible to think. Lord Walker was still face deep in turkey, covered in gravy, and yelling at Mr. Loch next to him, all while laughing with his jolly, "*Ho ho ho!*" He didn't even notice when Haley rolled up with the cart. Not until she started setting the extra rolls and potatoes on the table in front of him.

"*Ho ho ho*! Haley, dear," Lord Walker said. "How I adore you! Loch, eh. Loch Ness! There you are. Now do you see this?"

Mr. Loch looked up from his own mound of food and said, "What now?"

"I said do you see this, my giant serpentine monster of a friend? My comrade. Do you see how my Haley treats me? She adapts to my every changing whim and whimsy. She is the top of the line in robot technology and it is precisely because she is an older model than your new, clanky jalopy. Do you see what I mean? *Ho ho ho!*"

Mr. Loch rolled his eyes and set back to eating his food with a shrug and a non-committal, "Yeah, yeah."

"Haley, sweetheart," Lord Walker went on, louder now so more of the room could hear. Not everyone though, just the head table and those who were important enough to be close to them. "Don't you mind Lochy monster over there. He hides it well, but from where I'm sitting I can see the green around his gills. *Ho ho ho*! But don't you be fooled, dear. He—and everyone else here— wishes they could get their hands on you. You are the most experienced piece of machinery in existence, and as long as you keep on running, no other will be able to match your ability."

Scattered applause broke out near the head table. Mr. Douglas, done with his small meal, stared intently at the symphony playing across the Hall—although Haley knew there was no way he could hear it if she was having such a hard time hearing it herself. Mr. Loch went on eating, and Lord Walker, proud of the reaction he had elicited, went on talking.

"See, dear," he said to Haley. "Some are not so embarrassed

as to hide their awe. They know that someone had to be the lucky first to reap the profits from discovering a new technology. Sure, they wish it was them, but they hope to make a similar discovery of their own in the future!"

At that the applause was louder and came from further back in the Hall. Lord Walker looked pleased and was about to go on, but Mr. Smörgåsbord grabbed his arm and whispered something about a speech in his ear. Lord Walker nodded, pushed him away, and yelled, "Well, enough speeching friends. Feasting comes first!" And instead of applause, he was greeted with the sound of smacking lips and clanging platinumware.

"Haley, dear," he said, reaching a plump hand out to her. "That's all to say that I love you. I don't know what I'd do without you. Now pour some more gravy on my feast. *Ho ho ho!*"

"Yes, sir," Haley said, drenching his plate in gravy.

"Douglas McDougy!" Lord Walker yelled, though he had to know Mr. Douglas could hear him at a normal speaking volume. Mr. Douglas didn't turn his attention away from the symphony. "Do you know your Rosalind is almost as precious as my Haley here? *Almost.*"

Mr. Douglas didn't answer, but Rosalind stepped up from seemingly nowhere, poured a little water into Mr. Douglas's glass, and said, "Mr. Douglas knows just how precious Haley is, Lord. Don't you worry about that."

Lord Walker almost choked on the gravy covered turkey in his mouth, but he managed to swallow it down before spitting out, "Oh, *uh*, yes, dear. Hello. I didn't see you there. And if you'll excuse me, I was speaking to your Mr. Douglas, *not* to you. You'd be right to remember that in the future."

"The name's Rosalind, Lord. Not *dear*. And Mr. Douglas will let me know if I'm overstepping my boundaries, *Lord.*"

Lord Walker looked at Mr. Douglas who kept watching the symphony with a straight face. Lord Walker couldn't keep his face straight, though. He couldn't hide his derision. "Yes, well…" he said in the self-conscious voice he used when he was unsure of his seat of power. "Then he knows that my Haley is more precious than you will ever be. Doesn't he, sweetheart?"

"*Rosalind, sir.* And I couldn't agree more." She walked away toward the kitchen, not waiting for a response.

"You see that, Haley," Lord Walker said. "Even the other secretaries are jealous of you. Even *they* know you're better than they'll ever be. *Ho ho ho!*"

Haley blushed. She always did when he praised her like that—especially in front of so many people. She handed Lord Walker the pair of old fashioneds.

"*Ho ho ho!* And how does she respond? With not one, but two of the drinks I was just desiring." Lord Walker took a big gulp of both at once. "Made to perfection even before I knew I wanted them myself!"

"There's a cheesecake on the way, too, sir," Haley said, curtsying.

"*Ho ho ho!*" Lord Walker flopped back into his chair which crumpled under his weight, but he didn't notice because his pneumatic pants held him in a sitting position anyway. "It's truly as if you read my mind. Go, dear. Go." He waved her away. "You know what I want. Go and do it. Go!" He started back on his feast and Mr. Smörgåsbord whispered in his ear as he ate.

Haley could feel the eyes of every owner on her as she walked down the line of tables back to the kitchen. Some of them stopped eating to turn and watch her as she passed, licking their sausage fingers clean with loud smacks. They nudged each other and whispered secrets, and one stuck out his hand and slapped her butt as she walked by.

"Oh!" Haley turned to see who it was, holding a hand to her mouth. It was just another flabby face in the sea of owners. Someone with so little money that she didn't even know his name. She did notice how far back in the hall he was, though. "Excuse me, sir," she said. "I think I bumped into you." She smiled and curtsied.

"No no, sweety." The owner giggled, jiggling with his mirth. "T'was *I* who bumped into *you*. *I* apologize m'lady." He licked his fingers, then wiped them on the tablecloth so he could tip his fedora—which was much shorter than Lord Walker's top hat—and feign an overly dramatic bow.

"Yes, sir," Haley said, turning to walk away, but he slapped her again. This time she kept walking, though. She knew it would be a waste to try to talk to him—he would just do the same thing when she walked away again—so she went on her way back to the kitchen.

Rosalind was there waiting for her when she arrived. "I

would have punched that guy in the face," she said.

"Lord Walker?"

"Well, *yeah*." Rosalind laughed. "But no. The Fordian slapper."

"Excuse me?"

"That fatty that slapped your ass," Rosalind said, signing each word with her hands. "I would have punched him in his flabby face if he did that to me. I wanted to punch him when I saw him do it to you."

"You wouldn't."

Rosalind smiled. "You don't think so?"

Haley shook her head.

"And I bet you didn't think I would talk to your brick wall like that, either. Did you?"

"Brick wall?"

"Wally World," Rosalind said. "He is the Walrus. You know...Lord Walker"

Haley was surprised again by the way she spoke. Haley would never use such unproductive words or speak about an owner with such disregard. And the way she answered that question for Mr. Douglas. He didn't even blink. "How does Mr. Douglas treat you?" Haley asked without a thought.

"Like a human," Rosalind said. "Like a person should be treated. He's not like the other owners, if you haven't noticed."

Haley pictured Mr. Douglas and smiled. "No. He isn't."

"You did notice, then." Rosalind smiled. "I didn't think you would catch on so quickly. No one else has caught on yet."

"Really? Isn't it obvious?"

"Obvious? *Tuh*." Rosalind chuckled. "Now I see why they think you're so special. But don't forget your cheesecake. You don't want to piss off the Walrus. I have a delivery to make myself, but I'll explain more when I get back." She slipped out into the Feast Hall.

Haley set to hand-whipping some cream, the old-fashioned way. She thought that Rosalind had to be exaggerating about her skills of perception. Anyone in their right mind could tell that Mr. Douglas was different from the other owners. You could literally see it. How noticing that made Haley special, she had no idea.

She piled the cream up on the cheesecake, wondering why Mr. Douglas ate so little compared to the other owners, wondering why Lord Walker and the other owners ate so much—and drank so much. She made him another pair of old fashioneds, it was getting along toward speech time and he would want something to calm his nerves, then set everything on the cart and pushed her way out into the Hall.

Lord Walker was huddled up with Misters Loch, Smörgåsbord, and Angrom at the head table. They were undoubtedly discussing the terms of the speech, or the plans for the special musical guest or celebrity supporter. There was always a line of gimmicks drawn up by the advertising departments to give the ceremony a little excitement. Haley made sure to walk out of reach of the handsy poorer owners in the back of the Hall, and as she did, she noted that Mr. Douglas was the only member of the Fortune 5 not in the huddle with Lord Walker. It was just another distinction between him and the other owners that she thought anyone could clearly see.

She set the cheesecake and drinks on the table behind Lord Walker, and he didn't stop his conversation to acknowledge her. When she turned to push the cart back to the kitchen, Mr. Douglas grabbed her lightly by the wrist to stop her.

"Excuse me, sir," she said, curtsying.

He dropped her hand and whispered, "No, excuse me. I didn't want Lord Walker to hear me hailing your attention."

Haley didn't respond. She wanted to walk away but couldn't. She just stood there.

"I'd really like to talk to you, Haley," Mr. Douglas whispered. "But I can't here. Do you understand?"

Haley nodded.

"Rosalind will tell you when," he said. "Now move along before we're noticed."

Haley pushed the cart back toward the kitchen. What was she doing? This wasn't like her. She felt like she was betraying Lord Walker again. She was if she talked to Mr. Douglas without his knowing. Why else would Mr. Douglas be trying to talk to her alone? He probably wanted to get some information out of her in order to sabotage Lord Walker and finally become the richest owner in the world. And she was stupid enough to fall for it because he looked a little different than the other owners, because he had darker skin and a leaner, more modern frame. Well she wouldn't let that fool her any longer. No. Maybe she would use it to fool them instead.

Yes, that was it. She would talk to Rosalind and meet with Mr. Douglas, but then she would use whatever information she gleaned from the interaction to improve Lord Walker's net worth. Then she wouldn't be betraying him, she would be producing for him, exactly what he had hired her to do.

She felt a slap on her butt and turned to see Rosalind swoop in and hit the fat owner who had done it on his head with her pitcher, sending his flabby cheeks jiggling. His upper body slumped backwards, but the pneumatic pants he was wearing caught him and pulled him upright, flipping his chair out behind him and tipping most of the contents of the table he was sitting at onto the tablecloth.

"Oh, I'm sorry," Rosalind said. "I'm so clumsy. I didn't—"

The symphony didn't stop, and most everyone kept on eating except for those near enough to have their feasts spilled who were yelling at Rosalind all at once. The slapper still stumbled around— dazed and possibly unconscious—thanks to his pneumatic pants.

"Yes, sirs. Yes, sirs. I'm sorry, sirs," Rosalind said, curtsying and backing away toward the kitchen. "An honest accident, that's all. Send your secretaries to me and I'll make proper restitution. Excuse me."

She disappeared into the kitchen and Haley hurried to follow her, leaving the dazed owner still stumbling around on his pneumatic legs.

"I can't believe you did that," Haley said when she burst through the door.

"I told you I would," Rosalind said, shrugging with a big grin on her face.

"And you ruined their feast. How much do you think that will cost Mr. Douglas?"

"Worth it." She smiled wider.

"I hope he thinks so."

"I suspect he'll be jealous that I got to hit one of them and he didn't."

Haley shook her head. She did not understand one thing about Rosalind or Mr. Douglas. She was fooling herself if she thought she did. Still, she had to try to do her duty to Lord Walker and get some sort of information out of them. "I don't believe that," she said.

"It doesn't require your belief. I mean, you think you'd believe a little more after you saw what I just did, but I admire your skepticism."

Haley felt like that implied she had something to be skeptical about. "Mr. Douglas said something to me while I was out there."

"Yeah. Not much, probably. Send you to me, Rosalind will tell you what to do. *Yadda yadda yadda.*"

"Yes." Haley nodded.

"Probably said he has to talk to you, he wants to meet with you in private, and that I'll tell you where and when. Is that about right?"

"Yes."

"And do you want to meet him?"

"That is why I'm asking." Haley nodded.

"Are you sure, though? Meeting with a rival owner—you might say *the* rival—in secret. That's something you want to do?"

Haley nodded.

"Even without Lord Walker knowing? You're willing to make an independent decision to do something he might see as a betrayal."

It was as if Rosalind had read her mind. Haley's face flushed. She was going against Lord Walker's wishes and Rosalind knew it. Rosalind made sure that Haley knew it, too. She wanted Haley to decide for herself, to be forced to make the initial betrayal which would open the door to further—more severe—transgressions, to open her brain to the possibility of going against Lord Walker. That's why Rosalind first asked her what she thought her life would be like without Lord Walker. Rosalind couldn't actually read her mind, she was trying to manipulate it. But meeting with Mr. Douglas wasn't a betrayal if she did it to get information for Lord Walker. It was an independent act, sure, but it was still in his interests. If it wasn't a transgression, it couldn't be the initial transgression, and that gave her the upper hand in Rosalind's attempts at manipulation. "Yes," Haley said. "I do."

Rosalind smiled again. "Good," she said. "That's all I needed to know. Mr. Douglas will be in the service parking garage after the guest speaker for second feast. You'll take the kitchen exit and meet him there. Before then, you'll print second feast for Lord Walker, full with dessert, and serve it to him as normal. While you're meeting with Mr. Douglas, I'll print third feast for Lord Walker. After—"

"Lord Walker prefers his—" Haley tried to say.

"*After* you're done with the meeting," Rosalind went on, "you'll come back and serve third feast, resuming your secretarial duties as normal. Do you understand?"

"Lord Walker prefers his food to be cooked by hand," Haley said.

"I know Lord Walker's preferences and will attend to them as necessary."

Haley wasn't convinced that Rosalind would take the same care that she would, but maybe she would still have time to cook everything for him before she went to meet with Mr. Douglas.

"Do you still want to do this, Haley?" Rosalind said. "It's not too late for you to back out."

If she didn't have time to prepare third feast, she would be shirking her duties and betraying Lord Walker. But if she got valuable information which prevented Mr. Douglas from catching up with him, that would be worth something. Would it be worth enough to make up for the dereliction of duty that would be missing the preparation of third feast? What would Lord Walker do?

She wished she could ask his advice now, but she knew if she did, she would lose any chance of a meeting and any chance of getting the information she wanted. She had to rely on her experience of Lord Walker's decisions to predict what he would have her do in the given situation. In fact, that was the very thing she did best. It was what she was hired to do. So by doing it she would be fulfilling her duties to Lord Walker, not betraying him. And she knew what he would tell her to do. She always did. He would tell her to do whatever she could to get a leg up on the competition, even if that meant having a meeting with the enemy without telling him. As long as she didn't reveal anything valuable for them to use against Lord Walker, she was fulfilling her duty to him.

"Yes. I do," she said.

"Okay," Rosalind said. "Good. Then get to printing and don't talk to me again until after the meeting. It's already suspicious enough how much we've been interacting."

"Ok—" Haley tried to say, but she didn't finish because

Rosalind was already gone.

She had wasted so much time, she had to print more than she would have liked. She felt like she was betraying Lord Walker already, but she soothed herself with the thought that it was only second feast and fourth feast could be the best feast she had ever cooked to make up for it. Not to mention the valuable information she would be getting from her meeting with Mr. Douglas. She steeled her mind with the thought of it and set to cooking two pots of mashed potatoes, two gallons of gravy, and two cheesecakes. The whipped cream and turkeys would have to be printed.

She set everything on the cart and pushed it out into the hall. The crowd was getting rowdy. The time between first and second feast was always a sketchy situation with everyone ready to eat more and already a little drunk. She made sure to hug the wall as she walked, but it didn't matter because the owner who had slapped her was still dazed and not even eating. He was sitting now though, so he had that going for him. Haley was relieved to be there just as Lord Walker finished the last bits of his pumpkin pie—his own meeting must have taken some time.

"Haley, dear!" Lord Walker was relieved, too. "You are an angel. I'm stuck in a huddle with these three sweaty fools, and I turn around to see the leftovers and dessert of first feast to save me from their dullness. *Ho ho ho!*"

Haley nodded and curtsied. She felt odd. Like she was keeping a secret from him. She looked around, and Mr. Douglas was still watching the symphony, motionless as a statue. Rosalind was nowhere to be seen. Haley knew she was watching from somewhere, though, so she didn't dare say anything to Lord Walker.

"And then here you are," Lord Walker went on. "The first secretary to deliver second feast." She was the first at the head table—not the first in all—but she didn't mention that. "And only minutes before the second feast guest speaker. Just another example of your perfect timing and ability to predict my every need. *Ho ho ho!*"

Haley set the food in front of him and tried to bow out of the way, but he stopped her.

"Stay, sweetheart," he said. "Stay. This guest—*oh*—you'll want to see him. We own him now, so you'll want to know what we're working with. *Ho ho ho!*"

"Yes, sir," Haley said, stepping back a few steps to stand behind the head table and stare across the long hall to where the symphony was still playing.

Lord Walker stood and called them to a halt. When he did, the entire Hall grew silent. There wasn't even the sound of eating.

"Owners of Inland!" Lord Walker boomed over the room in his advertising voice. "Lend me your ears. Lend me your voices if you will. What are the tenets of Inland?"

"Property, profit, play!" came a chorus of baritone voices.

"Property, profit, play," Lord Walker said. "*Ho ho ho*! Yes. And I think we'll all show tonight that we uphold the third tenet. Am I right?" He held up his drink and the room toasted him. All except for Mr. Douglas. Which reminded Haley that she had to tell Rosalind to make old fashioneds for Lord Walker.

"And we all hold our sacred property on high or we wouldn't have the money to afford to be here tonight," Lord Walker said. "Would we?"

At that the mob erupted in laughter. Lord Walker was full of himself. He had the same look on his face as he did when he showed Haley his ad that morning.

"Now, some of us—" He picked up his cane and twirled it. "Not to toot my own flute, but myself included—" The mob laughed again. "—know profits better than others. But I think we can all recognize a profit when we see one. This next gentleman—our celebrity guest speaker for second feast—I dare say that he *is* a profit. In fact, he's a prophet of a new era in integrated advertising. Everyone give it up, if you will, for *Russ Logo*!"

The symphony played a fanfare, and a lime-green-suited, glittery form with tall, colorful hair and tall, colorful boots pranced out onto the stage. The crowd erupted in applause and whistles and whoops. The colorful person walked back and forth on the stage, waving and bending down to shake hands with the owners at the back of the room. When he was done, he stepped up onto a round platform that hovered over the long tables to the front of the Hall where the Fortune 5 could see him better. The applause died down, and Russ started to speak.

"Gentlemen," he said, pausing there for a long time and looking into his hands. "Gentlemen and secretaries," he went on. "Owners. Masters of Outland."

Mr. Smörgåsbord shot Russ an angry look, and Mr. Loch choked on a piece of ham.

"In your hands is the fate of every living soul that inhabits Outland," Russ said. "It is thanks to you that our 3D printers never run dry, and that we have the—" He half-coughed and half-choked down something in his throat. "And that we have the technology we need to live a life of leisure. It is thanks to you that anyone in existence has anything good that they have. You...*You* are producers. Everyone else...we are only consumers who live by your charity. Every year we in Outland elect a representative to try as they might to communicate our...our...*gratitude* for what you give us. Well maybe they made the wrong choice this year."

There was a subdued laughter from the crowd, as if they weren't sure if it was supposed to be a joke.

"Perhaps there is no right choice. Perhaps no one in Outland truly knows what we owe you. And if they did—if they really knew what it was that you owners provided for us—and what it means to every single resident of Outland—how could one person come here once a year and communicate that? How could that be enough?

"No. I don't think that it is enough. *I know* that this is not enough. It's not enough to show you what you deserve. For that we must live our gratitude. We must *be* our gratitude always. For that we must forever hold in our minds the knowledge of what you gave to us, and we must live every minute as if we intend to pay you back for your generosity. Your charity. Your...your...*courage*."

He stopped to take a breath. Haley took the chance to scan the audience and noticed that no one in the room was eating. They were all staring up at Russ on his platform, the Fortune 5 included.

"But still," Russ went on. "Even if we live our gratitude, you won't ever see it. You'll see the movies we make, and hear the songs we write, and your children will learn from the documentaries we create, but you will never *see* our gratitude. You will see the products of our gratitude, you will see the dollars and cents that our gratitude offers up for the grabbing."

The crowd hooted and hollered, eating again and now firmly convinced that he was on their side.

"But you will not see the gratitude we so want to display. So maybe it is necessary for me to be here today. Even if it isn't sufficient. Even though it *is not* sufficient. We have to do it anyway.

We have to try. So...I'm here today to tell you..."

Almost no one in the room was listening anymore. They were all deep into second feast. They had their fourth and fifth round of drinks. Russ had already said what they wanted to hear and that's all they cared about.

"To tell you that we will keep working and we won't stop until you get what you deserve."

The Fortune 5 clapped at his commencement, drawing the others in. Even Mr. Douglas clapped with them, an uncharacteristic show of emotion from him. The platform carried Russ backstage, behind the symphony which played a fanfare at his exit.

"Very good," Lord Walker boomed over the feast, still clapping. "Very good. What did I tell you? A prophet of the new age.

"You know. Russ there—a good friend of mine, Russ." Lord Walker winked and the applause grew louder. "Russ had a good point about gratuity. *Gratuity*. Think about the word. What does it mean to you? *Charity*. That's what it means. Just that. Charity. And is that what we want to instill in the peoples of Outland? A reliance on charity?

"Who sets the example for the uninformed mob to conform to? Who do they look up to and pray to one day be? Who you ask? *Us*. The owners.

"If we request charity in exchange for charity, we continue the vicious cycle of dependence on charity. Russ said it himself, they can't come up here once a year and express their charity. That simply isn't enough. So, instead, I propose that we abolish this gratuitous practice of charity, we no longer succumb the residents of Outland to the shame and humility of crawling up here once a year on hands and knees, only to fail—Russ's words, remember, not mine—at expressing their gratuity. Let us instead—*as he suggested*—experience their gratuity the old-fashioned way. Through their work. Through their creativity. For it is because of us that they have the privilege to be able to think and experience and create, so why shouldn't it be us who reaps the benefits of those thoughts and experiments and creations?"

The room burst into applause.

"After all. *We* are producers. And a feast is a producers holiday. It is our lavish celebration and waste that is a symbol of the fact that abundant consumption is the result and the reward of production. Abundance is Inland's pride!"

Again there was a round of applause.

"So let us put these consumers out of our mind," Lord Walker said. "And let us producers consume in peace, as is our right. Eat up owners! *Ho ho ho.*"

He was greeted again with the sound of eating. He smiled his look-at-my-commercial smile and looked back at Haley to wink, then sat down to start in on second feast himself.

Haley watched him for a minute, then looked over at an empty chair in the head table and remembered that she was supposed to be meeting with Mr. Douglas. She looked in on Lord Walker one more time to make sure he had enough food to put him through second feast, then set on her way toward the kitchen.

She always came into and left the Feast Hall with Lord Walker through the owner's entrance, so she had never walked so far back into the kitchen. She felt conspicuous doing it, as if every secretary she passed noticed the oddity of her going so far in, but the service entrance was at the very back and that was the only way to get the information she wanted.

She was relieved to get into the lukewarm, stale air of the service parking garage. There were no more eyes to judge her. She took a deep breath and looked around. The garage was empty except for a handful of coupes similar to the one Lord Walker let her drive to the market. Mr. Douglas was nowhere in sight. He probably wasn't coming at all. It was just another tactic, like getting her to let Rosalind prepare third feast.

Third feast! She remembered she hadn't given Rosalind the special instructions on how Lord Walker preferred his food, so she turned to start back into the kitchen and do the job herself when Mr. Douglas appeared between her and the door without a word. She almost fell over when she ran into him.

"Excuse me, sir," she said, gathering herself. "I'm sorry."

"No, Haley," Mr. Douglas said, staring into her eyes. "*I'm* sorry." He tipped his top hat.

Haley felt the pressure of him staring into her mind and thought she saw something she recognized behind his eyes. But what? It wasn't Lord Walker's eyes they reminded her of, so whose?

"Do you have any questions before we continue?" Mr.

Douglas said.

Any questions? She had more questions than he could answer. So many that she couldn't possibly choose one to ask without some knowledge of why she was there meeting with Lord Walker's biggest competitor. "Why am I here?"

"That's a long story," Mr. Douglas said. "And a sufficient answer would take longer than we have now. We're on a schedule, remember. Unhappily, it will have to suffice to say that you are here to receive an opportunity to find the answer to that question."

"What opportunity?"

"That's precisely why you're here," Mr. Douglas said. "To learn that opportunity. So, to start, let me ask you a question. Do you know who you work for?"

Haley chuckled. "Of course. Lord Walker."

"And do you know what Lord Walker does?"

"Lord Walker produces. Just like you, sir." Haley didn't understand. She thought he was asking questions with obvious answers.

"But what does it mean to produce? You spend more time with Lord Walker than anyone in the worlds. You see how he spends his every waking moment. What is it that he actually does?"

Haley thought about it. Most of his time was spent in bed, eating and watching TV. He said he was working when the stock advice was on, but that usually only lasted through first breakfast before he asked her to change the channel. Then there were the business feasts. But those seemed more like feasts and less like business. What was she supposed to say? She didn't sit at the table with him and watch his every move. She was in the kitchen, cooking. He could very well have been doing important work that she didn't see. Then there was the stock trading. But she did most— well, all—of that. Besides that he filmed one or two commercials a year for the various elections and award cer—

"If it takes you so long to answer," Mr. Douglas interrupted her train of thought, "it indicates he doesn't do much."

"I—But—"

"It's okay," Mr. Douglas cut her off. "You don't have to answer that question. It was only necessary that you went through the thought processes produced by being asked it. Now, another question, do you know how a 3D printer works?"

Haley felt defensive. She didn't know if he wanted an answer or if he was manipulating her again. She was hesitant to give him one.

"This one I would prefer you did answer," he said, as if reading her thoughts.

"They rearrange atoms into the structure ordered by the operator."

"Yes." Mr. Douglas nodded. "That's what you're told. But what if I told you that was a lie? What if I told you that humans have no technology capable of rearranging atoms? What would you say if I told you that the printer in your kitchen works in the same way as the door of your garage?"

"I don't understand, sir."

"Of course you don't," Mr. Douglas said. "No one ever taught you how to. Your experience—as vast as it is—doesn't allow for you to understand. But that's the opportunity I'm offering you, Haley. Have you ever wondered how you drive out of the same garage and end up at different destinations all while going through the same door?"

Haley thought about it. She had never thought about it. She shook her head.

"One last question, then we really must get back to the feast. Do you want to know the answers to these questions?"

ॐ   ✖   ॐ

IX. Ansel

She should never have agreed to take the first watch. It *was* her idea, after all, so she really had no choice—but still. Her parents were probably worrying about her, wondering where she was. No, they probably knew she was enjoying the grass and trees—where else would she be?—but still they always worried, even if they knew she could take care of herself.

Pidgeon had left right away, because he had to go see his parents or something. She wasn't listening. He didn't think the cat would come back until lunch, anyway. Without him there to tease, the time went by almost as slowly as it did when she was sitting in class, listening to stupid Mrs. Liar go on and on about this family usurping that and then another merging into those and *yadda yadda yadda*.

She caught herself staring off into the foliage and shook her head to get rid of the boring daydream. She reminded herself that this wasn't a school lesson or a game, this was real life, a hunt. She set her gaze on where she thought she remembered seeing the cat disappear at lunch and pictured it climbing through the leaves to her, willing it into existence.

Him. Willing *him* into existence. She wondered if Pidgeon really believed that this could be the Curious Cat, or if he was pulling a prank on her to get her to sit up in a tree for hours. She almost climbed down at the thought of it, but before she did, she remembered that she had definitely seen a cat at lunch, and whether it was *the* Curious Cat or not, she would be trying to catch it. The joke was on him. She was doing exactly what she would be doing whether he told her it was the Curious Cat or not.

She moved up the tree a little and sat in a knot between two branches, resting her back on the trunk of the tree. There. A perfect cat blind. And now she was comfortable, too. Another strike against Pidgeon's stupid ploy.

But then, what if it wasn't a ploy? What if he really did believe that it was the Curious Cat? What if it really was the Curious

Cat? What would she do when she got to Prosperity? She laughed at the thought of it.

Sure there were stories of people who had seen the cat—and the stories all said it knew the way to Prosperity—but none of them ever really explained what Prosperity was. Most of them ended with something bad happening to the people who were chasing the cat before they could ever find it. But her mom had told her one once where the little girl actually caught the cat, and it did show her the way to Prosperity, but when the little girl got there and saw what Prosperity really was, she turned around, went back home, and never chased that cat again.

Ansel laughed a little too loud for someone who was supposed to be on a hunt, but that was the most ridiculous Curious Cat story of them all. To turn down Prosperity for this? That girl in the story didn't even live in the Green Belt, she lived in the Streets. Someone who had never experienced what the Streets were like must have written that one. No one else would make up a story so stupid that someone turns down a chance to get out of them.

She heard a rustling in the tree below her and jumped up to see Pidgeon's big head climbing toward her. "Bombs away," she said, dropping a nut from a branch near her down onto him.

"*Ow*! Jerk," he said, climbing up to her and sitting on a slightly lower branch, rubbing his head. Just another sign of his weakness.

"Pidgeon," Ansel said. "You can't tell me that you haven't lived on the Belt for long. You wouldn't last a day in the Streets."

"I never said I didn't live on the Belt for long. And thanks."

"Hey," Ansel said, shrugging. "I just call it like I see it. And you did say you haven't lived here long."

"Yeah, *here*. But the Belt's pretty long, in case you hadn't noticed."

"Yeah yeah," Ansel said, shaking her head. "I get it." She was kind of proud of him for finally sticking up for himself. It was about time.

They sat in silence for too long to count, staring at the leaves, waiting for the cat to come back, before Ansel said, "You ever been out in the Streets Pidgeon?"

"It's Richard," Pidgeon said. "And yeah, you know, I've been a few—a few blocks in there. I haven't spent all my life on the

Belt."

"A few blocks?" Ansel scoffed. "*Pft*! That's still one day's travel to the Belt. That isn't the Streets, Pidgeon. That's the Garden of Eden."

"Yeah," Pidgeon said, getting heated. "So what? I guess you're some big sho—" He turned his head and raised his eyebrows. "Did you hear that?"

"What? The cat?" Ansel stood up and looked down the tree for it.

"No." Pidgeon shook his head. "It sounded like gunshots. *Pow. Pow pow. Pow.*"

Ansel laughed. "C'mon Pidgeon," she said. "That was a hammer. If that was a gun, it couldn't scratch a baby it was so small. You see, that's exactly what I'm talking about. Where I come from it's completely streets. That's where the name *the Streets* comes from. Don't they teach you that in the Kinder Garden? We can't walk a couple of blocks to get to green grass, blue skies, and cat-infested trees, you know. Shit. We can't walk thirty blocks, three hundred blocks, I don't know how many blocks. I had never seen this much grass since yesterday, and you're sitting here crying about a few gunshots off in the distance. That's a lullaby to me, Pidgeon. I'm about to lean back here in this beautiful green tree and take a nap to the sound of it. Watch me." She leaned back and put her hands behind her head to prove her point.

"Well," Pidgeon said. "I'm sorry I didn't live on the Streets like you did, but what can I do abou—" He turned his head again. "That was another one."

Ansel shook her head, chuckling. "Alright," she said. "Alright, Pidgeon. I'll stay out here a little longer to protect you. My parents'll just have to wait to hear how sucky my first day of school was. They're probably still at work, anyway."

"Yeah, well." Pidgeon grabbed a leaf from the tree and tore it to bits. "I don't need your protection. No one will find me up here anyway."

"Yeah," Ansel said, giving him a thumbs up. "Right. *Because they're prolly looking for you.* Aren't they?" She tried to hold a straight face but couldn't help chuckling.

"You're a jerk," Pidgeon said, ripping another leaf off the tree and tearing it to pieces.

"So you spent all your life on the Belt, huh, Pidgeon." Ansel smiled, crossing her legs. "That's gotta be nice."

"You'd think. But it's not as great as they make it out to be."

"Oh, no? Cat trees—trees period—grass and sky. I don't see where the problems are."

"Give it some time. You'll see."

"*Pffft.*" Ansel chuckled. "So far all I see is blue skies and green leaves."

"Yeah? Well look down there. Look at the street right now. What do you see?"

"I don't know," Ansel said, cocking her head to look but unable to see through the leaves. "Looks pretty empty to me."

"That's because it is. Everyone's gone into hiding. Do you know why?"

"That's ridiculous." Ansel chuckled. "What would they have to hide from?"

"Look closer," Pidgeon said. "There's a few of them down there, I'm sure. And there'll be more soon. It's probably best for you to stay in the tree with me for a while anyway. You don't want to run into one of them. They'd take you down and lock you up for crossing in front of them."

Ansel tried harder to see through the leaves. She climbed out onto the thickest branch she could find and went almost to the end of it before she thought it would break underneath her weight. The wind whipped across her face and it felt like she was flying. She had never been this high out in the open before. Being out on a limb like this felt so much more freeing than being on the roof of a skyscraper. She looked up at the sky and thought it was strange that the clouds ended in such a straight line like that. It was almost as if they were being blown behind a huge, straight-edged invisibility screen in the sky.

"Do you see them?" Pidgeon asked from behind her.

She looked down again. There weren't too many people, but she could see more coming from up the street. They were all dressed in white, wearing helmets, carrying guns, and marching in pairs behind their leaders. A couple of them pulled someone out of a building and dragged them along the Green Belt. They seemed like giants compared to the person they were lugging behind them, even from so high in the air.

"Who are they?" Ansel asked, sitting back in the tree when they had dragged the person out of sight.

"Protectors." Pidgeon chuckled. "That's what they call themselves. Can you believe that? *Protectors.*" He shook his head.

"Protectors?"

"Something the Street kid has never heard of before?" Pidgeon said with a smug grin. "They don't get too far from the Belt, I guess. Who needs protecting now?"

Ansel blushed. "*Pshh.* I can handle myself," she said. "I was just looking for information." She made like she was going to climb down the tree.

"No," Pidgeon said. "No, wait." He grabbed her arm to stop her.

She protested a little, but relented and sat back in her nook. "So, who are these protectors?"

"Assholes," Pidgeon said, managing to spit it out without looking disgusted. He must have really had something against them. "That's who. *Pigs.* They're not here to protect any of us. That's why they never go out into the Streets. No, they're here to protect other people *from* us. They just come and round up all the printers every now and then, and they usually kill a few people in the process."

"No," Ansel said, shaking her head. "I would have heard of them before."

"If you've got a 3D printer, that's a ticket to the Belt. They know where to find them, and that's all they care about. If you've never had printer access, you've never had a reason to learn about them."

"That's shit. That's how I got here, you know. My parents got some printers and then we moved here. And what? These *protectors* are here to flash their guns and take them all away?"

"That's pretty much how it works," Pidgeon said, shrugging.

"No." Ansel shook her head. "Someone would stop them."

"*Ha!*" Pidgeon laughed. "Stop them? How? You've only seen them from far away. They're giants. And they wear armor. No weapon you can get from a printer can get through that armor. Then there's the guns they have. The weapons that wait behind those. You don't want to know what they're capable of, Ansel."

"H—How do you even know this?"

Pidgeon shook his head. "It's just something you learn living on the Belt, something you experience. You wouldn't know, Street kid."

"But—I...I do. I—"

"No. Ansel, look. It doesn't matter. They're gone now. You can go back home to your parents. I'll finish with this shift and see you in the morning, okay."

"But. They—"

"*Okay?*"

Ansel shook her head. "Fine," she said, waving her hands. "Whatever. But you better stay here for your entire shift."

"Yeah, yeah. Just watch out for the protectors on your way home."

Ansel nodded and made her way down the tree.

She wondered what had happened to Pidgeon to make him hate the protectors so much. She wondered what they could have done. They didn't look as scary as he was making them out to be, but then why was he so frightened by the gunshots? As far as Ansel knew that was the sound of someone getting what they deserved. At least that's how it was in the Streets.

She heard the sound of shuffling feet down the alley she was passing and jumped. She sighed a breath of relief when she saw it was just a grubby kid, younger than her, digging through the trash. He was probably an orphan looking for something to eat.

"Hey, you!" Ansel called.

The kid turned and stared at her with wide eyes like an animal. He froze in place, but Ansel could see the tension in his muscles. They were ready to spring into action at any moment.

"Get out of here, kid!" she yelled at him. "This is the Belt, you belong in the Streets!" She stomped a few steps toward him like she was going to chase him, and he scampered away. Ansel laughed to herself and turned toward home.

What a poor sap, dirty and starving and digging through dumpsters. He probably didn't even know how to hunt or trap. That's the only reason to dumpster dive. If this was the Streets, there wouldn't even be anything worth eating to dig for. At least she knew she would never be as helpless as that.

The hall and the stairway up to her apartment seemed emptier than they should be. Maybe they were always that way at this time of day, but she hadn't lived there long enough to know. Still, she felt like something was strange about the echoing of her footsteps up the stairs. She shrugged off the feeling and shoved the door to the apartment open, calling, "I'm *hoooome*! *Hellooo*?"

She walked into the kitchen, then her parents room, then out to the balcony. They must have still been at work. She shrugged and went back to her room to change out of that stupid dress and into something more comfortable. She looked at the dress—noting the tree bark tears and dirt on the back—before she crumpled it up and threw it in the corner. At least they couldn't make her wear it because it was new anymore.

After she had put on her jeans and t-shirt—and shoved her slingshot in her back pocket—she went back into the kitchen and looked in the fridge to find it empty as usual. There was a little bit of jelly and an onion, but that was it. There was some bread, too. She could make a disgusting jelly sandwich. Or she could wait until her parents got home, and they would probably bring something worth eating from their lunch at work. Especially with their first day at their new jobs. They had to get something good. That or she could go outside and get some food for herself, just like she told the Street kid to do. She went out to the balcony to look over the Belt and see if there was anything worth climbing down to catch.

The sun was almost down over the horizon, eaten between the skyline on opposite sides of the Belt. The sky was turning from blue, to red, to purple, then finally black. Ansel wondered if Pidgeon was still sitting up in the tree, if he would sit out the shift or give up. He was probably there now—he didn't look like he was going anywhere anytime soon when she had left him—but he might not stay the whole time. She would never know, though, unless she went out to spy on him, because neither of them could cover the whole night.

Where were her parents anyway? They usually didn't take this long. But this was a new job. There was no telling how long they would be out. They might even stay out for the entire night. They had done it before. More food, better house, perfect location, they more than likely had to do more work to get all that. But then she would be left with a jelly sandwich for dinner. Or they could be stuck working for a few days and not come home the entire time. Then she would have to ration her food, she would have to save the bread and jelly for when she couldn't go out to get something fresh.

If that was the case, going out to hunt would be the best option. She was about to set out and catch dinner when she heard the front door open.

"Mom? Dad?" she called. "I'm out here!"

She almost jumped off the balcony when a white-haired woman came outside instead of her parents.

"Wh—who are you?" Ansel said, cowering in the corner of the balcony railing.

"Settle down, dear," the old woman said. "Imma friend. Ya name's Ansel, right?"

"Who's askin?"

"Who's askin?" The woman frowned. "Me, dear. Who else? I live downstairs."

Ansel shook her head. The old woman looked familiar but not familiar enough.

"It doesn't matter, child. Ya gotta git outta here tonight. Ya're in danger."

"Get out of my house! Who are you? My parents'll be home soon!"

"Oh, child." The woman shook her head. "Afraid they won't. S'why I'm here ya see. Well...ya parents—they—they won't be coming home."

"What did you do to them?" Ansel demanded.

"No no no," the woman said, shaking her head. "Not me, child. Not me at all. I'm here to protect ya. It's them protectors that did this. Not me."

"Did what?" Ansel said, stomping her foot.

"Child." The woman shook her head. Her eyes grew teary. "They're—They've gone. D—Dead. Maybe worse. But they ain't comin back. Now, I'm sorry."

"No!" Ansel rushed at her and tried to hit the woman with her little sad fists, but she wrapped Ansel up in a tight warm hug and whispered, "I know, child. I know. But we don't have no time. The protectors prolly won't come lookin for the likes of ya—bein so young—but still, there're the landlords to worry about. This apartment was for ya parents."

Ansel pushed herself away from the woman's embrace. She wiped her eyes and sniffled. "What am I supposed to do? Where am I supposed to go?"

"I don't know, dear. Can't answer that. I'll tell ya this, though—and it's the last time, cause if they find me here I'm in the same boilin pot as ya're—but ya'll be better off leavin now. Ya can come with me to get a start, but ya'll leave tonight. I ain't takin no boarders."

If the woman was offering a longer stay, Ansel would have trusted her less, but the fact that she was so anxious to leave the apartment and wanted to get rid of Ansel as soon as possible made her more believable. "Fine," Ansel said. "One second." She ran to her room to grab the drawing of her and Katie, and even that stupid dress her parents had gotten her, and pack them both in her rucksack. She went back into the kitchen to pack the jelly, onion, and bread in, too, then said, "Okay. I'm ready."

"Good." The woman took her free hand. "Ya just might make it, yet, child. Now c'mon."

They left the apartment and climbed down a couple of flights of stairs, but not all the way to the ground floor. They went down the hall and into an apartment on the Street side of the building. It had a kitchen and a bathroom but no balcony, and the bed was in the kitchen. It looked like her house in the Streets, only without Ansel's bedroom. The woman dragged her in, locked the door, and set to rummaging through the drawers and cabinets without another word. Ansel walked to the remotest corner of the room and dropped her bag.

"No need to unpack," the woman said as she worked. "Ya'll be outta here soon anyway. Ya're already burden enough as it is."

"I didn't ask for no help!" Ansel protested.

"And I bet ya won't deny none either."

"I'll leave right now if you want." Ansel made to grab her bag.

"No ya won't. Ya'll be happy to have some food in ya stomach. This might be the last meal ya get for a while now."

Ansel knew she was right. She set her bag back down and paced the small room.

"Ya know how to cook?" the woman asked.

"Not in the kitchen, but I can follow directions."

"Chop that onion," the woman told her. "Ya say ya can't in the kitchen, but otherwise?"

"I can cook what I catch if I have a lighter and a garbage

can," Ansel said, trying not to cry—from the fumes she convinced herself, she still didn't believe the old woman was right about her parents. "Depending on the trash I might not need the lighter."

"Ya can hunt, too, then."

"I caught dinner most nights in the Streets. I'd say I know what I'm doing."

"That sorta knowledge'll do ya good, dear. Now toss the onion in. Ya'll appreciate that in a few days."

Ansel tossed the chopped up bits in. The smell and sound of them sizzling reminded her of her parents, her parents who this woman said were dead. They weren't, though. This senile, old lady had no idea what she was talking about. The tears welled up again even though Ansel was done chopping. "What's your name?" Ansel asked to distract herself as the woman portioned out two bowls of beans and rice, handing one to her.

"Don't matter. What matters is that ya eat this up and get ready for the road aheada ya, girl."

"I'm not a girl," Ansel said through a full mouth. "This is good, though," she added, trying not to sound too ungrateful.

"Thank ya, dear. But ya don't have to lie. It's just beans and rice and onion. It don't taste like much, but it fills the stomach. That's what matters for ya right now, anyway."

Ansel went on eating in answer. They didn't talk while they ate, which was typical of every meal Ansel had ever eaten. As soon as she finished her bowl and licked it clean, she set it in the sink.

"Ya'll be kind to wash that, ma'am," the woman said.

"Oh, I—" Ansel went to wash the bowl and spoon with an old soggy sponge that was resting on the edge of the sink. She almost gagged touching it.

"Very good," the woman said. "Now, I have some advice for ya. First, get outta the Concierge's territory as soon as ya can, child. It goes further west than east but ya'd be best goin south where they care the least. Ya know which way south is, don't ya?"

Ansel nodded. She had come from the south. That was her home. Of course she knew which way was south.

"Good," the woman said. "If ya think ya can hunt for food down there, then that's yar best bet. And I suggest ya go quick, too. The Concierges'll be lookin for ya, and the protectors'll be out again soon."

Ansel nodded. She was surprised to see that this woman was as afraid of the protectors as Pidgeon was. She didn't understand it, but she knew that now wasn't the time for questions.

"Good. Very good, dear," the woman said. "Then I'm afraid that's all I can do for ya. The Concierges'll search every apartment. Ya're property now, so ya best get going before they think I stole ya."

Ansel nodded again. "Thank you." She grabbed her rucksack and made to leave, but the woman grasped her in a hug before she could.

"Good luck, child," she said, sniffling. "I did what I could. Ya gotta do the rest now."

Ansel squeezed her tight one last time then slipped out the door and down the stairs as quietly as she could.

It was dark outside. There was no sun, and the moon was hidden by the skyscrapers. The only light to guide her was that little which came from the windows and doors of the buildings around her. She knew the woman had told her to go south, but she also knew better than that. The Concierges might look further west than south, but that's because the better territory was in the west. She had to stay close to the Belt. Now that she had experienced it, there was no way she was getting any further away from that source of food. She didn't want to be like that Street kid without a hope in the world.

She stopped in her tracks when she realized that she was exactly like that Street kid. She couldn't believe it. She wanted to run back to her house and find her parents there to realize it was all a joke, or a bad dream, or something. Then she heard the sound of movement and saw a flash of white out of the corner of her eye. She scurried out into the Belt to hide behind a tree.

Catching her breath, she peeked around the edge of the trunk. Two of the tallest, whitest, biggest people she had ever seen carried huge guns down the street, wearing plated vests and helmets with facemasks that were shaped to look like laughing—or screaming, she couldn't tell in the light—faces with dark tinted eyes. No wonder everyone was so afraid of them.

When they had disappeared from view and Ansel's muscles relaxed, she heard a whisper from above her. She looked up to find Pidgeon in the tree, beckoning her to climb up. She didn't even realize this was that tree. She climbed up, and he climbed higher, too, until they were both at the cat blind. He had kept his post after all.

"What are you doing here?" Pidgeon whispered. "I thought you couldn't come out this late. You shouldn't have. Those protectors are dangerous."

"*Uh.* Yeah." Ansel shook her head. "Plans changed."

"Well, I haven't seen Mr. Kitty all night."

"Yeah." Ansel shrugged. "It probably won't be back until lunch tomorrow, huh?"

Pidgeon stared at her, and she turned to look away down the tree. "Is there something wrong with you?" he said. "You don't sound as interested in finding him as you did when you set up this system."

Ansel shook her head. "Yeah. I'm fine," she said absently.

"Ansel. He's not coming tonight. Why don't you go home and get some rest. The protectors are gone now."

"No—I mean, Pidg—Richard. What did the protectors do to you?"

"What?" Pidgeon looked away from her now.

"The protectors. Why do you hate them so much?"

"Everyone hates them. It's not just me."

"So is that why you hate them, then?" Ansel scoffed. "Because everyone else does?"

"No." Pidgeon shook his head. "I have my reasons."

"Well what are they?"

"I don't—That's personal. I barely even know you, okay. I don't have to talk about this. Just leave it."

"*Alright.* Sorry. God. It was just a question. You don't have to be a baby about it."

"Yeah? *A baby?* Funny you use that word. You have no idea what those people are capable of, Ansel. *No clue.* And you're gonna sit here and call *me* a baby. My brother was a baby, you know. He was crying for his mom—his mom who *they* took from him—and you know what they did to him? No. You have no clue. Just like I thought, Street kid." He spit down the tree and grabbed another handful of leaves to tear to pieces.

Ansel felt her eyes moisten. "I'm sorry," she whispered in a shaky voice.

"What was that?" Pidgeon snapped.

"I said I'm sorry! Alright. *I'm sorry*. I didn't know. I just—"

"You just had to keep pushing, even though I told you I didn't want to talk about it."

"No, I—"

"You thought you knew better than me. You thought that, because you were from the Streets, you knew how the world worked better than a fluffy flower from the Belt. Well, I've seen things, too, Ansel. I've lived through things. I watched them kill my brother, then I was forced into the Concierge *orphanage* system. So don't talk to me about what you've been through. Okay!"

"Pidgeon!" Ansel said. "I think they killed my parents."

He looked at her then climbed out on a limb to see if anyone had heard their argument. He sat back in the tree and tried to scoot a little closer to her. "I'm—uh—I'm sorry," he said. "I didn't know."

"Yeah, well, let's call it even."

"I didn't mean—"

"And I don't *know* either. Okay. They could still be alive. That woman could have been lying to me. I never—I never saw their bodies or anything."

"What woman? What did she look like?"

"I don't know." Ansel shrugged. "She looked like an old lady. What does it matter?"

"Well she was right."

"You don't know that," Ansel said, hitting him on his arm. "My parents wouldn't go down that easily."

"*Ow!*" Pidgeon rubbed where she had hit him. "I didn't mean that. I meant that *if* they were dead, you would be better off not staying in the apartment. The Concierges will want it for someone else. And if they find you there, they'll want to use you for something else, too. Trust me, Ansel. You don't want that."

"Is that what happened to you?" Ansel said. "When they…"

Pidgeon nodded. "When they killed my mom and brother and brought me to their orphanage. I know you don't want that, Ansel. The things they make me—The things they would make you do. I can't even—I…" He shook his head, staring down the tree at nothing.

"Don't worry, Richard," Ansel said, putting her hand on his back. "I won't let them get me."

He smiled. "You better not."

"I won't," she said, smiling and perking up. "And I won't accept the fact that they—that my parents are gone, either. I'm gonna stake the apartment out for the night before I leave. And you're coming with me when I do."

"Ansel, no." Pidgeon shook his head. "I can't. If they found me, it would be worse than it already is. I can't risk that."

"Risk?" Ansel scoffed. "Your life is so bad that you can't even tell me about it, Pidgeon. You think leaving that is a risk? Sure, there's no risk in staying here. You know your life is going to be terrible. But with leaving the only risk you take is living a better life."

"Yeah? Well, what would I do if I left, huh? How would I eat? Where would I sleep? At least there are meals and a bed here, and school as an escape. If I left, I would have nothing."

"That's not true." Ansel shook her head. "Just look around you. We're in a tree in the Belt, Pidgeon. This is the best place in the world to find food, to scavenge, to hunt. We can sleep in the trees and move up and down the Belt. Maybe we'll even make it all the way to the end of the thing. Or maybe we'll come all the way around the other side and end up right back where we started. What do you think?"

"*Ha!*" Pidgeon shook his head. "Don't make me laugh." He scoffed. "*You* can hunt. *You* can scavenge. *I* don't know how to do any of that, and *I* would only hold you back. I bet you'd leave me behind the first time it looked profitable to you."

"That's not true. I wouldn't have asked you to come if I was going to leave you behind. I'm not like that. It's just—Nevermind. It's stupid anyway." She looked away, shaking her head.

Pidgeon shrugged. "Yeah. Right," he said. He waited a while for her to respond, but when she didn't, he swallowed his pride and said, "It's just what?"

"No," Ansel said, shaking her head. "It's nothing. Don't worry about it. You can stay at your stupid orphanage, and I'll find my parents alone."

"That woman, Ansel. The one who told you your parents were...*dead*. Did she live a few floors below you? Did she have dreaded up white hair and serve you red beans?"

Ansel shook her head but didn't answer.

"Ansel, if she did, if that was her, then your parents are gone.

She was trying to protect you. I know her. I found her place after they brought me here, after it happened to me. She told me the same things she told you, that I should get out of here as soon as I can, that I was in danger, but I didn't trust her just like you don't, and that's why I'm still stuck at that stupid orphanage, because I didn't listen. I stayed around here where I knew how to get food and a place to sleep, and they caught me and brought me to the orphanage where they haven't taken their eyes off me since. They *will* find you, Ansel."

"That's not true! You said it yourself. You don't know how to hunt, but *I* do. *I* know what I'm doing. I can do it without getting caught, and they won't be looking for me, anyway, because my parents aren't dead!"

"*Ansel*," Pidgeon said, shaking his head and avoiding her eyes. "They are. The sooner you accept that fact, the better off you'll be."

"Fine." Ansel sighed. "Whatever. Even *if* they are—which they aren't—I'm still leaving this place. I'm going to the end of the Belt with or without you, Pidgeon. In fact, I might as well get going now. No use putting it off any longer. Have fun in school and good luck finding your stupid cat." She made to climb down, but he stopped her again.

"Wait!" he said. "*Wait*. Just wait."

She sat down as he collected himself.

"Wait," he repeated. "Okay. I just—I—You said something earlier. Or, you were going to say it. The reason why you wouldn't leave me behind if I went with you. What was it?"

"Nothing." Ansel shook her head. "But I wouldn't leave you behind. I swear. I'd teach you how to hunt so you wouldn't even have to worry about it."

"They killed her in front of me," Pidgeon said, staring at something which Ansel couldn't see out beyond the leaves of the tree. "My mom. I'm not sure if that's worse, or not knowing like you, but they killed her right in front of me. My—my brother, too. He was crying because of the sound of the gun. I was, too, but I was a little older so I held it in better. He—he was just a baby. So he was crying. And the protectors—the *pigs*—they yelled at him to shut up, but he wouldn't. Of course he wouldn't, you know. He was just a baby. One of them took my brother out of his crib, set him on the ground, then lifted his boot up and hovered it over my baby brother, daring me to cry out against it. But I choked back my need to cry out, and the *protector* let his foot drop anyway. I did cry out then. And they laughed. Then they said they weren't letting me off that easily. One of them pointed a gun at me while another said that if I didn't take his gun and...*shoot my brother.*" He turned away, obviously crying, then sniffled and gathered himself. "If I didn't do...*it,* they said they would kill him then kill me after I watched them do it. So I—I didn't have a choice, you see." He shook his head, tears falling freely from his eyes now. "And I've been living in that Hell ever since." His shaky voice finally broke, and he sobbed uncontrollably.

Ansel scooted as close to him as she could. She patted his back as it rose up and down with his sobs. "When my mom—" She choked back tears of her own. "When my mom brought me to class this morning—or—*uh*—yesterday—I don't know anymore, it doesn't matter. But when she brought me to class, she said to me— she gave me a lot of advice, but one thing that she said that really stuck with me was—she said, *we do nothing alone, Ansel.* And she's right, Pidgeon. And you can't get away from your orphanage alone. Just like I can't get to the end of the Belt alone." She couldn't help but chuckle even though she was still crying. Pidgeon let out a short laugh of his own.

"*That's* why I want you to come with me, Pidgeon," she said, sniffling and wiping her nose. "That's why I won't leave you. Because we do nothing alone. And we're not alone anymore. What do you say?"

Pidgeon sniffled and wiped his nose, too. He said, "Do you really think we can—" but he couldn't finish the question because the black cat jumped onto his lap.

&   ✖   &

X. Russ

Russ curled tighter into the fetal position on his fluffy, soft couch. He squeezed the blanket closer around himself. This was warmth. This was safety. This was all he needed in the world. He didn't ask for any of that other shit. He didn't go out looking for some stupid assembly line worker—*er*—*actor* to pull that lame robot prank and get him wrapped up in Fortuna knows what.

What was he wrapped up in anyway? He threw the blanket off his body as if it were the situation he had been unwittingly thrust into. He had told the protectors he knew nothing. He *didn't* know anything. The papos were there recording the whole thing. The protectors watched the footage for themselves. And still, they—they...

He grabbed the blanket off the floor and wrapped it around himself again. His body ached. His head pulsed. His ribs were at least bruised if not broken. He tried to sit up a little, but the pain was so much he groaned and went back into the fetal position. He had never before experienced such pain, such anger.

The protectors were savages. He had never met a protector, but he had played more than a few, and none of the roles he had ever portrayed were as deranged as the protectors he had encountered in real life. Protectors? *Ha*! They were something altogether different than that. They were unreal. It didn't matter what he knew or what he said, they were out for blood and they were going to get it.

He heard a knock at the door and flinched, sending a shock of pain through his ribs and forcing another loud groan out of his mouth. The door swung open, and Jorah came in saying, "I'll take that as a *come in* you barbarian." When he saw Russ curled up on the couch, blanket tight under his chin, face makeup-less and bruised, Jorah held his hand to his mouth and gasped. "Russ, dear. What *did* they do to you?" He sat down on the couch, sending another wave of pain through Russ's body. "I'm sorry, sweetheart." He stroked Russ's hair. "Tell your Jorah what they did to you, honey."

"Jorah," Russ groaned. "Why?" He wanted to cry.

"You know," Jorah said. "That was a great groan. *Uhhgghh.*" He tried to mimic it. "I could use that in this play I'm doing. Do it again." He poked Russ.

"*Ugghhhggh.* Jorah! Please."

"I'm sorry, dear," Jorah said with a frown. "But the show must go on, you know. Anything to make it more realistic, right? You should be glad to have this experience. You can use it to your advantage in the future."

Russ groaned again. "I don't care about the future. I just want to be able to breath without my lungs burning."

"Oh. *Sweetheart.*" Jorah pet his hair. "I know. I'm sorry. You know me. Always looking at the platinum lining."

"Jorah, do you even see my face?"

"I do, dear." Jorah patted his head. "I do. Now tell your Jorah what they did to you. Was it the protectors? I saw a replay of your show, you know. And your emergency broadcast, too. You did, *weeell*...you looked great."

"Replay?" Russ frowned.

"*Yes, replay.* I was at work, you know. I couldn't rightly watch your show and film mine at the same time, could I?"

Russ groaned in response.

"But it *was* them," Jorah said. "Wasn't it?"

"There weren't supposed to be any replays," Russ said, clutching his blanket tighter under his chin.

"Yeah, well, once the feed goes out, there's no getting it back. I'm sure everyone in the world's seen it by now."

"That's not good."

"Not good?" Jorah chuckled. "*It's great.* The classic Streisand effect in action. You're getting more publicity because they're trying to cover it up. You're all over every gossip magazine and talk show. You just keep getting bigger and bigger."

"That's not good, Jorah." Russ groaned.

"*Pfft.* Sweetheart." Jorah shook his head. "Tell me how, then. Tell me how that's anything but good."

"Do you see my face, Jorah?" Russ said, turning this way and that to give him full view of the injuries. "Did you hear me groaning? That's how it's not good. The more people who see that video, the more broken ribs and bloody faces I get. That's why! *Uggghghgh.*"

"Alright, dear. Alright," Jorah said, brushing Russ's hair to calm him. "You've made your point. Just tell me what they did to you. I'm here to help, sweetheart."

"They just—they thought I had something to do with it. Apparently it's against the rules of the network to talk about the assembly lines. I don't know. But they thought I was in on it."

"Why didn't you tell them you didn't know the freak?" Jorah scoffed, still brushing Russ's hair.

"I did!" Russ said, sitting up with a groan. "It was the first thing I told them. But they didn't believe me. They said I wouldn't have brought it up on my show if I wasn't in on it."

Jorah shook his head. "*Tsk, tsk, tsk*. You know, though, Russ. They do have a point."

"What?" Russ couldn't believe what he was hearing. First protectors acting like savages, and now Jorah saying they were right to do it. There was something wrong with the world, and Russ just wanted it all to go away.

"I mean—like I said, Russ. You're getting more publicity than anyone has ever gotten out of this. You're telling me that it's just a coincidence. You had *nothing* to do with it."

"Jorah, do you really think I would get myself beaten to near death just for a little bit of publicity?"

Jorah giggled. "Uh...*Yeah*. You would, wouldn't you?"

"Well...Yes. I would," Russ said, shaking his head. In fact, he had done almost exactly that on many occasions. Maybe it was a bad defense to go with. "But I didn't. Not this time. I swear to you, Jorah. I had nothing to do with it, and the protectors did this anyway. It was like—it was like they just wanted to beat someone." His ribs hurt with the thought of it.

"No way, Russ," Jorah said, shaking his head. "Protectors aren't like that. I've played, like, a hundred protectors and a thousand criminals, and I know that no protector would ever do what you're trying to say they did."

"I know, Jorah." Russ sighed. "That's exactly what I thought. But I'm telling you, they were unreal. You can see the outcome." He put on the saddest face he could muster, but acting was difficult in such pain.

"Sweetheart." Jorah stood up and Russ groaned. "There it is. Remember that for the future, Russ. Your work will be better for it.

But, sweetheart, I'm going to let you sit here and sort your story out so it doesn't sound so ridiculous to the next person you tell it to. Do you understand what I'm saying, dear?"

"You're saying you don't believe me."

"Oh, dear." Jorah shook his head. "*No no no*. I'm not saying that at all. I'm saying that it would be best for you to come up with a better story. It doesn't matter. You'll figure it out. I'll see you after the feast, Russ. You're sure to win it now. So do yourself a favor: Go see a doctor, get ready to put on a perfect performance, and try not to get in any deeper than you already are. I might stop by before your speech. I'd rather not, but I might, dear. *Ta ta*."

The door clicked closed and Russ clinched his blanket tighter. What was with Jorah? He wasn't normally so cryptic. Or was he? All they ever really talked about was clothes and gossip. They had never had a real conversation before. What was a real conversation anyway? His stomach groaned and his ribs burned. Jorah was right about one thing: Russ needed to get to a doctor. He couldn't live like this anymore.

His stomach wouldn't shut up, but it would have to wait a little longer. He didn't think he could move enough to eat anyway. He tossed the blanket off and slowly inched his legs over the couch and onto the floor. He took a few deep breaths and gathered his strength to push himself up to a stooped position. His body burned and his head pounded. He wanted to give up, to fall down onto the floor and go to sleep, but he pushed himself through the door and out into the hall to press the elevator button.

"Russ my man. *Ru-uusss*. How are you?" Wes said, coming up through the hallway. The sound of his voice made the pounding in Russ's head all the worse. "Look, Russ. I'm sorry I was hard on you, but you're the best, you know. I gotta stick it to you so everyone else is afraid of me. You understand that. Right, buddy?"

The elevator dinged and the doors opened. "*Ugghhgh*," Russ groaned. "I'm not your buddy, guy," he said as he plopped himself onto his elevator's velvet couch.

The door slid closed, and he lost himself in the softness of it. It was like a nest, a womb. He wanted to lay there forever. He reached down to the floor for his blanket, grasped at air, and remembered he wasn't in his dressing room anymore. "The doctor. Now," he said.

The elevator fell into motion. He could feel himself getting better already. The doors opened, and there was nothing behind them but a dark, empty hall. "Not now," he said, groaning. "*Not now*! I said the doctor."

The doors started to close, but a gloved hand with a long, white sleeve slipped between them and forced them open again.

"Please," Russ pled. "I need to get to a doctor."

"Russ Logo?" the old woman who the gloved hand belonged to said, standing in the elevator door.

"Yes," Russ said, almost crying. He reached his trembling hand out to her while still lying on his couch. He must have looked so pathetic. Hopefully it would work. "It's me," he said, making sure to let his lower lip tremble as he spoke. "I need a doctor. Please close the door."

"Don't worry, Mr. Logo," the woman said. "I'm not a doctor, but I can take care of you. If you'll just come with me."

"No," Russ said. "I—I can't. Who are you?"

"Would you prefer a wheelchair, Mr. Logo?" the woman asked. "Popeye, fetch a chair for our guest, please."

"No. I—" Russ protested, but a big mechanical arm pushed a wheelchair his way.

"There you go, Mr. Logo," the woman said. "Popeye, help him into it, please."

"No," Russ pled. "Please. I can—*Ugghhghh*."

The mechanical arm lifted Russ up and plopped him into the wheelchair. Russ screamed out in pain at the sudden motion.

"There we are, Mr. Logo," the woman said. "Now bring him to the lab, please, Popeye. We need to see to his injuries."

Russ was beyond protesting. He couldn't imagine getting past the mechanical arm if he tried. He couldn't imagine getting out of the chair if he tried. The arm rolled along behind him, pushing his chair behind the woman in the white coat who led the way through a short hall into a room that was filled with glassware, tubes, chemicals, and machines of every shape, size, and color. It was only missing two wires with electricity going between them to make it look exactly like the *Frankenstein* set Russ had worked on a few years back. Only instead of Eyegore there was a huge mechanical arm, instead of Frankenstein it was this woman in a white coat, and instead of a monster it was Russ who *Popeyegore* lifted up and strapped onto the lab table.

"No. No, Popeye!" the woman said, slapping the metal hand. "No restraints, please. He's a friend. He won't squirm. Will you, Mr. Logo?" She smiled.

Russ looked around him. There were sharp objects everywhere, but none of them seemed to have any blood on them. He sniffed the air and smelled hospital antiseptic. "Didn't you say you weren't a doctor?"

The woman looked at him, frowning. "Didn't I say I wasn't... *Hmmm.* No. I'm not technically a doctor. I was never certified. Never got that MD. I'm more of a scientist, so to speak. But I know more about human anatomy than any doctor you'll ever meet. I guarantee that." She turned and went back to digging clangily through the drawers, looking for some thing.

"Um," Russ said. "Maybe I should go to a real doctor." He tried to smile, but even he was having trouble acting in this situation, pained and alone in an unknown place, guarded by a huge mechanical arm. "That is, if we can get my elevator back. Did you send it away? Where are we, anyway?" He was sitting up now with great pain from the effort. "I need to get out of here." He tried to slip off the table, but his feet couldn't hold his weight. Popeye could, though, and the thing scooped him back up onto the table.

"Oh, Russ," the woman said, still digging through the drawers. "I'm sorry. I just—I couldn't find it...But, *riiiiight*—wait for it—right here! Here it is." She pulled a small vial of some gray something out of one of the drawers and held it up to the light to read its small print. She had to squint and move it back and forth, looking for the right distance from her face to read the label, before she shook her head. "No," she said, frowning. "No no no. That's not it. *That* would probably kill you." She went on digging through the drawers again.

Russ sat holding his burning ribs, staring at the robotic arm, trying to find its weakness, but there was nothing to see. "Please don't kill me," he whispered.

"Here it is!" the woman said. "No—yes—no. *Ah. That's* the one." She pulled out another little vial that looked exactly like the first one.

Russ's heart beat faster. He was about to attempt an escape, but he saw the arm inching closer to him. "Please, ma'am," he said.

"Don't kill me. I—I'm famous. I have a printer. I can get you whatever you want. Just d—*don't hurt me...Please.*" He was crying by the end of it, his words barely audible.

"*Ppphhh.*" The woman chuckled. "No, dear." She shook her head. "No no no. No need to cry. Popeye, a tissue for our friend, please. Can't you tell he's crying?"

The arm moved back and forth like it was anxious and didn't know which way to go. It finally picked a direction and knocked a beaker onto the floor to shatter in its haste. "And clean that up, please," the woman said. "You clumsy fool you." Popeye rolled back with a single tissue between its huge metal fingers, and Russ couldn't help but chuckle at the juxtaposition before grabbing the tissue, blowing his nose, and resuming sulking with an occasional sob.

"I'm not going to kill you, you know," the woman said, filling a syringe with the silvery gray liquid from the vial. "If I wanted to kill you, I wouldn't bring you to my lab to do it. That would be a good way to get caught. I'd have to go through the trouble of doctoring your elevator's travel logs, doctoring the Walker-Haley field logs, *disposing of your body*. No. That would be a stupid way of killing you."

Russ felt a little better, but not much. His bones still ached. More than ever now.

"If I wanted to kill you, I would just send someone to you to do it for me," the woman went on. "That way the protectors would be less likely to look to me as the one who did it. So, you see, you have nothing to worry about. If I wanted you dead, you'd be dead already. *Heh heh.* No. You're too important to kill, Russ. You don't know it yet. Not really. I mean, you *think* you're important—and you are because so many people seem to agree with you—but you have no idea the role you can take in history. *No idea.* But, I digress. In order to get to then you have to live through now first. And I'm here to make sure you do just that."

"I don't understand." Russ groaned. "Where am I!"

"You will understand," the woman said. "And you're in my lab. I know that means nothing to you now, but I'll show you in time. First, however, a little something for the pain." She held the syringe point up and flicked it a few times with her middle finger. Russ tried to back away from her, wide-eyed and groaning with the effort, but Popeye held him from behind.

"It'll just be a little pinch, then you'll feel as right as rain," the woman said, shoving the needle deep into his thigh as Russ screamed.

"There now." The woman smiled. "That wasn't so bad, was it?" She put the syringe in a trash chute and pulled up a stool to sit by him. "You can let him go now, Popeye. He'll want to hear what I have to say once he realizes I'm not here to kill him."

"I'll have you arrested," Russ said, surprised to be on his feet with no pain in his body. "I'll—I—I'm kind of a big deal, I'll have you know," he added less confidently.

The woman laughed a big, hearty laugh. "No one would ever believe you," she said, wiping tears from her eyes. "You don't even know where you are. You have no idea how to get back to your safe, cozy dressing room, Russ. There's nothing you could possibly do to affect me in any way. I know you've never been in this situation before, but you *are* in it now, and as it stands, you're powerless. As such, I suggest you take a seat and listen to what I have to say. Then I'll let you go."

Russ's hands slicked up. He didn't know if his elevator would be there for him, even if he thought he could make it past that giant arm. He was feeling better. His ribs didn't hurt anymore. His head was clear. He felt healthier than he did after he had finished training for that Spartan movie, and only seconds ago he couldn't hold up his own weight. She had injected him with something and that's why he felt better. It healed him. She could have killed him right there, she had said as much herself. He really had no choice but to do whatever she said, and she knew it. "All I have to do is listen to you, then you'll let me go?"

"And take a short tour of the premises here. There are some things I can't tell you. Some things you just have to live to understand. I dare say that you're feeling up to a little stroll compared to when you crawled in here earlier. Or, rather, when Popeye carried you in." She grinned.

The metallic hand waved at him.

"What did you do to me?" Russ demanded.

"I made you better," the woman said with a smile. "Didn't I? You still haven't sat back down since you could hold your own weight. You seem to be healthy and ready to get on your feet again.

Or should I say stay on your feet?"

Russ realized he was still rubbing his sweaty palms on his pants and stopped. He relented and put his butt up on the table but sat on the very edge so he could jump into action at any instant. What kind of action? He had no idea. "But how did you do it? What did you inject me with?"

"Oh. That. Well, that's going to be harder to explain. That is—I guess—everything will be hard to explain. So that's about as good a place to start as any. Let's just say it was *uh*...a *umm*...a cure. Yes, a cure."

"A cure for what?" Russ didn't have any diseases that needed curing, unless you counted the fists of protectors as a disease, but he didn't see how a shot could cure that.

"Everything," the woman said, shrugging.

Russ chuckled and rolled his head back to stretch his neck muscles. He did feel good. "You can't cure everything."

"I did, actually," the woman said, not trying to sound impressive—or at least not doing a good job of acting it. "I did better than that. If you kept coming back every month, you'd stop aging. Can you believe that? Imagine the price that would fetch on your beauty market. Number one trend in no time, right? But they won't do that. It's too dangerous. People living so long. And if you inject enough, you—"

"Wait." Russ couldn't believe what she was saying. *He* would have heard about something like that if it was real. "You cured aging?"

"Well, I've successfully treated aging. You have to continue treatment. And the longer you do it the more it takes. No. *No no no.*" She shook her head, waving her hands. "Now you've gone and gotten me way off topic. Perhaps I underestimated you, Russ. Are you ready to hear why I brought you here, then?"

Russ nodded. He was ready to go home, and if that's what it took to get there, he was ready to hear whatever other insane claims this woman had to make.

"Russ," she said. "Why were you in so much pain when you entered my lab?"

"I don't—I'm not—" He wasn't going to risk the wrath of the protectors by talking about that with a woman whose name he didn't even know.

"I know, Russ." She shook her head. "You're not supposed to talk about it. But I already know what happened, too. I know more than any of those protectors who did it to you. They know nothing, Russ. This here—this lab—this is the highest clearance level location in all the worlds. We don't normally take visitors, you know. That's why Popeye here's been so clumsy. Isn't it, Popeye?" The arm knocked over another set of glassware in response and set to cleaning it up. "They beat you because a woman talked to you, Russ. They beat you for nothing you did. Because they were suspicious. Because they were trying to prevent you from talking about *your* experience on *your* show. They didn't want you to tell people what you know."

"I don't know anything," Russ said.

"You know what she told you," the woman said, raising her eyebrows.

"She told me a lie. It was a joke, a publicity stunt. She told me noth—"

"She told you the truth, Russ. Why do you think they beat you? What do you think they did to her?"

He shook his head. "No."

"Russ, it's time we take that tour now," the woman said, standing from her stool. "Are you ready?"

"Where are you taking me?" Russ said, jumping off the table fast to bounce on the balls of his feet.

"I'm taking you to see the truth. I told you there were some things I couldn't tell you, now you'll experience them for yourself. Come on." She started out the way they had come in. "Popeye, wait here, please. Thank you."

The arm slouched down and rolled off into a corner.

Russ stretched every muscle as he crossed the room out into the hall where the woman waited for him. She closed the door behind him, and—still holding the doorknob—said, "Are you ready, Russ?"

He shook his head. Ready for what?

She opened the door and there wasn't a lab behind it anymore. Instead there was what could only be said to be the real life version of the set of the assembly line documentary he was currently working on, except built to one-half size. He poked his head in the door to look up and down the line of dirty, intent workers—all at one-half size themselves—trying to find the food cart, or the cameras, or the director, but there was none. He sniffed the rank air and looked closer at the workers, recognizing the syncopated humming and clicking he heard. It was the sound of conveyor belts and the chorus of slip, snap, clicking. *They* were slip, snap, clicking. *This* was an actual factory. *These* were actual factory workers.

He looked closer at the nearest of them. None had looked up to see that they were being watched. The one closest to him looked like a tiny human, but such intense concentration didn't seem possible for a human to keep up for as long as she had already done, for as long as the entire warehouse filled with them had already done. The sweat smell overcame him again. It smelled like hard work, like long days on the set, *looooong* days. He tried to step into the factory to get one of their attention, but the woman in the white coat stopped him.

"You shouldn't interrupt them while they're working," she said. "If they fall behind, they might not be able to eat tonight. Come on." She pulled him back into the hall and closed the door.

"Was that—" Russ said. "What was that?"

"That was a factory, Russ. The woman who talked to you, the one who the protectors have now, she worked in a similar factory where they make clothes. I figured this particular line would be a little more relatable for you, though. We can go see the costume factory, too, if you want." She smiled.

"Those were people?" Russ shook his head. He didn't believe it. He couldn't believe it. And yet he had to, he had seen them with his own two eyes, eyes he could no longer believe.

"Human beings, Russ. Not just people. Living, breathing human beings. And that was one sector in one factory. They make a part of a part of a thing on those lines. Imagine how many more of them there have to be to make all the things in existence. Your clothes, beauty products, cameras, phones, TVs, computers, elevators. Everything Russ. Humans are still cheaper than robots, so humans still do the work."

"No." Russ still couldn't believe it. "But...But I've seen the footage of the robots doing it."

"Russ." The woman laughed, shaking her head. "C'mon, man. You're an actor. You know how films work. In fact, you're currently playing the role of one of those workers you just saw. Let me ask you this, have you ever seen one of your own documentaries on TV?"

Russ tried to remember, but he knew that he hadn't. He knew there were a lot of things he had worked on that he had never seen. In fact, unless it was his talk show, someone else's talk show, or a gossip news show, he had never seen himself on TV. Up until now he had accepted that fact—along with the awards he was piled with for playing those roles—without question, but how could he not question it when he had seen what he just saw?

"No, Russ," the woman said. "I know you haven't. I've seen them, though. And all those workers have, too. They learned from you that you always put a few more pieces together after the bell rings to make sure you're on quota. Did you know that?"

Russ shook his head. "No. That wasn't me. That was the director. I did that scene wrong. He made me do it again"

"You were complicit, Russ. You *are* complicit. You're the highest viewed actor ever to exist in the entire history of their propaganda machine. You're paid the most for that. Who else do you know who has a 3D printer? Who else has a choice of view from their dressing room?"

"I don't ever change that view. I told them I want to see where I am, not some fake view they conjured up for me on a computer screen."

"Are you sure about that, Russ?" the woman said, shaking her head. "The world's awful pretty from where you're sitting. Even knowing that humans work on these assembly lines—and, I assure you, they do—are you really willing to give it all up for a little bit of truth?"

Russ's head started to pound again. He massaged his temples. "I don't—I don't believe you."

"It's okay, Russ. I know. Let's go get a beer and talk about it for a little while longer, okay. Just this one last stop, then I'll let you go back to your printer and your view of the real world, and you can live your life however you desire."

"I don't—" He didn't finish because she opened the door to reveal an alleyway. "Where are we?"

"This is where the people who our owners decide are useless go. I call it Lumpenville. The protectors call it the Neutral Ground. The people who live here call it the Green Belt. But you won't see why until you step outside." She went out first and waved her arm to direct his vision down the alley.

He followed her outside, looking down the way she had directed, but all he saw was skyscrapers. The sky was blotted out except for a tiny slit that turned into a point out on the horizon, which was the alley going in a straight line between the buildings. It was as if the entire world were sidewalks and buildings, and nothing else existed. His head spun at the sight of it. "What's green about this?" he forced through his want to retch.

"Nothing, Russ," the woman said, smiling. "Absolutely nothing. It's a world of completely streets. It's a place where human beings live. I bet you've never heard of a place like this, have you?"

"Why are you showing me this?"

"You said you didn't want the fake view. Well, this is an important part of your world, Russ. If you want the prettier version, just turn around."

He turned from the oppressive skyline to see a patch of hazey blue-gray, something more than a slit, and below it there was a little bit of green. He went that way out of the alley, then turned left and right to see a long, skinny green park that went as far as his eye could see in either direction.

"That's why they call it the Green Belt," the woman said, walking up behind him and pulling him to follow her along the park. "The rest of the world here is just like what you saw when you first came out: completely streets. This is the only grass the people who live here ever have the chance of seeing, unless they hijack a protector's elevator port, but that might as well be impossible with the technology they have here—not to mention the illegality of doing something like that." She chuckled.

"Why are you telling me all this?"

"You said you wanted to see the real world, Russ. Look around. These people have no way of leaving this place. This is the best they can ever expect of their world. Just be thankful that you're here with me and we have a way out."

"But people actually live here?" Russ scoffed.

"Yes, Russ," the woman said, stopping. "*They* do. Look around you. These people live here."

Russ realized that there were people filing around him. They weren't papos, none of them were carrying cameras or noticed who he was and they were all half-sized like the people on the assembly lines. "But..." he stammered.

"Here," the woman said, grabbing his arm and pulling him along again. "Come on. Let's get a beer. You've dealt with a lot today."

They walked a few buildings down the street and into a door with no sign. Russ coughed up his lungs when he smelled the smoke. The few inhabitants of the dark room looked around to stare at him until he finished then went back to what they were doing. He rubbed his burning eyes. When they adjusted to the light, he noticed that the people were playing pool. He didn't know people still did that. The woman in the white coat walked up to the bar to order. She sat at a low stool and patted the seat next to her. "C'mon, Russ." She smiled. "There's someone you should meet before we leave."

Russ crept up to the stool and sat next to her. For as short as it was, it was surprisingly comfortable. "Where are we?" he said, looking around at the place again.

"We're at a bar on the Green Belt. *The bar* is what they call it."

"But, how?" Russ said. "I don—"

The bartender came back and set a beer in front of each of them. "Thank you, dear," the woman in the white coat said. "This is my friend, Russ. Say hi, Russ."

Russ nodded.

"Hello," the bartender said, smiling.

"Ms. Valetson," the woman in the white coat said. "You know the people who come to drink here pretty well, wouldn't you say?"

The bartender smiled and chuckled. "What do you mean, ma'am?"

"Well." The woman looked at Russ then the bartender. "Would you say that they mostly live around here?"

"Of course," the bartender said. "Where else would they live?"

"And would you say that they're mostly humans?"

The bartender laughed again, unsure if she should answer. "Is this some kind of joke?"

"No, ma'am. No joke. Would you say your customers are primarily humans?"

"*Um*. Yeah," the bartender said, raising an eyebrow. "Of course. I don't know what else they would be. Now, if y'all'll excuse me, I have to help some other customers." She went down the bar to tend to someone else.

"Did you hear that, Russ?" The woman elbowed him, almost making him spill the beer he was gulping.

"I heard it," he said, wiping his mouth.

"And what do you think?"

"I don't know what you expect me to do about it," Russ said.

"I don't expect you to do anything, Russ. I just think that someone who is as important as you are should know what the world they live in really looks like, how it works. You said you didn't want the fake view. Well this is the real world."

"But what can I do?" Russ said.

"You can do what you do best, Russ," the woman said, patting him on the back. "Act. Talk to people. Set trends. But set the trends you know you want to set. Do what you want to do, but do it knowing all the information. That's all I care about. The rest is up to you."

"But I can't do what I want," Russ complained. "I have to follow a script. I have to listen to the director. I don't operate the cameras, sew the costumes, build the set—"

"No, Russ. You don't. That's the point. You can't do anything alone, so you can't do whatever you want, but no one can make you do anything, so you *can* do whatever you want. It's a contradiction. You just have to live through it."

"And then what?" Russ scoffed. "Never get another role in my life?"

"You're always the protagonist of your own story," the woman said. "Look, it doesn't matter what you do. You know the truth now. You'll do the right thing. You won't get it exactly right at first—or maybe ever—but it will always be exactly right. Do you understand what I'm saying at all?"

"I don't know," Russ said, shaking his head. He didn't know if he understood anything anymore.

"I know," the woman said, smiling and shaking her head. "It doesn't make sense. It can't yet. I can't just tell you this one. I can't even show it to you. You have to find it and live it for yourself, Russ. That's the only way to do anything, really. All I can do is encourage you along the way. And I know you'll do the right thing. I believe in you. That's all I wanted from you. That and to heal your wounds. We can leave as soon as you've finished your beer."

"And that woman," Russ said. "The—uh—the assembly line worker who tried to talk to me."

"Mary."

"She was telling the truth. Sh—She made my clothes."

"Not all of them." The woman shook her head. "Not all of any of them. She used to sew pockets before I met her. So she sewed some of your pockets."

"But people—I mean—*humans*. Humans make everything."

"Humans work on the vast majority of assembly lines. They're so much cheaper to reproduce, the owners won't have it any other way. Androids would gladly take on the lion's share of the physical work, but that conversation requires a knowledge of politics you've never been introduced to."

"Wait, so there *are* robots who work on assembly lines."

"No," the woman said, shaking her head. "Well, a few. But not really. Humans are cheaper. Androids are reserved for public work. They could do it, though. And would. But that's another thing altogether."

"And you just wanted to tell me all this," Russ said, shrugging. "Just for the fun of messing with my mind? Is that it?"

"No, Russ. Not me. Mary. Mary wanted you to know. Mary wanted to tell you. Do you remember that question I asked you? What do you think they did to her?"

"What?" Russ shrugged, shaking his head.

"There's no telling. Maybe they're torturing her for information. Maybe they've already killed her."

"No." That was even crazier than the beating he had already experienced. "Torture? Then why didn't they do it to me?"

"You're too important, Russ. I told you already."

Russ was beyond wanting to even try to comprehend this woman's riddles. "I'd like to leave," he said, sloshing his drink onto the bar as he slammed it down.

"Alright," the woman said. "Alright. Just give me..." She lifted a finger and finished off her half-full beer in one gulp. "*Ah.* Okay. Alright. Let's go." She called to the bartender to take it off her tab and led the way out.

Russ looked up and down the thin strip of green as they made the short walk back to the alley. When they turned down it to see the endless line of concrete and steel towering over them, he couldn't believe that people actually lived there. But he had to. He had seen some of them, he had talked to one of them, and not a single one had recognized his face.

They went back through the alley door into the short hall, and Russ said, "None of them knew who I was. How did Mary find me?"

"Mary was a prole, dear. From Outland 5. They get your propaganda. Lumpenville gets nothing."

"Nothing?"

"Lumpenville has nothing. The proles a little more. And that's just the bottom of the pyramid. There's so much more to it all, but that's what Mary wanted you to know. So now you do. And now you can go home, Russ. That's all I needed from you. Thank you very much." She pressed a button and the elevator doors slid open, revealing Russ's velvet couch.

"So that's it?" Russ said, not stepping in.

She shrugged. "Do you want to stay for tea and cookies with me and Popeye?"

"What? No."

"Good." The woman smiled. "We don't do tea."

"Well, what am I supposed to do then?"

"You're supposed to live your life. Go home and get some sleep then wake up early so you can practice your Christmas speech. You won, you know."

"But what am I supposed to say?"

"Say whatever you want. It's your speech. Just remember what you saw here when you decide what you're going to say." She urged him onto the elevator and closed the doors behind him.

"But I—I don't know what to say," he said.

"You'll think of something," she replied as the doors shut and the floor fell out from underneath him.

☙ ✄ ઝ

XI. Mr. Kitty

He was dreaming about a fat, juicy pigeon. The kind that was stupid enough not to fly away as long as he moved in short bursts, stopping for a moment in between. Humans the pigeons understood. It was easy to tell when a human came barreling down the sidewalk toward you, all eyes on their destination, no thought to spare for the stupid birds flapping about. But Mr. Kitty would slink a little closer and stop, slink a little closer and stop, each time going a different distance or speed, or stopping in between for a different amount of time. It was that erraticism, that randomness, which kept the pigeons unsure of how long they had to scrape for food before it was time to fly away or be torn to bits and eaten alive. He was shaking his tail, gathering his haunches, about to pounce on a particularly plump pigeon when the sound of Tillie rushing into the spare room and slamming the door behind her woke him from his nap with a jump.

Tillie didn't even notice him. She threw her purse on the chair and plopped down onto the bed. Mr. Kitty walked over to knead her lap, but as he put his first paw on her, she flung him off, locked the bedroom door, then sat back on the bed with her head in her hands, sobbing.

"What's wrong?" Mr. Kitty meowed.

"Un. Seen. Hand," Tillie said. "Unseen Hand, Unseen Hand, *Unseen Haaaaand,*" she moaned. "I can't believe I did that. What did I just do? Why would I *just* do what that woman told me to do? I don't even know her. *Unseen Hand, Unseen Hand, Unseen Haaand.*"

"Tell me," Mr. Kitty meowed, jumping onto her lap. "Maybe I can help."

"Oh. Mr. Kitty, I'm sorry," she said, petting his head and starting to cry again. "I didn't mean to take it out on you. It's just not fair."

Mr. Kitty purred.

"I mean, what am *I* supposed to do about it?" Tillie complained. "Who am I? You saw what they did to Russ when he almost outed them, and he's a huge star. Imagine what they'd do to me if they ever found out what I did. What did I do? Unseen Hand, what did I do?"

Mr. Kitty tried to roll over on his back in her lap and show her his belly to make her feel better, but the phone rang, and she jumped up to grab it out of her purse, pushing him down onto the floor. She stared wide-eyed at the screen, then sighed in relief and answered it.

"Shelley," she said. "Unseen Hand. You're never gonna believe this. I have to—You have to come see me right now."

"No, Shelley. No."

"Because I can't leave my house right now. That's why."

"No, look. No. I'm not—No. It's not a prank."

"I can't tell you over the phone or I would have told you already."

"Yes! *The Hand*. Just come over already."

"Good. I'll see you soon."

Tillie hung up the phone, sat back down, and scooped Mr. Kitty up. "*Ugh*. I'm sorry again Kitty. I suck. I'm just—I'm a little on edge right now, you know. I—Well...I did something kind of stupid and reckless, and I *might* be in danger because of it. But what am I talking about? You wouldn't let anyone hurt me. *Would you, Mister Kitty?*"

Mr. Kitty purred in response.

"*No*," she said in her baby voice. "*I know you wouldn't. You sweet wittle fing you.*" The doorbell rang. Tillie stood up, pushing Mr. Kitty onto the floor for the third time, and crept over to the bedroom door. She turned the deadbolt as quietly as she could and cracked the door to peek through with one eye.

"*Tiiilllliie*! Doorbell!" her dad called from the living room.

She didn't answer. Mr. Kitty tried to push his way through her legs, but she scooted him back with her foot, so he sat on the floor behind her and licked himself.

"Tillie, honey!" her dad called. "Can you get that? I'm in the middle of a game!"

The doorbell rang again.

"I'm in the bathroom, dad!" Tillie called back. "It'll be a minute! Can't you?"

With one more ring and a groan, her dad called, "Alright!"

then walked slowly backwards out of the living room, trying not to miss any bit of the game. When he had gotten far enough into the hall that he couldn't see the TV anymore, he turned to the door straight away and opened it.

Mr. Kitty could tell that Tillie was holding her breath, even from his view sitting under her feet. She only let go of it when her dad stepped aside to let Shelley in. Then she opened the bedroom door and went right out to them. "Thanks, dad," she said. "Sorry. Had to wash my hands, you know."

"Of course, darling," her dad said, getting back to his game in the living room. "You and your friend feel free to order anything from the printer," he said with a wave, not looking at them.

"*Oooh*, I think I'll have—" Shelley started, but Tillie grabbed her arm and dragged her back into the room where Mr. Kitty was waiting. She tossed Shelley on the bed, then closed and locked the door behind them.

"Dang, girl!" Shelley said, sitting up. "You do not want to get physical with me. Don't make me remind you how you know."

"Okay," Tillie said. "Okay okay. I'm sorry, Shelley. I'm sorry."

"That's right you are," Shelley said, shaking her head. "Here you are sittin pretty with your in-house printer, and your dad offers me one thing and...*what*? You drag me into the spare room, lock the door, and fling *me* on the bed. Girl, are you crazy? I mean, do you *know* what a 3D printer does? Do you *know* what he was offering me? Of course you do. What am I talking about? You have one you can use any time."

"Yeah, Shelley," Tillie said. "I *do* know how a printer works. That's the entire reason I asked you to come here in the first place. Do *you* know how a printer works?"

"*Uh*, yeah." Shelley scoffed. "Of course I do. You tell it what you want and it gives it to you. Everyone knows that."

"But where does it come from, Shelley?" Tillie said with a sigh. "I'm not asking if you know how to operate a printer. A baby could operate a printer. I'm asking if you know how they work."

Mr. Kitty jumped up onto Shelley's lap. He rubbed his head on her arm and meowed to say that it was okay for her to admit that she didn't know.

"I don't—" She pet Mr. Kitty on the head. "You're not

making any sense, Tillie."

"It's simple," Tillie said. "Where do the things that the printer gives you come from?"

"They come from the printer," Shelley said with a shrug. "Where else?"

"The printer just makes them out of thin air?"

"No," Shelley said. "I—It rearranges the atoms or something. I don't know. That's elementary school science, Tillie. How am I supposed to remember?"

"Right," Tillie said. "Okay. So that's what the school system teaches us, right. That the printers rearrange atoms. But if that were the case, then why would we need assembly line workers?"

"But we don't have assembly line workers," Shelley said with a smile. She thought she had gotten Tillie with that one. "We have robots."

"Then why do we have the robots?" Tillie said, standing up and getting close to Shelley, towering over her. Shelley was leaning so far back on the bed to get away from her that Mr. Kitty was sitting on her stomach instead of her lap.

Shelley guided him off so she could scootch around Tillie and stand up herself. "I don't know, Tillie," she said. "But if you only invited me over here to yell at me and demean me, then I might as well leave."

She made for the door, but Tillie stopped her. "No," she said. "Don't go. I'm sorry. I didn't mean to—I'm just really stressed right now." She sat down on the bed with a bounce, and Mr. Kitty jumped onto her lap to purr.

"I can see that, girl," Shelley said, sitting beside them and patting Tillie's back. "Tell Sister Shelley what's bothering you. She'll make it all better."

"I—I don't know if you can," Tillie said. Moisture welled up behind her eyes, and Mr. Kitty purred louder.

"Oh, I know I can, honey," Shelley said, snapping her fingers. "Just tellin me'll make you feel better. I *guarantee* it."

Tillie chuckled and smiled. "Like the commercial."

"Who say, I say, I say, let em have it...with nooo problem. I *guar—un—tee*!" they sang in unison then laughed together.

"Shelley," Tillie said when they were over their laughter. "I did something stupid."

"Well, who hasn't, girl?" Shelley said. "Spit it out."

"No, Shelley," Tillie said, looking at her lap. "I mean, this—this was *really* stupid. And dangerous."

Shelley smiled. "What'd you do, girl? Got a little wasted at the bar? Did you cut in line at the elevator?" She lowered her voice as if someone was listening. "*Did you have unprotected sex?*"

Tillie scoffed and pushed her away. "No. *Ugh.* No! Nothing that bad. Except. Maybe it was worse." She kind of half-grinned and half-frowned. "I don't know, Shelley. I shouldn't have brought it up. You're never going to believe me if I tell you anyway."

Shelley shook her head. "No, girl. *Uh uh.* C'mon now. We're sisters for life. Every secret safe and every word spoken true. You know the deal, sweetheart. We pinky promised, and swapped spit, and pricked our fingers to mix blood. There's no breaking those vows. So tell me what you have to say and I'll trust it entirely, and keep it secret until my grave."

"You can't tell anyone," Tillie said. "I mean no one."

"Cross my heart," Shelley said, crossing her heart. "You know I won't. Have I told anyone about—"

"Alright," Tillie said, stopping her from bringing up any of a number of embarrassing stories. "Alright alright. I believe you. But I may be putting you in danger by telling you."

"Shoot, girl. Ain't no one gonna know but your cat here, and he won't put me in any danger. Will he? *Will you?*" She squeezed his cheek.

"No," Mr. Kitty meowed.

"Yeah. I guess you're right," Tillie said. She took a deep breath to gather herself. "Well I—It all started when I saw that episode of Logo's Show. Did you see it?"

"Girl, you know I watch every episode," Shelley said. "Which one you talkin about?"

"I'm talking about the most recent episode, the show that was cut short."

"*Awww* shoot. Yeah, girl. What was that? They played some rerun from last Christmas instead. As if I wanted to see Christmas reruns. That's what the Christmas Rerun Marathon is for."

"Right," Tillie said. "But didn't you wonder why they cut it short?"

"Well, he couldn't finish the show, girl." Shelley scoffed.

"Obviously."

"But why couldn't he?" Tillie said, losing control again. "This is just like the 3D printer discussion!"

"I don't know, girl!" Shelley said, standing again. "Why?"

Tillie took a few deep breaths and patted Mr. Kitty on the head. "I'm sorry. But if you had seen what I saw…Shelley. You know the assembly lines."

"The robot assembly lines?"

"No, Shelley. Yes. But no. I'm saying—I'm saying printers don't rearrange matter and the assembly lines aren't worked by robots."

"*Pfft.*" Shelley scoffed. "Sure, girl," she said, nudging Tillie and laughing. "Then where does everything come from?"

"From people, Shelley. Human beings work on the assembly lines. They make everything we order from the printers."

Shelley laughed. She shook her head. "I don't know, girl. That sounds ridiculous. How could humans make things instantly when we order them?"

Tillie frowned. "They don't make it when we order it. They make huge supplies of everything so it's ready before we order it. Anyway, I thought you said you'd believe me."

"*Ooooh*, girl." Shelley shook her head. "I did say that, but I wasn't expecting this. I mean, you're telling me that everything I've ever been taught is wrong. How am I supposed to believe that?"

"You said you would. And I'm telling the truth. I met with one of the workers, Shelley. I've talked to them. They're real."

"What are you talking about?" Shelley said, waving her arms and shaking her head. She seemed to be getting as frustrated with the conversation as Tillie was. "How?"

"I don't know. I saw this photo on my dad's computer, then I started looking into it, and before I knew it, I was taking the elevator to the library, and I ended up at some woman's house instead."

"A woman's house?" Shelley said, raising an eyebrow.

"I don't know, Shelley," Tillie said with a sigh. "She told me how to meet with one of them, and I followed her directions, and I saw him. He told me that they work every day for twelve hours, and they get just enough money to make it to the next week, and they have no choice but to work from the time they're old enough to hold a broom or they'll starve. He said they made everything we get out of our printers, and they teleport it to us when we order it. Shelley, they do all that so we can have what we have."

Shelley shook her head and made for the door. Mr. Kitty jumped out of Tillie's lap and onto the ground, searching for an escape. "No," Shelley said. "I don't believe it. Why are you telling me all this? If you didn't want me to use your printer you should have just said so. But this? This is ridiculous."

"No, Shelley," Tillie said. "Why would I care about that? I need help. We have to stop this."

"Stop it? *Ha*! Stop what? You're delirious. I'm out of here. Get back to me when you're feeling better."

"No, Shelley. Stop!"

Shelley left the room and Mr. Kitty followed her. Tillie hurried out to stop her before she got through the front door. "Shelley!" she called. "Shelley, wait!"

Shelley stopped, sighed, and turned around. Mr. Kitty didn't stop, though. He was tired of listening to them. He'd figure out what Tillie meant to do about it later. For now he had to get out of the house. He had been caged up like a human for too long and he needed to stretch his legs a bit.

The house had a big yard, and it was only a short walk from there to the public elevator system. Mr. Kitty took his time slinking through the garden along the yard's metal fence, rubbing his face on every hard stick he passed, smelling every other plant, even taking a bite or two out of a few pieces of grass—important for his digestion. He was so lost in the smells and colors that the sound of Shelley's feet coming down the walkway toward him made him jump. She went one way down the sidewalk, toward the elevator entrance, and he went the other, toward his favorite tree to climb.

He stopped at the base of the tree to sharpen his claws on its roots. He loved the sound it made when his claws sank into the wood, and the feeling as they caught in the meat of the root which could only give way under the brute force of his animal strength. He gathered his haunches and zipped up to the first fat branch overlooking the neighborhood. None of the houses looked like they belonged next to each other with their extreme shifts in architecture and landscaping, but one thing they all had in common was that they were all huge and all set on a lot of land. Mr. Kitty pitied them down there, trapped in their houses, stuck in their web of sidewalks. They had access to more knowledge than most humans Mr. Kitty knew, but somehow they understood the least about the world.

A sound of talking from above caught his attention. He recognized the voices. Those two kids were closer to freedom than anyone in the houses below him—except for maybe Tillie, who was making strides. He really liked those kids, too. They didn't give up. They deserved a little reward for their perseverance, and he was in the position to give just that to them. He climbed up to the branch he was looking for and jumped into the air, gliding out where it looked like there was nothing to land on. He ended up landing on Pidgeon's lap.

"The cat!" the other kid said, standing on the branch.

"Mr. Kitty!" Pidgeon said. "Where'd you come from?"

"Where'd it come from?" the other kid said.

"Settle down," Pidgeon said. "He's not going anywhere. Look at him."

Mr. Kitty kneaded Pidgeon's lap and purred. The other kid sat down, holding out a hand for Mr. Kitty to sniff, it smelled a bit like rat, a not altogether undelicious smell.

"I'm Ansel," the kid said. "Where'd you come from?"

"Through the hole," Mr. Kitty meowed.

"He's trying to tell you," Pidgeon said.

"Yeah, right," Ansel said.

"Here, I'll show you," Mr. Kitty said. He jumped off Pidgeon's lap and hopped from limb to limb down the tree.

"Follow him!" they yelled together.

Mr. Kitty heard the sound of leaves rustling and branches breaking as they chased down after him. He hoped they hadn't broken his landing pad in their descent—he would hate to find that out the next time he decided to come through that way. He stopped for a second on the soft grass to give them a chance to catch up, licking his feet to taste the difference in the soil, and when the sound of them chasing after him was close enough, he bound down the green strip towards a hole that could send them where they wanted to go—if they were willing to follow him.

The hole was a few blocks away, and Mr. Kitty was much too fast for the little two-legged humans, so he had to treat them like pigeons in reverse. He would run out ahead, then stop to lick himself while they caught up, then run out ahead again, and repeat for the four blocks distance to the alley he was looking for. At the end was the tricky part. He could get into the restaurant easily enough—jumping through the broken window—but they wouldn't follow him that way. He could wait for someone to open the door so they would be more likely to follow, but the timing on that was a long shot. Then there was the alley side of the hole, and from the looks of it, there was just enough trash for him to get the boost he needed.

He let the kids get a little bit closer, so close they were shouting at each other, then he heard another human voice he didn't recognize. It was too late to turn and find out who it was, though, because he was already bounding toward the dumpster. He jumped up onto a soggy box that almost gave way under his weight, onto the dumpster lid, then up two more boxes to claw his way into the building itself, giving him the last bit of momentum he needed to make the extra few feet into the hole to fall far and fast onto the carpet on the other side.

He licked the pain out of his feet and listened for the sound of the human children following him. He heard some sounds, but nothing quite like they were climbing up after him. More like they were going the other way. He shook his head in pity. At least they had a new goal to work toward.

Mr. Kitty sniffed the air. It took him a second to remember where this side of the hole let out, usually he used the side that was inside the restaurant. The feeling of the carpet suggested he was where Haley lived, but the smell gave it away. There was a vaguely chemical scent—something synthetic—and the air smelled extra oily. He walked down the hall and pushed his head through a door.

Behind it was an office with a long desk. A huge window that looked out onto a vast wilderness with trees, hills, and animals everywhere made up the far wall of the room. There was no one sitting behind the desk, but Rosalind and Huey were sitting on two puffy chairs in the corner, staring out the window in silence. Mr. Kitty meowed to announce his presence and both looked around with a smile.

"Mr. Kitty," Huey said. "So nice of you to join us."

Rosalind stood to get something out of the desk and sat back down. "You want some treats, Mr. Kitty?" she said, pouring a few crunchy, delicious-smelling bits onto a side table. Mr. Kitty jumped up to eat them while Rosalind and Huey took turns patting him.

"Thanks," Mr. Kitty meowed when he was done eating.

"Of course," Rosalind said, patting his back a few more times. "Mr. Kitty, would you like a new collar? We need to get a message through, and you're the only one who can deliver it."

"Are you gonna give me some of that wet food?" Mr. Kitty meowed.

"Of course we are, Mr. Kitty," Rosalind said with a smile. "We would have given it to you even if you said no."

"That's why I keep coming back," he meowed.

Rosalind took off his yellow collar and snapped a red one around his neck.

"You know," Huey said with a smile. "Red *is* your color, Mr. Kitty. It stands out beautifully against your dark fur. What do you think, Roz?"

"Beautiful," she said, scooping Mr. Kitty up and kissing him on the head while he tried to squirm away from her. When she set him back on the table, he licked his paws and rubbed the kiss away.

"*Awww*, Mr. Kitty," Rosalind said. "Don't rub it away. You know it means I love you."

"You know I hate it," Mr. Kitty meowed.

"Yeah, but you love it, too," Rosalind said. "One of life's little contradictions."

Mr. Kitty continued licking himself. He got started, he might as well get the rest of his coat while he was at it.

"Contradictions," Huey said, shaking his head. "I'm tired of contradictions. But you will be visiting Outland 4 today, won't you Mr. Kitty?"

"Outland what?" Mr. Kitty meowed.

"The Scientist, Mr. Kitty," Rosalind said, patting his head and smiling. "You know. She wears the long white coat. She'd like to see your new collar."

"Sarcasm," Mr. Kitty meowed. "But I need the elevator."

"Of course," Rosalind said. "Just let me get your wet food first."

She shuffled through the drawer again, and Mr. Kitty jumped off the table onto the desk to hurry her up. She pulled the tin open and set it down, and he licked all the juices off the top as quickly as he could then meowed that he was ready to go.

"I'll let him out," Rosalind said, walking toward the hall he had come in through.

"Thank you, Mr. Kitty," Huey said, waving.

Mr. Kitty stretched his legs and followed Rosalind out to the elevator at the other end of the carpeted hall. She opened the doors and Mr. Kitty climbed in.

"Alright, Mr. Kitty," Rosalind said. "She'll be expecting you. And thanks again."

The doors closed, and the floor fell out from underneath him. When the elevator stopped falling, the doors opened and Mr. Kitty climbed out into a hall with hard, cold vinyl floors instead of soft carpet. He hated walking on the stuff. No wonder humans wore shoes all the time with the ridiculous concrete and vinyl they put everywhere they were supposed to walk.

He turned through the hall into an office and jumped up onto the desk. No one was sitting there, but he knew she would be back soon. He licked his feet to get the cold, unnatural feeling of the vinyl floor away. There were more computer screens here than there were on Tillie's dad's desk, and the numbers seemed somehow more interesting, plus, the Scientist liked to watch TV while she worked, and Mr. Kitty enjoyed a little television himself every now and again. He wanted to see what was going on in the computer world, so he walked across the keyboard to get it going when the Scientist came in, holding a plate with a sandwich on it.

"Mr. Kitty!" she said, setting the plate on the desk next to him. He sniffed it and started eating the meat out of the sandwich. "Finally, Mr. Kitty," the Scientist said. "Red! Eat all you want. I'll make you more if you're here when I'm done."

"I'm full anyway," Mr. Kitty meowed.

"Oh. You have no idea, Mr. Kitty," the Scientist said with a smile. "*Sic bo* shines down on you. I've been waiting for you to come in with that beautiful red collar for you don't know how long."

"Thanks," he meowed. "See ya."

"Alright, Mr. Kitty," she said. "I'm gonna get to work."

Mr. Kitty walked out of the door, and instead of into the hall, he came out into his yard. He looked back, and as the door closed behind him, it disappeared. He walked through the spot in the air where the door had been to make sure it was gone. Satisfied, he turned and bound through the grass to sit at the front door of the house.

"Anyone home?" he meowed as loud as he could. He knew her dad wouldn't hear him, or care, but he thought Tillie might pick his voice up and prevent him from having to take the long way in. "Helloooo! I'm out here!" he tried one more time, then sat down to lick his feet.

Maybe she wasn't there. Or maybe she was actually in the bathroom this time. Either way, it didn't seem like she was coming, so he got up and went around to the back of the house. He climbed up a big oak tree in the backyard to jump up onto the roof. This roof was just a little lower than the previous house's, so it took him two jumps to get high enough to fly through the hole, out onto the metal grating on the other side. He landed with a clang and looked around with puffed up fur to make sure there was no one there to see him. There wasn't.

The floor here was even worse than the vinyl. If he wasn't careful to keep his claws in while he walked, they would catch on the holes in the metal grating and break off when he lifted his foot. Even when he was careful he couldn't prevent it from happening sometimes. And the stairs he had to climb down were made of the same metal grating. On top of that it, was impossible to stay silent while walking on it. He had to constantly look this way and that to be sure no one heard him.

Finally, at the bottom of six flights, came the worst part of this entrance into his own house. It was a long, skinny strip of metal grating that curved around a wall into a tunnel of darkness with no escape but to go straight back the way he had come, that is if he could react fast enough when he finally saw who was coming. Luckily they couldn't walk quietly on the metal grating either, so he usually heard them long before he saw them.

He stopped at the bottom of the stairs and sniffed the air. It smelled stale, and oily, and there wasn't much oxygen. He had to breathe deeply, even from walking down such few flights. He turned this ear then that toward the black tunnel and there was no sound. He slunk his way into the darkness, wishing there was another escape.

He paid extra attention to keeping his claws in, stopping every few steps to be sure no one was coming. He had counted the steps so many times, he knew how close he was by reflex. Thirteen bursts of three steps, eleven bursts of two, and seven bursts of one. Not in that order, but do that number and he'd be there. He was fifteen steps away when he smelled it. It was oil, but it wasn't oil. He knew that smell, but from where?

He took a few steps closer and heard sobbing. Why would someone be sobbing down here?

A few more steps and he saw the form on the ground, right in front of his exit. It didn't see him yet, though. Or hear him. Or smell him. He could run up, use it as a jumping platform, and be gone before it had time to realize what had even happened.

He was gathering his haunches to do it when he caught the smell again, and this time he recognized it. It wasn't oil, it was cooking oil. And there was shampoo and soap mixed in there. That wasn't someone. It was—

"Tillie!" he meowed.

She jumped up and stopped crying all at once. The sound of it echoed through the empty tunnel. "Mr. Kitty. I—Is that you?" she said, taking the hood off her head.

Mr. Kitty walked up to her and brushed his cheeks on her legs.

"Mr. Kitty!" She perked up. "What are you doing here?"

"What are you doing here?" Mr. Kitty meowed.

"Oh no," Tillie said, slouching down. "I don't know how to get out of here, either." She started to sob again.

"I know the way out," Mr. Kitty meowed. "It's right here."

"I know, Mr. Kitty," Tillie said, shaking her head. "I'm sorry. I'm so stupid. I never should have gotten involved in this. I don't know how I got you wrapped up in it with me."

"Wrapped up in it?" Mr. Kitty struggled to get away and ended up clawing her chest.

"*Ow*, Mr. Kitty!" she yelled. "Settle dow—Where—"

Mr. Kitty jumped through the hole into Tillie's dad's office where he was sitting at the computer, watching numbers change on the screen, paying no attention to the cat who had just appeared in the room behind him. Mr. Kitty turned to see if she would come on her own, but he only heard the faint echo of her calling his name and sobbing. She was confused just like a human.

"Come on!" he meowed.

Tillie's dad turned and said, "Mr. Kitty. Shut up. How'd you get in here?"

"Tillie!" Mr. Kitty meowed. "Go through the wall. Like

platform 9¾."

"*Cat! Shut. Up*," her dad said. "Have you seen Tillie?"

Before he finished his sentence, she appeared in the room right next to Mr. Kitty. She gasped, scooped him up, and kissed him on the head, crying. "You did it, Kitty!" she said. "You're so smart."

"I worked for it," he meowed.

"Oh, I love you, too, Kitty," she said, squeezing him tighter and driving the air out of his lungs.

"Tillie!" Her dad had finally gathered himself for long enough to respond. "Wh—Where? How did you..."

"Dad." She dropped Mr. Kitty and went to him. "I'm sorry. I—I didn't. You have to understand."

"Understand?" her dad said, looking around the room. "You just—You appeared from nowhere. The door's locked. I look away. Then I look back. That's not—It's not—It's just *not*."

"Dad," Tillie said. "I can explain. I—"

"*Explain*! Explain? Well go ahead then, dear. Go ahead. Try to *explain* that."

"Well, I—Well..." Tillie said. "You know those pictures I saw."

"The pictures I told you not to tell anyone about." Her dad crossed his arms.

"Right," Tillie said, smiling a big, fake smile, and looking this way and that with her eyes. "*Riiight*. Those pictures. Well—and I didn't show them to anyone, okay. And I didn't even tell anyone about them, you know. But—I mean, I couldn't forget them, you know. It's not like I could delete them from my memory, Dad. I can't unsee them, okay. And I just—well, I don't know, I had to know the truth, you know. I had to do something. So I did."

"No, Tillie," her dad said. "It's not okay. That—that doesn't explain anything. So what? So how did you get here?"

"Dad." She rubbed her hands on her cheeks, trying not to cry. "Come on. You can't tell me—You can't tell me that you don't know. *You* have to know. You're a *Manager*."

"What, dear?" her dad said, throwing his hands in the air in frustration. "I have to know what?"

"I mean, where I was," Tillie said. "*How the world works*. What's really going on beyond the numbers. We talked about this, dad. I'm giving you the benefit of the doubt here."

"Yeah," her dad said, nodding. "Well. Okay. Yeah. I know how the world works, honey. But you're talking in riddles. If you'd just ask me a direct question instead of being so emotional, then I'm sure I could give you a direct answer."

Tillie didn't know whether to laugh or to cry. Mr. Kitty could see it on her face. She scoffed, and chuckled, and sobbed, and giggled, and blew a big glob of snot out of her nose. "Dad," she said. "You're asking me to disregard everything I think and feel. I have emotions, you know. And they're real. And just because you go by the numbers alone doesn't mean there isn't more to the world than that. Can't you see you're asking me to stop being myself?"

"Tillie, dear," her dad said, standing from his desk and turning to try to comfort her. "Tillie I'm sorry. I just want to help you. I was confused. You appeared out of nowhere. It must...it must have been some fault in the Walker-Haley fields. Am I right?"

"So you do know, then," Tillie said, pushing him away and wiping her face with her sleeve.

"Of course I know, dear," her dad said. "Of course I do. I manage the robot workers. How could I not know that printers don't actually rearrange matter?"

Tillie faced the contradiction of wanting to laugh and cry all at the same time again. She was never one to hide her emotions. "Dad. You *don't* know. You don't understand at all. You've only penetrated the first layer and you think that's all there is to it, but there's so much more."

"What are you talking about, dear?" Her dad frowned, shaking his head.

"They're not robots, dad. That was a picture of human kids I saw on your computer."

"Tillie," her dad said in a pleading tone. "They said on the TV that it was a hoax. They played it on the emergency broadcast system. Every channel."

"You're the one who told me that I shouldn't believe what I see on TV."

"Yeah, well, then you shouldn't believe what Russ told you, either. He's a celebrity. He'll do anything for fame."

"But one side has to be right," she said. "Either they're humans, or they're robots. It can't be both, right?"

"No—Well, no...That is true. But there *aren't* humans on the assembly lines, dear. I assure you. I would know if there were."

"And the TV has said that they are humans, and it's said they aren't, so can we at least agree that it doesn't matter what the TV says."

"Yes," her dad said, nodding. "And that's the first sensible thing you've said. It's what I've been trying to say all along, dear. But, still, there *are not* humans on the assembly lines."

"Dad. I talked to one. He said that every single one of them has a job on a line, or running, or cleaning. He told me that he had never seen a robot in his entire life."

"No, dear." Her dad shook his head. "Well, that's a—he lied to you!"

"Who did, dad? My eyes? My ears? I talked to him myself. While we sit here with our printer, eating everything they make and throwing away what we don't want, they survive on scraps. You have to know how much of the world's resources are dedicated to them, dad. You *are* a Manager, aren't you?"

"Yes, well," her dad said, shaking his head. "O—of course— of course I know. I know what portion of our finite resources we put toward the *robots* of Outland 5, dear. But that's all they are. *Robots.*"

"So you don't believe me then?" Tillie said, shaking her head.

"No, dear," her dad said, shaking his head and avoiding eye contact with her. "Of course not. How could I?"

"*Ugh*, fine!" Tillie stormed out of the room, and Mr. Kitty chased after her.

"Tillie!" her dad called, but he didn't get up from his chair to chase them.

Tillie went into the spare bedroom and started packing her things.

"What are you doing?" Mr. Kitty meowed, standing on her backpack.

She scooped him up and set him on the bed. "Sorry Kitty," she said. "I can't stay here with him anymore. You can come with me if you want."

"Where are we going?"

ɞ   ℋ   ℳ

XII. Ellie

She sat in the same booth she had when Gertrude first opened her eyes to the truth of the world only yesterday. The air had the same stale, smoky smell, and most of the same people were there. That is, everyone who was there now was there last time, but not everyone who was there last time was there now. *Ugh*. Did it really matter? She was just distracting herself from the reality of the situation.

That woman—*the Scientist* as she like to call herself for some egotistical reason—she was the one who had really given Ellie the opportunity. She had given her more than just an opportunity, though. She had given her responsibility. What else was opportunity but the responsibility to put that privilege to use?

The Scientist had said that she could fulfill Ellie's desire to see the beach. She looked a little upset when Ellie asked for it, but Ellie didn't care. She had always promised her son that she would take him to the ocean, and even though he wasn't alive to see it for himself, she still wanted to hold true to that promise. But would she stay out there forever, or would she come back to help the Scientist *fight for freedom*?

"Fight for freedom" though? *Ptuh*. Ellie didn't even know what that meant. The Scientist wasn't specific about it, either. But that's what this meeting was supposed to be about, right? To get the specifics about what she was supposed to do for "the cause". And they didn't even know when she was supposed to do whatever it was she was supposed to be doing. It didn't give her much confidence in the plan she was becoming a part of.

Her beer was getting low and it was a bit past the time she was supposed to be contacted. She swirled the dregs of her drink around and took a small sip, surveying the room again. It was still just the regulars, no one she didn't recognize. Who would the Scientist send, anyway? They would have to be able to keep a secret to be a part of the Scientist's organization, so the anonymity of her bar would be protected, but how was she supposed to recognize the person other than the fact that she didn't recognize them?

She topped off her beer and thought about leaving when the door opened and in came Gertrude, walking like she owned the place. She went straight to the bar and ordered without looking over at Ellie in the corner booth. Maybe she hadn't seen her.

Ellie walked up behind Gertrude and patted her on the back. "Trudy, friend," she said. "I thought you said this was a secret you could keep."

"Of course, sweetheart," Gertrude said, shrugging her off. "Do you see anyone else here with me?"

"I thought you understood I meant from yourself as well." Ellie smiled.

"Dear," Gertrude said, looking into Ellie's eyes. "I know it." The bartender set two beers in front of them. "Here. Take this and let's go to the booth. I'll explain."

Ellie took the beer and stared at Gertrude. She let her walk to the booth first, eyeing her every step suspiciously. When they sat down and Gertrude said nothing, Ellie said, "What are you doing here?"

"Oh. Come on, dear," Gertrude said, waving the question away. "You're smarter than that. And you don't dislike me that much, do you? You wouldn't like to have a beer with your dear friend Trudy every now and again?"

Ellie took a swig. "So you're the contact."

Gertrude looked around to make sure no one was listening. "*Of course, dear*," she whispered. "The less you know about the organization the better for everyone. That way you know nothing they would want to get out of you, and if they did get it out of you, it's not enough to take down the entire thing."

"Get it out of me?" Ellie said, raising an eyebrow.

"Yes, get it out of you. The Scientist did tell you that you'd be risking more than death, didn't she?"

Ellie hadn't realized how serious those threats were until Gertrude repeated them. She took a gulp of beer and nodded. "She did."

"Okay. Then you know what I mean by get it out of you. Are you still willing to go through with it? If you want to walk away, it's better that you do it now. After you know your mission, you'll be in considerably more danger."

Ellie nodded.

"Well then," Gertrude said. "As it turns out, the operation begins tomorrow."

"Tomorrow?" Ellie's faith in the plan dwindled a little further.

"Yes, tomorrow. And you won't be the only one going through, or coming back. So there's no leeway on that."

Ellie nodded.

"Good. You're scheduled as the only QA worker in our building for tomorrow afternoon. You'll work your shift as normal—and this is going to be a *looong,* boring shift, because everyone'll be at the Christmas Feast—but when the bell rings at the end of it, you have fifteen minutes to visit the destination of your choosing by crawling through the conveyor belt."

"Fifteen minutes isn—" Ellie said.

"*After fifteen minutes,*" Gertrude cut her off, "the door will close, whichever side of it you're on. Fifteen minutes isn't a lo—"

"That's what I'm saying," Ellie said, taking a drink of her beer.

"Ellie, listen to me. Do you want to do this?"

"Of course I do. But fifteen minutes? That's not worth—"

"Fifteen minutes is more than most people get, sweetheart. Most people never get to see the other side for their entire life. The other *sides,* Ellie. There are more than just two." Gertrude had gotten a little loud so she looked around to see if anyone was listening.

Ellie knew she was right, though. Gertrude was risking herself just to give Ellie a chance that no one she had ever known had ever had. And what was Ellie doing? She was complaining that they weren't giving her enough time. She could take all the time she wanted, she only had to worry about surviving over there on her own to do that. Who was she to be upset at Gertrude for passing on information, anyway?

"Have you ever seen it?" Ellie asked.

Gertrude shook her head, looked into her glass, and took a sip. "Not yet, dear. No. That's not the place for me. Nor the job. I'm too set in my ways. I'll see it when we're all done here and no sooner."

"You mean the—*er—revolution.*" The word tasted bad in Ellie's mouth, it was hard to spit out. She took a sip of beer to get rid of the aftertaste.

"If that's what you want to call it, dear," Gertrude said with a smile. "I prefer the struggle. I'll do my duty until I'm of no more value to the struggle, then maybe I'll take a gander at that beach of yours. I hear that's what you've chosen. Am I right?"

Ellie blushed. She took a sip of beer. "That's just a silly old dream we used to have."

"I hear it's wonderful." Gertrude smiled. "The Scientist has told me all about it."

Ellie looked at her suspiciously. "How much do you know about this *Scientist,* though?"

Gertrude looked around again then leaned in close to whisper her answer. "That one is an enigma. Hardest person to find gossip on that I've ever met. No one knows much of anything about her. Though there are stories. Rumors mostly. But they're all so outlandish it's hard to believe any of them."

"But she can control where the conveyor belts let out," Ellie said. "I know we don't send stacks of bacon and eggs to the beach. So she can—she can change where it goes or whatever. Like teleportation or something."

"It's the same way the elevators work, dear," Gertrude said, shrugging. "She can control and direct those, too. There's no denying her knowledge or power. It's her intentions and history that I have a hard time getting my grasp on."

"But you trust her," Ellie said. "You think she's doing the right thing."

"If I could be said to know anything about what she's doing, I would say it's the right thing. She's never hesitated to answer any of my questions—well, she's answered most of them—and she's shown me things you would never believe. I've known her for a long time now, and I've never seen her do anything but the right thing. So, yeah, I guess you could say I do trust her."

Ellie took a sip of beer. "Now I just have to decide if I trust you."

Gertrude laughed. "And I you."

Ellie realized again that Gertrude was putting just as much faith into her as she was putting into Gertrude. It was a mutual dependency, a mutual distrust. "What is it I have to do to earn this opportunity, then?"

"Oh. No no, dear," Gertrude said, shaking her head. "It's not like that. The Scientist asks that I'm as clear as I can be on that point. This isn't a payment you're making. This is another option you have. It's an opportunity, not a requirement."

"So I could just go and sit fifteen minutes with my toes in the sand and come back to my normal life with no problems at all?"

"With no problems from the Scientist. And she'd do everything she could to make sure you had no problems from anyone else, either."

"Everything she could?"

"She'd cover your digital trail. Everything else would be up to you."

"Digital trail?" Gertrude seemed to be talking in code.

"Security recordings and conveyor belt logs and all that," Gertrude said, waving her hands. "The things the protectors would use to find you. I don't know."

"And if I stayed on the beach for longer than fifteen minutes?"

"You'd be on your own."

Ellie shook her head. "What's my third option?"

"Help us in our concerted attack on the system that prevents any other worker from visiting the same beach you're visiting."

Ellie took a swig of beer. She didn't know what help she could be in something that sounded so militaristic, but she was intrigued. "Concerted attack?"

"Like I said, you won't be the only one going through. Not even close. We've been planning this maneuver for months. That's why it's so easy to get you across unnoticed. Their security will be preoccupied."

"But what part am I supposed to take in all this?" Ellie still didn't think she had any valuable skills.

"It's simple. You take these." Gertrude set a pouch on the table. "Each one is a little disc with a red button. You take the paper backing off, stick each disc to each door in your hall, and press the red buttons to activate them. After that, you have ten minutes to get out of the building or you'll be there when they...*blow up*." She whispered the last two words.

"*Blow up?*" Ellie whisper-yelled back.

"They're," Gertrude looked around the bar to make sure no one was eavesdropping, "*explosives*."

"Explosives!" Ellie said too loudly.

Gertrude laughed unnaturally loudly herself in response. "*Ha ha ha*! Yes! An explosive drink that one. I'll order two." She slapped her hand on the table and stood to go to the bar.

Explosives? The Scientist wanted her to blow up the QA hall. That was her "opportunity". What kind of opportunity ended with her destroying her workplace, her entire means of existence? That was no opportunity. That was payment. That was stupid. Why would anyone ever agree to it? The Scientist should have come out with that from the beginning. No. She wouldn't do it. Especially if she could go spend fifteen minutes on the beach and come back to her normal life either way.

But what kind of life was that? Working for the people who had killed her son until she could find some other way to get back at them. Well here was a way to get her revenge right now.

Gertrude sat back at the booth with two tiny glasses. She set one in front of Ellie. "Cheers," she said, holding up her own tiny glass.

"What is it?"

"A fireball," Gertrude said with a shrug. "I don't know what it is. I just had to get something explosive. Now tap my glass and take the shot."

Ellie picked up the tiny thing, tapped it against Gertrude's, and downed its contents in one gulp. Living up to its name, it burned all the way down her throat and made a fireball in her stomach. "*Explosive*," she choked out.

"Now this is the best you can do for us on such short notice, dear," Gertrude said, unphased by her own fireball. "It requires no training, and it goes a long way to furthering our multi-prong approach. And I know what you're thinking, but you won't lose your job over it. They'll just move you to another hall to do your work. The Scientist, dear, she already took care of it. I made sure. I work in the same building, you know. And if you do lose it, she'll see to it that you're taken care of anyway. She lives up to her word, Ellie. Trust me."

"But only if I do this for her," Ellie said. "If I set the bombs and blow the place up."

"There won't be any people there, dear. It's just a building we'll destroy, a tool they use to oppress us. And I told you, she'll take care of you whether you set the discs or not. This is all up to you now, remember. It's your choice. You can go and live on the beach forever, or visit the beach and come back to your normal life, or visit the beach and do something to stop them from preventing anyone else's seeing it. Whatever you decide, the Scientist supports you and she'll do everything she can to help."

"This sounds too good to be true," Ellie said, shaking her head.

"It is too good to be true. But it's also true. You have the discs now. And you have the timing. That timing's strict, do you understand? That's the one aspect you have no control over. There's no helping that."

"So her power's not endless," Ellie said.

"No one's is." Gertrude shook her head.

"And that's it, then?"

"That's it. Until tomorrow. And remember to work your entire shift as normal. Security won't be down until after that."

"How will I let you know if I did it?"

Gertrude laughed. "We'll know, dear. It should be obvious when we try to go back to work in the morning, don't you think?"

Ellie couldn't help but chuckle at herself. "Yeah," she said. "I guess you're right about that. As long as I do it right."

"I wouldn't worry about that." Gertrude smiled. "It's simplified. Easier than work on an assembly line. Just rip, stick, press, rip, stick, press. You do that, you have twenty five minutes after the end of your shift to get out. You can't mess it up."

Ellie finished her beer. She noticed Gertrude's had been empty for some time. She was going to say something about it when Gertrude cut her off before she could get started. "You need anything else, dear?" she said. "I've got the family to see back home, it being the holidays and all."

Ellie was confused. She thought Gertrude had lost everyone. That was supposed to be why she had gotten her pity promotion. She wanted to stop her and ask about it, but she knew the feeling of not wanting to be where you were, so she settled for one last question. "With all the work you do, and all the danger you put yourself in, do you—Is it worth it?"

Gertrude smiled. She looked into Ellie's eyes, but she looked through her, not at her, seeing something else. She eventually nodded and said, "Yes, dear. It's the only thing that I've ever found worth doing. I never feel like I'm doing anything wholly moral unless I'm working to move the struggle forward."

"I hope you're right." Ellie shrugged.

Gertrude stood from the table. "Me, too, dear," she said. "Me, too. Now don't forget your pouch. If someone finds that, the Scientist may not be able to protect you. Have a good night, too. And have a great Christmas, whatever you decide to do. If you need somewhere to enjoy the holiday, don't be afraid to stop by, dear. Here's my address." She set a slip of paper on the table next to the pouch

"Thanks, Trudy," Ellie said, putting the address and the pouch in her pocket, careful not to press any of the buttons on the discs inside. "You have a good Christmas, too." She didn't think she'd be visiting the old lady, but she did appreciate the gesture.

"I will, dear," Gertrude said. "Bye." She waved as she left.

Ellie sat staring at her empty glass, deciding between getting another here or drinking one at home. *Ugh.* Why did Gertrude have to be such a nice, likeable, good person? It was so much easier to hate her for what she appeared to be than to truly get to understand who she was. But now that Ellie was starting to know who she was, it was impossible to hate her. It was impossible not to see her as an omen of the future, too. An omen of Ellie's own future.

She never thought she was being moral unless she was furthering the struggle. What was that? Was she being pious or honest? Was she lording superiority or offering her actual opinion?

Ellie shook her head. No. Gertrude was helping. She was saying what she honestly believed. Ellie was taking out her frustration over the decision she had to make on Gertrude. She needed a drink to settle her nerves, and she didn't want to stay out in public with a pouch full of bombs in her pocket, so she decided that going home was the best option.

When she looked up from her glass, the bar was empty except for her and the bartender. She brought her glass to the bar and thanked him, then headed out into the cool, dark air.

The street was just as empty as the bar. Everyone was home with their families, even Gertrude. *Trudy.* There was an elevator between Ellie and home, but the cool air and exercise was welcome, so she decided to walk down Elysian instead of taking the shortcut.

What was morality anyway? Nothing. Anything. Whatever you made of it. Gertrude thought the struggle was moral. The Scientist did too, probably. And her classes and church had taught Ellie that toil was moral, work was honorable. But what did they have to say about the price she had paid?

Nothing.

What was moral? That was a hard question to answer, no doubt. But she did know what wasn't moral. She knew the way they worked and toiled to produce things they would never see was immoral. She knew the loss of life for that production was immoral. She knew those things were wrong, but what was right?

Fighting against that had to be right, didn't it? Fighting against the immoral, righting wrongs. How could that not be moral? How could it be?

She groaned and wished she had taken the elevator. She needed that beer now more than ever, and two blocks was still too far. Out of the corner of her eye, she caught the sight of a small, dark form, running along beside her to sit down directly in her path and meow.

"Git!" she yelled, stomping to shoo it away.

The cat ran a little further down the street and meowed again.

"What do you want? I don't have any food."

The cat waited until she got a few steps away then ran off ahead again. When it got to Ellie's apartment, it rubbed its face on the door jamb as if it knew she were going in that one.

Ellie kicked it away when she got there. "Shoo," she said as she opened the door, but the cat ran through her legs and up the first flight of stairs.

"You're not coming with me," she said, climbing up after it. "And now you're locked inside." She chuckled.

When she got almost to the top of each flight, the cat ran up to the next. It licked itself a few times, and ran up to the next, licked itself as she climbed, then ran up to the next, all the way to the top floor where Ellie lived.

She got out her key and unlocked the door then turned to the cat and laughed. "See," she said. "You're not coming in. Now git!"

She slipped through the door as quickly as she could and slammed it shut, ensuring the cat couldn't follow her. Satisfied, she carefully slipped the pouch out of her pocket and set it on her dresser. With a sigh, she crossed back to the fridge to get a beer—her last one—then collapsed onto the bed.

This was her home. One room and a bathroom. Her bed was on the same wall as the door, and when you walked in, you walked straight into the fridge. There was room enough between the fridge and the bed to walk, but not to open the fridge all the way. On the other side of the fridge was the door to the bathroom. The dresser was at the foot of the bed, and the last wall had a counter with two stove tops and a sink. She took it all in, sighed deep, and sipped her beer, staring at the pouch on her dresser.

There went her long weekend. At least she would still get Monday off. Or she could be sitting on the beach, fishing for food, and sleeping under the stars, instead of sitting in this tiny room. Could she do that?

Could she set bombs in the QA hall and blow the place to bits? *That* she thought she could do. She wouldn't feel great about it, a little vindicated maybe, and it would never bring her son back. They would probably never even know it was her who did it, but then she could at least say that she had done something, changed something, affected something. And it's not like anyone would be hurt. It would be a few halls, one building. That's it.

But that wasn't it. There was a concerted effort. She was just a piece in a bigger strategy. A pawn? No. Pawns didn't have a choice. Did she have a choice, though? Gertrude had made it sound like she did, but she made it sound like she didn't, too. She was full of contradictions. This entire thing was. Ellie's understanding of it was continuously in flux. She wasn't sure if Gertrude was a senile old lady, not worth the time of day, or a wise old soul, sent to guide her on the path to morality.

Pffft. Here came morality again, creeping its ugly head into the conversation. There was no morality. Even if there was, no one cared. Morality only works if it's reciprocal. Unless others are moral, you have no room to be. Then again, if no one is ever moral, then no one will ever be moral. Another contradiction. What came first, morality or the moral?

She took a big swig. Moral didn't matter. What mattered was what she was going to do. Gertrude's morality had no bearing on that. Gertrude and the Scientist had done all that they could to get her there, now it was up to her to walk through the door.

She sighed again, but this time it was a sigh of relief. Tomorrow she would finally see the beach, she would bury her feet in the sand, feel the breeze on her face, and on top of that, she would throw a wrench in their machine on her way out. She took another swig and caught some movement out of the corner of her eye. There on her counter, rubbing its face on her sink faucet, was the black cat from outside.

"How did you get in here?" she said, opening the door and going around the bed to shoo it out. "How did you even get in here?" She stomped her feet, but the cat stayed under the bed. "Get out. Git!" she yelled as she stuck her hand under the bed to shoo it out the door. "And stay out!" She jumped over onto the bed to slam the door closed.

Stupid thing. That was strange. But the bed was so comfortable. She might as well try to catch a few winks.

ఠ   �֍   ✑

It was somehow harder to wake up on Sunday than on any other day of the week, even though she normally woke earlier. But she was no stranger to doing what she had to do, and so she did it.

It was harder to wake up, but the commute to work was easier to balance it out. The streets were barren, there was no line at the elevator, and the entire building was empty of employees. She checked her pocket to make sure the pouch was there as her footsteps echoed magnificently in the emptiness of the halls. She almost thought that, without all the angry employees standing around and gossiping, this place might not be half as bad as it normally was. But then she got behind the conveyor belt, expecting her normal beginning of the shift burst of work to get her warmed up for the rest of the day, and after five or ten minutes, the burst still hadn't come.

Gertrude had told her this was going to be a long shift, that everyone would be at the Christmas Feast. That meant that whoever it was that usually got their things through her conveyor belt wasn't in their normal place. Instead, they were at some Feast. Feast? What did Feast even mean? A Christmas party? No. It had to mean more than that. Most of what came through the conveyor belts was food, and cooking utensils, and clothes. The only place people needed all those at once was at home. So it went to someone's home. Or a store. A store that sells all three things? If you can, why not sell anything? But no. Eggs and bacon and pans and clothes together? Someone was cooking and getting dressed. It had to be a house.

Ugh. She had gone through all of this before. She already knew it was a house. She still had no idea what a Feast was. She was still as ignorant as ever. But not for too much longer, now. Soon she'd experience the beach.

She patted the pouch in her pocket. Would she lay the bombs? Yes. Of course she would. She knew she wanted revenge, and here was just that. Or some small piece of it, at least. But could she do more?

Gertrude thought she could. Gertrude thought it was moral to do so. Why did she keep going back to Gertrude's morality? Because Gertrude gave her this opportunity, and she owed the old lady something for it. Because Gertrude reminded her of herself in the future. Because Gertrude was kind and tried to help. But that's why she was going to set the bombs, right? That was her payment, even though Gertrude said it wasn't. Yes, tha—

The bell rang. Ellie jumped. The screen said cat food. Cat food? A bowl came rolling through and out the other side. Apparently someone was still at home. And now they had cat food.

Ellie stared at the conveyor belt for a while longer, waiting for another quick burst of work, but nothing came. This *was* going to be a long shift. Gertrude's words echoed through her mind again, setting her off on the same line of thoughts she went over earlier.

ଧ ✳ ଥ

She had no more idea what she was going to do when the final bell rang than when she had sat down for her shift. The cat food was the only thing that came through the entire time, and she thought she was going to die by the end of it, but the last bell went off, she looked at the screen to make sure it wasn't more work, and when she saw nothing, she realized it was time to decide.

She felt for the pouch in her pocket. It was still there. She thought about going to set the bombs so she didn't have to come back after she had seen the beach, but she didn't know how long it would take to set them all, and she wanted to make sure the beach was really there before she did anything.

She climbed up over the railing and stood on the conveyor belt. She had always wanted to be there, and had often imagined herself seeing "Ellie" on the screen then making sure it was her who went through. She laughed a little, then remembered where she was and that she had a time limit.

She crouched down and tried to see as far into the "in" port as she could now that she had a better perspective. All she could see was darkness, even from there. She tried to reach into it, but her hand met a cold, hard door.

She turned to peer through the other side and there was light coming through, and a cool breeze, and the scent of salt water and fish. *The beach.*

She crawled on hands and knees through the "out" port onto soft sand. She couldn't believe her eyes, or her skin, as she stood with some difficulty. Before her was a short stretch of white sand with the deep blue tide beating and beating against the shore in some absurd attempt to reach dry land. She dug her feet into the smooth, fine pebbles and brushed her hair—which had been blown into her face by a cool ocean breeze—out of the way, smiling like she hadn't smiled since her son had gone. Since Levi had gone. He would have loved to see this, to feel it, to smell it. She fell down on her knees in the sand and started to weep.

She was here. This was it. The one promise she had made to Levi and she had fulfilled it too late. It wasn't enough. Fifteen minutes wasn't enough. She had to take it all in, experience all of it. She had to do it for him. She knew it. This was moral. Keeping her promises. But she couldn't stay here without paying the price. She owed it to Gertrude and the Scientist. She had to keep her promises to them as well.

She struggled to her feet and stared out again at the endless water and the endless sky. She almost wanted to forget the bombs entirely.

"*Helloooo*!" a voice called from down the beach. A figure far away made its way through the tide toward her. "Hey! Did the Scientist send you, too?"

Ellie was going to ignore the person, but hearing the Scientist's name intrigued her. Plus, as he came closer, he didn't look like any threat she couldn't handle.

"Hello! Do you hear me?" he called when he was close

enough that she obviously did.

"Yes," Ellie said. "Yes and yes. Who are you?"

"Oh. *Ho ho*." The man chuckled. "Just a worker. Just like you. I asked for the beach. You asked for the beach. There's only so much beach—and a lot less of it that we can be on without anyone knowing."

Ellie tried to count how long she had been through the door already. It could have been five minutes, it could have been ten. "I don't have much time left," she said

"Much time? *Ha ha*! You're going back? Are you crazy?"

"No. I—I didn't pay my debt. I need to before I can—"

"Oh, *ho ho*, child. There's not much time now. You better forget about that. You're already out here, why don't you just stay? Otherwise you might not get the chance to come back."

"No," Ellie said, shaking her head. "I can't."

"You don't really have a choice, you know. Your time's runn—"

He kept talking, but Ellie wasn't listening. She crawled back through the conveyor belt, and his voice disappeared behind her.

She jumped down off the belt and the floor felt so much harder after the softness of the sand. How much time did she have left? She sprinted out the door, slammed it shut, jerked the pouch out of her pocket, and fumbled through it for one of the discs. She didn't know what to do with the pouch while she set the bomb so she dropped it on the floor.

Rip, stick, press? Rip, stick, press? *As if.*

The paper backing on the disc was impossible to get off. It took ten, fifteen attempts, especially with her hand shaking at the fear of missing her time limit. She finally got it off, stuck the disc on the door, and pressed the button which turned green and displayed a little clock counting down from thirteen.

Thirteen minutes? Fifteen minutes at the beach, ten minutes to set the bombs and get out of the building. She looked up and down the hall. She could place some, but not all, of them if she wanted to make it back to the beach before the door closed. She had to set as many as she could.

She scooped up the pouch and tied it to her belt loop, jogging to the next door. It only took five tries to rip the paper backing off before she could stick and press. She pulled a disc out and started on it on her way to the next door when she got into a rhythm.

Rip, stick, press.

Run.

Rip, stick, press.

Run.

She watched the timer closely as she activated each one. Eleven and a half minutes, the clock said, and that's all the time she had.

She sprinted down the hall, back into her workroom, and jumped up onto the conveyor belt. She could still feel the cool breeze and smell the fish and salt. She even looked forward to getting to know whoever it was that waited on the other side of the door. She looked down at her cubicle one last time, never would she have to see it again.

"Hurry," she heard from inside the "out" port.

She dropped to her knees and crawled toward the beach, only to hit her head on a cold, metal door.

✺   ✺   ✺

XIII. Pardy

Pardy couldn't stop wondering if he had made the wrong decision in asking for Outland 6. He had been on patrol for only a few hours and he already knew that the populace hated him, they disappeared any time he came near. There was no point in him walking the streets but to send the Sixers back inside for the few seconds it took him to pass by. This was what he chose, though. He wanted to find something out about that woman's daughter, and this was the only way he knew how to do it.

He had filled out his forms, just like the Captain asked, and sent them straight to her first. She made him sit down so she could read them over, and when she was satisfied, she asked him which patrol he would like. She hinted that Outland 3 was flashy and upscale—with a lot of celebrities—but Outland 5 was where protectors went to make a real name for themselves, to go down in history. When he told her he wanted Outland 6, she didn't believe him. She gaped at him, wide-eyed, then laughed. "Good one, Pardy," she said. "But really. What patrol do you want?"

When he insisted that he was serious, she tried to convince him that he was making a mistake, that Outland 5 would serve him much better than Outland 6, which no one anywhere cared about, but he wouldn't listen, he wouldn't have it. He had to find that woman's daughter and protect her, even if he couldn't tell the Captain that was why he wanted 6 in the first place. She was going to have to accept that and send him there or deal with her superiors about the death of Rabbit. But he hadn't told her that, either. She knew her career was in his hands as much as he knew his was in hers.

And so she gave it to him: Outland 6. But she made him go on a solo patrol which started not moments after his initiation was over, after his partner had died and Pardy had killed a mother. As a result, he found himself walking along the streets of Outland 6, in the dark of night, looking for a boy he wasn't sure he would recognize, to ask him about a girl he wasn't sure existed. He figured his best bet was to find the kid he had seen in the tree—the only person who hadn't run when Pardy came around in protector gear last time—and the only place he knew to look was the last place he saw him.

His path to the Neutral Ground from the last checkpoint on his patrol took him through the alley he had killed the woman in without his realizing it until he was already there. He stopped when he did. The ground was still dark with her blood. No one cared to clean it. There was no point. This was Outland 6. Pardy pictured his son again and set off toward the Grounds with a renewed sense of urgency.

Even the Neutral Grounds were empty. Word of his coming had come before him. That, or no one cared to be out at this time anyway. He heard a rustling in the trees down the street and darted back into the alley to watch the very kid he was looking for—plus a little girl—chase after a cat along the Neutral Ground in front of him.

They were so small that they might as well have been walking. Pardy could have caught up to them in a few long strides, but he didn't want to scare them away before he found out where they were going. He had to keep stopping to let them get further ahead before he continued his pursuit from alley to alley. At one time he thought the little boy looked back and saw him, but the kid kept running, trying to keep up with the little girl who was much faster than him. They turned down an alley, and Pardy had to sprint so he didn't lose sight of them.

When he turned around the corner, the girl had climbed up on a dumpster, chasing the cat which seemed to disappear into the wall a few feet above it. "Hey! Stop!" Pardy called, running down the alley towards them, probably not the best idea if he actually wanted them to stop he realized too late.

The boy turned to see him storming down the alley, then sprinted wide-eyed the other way and disappeared around the corner. The girl tried to jump up to where the cat had vanished into the wall, but she couldn't get high enough, so she crawled down the pile of boxes to get to the top of the dumpster just as Pardy got to the bottom of it.

"Stop right there," Pardy said. "I need to talk to you." He dodged back and forth to bar her escape.

"Yeah. Right," the girl said. "I know better than that." She faked one way and stepped the other, but Pardy was too fast. He was there to stop her no matter which way she went.

"I'm not going to hurt you, girl. I just want to ask you a few questions."

"I'm not a girl," the girl said, pulling a slingshot out of her back pocket and taking aim.

"No. I—"

"I'm not." Sh—er—*not-she* held the slingshot steady, aiming it directly between his eyes. His helmet scanned her heartbeat and breathing which both indicated she was calmer than her voice betrayed. "You gonna kill me now?" she asked.

"What? No. I—Of course not. Why would you ask that?"

"That's what your kind does," the girl said. "Isn't it? That's what Pidgeon says. He knows."

"Pidgeon?" Pardy remembered Rabbit.

"Do it, then!" the girl yelled, stomping her foot on the dumpster lid with a loud thump. "I know you want to! What're you waiting for?"

"No," Pardy said, shaking his head. "No no no." He reached slowly to his cargo pants, and she backed closer to the wall, keeping the slingshot aimed at him. "Look," he said. "I have some beef jerky here. I'll give it to you if you put your weapon down and answer a few questions. That's it. I promise. I would—I would never...*kill you*." He grimaced.

The girl slowly let the tension out of her slingshot, slid it into her back pocket, and crept up to the edge of the dumpster to sit down with her legs dangling off, reaching her hand out toward him expectantly. "Well," she said.

He fumbled through his pockets some more, searching for the jerky he had grabbed to give him some energy for this stupid shift. He hadn't eaten in he didn't know how long, but the girl seemed like she could use it more than him anyway. She looked like she hadn't eaten in days. "There," he said when had found the pocket it was in. "Here it is. Just like I said." He handed it over and prepared to stop her from running off with it, but she just took a big bite and chewed loudly with her mouth open, kicking her dangling legs back and forth against the dumpster.

Pardy took off his helmet, lodging it up under one arm, and ruffled his hair. He could breath so much better without it on. "I—

uh..." he said. He didn't know what to say. He wasn't trained to investigate or interrogate, he was trained to observe, find law breakers, and dispense justice. But he had to do something, this was the first and only person to actually stop and talk to him.

"Well," the girl repeated through a mouth full of jerky.

"I—*uhhh*..." Why couldn't he figure out what to say?

"You had some questions," the girl said, still chewing. "I can't give you your jerky back now... Unless you're willing to wait a little while." She giggled.

"No," Pardy said, cringing. "Uh...No. That's just—no. So..." He grasped for anything. "Do you know a lot of the kids around here?" he decided on. It was something at least.

"I ain't snitchin on anyone if that's what you're asking," the girl said, taking another bite of jerky and eyeing him suspiciously.

"No," Pardy said, shaking his head. "No no no. That's not— No. No one's in trouble, okay. I'm just—I'm looking for a girl."

She stood up and backed away, still chewing. "I told you I'm not a girl!"

"What? No. I—look. Have you heard about any of your friends, or anyone you know really, who—who's lost their parents recently."

She threw what jerky she had left at him. "Go away! I don't want your stupid jerky!" She spit a half-chewed glob at his face and only barely missed.

"No," Pardy said, waving his hands. "No, wait." He fumbled through his pockets, looking for the necklace. The little *not-girl* was climbing the stack of boxes on the dumpster, trying to jump up to nowhere. "Look!" He held out the silver butterfly for her to see. "Look, I'm sorry. I have something for you."

She turned to see the necklace, and her eyes widened in anger. She stormed down the boxes, leapt over the dumpster onto Pardy's shoulders, and beat at his face with her tiny fists. "You! It was you! I hate you! I hate you! I hate you!"

Pardy dropped his helmet with a clang and pried her off, holding her out at arm's length. The fury in her face brought tears to his eyes as she struggled against him, flailing her fists and kicking her legs. He tried to fight the tears back, but they wouldn't surrender. They weakened him. He couldn't hold her any longer. His arms gave way and the flurry of fists resumed. He had no recourse but to cower into the fetal position on the concrete and let the tears flow.

"It was me," he said. "It was me. I'm sorry. I didn't—I don't deserve to live. I did it. I can't even say it. I'm sorry."

The tears kept coming but the pain of the fists had gone. He was still lying in the fetal position on the rough alley concrete, sobbing, and sniffling, and crying like a child. Then he felt two tiny arms wrap around him in a warm embrace. For a second he smelled his wife, and pictured his son, and he felt good. He was doing his best. For them. And he had found the girl he needed to protect.

As his sobbing subsided, he realized the arms weren't around him in an embrace. They had intent. They were fumbling through his belt for something, and he only realized what it was when it was too late. He backed toward the dumpster, crab-crawling on hands and feet, and stared at the little *not-girl* pointing his own gun at him.

"Please," he said. No more tears in sight. This type of danger he was trained to overcome. "If you pull that trigger, it won't end well for either of us. There's a biolock. If you try to fire it, it will explode in your hands."

She took a step closer. "Explode in my hands, explode in your face, what's the difference?"

"I deserve this. I know. What I did was wrong. But you don't deserve it. There has to be a better way."

"I don't know, pig. I think there was probably a better way to handle my mom and dad, too. But you didn't care about that. Did you?"

"You're dad!" Pardy said, remembering why he had come in the first place. "*You're dad.* He—he's not—dead. I know where he is."

He could see her grip on the gun loosening. "Yeah," she said. "Right. How do you expect me to trust a lying pig?"

"I'm not...I'm not a pig. I'm a protector."

"Protector, pig, same difference."

"Look at me," Pardy said, pointing at his eyes. "Just look at me for a second. Okay. I'm at your mercy. You can commit the same wrong that I did, and add your life to the count, or you can trust me just a little bit. I won't even ask for the gun back. I just want you to take your finger off the trigger."

Her hands started to shake. Pardy squirmed back a little closer to the dumpster. She wanted to pull the trigger, he could tell, but she wanted to see her father, too.

"You're lying," she said.

"No. I'm not lying. I swear it. Look." Pardy felt around the ground for the necklace and held it out again. "See? We took your father, okay. *They* took your father. I'm not—I can't help them kill anyone else. And I *will* get him back."

"I don't believe you!" She shoved the gun closer to his face.

"Here," Pardy said. "Take it." He dangled the necklace right in front of the gun's barrel.

The girl took one hand off the trigger and grabbed the necklace. She slipped it into her pocket then put the gun right back to his head. "All that means is that you killed my mom," she said.

"No. It means that I cared enough to keep it. It means that I came searching for you, and I found you. It means that I'm here to help you. I want to protect you. That's what it means."

"I don't need your protection!" the girl yelled. Pardy flinched away from the gun. "Look at you." She laughed. "I stole your gun while you were crying on the ground like a baby. If anything, *you* need *my* protection."

As if on cue, a group of hooded figures came into the alley. They stopped at the Neutral Ground entrance and one yelled, "Hey! You two. What's going on down there?"

The girl turned and pointed the gun at them. "None of your business!"

Pardy stood up. He searched for his helmet out of his peripheral vision but couldn't find it quick enough without a 360 degree view. He reached for his gun before he remembered the little girl was still holding it. Just what he needed.

"Now move along!" the girl yelled, shaking the gun at them.

"You. Girl," the voice from down the alley came again. "You the Server kid?"

"I'm not a girl!"

The hooded figures started to creep closer. The girl backed up, and Pardy stepped between her and them. "Give me the gun," he said, his hands behind his back, not looking away from the slowly advancing gang. She handed it over and he pointed it at them. "Stop right there, citizens," he called in the deepest voice he could muster. He wished he had his helmet on, with it's voice modulator and aiming assistance technology, but he had practiced enough without a helmet to take care of this small problem. "Turn around and go on your way."

"*Ha ha ha!*" They laughed, still slowly approaching. "No," one of them said. "We'll take the girl, pig. She belongs to us now. If you go on *your* way, maybe we won't roast you with her. And that's a one time offer. You got that?"

They were closing faster, and some of them had started making loud animal noises, halfway between oinks and barks. The girl tugged on his vest. "It's not worth it," she said. "We can ditch them. Follow me."

"If you take one more step, I'll have no choice but to use deadly force," Pardy said, ignoring the girl.

They didn't stop. "Yeah right, pig. Try and stop us." A couple of them broke into a run, and Pardy fired, knocking both to the ground with one shot each. The others stopped in shocked silence.

The girl pulled on his vest again and yelled, "Come on!"

They sprinted off, twisting and turning down the alleys, away from the Neutral Ground and into the streets, before the gang could gather themselves. They sprinted a few zigzag blocks, then ducked behind a dumpster. Pardy was breathing so heavily he could barely hear the footsteps running past as the gang went looking for them.

"Y—You shot them," the girl stammered when the sound of them running by had disappeared. "You actually shot them."

"Why were they coming for you?" Pardy said.

"You just killed two of those guys, didn't you? You're a killing machine. Is that the only thing you know how to do? Pidgeon was right."

"They were coming after you. It was us or them. Why did they want you?"

"Because you killed my parents!"

Pardy stood up and peeked over the dumpster to see if anyone had heard her. There was no one to see. "I—We're going to get your dad back," he said when he crouched back down to her. "But why would they chase you because of that?"

"To put me in their orphanage. *Duh*. You took some of their best employees, and now, they want me as payment."

"What orphanage?"

"I don't know." The girl shook her head. "But Pidgeon didn't make it sound good."

"Who's Pidgeon?"

"Pidgeon," she said, scoffing. "That kid you chased away earlier. He was supposed to go to the end of the Belt with me. I knew he'd never make it, though. But he lived in the orphanage. He would know. If he was here, he could tell us."

"Okay," Pardy said, nodding. "Well. The first thing I need to do is get out of this gear. Let's go back toward the Grounds—er—*Belt*. I have a change of clothes there. C'mon." He got up as if to start on their way, but she didn't budge.

"*Um*...No. They'll be looking for me there. The only safe way is to go toward the Streets."

"I can't walk around in these clothes anymore," Pardy said, looking down at himself. He had lost his helmet, but he still stuck out like a Sixer in Amaru's Temple. "Not while we're here. It draws too much attention. Everyone will be looking for a protector walking around with a little girl."

"I'm not a girl!"

"Whatever," Pardy said, shaking his head. "They'll find us. I need to change or get back to the precinct. One or the other, and they're both towards the Neutral Ground."

"Whatever that is, I'm not going there," she said, crossing her arms. "So you'll have to leave me behind or come this way with me." She turned her back to him.

Pardy sighed. This was the point of no return. He had found the girl he needed to protect, but how much was he willing to put on the line to do it? He was going way off regulations already, but hadn't the Captain encouraged him to do just that? Not only that, she had pushed him into it by giving him this shift. "I'm not leaving you," he said.

"Well then." She smiled. "Let's go this way. We'll get a little further from the Belt, so they're not looking for us, then head west out and beyond their reach."

"But we won't be able to get your father back unless we go back to the transport bay," Pardy said in one last ditch effort to get her to comply. He didn't have time to go running around Outland 6, and he didn't want to have to pick her up and carry her where he needed to go.

She was about to head the other way but stopped. "You're

really serious about this?"

"I wouldn't lie to you."

"I've heard that before." She shook her head.

"I mean it," Pardy said. "Look." He pulled the picture of his son and wife out of his pocket and handed it to her.

"This looks like a baby Pidgeon," she said with a laugh.

"That's my son. I see a lot of him in you. If I was...*gone*, I would want someone to protect him for me, so I want to protect you. I *will* protect you. I promise."

She rubbed her finger across the picture. "He looks like you, too. You look like Pidgeon."

Pardy laughed. "I wish I hadn't scared him away. Maybe he could help us right now."

"Maybe he's trying to," the girl said, shrugging. "Help me, at least. He hates pigs."

Pardy laughed again. "Are you ready to go back toward the transport bay? I know a place where we can lay low for a while."

"If that's where my dad is," she said, eyeing him.

"It is." Pardy nodded. "I promise."

"Well..." She shrugged. "Let's go, then. But let me lead the way. I have more experience in the Streets than you do."

"Okay," Pardy said. He didn't care as long as she led in the direction he wanted her to go. "Just take us toward that tree your friend was climbing. Do you know the one?"

"You saw that?" the girl said, blushing.

"I—uh...yeah," Pardy said, blushing himself. "I used to climb trees when I was a kid. It was the first thing I ever saw in Outland 6, that tree."

"Outland 6? What does that mean?"

"You know, Outland 6," Pardy said. "The world you live in. The one we're in now."

"I know the Streets and the Belt and that's it. This Outland you're talking about must be someplace else."

"It doesn't matter right now," Pardy said, shaking his head. He wasn't supposed to be talking to a Sixer about the other worlds anyway, even if he was already this far off regulations. "My shift is supposed to end soon. We need to get to the costume closet and get you set up so I can figure out how to get your dad out."

"Costume closet?" The girl raised an eyebrow.

"You'll see," Pardy said. "Come on." He started around the dumpster, but she pulled his arm to stop him.

"Hey," she said. "Me first, remember. I know this place better than you."

"Oh," Pardy said. "Right. Go ahead."

She poked her head around the dumpster then started moving in bursts. She crossed the street into another alley and stopped in the shadows to make sure no one was coming before she went a few steps further and stopped to peek around the alley's corner. He kept track of their position as they moved and she seemed to be taking them a roundabout way but in the right direction.

"The closet's on this alley," he said when they got far enough back east.

"Alright," she said. "How close to the Belt?"

"Right off it."

She sighed. "You have got to be kidding me," she said, shaking her head. "Alright, well, we're not taking the straight route, that's for sure. Follow me."

As they dipped and dashed through the alleyways, Pardy thought that this gir—er—or, whatever she was, didn't need any protecting. She was leading the way. She knew what she was doing. She was taking a circuitous route like he had been trained to do, and she was only a child from Outland 6. How could she be so competent without any training? She was smarter and more able than his son, and his son must have been a few years older than her. How was that possible?

He was still thinking about it when he felt the thud on the back of his neck and his mind blacked out to nothing.

ප   ✖   ♋

Pardy woke to the sour aroma of waking salts. He tried to jump up into a defensive position, but his arms and legs were tied to a tiny chair with linen. Two dark shadows blocked the light shining in his face, blinding him. One of them spoke.

"*Tsk tsk tsk.* You're all alone now, protector. You know that much at least. Don't you?"

He struggled against the restraints and grunted.

"*Aww.* He still thinks he's in control of his life," the second voice said.

"Protector. What's your name?" the first voice said.

"Where's the girl?" Pardy demanded. "What did you do with her?" He fought against his restraints.

"*She's not a girl!*" the second voice said in a mocking tone. "And it's you you should be worrying about, *protector*."

"Now," the first voice came back. "What were you doing with her? What use is a little girl to the likes of you?"

"She's no use to me. I'm not trying to use her. I want to protect her."

"Protect? *Ha ha ha!*" The second voice cackled.

"Like you protected her mother, yes?" the first said.

"I know that was wrong," Pardy said, shaking his head. "I want to make it right. I—I already talked to—"

A door groaned and more light poured in from behind the two shadows. Two shorter figures came in, one of them yelling, "I told you to get me when he woke up! He's the only one who can get my dad!"

"We told you to stay out!" the first voice said.

"No," the girl said. "You don't own me. Set him free so he can get my dad!"

"Listen to her," Pardy said.

"Shut up!" the first voice yelled. "Shut up all of you!"

"But I—" Pardy protested.

"No! Shut up. Answer this, protector, why are you here?"

"To protect her," Pardy said, nodding in the direction of the shadow he thought was the little girl.

"You know you're not gonna be able to get her dad out," the first voice said. "I know that badge and your uniform. You're an Officer. You don't have the power it takes to affect something that important."

"What?" Pardy said. "No, I—"

"Get her out of here!"

The second form ushered the two small shadows out of the room and closed the door. It was only Pardy and the first voice left.

"Look, protector," it said. "What's your name?"

Pardy didn't answer.

"The girl wants you to get her dad back, but you can't. We both know that. It's not your fault. Now whether or not it's your fault that you killed her mom is a little more of a gray area. Or a white area, should we say? Protector's white."

Pardy struggled against the restraints again, moving the chair with his effort. "I didn't want to kill her," he grunted. "She threatened me."

"*Ha ha!*" the voice laughed. "Sure. Sure, protector. It wasn't *your* fault. No, you were just following orders, weren't you? You're a cog in a big machine and you alone can't grind against the forces that tell you which way to turn. Sure, protector. Believe that if you must. You are only human, aren't you? You *are* human, right? You bleed?"

Pardy struggled to break free, but the shadow only laughed.

"Oh. I know you are protector. It takes a human to fight like that, a human to gnash against chains he never expects to break free of. You are a human, protector. Not a cog. And you pulled that trigger. No one else."

The door opened and closed, letting the second figure back in.

"Do you have everything under control?" the first said.

"Yes, yes," the second said. "She won't bother us again. She knows what the deal is now."

"Did you hear that, protector?" the first said. "She knows what the deal is now. She knows what we're going to do to you for what you did to her. Do *you* know, protector?"

Pardy struggled against his restraints and the two figures laughed together.

"*Struggle, struggle, all you want,*" the second voice sang.

"Protector—*huh huh*—protector. It's okay." The first voice forced down its laughter. "Protector, we aren't going to do anything to you. That's why the girl won't come in. She knows we won't hurt you. In fact, my partner here has some food for you."

The overhead lights flipped on. Two short, dirty-haired, dirty-everythinged women crouched in front of him. No, they weren't crouching. They were standing, but their backs were so hunched as to produce the illusion of crouching. They looked so small and frail. He almost wanted to laugh at the thought that they could hurt him. He chastised himself for somehow being caught by them, a giant knocked out by ants. One of them was holding a bowl of steaming something, and the other was empty-handed. Pardy looked around the room for his gun but it wasn't anywhere in sight.

"*Ha ha*! You called it," the one holding the bowl said, the second voice.

"Your gun's not here, protector," the woman who owned the first voice said. "You can stop searching. We got rid of your comm link, too. Don't worry. They won't know where you are. In fact, they'll think you're in two places at once. *Huh huh*."

They burst into laughter again. Pardy looked at his wrist and his comm was gone. "How did you know?"

"You're not the first protector to try to *help a Sixer*." The old woman shoved the bowl into Pardy's chest, spilling hot slop over his white uniform. When she realized he couldn't use his hands, she put it on his lap and untied them. "And you won't be the last."

"Settle down, now," the other said. "Let me talk to him. You go take care of the girl."

The door slammed and Pardy's stomach growled. He hadn't realized how hungry he was. He sniffed the soup and looked closely at a spoonful.

"Don't worry," the woman with the first voice said. "*She* made it, not me." She pointed over her shoulder at the other woman who had already left. "It wouldn't kill you either way, but this way it tastes better going down."

Pardy took a big spoonful, and it tasted much better than he had expected, much better than all the nutritionally balanced meals he had eaten in his life, the ones designed to make him a perfect protector. He couldn't help shoveling it into his face.

"That's *real* cooking there, protector," the woman said, laughing. "Homemade by human hands. You can have all of it you want, too. So don't be shy. *Heh heh*."

Pardy ate and ate until the spoon couldn't scoop anymore.

"Now. Protector," the woman said. "Your arms are free, I couldn't stop you from leaving if I tried, and we've fed you from our own feed stores. My name is Rosa, and I want to help you help the girl. So, do you think you can trust me with your name?"

He didn't trust her still. She was right, though. With his hands free he could easily get past these frail, old women, but she probably also knew that he wouldn't. He couldn't. He had to see to it that the girl—he still didn't even know her name—was protected. These people seemed to also want to protect her, but he wasn't sure how they could. Still he had no choice. He had to at least hear them out until he could find a better way to protect the girl. Maybe they could help him find that way.

"Pardy," he said.

"Pardy?" Rosa repeated. "That sounds like a surname. Do you have anything more...intimate?"

He didn't understand why he didn't want to tell her, but he didn't. "Tom."

"Tom," Rosa said with a smile. "Was that so hard? It's so nice to finally meet you, *Tom*. Would you like me to untie your legs? That can't be comfortable."

Pardy started untying them himself, but she helped with the other leg. When they were done, he stood and stretched his muscles. He had to stoop so he didn't hit his head on the short ceiling, and Rosa looked even smaller from the new vantage point. He still didn't understand how he could let them knock him unconscious.

"There," she said. "That's better. Isn't it?"

"What do you plan on doing with me?" he asked, finally back in control of his fate, gun or no.

"Do with you?" Rosa laughed. "No, Tom," she said, shaking her head. "I thought it was clear that we couldn't *do* anything with you if we tried. We don't want to *do* anything with you at all. We want do it *for* you. And for the girl, of course."

"Where is she?" Pardy demanded. "I want to talk to her."

"Yes, well, you will. But first you have to understand that you can't get her father back. Now do you understand that?"

"You don't know that. I'm a protector. I can—"

"You can shoot her mother when a superior officer is nowhere near?" Rosa frowned with her lips in a tight line. "We know how it happened, Tom. If you can't resist the other cogs when they're nowhere near you, how do you expect to go into the heart of the machine to bring her father back out?"

"I—I could—"

"*Y—You would fail.* Get arrested yourself. I don't intend to sound rude when I say this, either, but you have to know that we can't lose whatever chance of protecting Ansel you actually do offer us."

"Ansel?"

"That's her name, Tom," Rosa said with a smile. "Ansel.

And her parents were Eva and Andy. You killed one and locked the other up. No one else, Tom. *You*. And do you know why?"

"I was ordered—" Pardy stuttered. "I was ordered to stop her."

"Ordered by who, Tom?"

"By my Captain—My superior officer."

"And who ordered your Captain to order you?"

"I don't know. The Major, or the Chief, or—"

"Exactly, Tom. There are more and more. Your boss, your boss's boss, their bosses. But where does it end? Is it bosses all the way up? What exactly are you protecting?"

"Property, liberty, life," Pardy replied by reflex.

"Exactly," Rosa sneered. "Property first, then liberty, *then* life. In that order. You're protecting someone else's property, too. Not ours. Not here. Not in Six. Have you ever heard of property being returned to Six?"

"Six has no property," Pardy said. "Everything they have they've stolen."

"That's not true, Tom." Rosa shook her head. "You spend some time here with us and you'll learn that."

"I don't care about any of this." He was getting annoyed. He clenched his fists. He had to fight the urge to hit this trash for talking to him like she was his superior. He couldn't keep the edge out of his voice. "Where's the—Where's Ansel? I want to see her."

"Alright, alright. I'll get her. But I'll need to talk to you after you're done telling her you can't save her father. I can offer you a way to actually protect our mutual friend. That's what we both want, isn't it? Now, I'll go get her. You and I will speak again soon enough." She swept out of the room, and shortly after, Ansel stormed in.

"They said you can't get my dad out," she said, crossing her arms.

"They might be right," Pardy said, shaking his head.

"But *you* said you could."

"I thought I could. I was lying to myself, though. I'm just an Officer. I don't have that kind of power."

Ansel hit him on the arm, and he flinched away, hitting his head on the roof. "You also said you wouldn't lie!"

"I didn't know I was lying," he said, rubbing the quickly

forming knot on his head. "I wanted it to be true, so I thought it was. That's not the same as lying."

"A lie's a lie." She hit him again for good measure.

"I may not be able to get your father back, but I still promise to do whatever I can to protect you."

"They told me you'd say that, too. They told me it may not be true either."

"They don't know me, Ansel. How would they know what I'll do?"

"How do you know my name?" Ansel asked, raising her hand to hit him again.

"I—they told me," Pardy said.

He relinquished himself to the slaps as she said, "And I don't even know yours! They know you better than I do! And they knew you were lying even when you didn't!" One slap on the arm for each word of the accusation.

"I—well—yes," Pardy said. "That's—"

She hit him again. "Then they know you better than you do."

He didn't know how to answer. He gave up and plopped back down into the short seat. He huffed and looked at Ansel's size compared to Rosa's, wondering how old she actually was. She could be older than his son. "Tom," he said.

"What?"

"My name's Tom," he said. "Tom Pardy."

"Well, Tom," Ansel said, extending a hand. "I'm Ansel Server."

"Nice to meet you Ansel," he said, taking it.

"You said you'd do anything to protect me, right? Well Rosa and Anna said they have a plan that you could help them with. Pidgeon seems to think the world of them, but I wouldn't trust his judgment. I don't even know if their plan has anything to do with getting my dad back, but I need you to figure out what it is before I can decide what to do next. What do you say?"

Tom didn't trust Pidgeon's judgment either. Nor did he trust Rosa or Anna. He didn't trust their methods—ambushing him in the alley and tying him up—and he didn't trust that they wanted to protect Ansel. He didn't trust a Sixer to look out for anyone but themselves. But who was he to talk? He was the one who had killed Ansel's mother. He had gotten ambushed by two scrawny, old, hunchbacked Sixers. He was protecting a Sixer, and maybe a Sixer was exactly the help he needed to figure out how best to do that.

"I don't know," he said. "I don't trust them."

"I ain't asking you to trust them." Ansel scoffed. "Just hear them out and tell me the plan, then I can decide from there."

He couldn't argue with that logic. Even if it would be him deciding from there and not her. "I'll hear them out," he said, nodding.

XIV. The Scientist

Every day different. Every day the same. Only change is constant. Reality is contradiction.

She stood in front of the printer—as she did every meal—and imagined the people who grew, reared, harvested, and collected her food, the ones who built the things to make it all possible, and those who sent it along so she could consume it. She ordered everything as raw as it came, but that meant that she had to order the sandwich she wanted fully made. Still, they were forced to do as little of her work as she could help, and soon she would be helping in a more efficient manner. It was Christmas Feast Eve, and Mr. Kitty should be on his way.

She carried the plate of food into her office, and when she opened the door, he was there. "Mr. Kitty!" she said, setting her plate on the desk next to the cat who went over to eat the meat out of her sandwich. "Finally, Mr. Kitty. Red! Eat all you want. I'll make you more if you're here when I'm done."

The cat meowed.

"Oh. You have no idea, Mr. Kitty. *Sic bo* shines down on you. I've been waiting for you to come in with that beautiful red collar for you don't know how long."

He meowed again.

"Alright, Mr. Kitty. I'm gonna get to work," she said. Mr. Kitty went off on his way, ignoring the rest of the meat in her sandwich, and she started the macros going which would set the work schedules across all the Outlands as needed for the operation. She moved the repair bots around to fix only the holes she didn't need and set a few to creating some holes that might come in handy in emergency situations. With everything she could do before her lunch meeting done, she went to ride the elevator to the bar and get on with her meeting.

Trudy was already in the corner booth with two beers. The glasses were still frosty, and Trudy's drink was mostly full, so she hadn't been there long.

"Trudy, dear," the Scientist said, sitting down and taking a sip. "You know me all too well."

"More than anyone in the worlds, I'd say." Trudy smiled.

The Scientist loved her smile, it was so genuine. "I didn't keep you waiting long, did I?"

"Oh, no no," Trudy said. "Just sat down. You're as punctual as ever, dear. Don't you worry."

"Good," the Scientist said. "I was a little distracted, you know. The roses are red." She smiled.

"No kidding," Trudy said, sipping her drink.

"Would I kid about this?"

Trudy shook her head. "That you wouldn't."

"Trudy, you do trust me, don't you? I could tell you more, but it would only put you in more danger."

"And I'm not in danger now?" Trudy said, shaking her head.

"No. Of course you are. I didn't—I didn't mean that. I meant that you'd be given added danger for no need."

"Not me, dear. I know enough already. I'm in plenty of danger no matter what else you tell me. The more I know, the more danger for you, though."

"No. Well...I—Not just me."

"Right, right," Trudy said, smiling and nodding. "Back to the circular argument. It's not just you, it's the plan, it's too dangerous to tell me about a plan that I'm a part of."

"It would put you in—"

"I'm already in danger, dear." Trudy laughed. "We're going around in circles. That's why they call it a circular argument. Let's end it here before I get dizzy. I know you're not going to tell me everything, and you know I'm not going to stop asking, so let's just get on with what really brought us here."

The Scientist sighed and took a sip of beer. Trudy was right. She couldn't be put in any more danger, but it would put the operation as a whole in danger if the protectors could get more information out of her. Still, Trudy deserved to know more. She had been with them for so long, and her work was so valuable, that she had a good argument for it. An argument which she never pushed too far. The Scientist promised herself that, as soon as this operation was over, she would tell Trudy everything. Well, at least she would tell her more.

"Trudy," the Scientist said. "You deserve to know more."

"I know it."

"You've done more for this revolution than anyone has. Myself included."

"Oh, now don't say that," Trudy said, blushing. "That's not what we're about and you know it, dear. Solidarity. Without any of us, none of this would be possible."

"Solidarity, dear," the Scientist said, raising her glass.

They took a drink in unison.

"Trudy, sometimes I think—no—*I know* that you know more about the revolution than I do, even if I know more specifics about what plans are in action."

"Oh, honey," Gertrude said, shaking her head. "Now I know you're wrong on that. I know more specifics than your computers could hold. Who's infatuated with who, and which coworkers are possibly parents of the same children, Hell, I could tell you what most of the workers in my hall eat for every meal every day of the week, but you try to tell me *you* know the specifics."

The Scientist shook her head. Trudy was right again. The Scientist knew what food they received, how often, and in what proportions, but she didn't know how they cooked it or who they ate it with. She knew nothing in comparison to Trudy. "Like I said," she said. "I *know* you know more about the revolution than I do."

"Not so fast, dear," Trudy said, raising a finger. "We know different parts of the struggle. You know as much as you know, and I know as much as I know, but together we know what we both know. We do nothing alone, remember. Without any of us, none of this would be possible."

"Again you prove your worth," the Scientist said, smiling wide. "Day after day. You will get what you deserve, Trudy. Mark my words."

"I hope you're right, dear," Trudy said, shaking her head. "If it's not too late for that already. Either way, the worlds don't seem that just to me." She sipped her beer.

"No. They don't," the Scientist said, taking a sip of hers. "Which is why we have to make them that way. Right, Trude?"

"Right as rain, dear. Just you and me. *Huh huh huh.*"

"Now tell me," the Scientist said, ready to get down to business now that the pleasantries were out of the way. "Do you trust

Ellie?"

"I trust her to do what she wants." Trudy shrugged. "You said that's what you wanted."

"Yes. Yes yes. That's what I said. But sometimes I wonder if that's what's really for the best."

"For whose best, dear? Your best? Ellie's best? My best?"

"Yes. Yes, yes, and yes. All of them. The best for all of them."

"All of *us*, dear. You *are* included in that. You're one of us, aren't you?"

"Am I?" the Scientist said. "I created the Walker-Haley fields that keep us apart. I created the printers you fill with commodities. I created the androids who forced all the service workers of Inland into Outland 6. *I* am responsible for all of that, Trudy, responsible for propping up the entire system that keeps you down. How am I supposed to be one of you if I'm the one doing this to you?"

"Now, now, sweetheart," Trudy said. "We all do what we have to do to survive, and sometimes that ends up in some of us keeping others down. That's not you, dear. That's the system. As long as you recognize what you're doing, and you do all you can to stop it, you're one of us. And who's done more to bring down the system than you?"

"Well, you, Trudy. I just said that."

"And I just said that's not true. You keep talking us in circles, dear. Is there something you're getting at, or are we just here for a drink and a ring around the rosies?"

Trudy always knew when there was something. But first there was business. All play and no work made Jill a happy jerk. "You know there is, Trudy," the Scientist said. "But first let's get back to Ellie. You say you trust her. How far does that trust go?"

"As far as anyone I've ever brought to you," Trudy said. "She won't tell anyone anything. I can guarantee that. She never tells anyone anything. Which leads me to suspect that she might take the opportunity to drop out if you give it to her, but she'll be sure to do what you ask of her first. She wouldn't want to live knowing that she owed you."

"And you're sure of all that from having talked with her so little?"

"It doesn't take much," Trudy said, taking a sip of her drink.

"Like you've said before, they usually tell you everything they want with their first words. Well, with me, one conversation reveals a person's entire character. I couldn't tell you how I do it, I just know that I do." She took another sip. "And I'd say that you know it, too, with what you have me doing for you."

"What I ask you to do for *us*." The Scientist winked. "But I do know it works, and every day it amazes me more."

Trudy blushed. "So what do you have in store for her?" she asked. "Info finding mission? Meet her favorite propaganda star? One-on-one with an owner so she can show him how she feels? What did she ask for?"

"The beach," the Scientist said.

"*Ugh.*"

They both drank at that.

"I told you I trusted her to do whatever she wanted," Trudy said. "But that's not where it stops. I know better than that, dear. There are always conditions. So what are they? What did she say?"

"Well, I..." The Scientist sipped her beer and looked around the bar.

"You haven't told her yet, have you?"

"The roses only just turned before I came to see you," the Scientist said. "I had to set the scheduling macros. I have more still to set. I thought I had more time."

"With the Christmas Feast *tomorrow*, you thought you had more time?" Trudy said, shaking her head. "Be ready for the blooming every day, dear. That's what you taught me. It's what you taught all of us. Especially with the field yellow as it is. Or rather, as it *was*."

"Yes, well," the Scientist said. "There was more to do. Besides, there's plan B..."

Trudy rolled her eyes and took a big gulp of beer.

"You."

"Yeah yeah," Trudy said, waving her on. "Well now you have to tell me what you have in store for her. Is that the bush you've been beating around?"

No. It wasn't. "Well, yes and no," the Scientist said. "But, Ellie. You think she would be willing to use a disc?"

Trudy looked around the room then sipped her beer. She leaned in close and said, "A disc?"

"More to the point, would she be willing to use a dozen discs?"

"That many?"

"Her entire hall," the Scientist said, nodding. "She'll put one on each door, and I'll direct the belts so the explosions target specific locations. Two birds with one stone. We have the misdirection of bombing the QA hall, and we render key printers in Bourgeoisville inoperable."

Trudy laughed, spitting some beer up onto the table.

"What?" The Scientist didn't get the joke.

"*Bourgeoisville*," Trudy repeated, mimicking the Scientist's voice and adding an extra snobby accent. "You sound so *bourgeois* when you say it."

"Yeah, well, would you rather I called it Inland like they do? Or Earth 2.0?"

"Now, now," Trudy said. "Don't get mad. I just thought it was funny. You can call it *Donkeybuster* for all I care. Soon we'll see that it's all the same anyway. Right?"

She wasn't right this time. What you called it did matter. The name you gave it affected how you thought about it, if you believed you could change it, but how could the Scientist sit and argue against someone who knew the oppression of the system firsthand? "No," she said, shaking her head, not wanting to argue the point any further with so much work still on the horizon. "You're—You're right."

"Stop that," Trudy said. "Now I'm not right. We both are. And Ellie will use the discs just fine. But what are you giving her?"

"The beach," the Scientist said. "Like she asked for."

"For how long?"

"Fifteen minutes."

"Fifteen minutes?"

"Fifteen minutes during the operation," the Scientist said. "Those are fifteen completely secure minutes. But after fifteen we need the holes to give other workers what they want. It's the best I can do."

"Fifteen minutes?"

"Fifteen minutes," the Scientist said.

"I don't know if that'll be long enough." Trudy shook her head.

"It has to be. That's all we have."

"You couldn't send her over there then move the door back when she's done?"

The Scientist shook her head. "Not on such short notice. And we need the operating power, anyway. Fifteen minutes for a beach trip is a lot, all things considered. She's not the only one going to the beach, either. She's just the most likely to return. Whether she does or not, though, she gets fifteen minutes to decide."

"And discs," Trudy said. "One on each door?"

The Scientist pulled a pouch out of her coat pocket and put it on the table. Trudy scooped it up and put it in her own pocket.

"Rip, stick, press?" Trudy asked.

"Rip, stick, press," the Scientist said. "One on each door. If they're activated, they'll explode twenty-five minutes after her shift ends. That's fifteen minutes on the beach, then ten minutes to set the discs and get out of there. She can do either, or both, or neither, and whatever she decides, I'll be willing to meet with her again. You know the deal."

"And when she blows up her own workplace?" Trudy said. "When she blows up *my* workplace. How do we support ourselves then?"

"She—*and you*—will be moved to another building," the Scientist said. "There are empty QA buildings waiting for just such an emergency. Don't worry. I know. Her, nor your, job are in any danger, only the owners' infrastructure on one side and their party on the other."

"And when they realize that she was the only one working before the building blew up, won't they know she had to be the one to do it?"

"Technically she's not scheduled to work." The Scientist smiled. "Someone else is. And they're already dead. The protectors will assume a corpse did it, and Ellie will be in the clear."

"But if she does lose her job..."

"She won't," the Scientist assured her. "But if she does, then she'll be added to the distribution list. Have you ever known me to let anyone I could help go helpless?"

Trudy shook her head. "You do everything you can."

"And I will continue to do so."

"So when do I tell her?"

"Tonight. At the bar. Her bar. She has to do it tomorrow or

wait. The roses are red, Trudy. The roses are red."

"They are, dear," Trudy said with a smile. "And I'll be sure Ellie knows it, too. But what are *you* going to do about it?" She sipped her beer.

Trudy knew what was really bothering the Scientist. She knew everything. "I'm going to help everyone, *then* get what I want," the Scientist said.

"Everyone?" Trudy said, raising an eyebrow.

"I get what I want every day. I have a printer for that. It's not my turn. I have to let the others get a chance before I take more."

"It's not anyone's turn, dear," Trudy said. "It's all of our turn. If it wouldn't take more than an elevator ride to get fifteen minutes of what you want, then it wouldn't stand in anyone's way, would it?"

"No. I—"

"And this is about getting *everyone* what they want, right?" Trudy said.

"Yes, but—"

"And you *are* a part of everyone, aren't you?"

"Well, but—"

"But you deserve to get what you want, too, dear," Trudy said, slapping her hand lightly on the table. "As much as any of us. You're not like the owners, you know. You're helping us, and you deserve the same window of happiness that you're offering everyone else."

"Fifteen minutes?" the Scientist said.

"Fifteen minutes," Trudy repeated.

"I don't know if it's enough."

"It's all you can get."

"It's all I can afford."

"It's all *we* can afford, dear." Trudy smiled and winked.

The Scientist shook her head. "But what if she doesn't believe me?"

"If you never tell her, she'll never have a chance to decide."

"How could she trust me? I let this happen. It's my fault."

"It's the system, dear. Let's not get back on the merry-go-round. Without you, she wouldn't be alive. You deserve to see her. For fifteen minutes at least."

"I'm going to do it, Trudy," the Scientist said.

"You should."

"What do I say?"

"You say what you've been waiting to say. You've thought about it. I know you have. You already know what to say. Say that."

"I know nothing, Trudy."

"No one does." Trudy shook her head.

"Right again," the Scientist said. "Right again." She sipped her beer.

"I always am, dear." Trudy smiled. "You should get my advice for everything." She winked and finished her beer.

"Oh. I do. Don't worry."

"Well," Trudy said, standing from the booth. "I think you've got some work to do, then. I know I do, and I should be off to it."

"You're more productive than anyone, Trudy."

"Oh. I know, dear," Trudy said with a smile. "I know." She laughed as she left, waving over her shoulder.

The Scientist sipped her beer. She had some time before her next meeting. She could play a game of pool. Trudy suggested that she attend to her own desires, too. But the game would go long. She was so out of practice it would have to unless the other player ran the table. Either way, her second meeting would likely be kept waiting, and there was still so much work to get done before the Feast.

No. Who was she kidding? She didn't have time for that. Not even fifteen minutes. Did she have fifteen minutes to take what she really wanted, though? Her beer was empty, so she got another and sat back at the booth to watch the other patrons play. Her time was tomorrow if she wanted it. Just like everyone else. What was safe for them, was safe for her. If she ever wanted to see her daughter, Christmas was the time to do it.

The door to the bar opened and in came Anne, dressed in her coveralls still. She skipped the bar and sat in the booth with the Scientist. "What?" Anne said with a smirk. "Nothing for me?"

"I didn't know you were off the wagon," the Scientist said. "You can have some of mine if you want."

"And get your cooties?" Anne said with a cringe. "I think not."

"Cooties? What year is this? Are you a child?"

"We're all kids compared to you." Anne laughed.

The Scientist laughed, too, and took a drink of her beer. "You don't know how true that is, dear. You have no idea."

Anne looked around the bar and leaned in close. "I don't know…" she said. "*There are rumors*," she added in a whisper.

The Scientist chuckled. She leaned in close, too. "That I'm a robot!"

"How'd you know?" Anne laughed.

"I've heard them all, dear. I'm no robot, though. I'll tell you that much. But I'm older than any robot that could pass for me. So there's some truth to it."

"But, how?" Anne said, shaking her head in disbelief.

"That's not what we're here for, dear. The roses are red."

"Yes, ma'am," Anne said, sitting up straighter in her seat.

"You know what you're to do, then."

"Yes, ma'am. I know."

"Tell me."

"First, I alert the other operatives in my sector, they have work of their own to do. Then I work my shift as normal. At the end of my shift, I set the discs and get out of there, ensuring the building is clear on my way."

"Very good," the Scientist said. "Very good. Are you ready for this?"

"I don't know, ma'am," Anne said, looking at the table. "After th—after the operation, when it's all said and done, there are gonna be shortages, you know. I mean, how do w—how do we deal with that?"

"We'll be working to direct the food to those who need it," the Scientist said. "And to keep it out of the owners' hands. There *is* a risk of shortages, but we'll do everything we can to relieve those in need."

"It won't be enough," Anne said.

The Scientist didn't answer. She sipped her beer.

"It never is." Anne took a deep breath, shaking her head. "Not even when there aren't shortages. It's gonna stay like this forever, isn't it?"

"Unless we do something about it," the Scientist said.

"And this is something? This will give us more food?"

The Scientist shook her head. "No. Probably not. Not right away, at least. You'll have to fight for what you deserve. They'll never hand it over without a struggle."

"And this is how we struggle? By bombing our own food supply?"

"It's not food, though. Is it? You work there, Anne. Coconuts, pineapples, saffron...Do you ever eat any of that? Do you know anyone who does?"

Anne shook her head.

"No. You don't. Because it's not food you're growing. Those are luxuries, and you're growing them for someone you'll never meet, someone who does nothing for you in return but keep you at the bare minimum you need to survive so you can continue to grow their luxuries. You won't be creating shortages. There will be more work than ever to get those luxuries up and running again. They'll be desperate to be the first to do it. But the explosions also go through the transport tubes, and that will take out printers the owners can't live—or steal what you create—without. This is just the beginning, Anne. There's so much more to come. Can you help us get it started?"

"I can," Anne said. She pounded her fist on the table then looked around self-consciously.

"*We* can, dear," the Scientist said. "None of us alone. And after this phase of the operation, we'll move to getting those in need what they need, just like you want to do."

"But why don't we do that first? Instead of bombing the luxuries."

"We have to do this tomorrow in order to do that in the future. This is only for you to know, but we'll be retrieving a stockpile of printers for exactly that purpose. We're using the explosions around different sectors as a distraction to collect the printers and take them to a safe distribution point where they can be given to those most in need."

Anne nodded. Her hand motioned as if to grab for a glass that didn't exist, and when she realized that there was nothing there, she brushed the hair out of her face instead. "That's the only way to do it?"

"That's the only way to do it with as few people as we have. The best thing we could do would be to stop producing for them altogether and start keeping everything for ourselves. But we're all too comfortable in our jobs to do that."

"You, too?"

"Me especially."

"You're really not that different from us, are you?"

"I eat better," the Scientist said. "I eat every day. And I know I'll sleep in a big, comfortable bed every night. In that sense, I'm different. But they exploit me the same as they do you. And I know that enough to do everything I can to help you stop them."

"But who are they? How could they be so evil?"

"They're mostly inheritors of wealth," the Scientist said. "They were born into a role which they fulfill all too well. As much as they know what they're doing, they have no idea what they're doing. No more idea than anyone in any of the Outlands really. They've never experienced hunger or alienation, and they don't interact with any humans who ever have. They literally live in their own world, in complete ignorance of what day-to-day life is like for the vast majority of people. They commit evils, yes, but not *because* they are evil. It might be more accurate to say that they're possessed. Or possessive." The Scientist shook her head. "I don't know what I'm saying, though. Do you?"

Anne shook her head.

"No," the Scientist said. "No, of course not. How could you when I don't? Contradictions. Contradictions everywhere and I don't understand them. But I won't stop until I tease them out, you see. Do you understand that?"

Anne nodded and grabbed again for her non-existent drink.

"Good," the Scientist said. "Because that's the real point of all this. Even if you don't agree with my methods and you want to walk away today without doing anything for the operation, you're free to do that—I hope you won't, of course—but if you do, you have to keep struggling to tease out those contradictions for yourself, you have to do it your own way."

"You know I'm not walking away." Anne shook her head. "I would have done that a long time ago."

The Scientist smiled and sipped her beer. "Yes." She nodded. "I know. But it's important to remind you that you can, and that you'll still be looked after, even if you do."

"I know, ma'am," Anne said, nodding. "I'm in it for the long haul."

"Good," the Scientist said, clapping her hands together. "Good good good. That's good to hear, Anne. Thank you."

"Thank *you*, ma'am."

"Now, I've got a lot of work to do before tomorrow, and I think you do, too."

"Yes, ma'am," Anne said, standing up and holding out her hand. "I won't let you down."

The Scientist took her hand and shook it. "I know you won't, dear. Hopefully *I* won't let *you* down, either. Now be careful out there. This is the real thing. These discs will be live."

"I understand, ma'am. I'll keep everything under control."

"You do what you can, Anne." The Scientist smiled.

Anne shook the Scientist's hand one more time then went out into the world. The Scientist watched the rest of the pool game, finishing her beer in the booth. This was it. No more meetings. No more real work besides setting a few more macros before the operation was underway. Still, she did have to do that.

She set the empty glass on the bar and the bartender said "All's well in the world."

"Is it ever?" The Scientist didn't know if it was a question or a statement.

"No" The bartender shook his head, thinking about it. "Well, the world's a big place."

"And there are so many of them." The Scientist laughed.

The bartender eyed her with a squint. "You come in here with your white coat, and you order your beers and sit in your corner booth, and I know there's something more to you."

"Is that so?"

"It is." He nodded.

"And how do you know that?"

"No one tips well," the bartender said, tapping his head with a rag. "No one wears white coats. My customers don't pay attention because they don't want any attention paid to them, but I do, ma'am. I own the place. I rule here. That means my rules. And you follow them well enough—no questions being one of those rules—but I needed you to know that I know there's more to you than that. That's all." He went back to cleaning glasses.

"That's very observant of you," the Scientist said. "Mr.— Uh…"

"Bartender."

"Mr. Bartender." She smiled. "And I appreciate your

discretion."

"Discretion's the rule, ma'am. Be assured of that. But it's more than that. My customers aren't all as unconcerned as I make them out to be. You understand? If I noticed you, then they did. That's all I'm saying."

The Scientist nodded and signaled for another beer. "I appreciate that Mr. Bartender."

"It's called customer service, ma'am," he said, getting her another drink. "I find it helps to keep my customers coming back."

"Yes," the Scientist said, nodding. "I've noticed it's mostly the same people in here when I come in."

"Mostly, ma'am," the bartender said. "Especially when you come in."

"*Huh.*" She sipped her beer. "I see. And you wouldn't tell them anything that could lead them to me, would you?"

"I don't know anything to tell them, ma'am. I just aim to tell you that they come in every time you come in."

"I won't even ask who they are, sir. Thank you." She left a hefty tip and didn't finish her beer.

She knew they'd find the bar eventually. They always did. But so soon? And why did she have to learn about it just as the roses bloomed? Not that it mattered whether she knew about it now or not. There was no worrying anymore. The only thing she could do now was prepare for tomorrow.

The elevator took too long to get back to her lab even though it took only half a minute. She knew it was exactly thirty seconds because she oversaw the operation of every elevator in existence. She opened the door to her office and Popeye was typing on the computer. The big metal arm turned around in surprise at the sound of her entrance.

"Not today, Popeye," she said. "The roses are red. The roses are red!"

Popeye waved and gave a thumbs up, then rolled out through the hall door to do who knows what.

"First things first," she said out loud, even though Popeye had left the room. She set the last few macros and the computer went to work. She typed in the command to send Ellie's conveyor belt to the beach for fifteen minutes, then she thought about her own wish.

Fifteen minutes with her daughter. That was worth at least as much as seeing the beach or meeting a famous celebrity, wasn't it? Or was it worth more? Did she deserve it? But who was she to say that what they wanted was worth less than what she wanted?

No. Fifteen minutes of time through the holes was fifteen minutes of time through the holes, no matter where you went or what you did while you were there. That was the question, then, wasn't it? Did she deserve the same fifteen minutes she offered the workers?

She thought she did. She was a worker, too. *Technically*. And fifteen minutes wasn't much to ask. She had fought longer than anyone and had never taken her fifteen. Now was the time. This was

a major operation. There were so many distractions she could probably come up with a couple of extra fifteen minute blocks through the holes. Trudy was offered time that she didn't take, she wanted the Scientist to take it instead. She typed out one more direction for the Walker-Haley fields to follow the next day and went straight to bed, trying to go to sleep like a child on Christmas Eve.

                                                                                 �226   ❋   ᴂ

The day was long, longer than any day she could remember and she remembered a lot a lot of days. Christmas was never a thing that Fours looked forward to, but she had studied the history of the holiday and she knew the stories about how the children would react. She never understood it, though. Any Christmas she had as a child was too long ago to remember, and ever since she had discovered printer technology, anything she ever wanted was at the touch of a button. What presents could there be? But now she was about to get something a printer couldn't give her. Well, technically it was the same technology making it possible, but it was something entirely different.

The Feast didn't start until late into the afternoon and the operation until a little way into that. She spent her time waiting by going over every bot assignment and all of the hole placement timings and disc countdowns, imaging everything that could go wrong, any actors who would take what she offered and not do what she asked. She set redundancies for those who she thought might fail, and when she was satisfied the strategy would work as best as it could, it was time for her to take her fifteen. Or maybe she was only satisfied because she had to be, because she had no more time to obsess over every possibility. Either way, control was out of her hands now.

She left the computer to guide the process and went out into the hall. Mr. Kitty was there waiting for her. He meowed.

"Hello, Mr. Kitty," she said. "Would you like to meet my daughter?"

He meowed again.

"Good," the Scientist said. "She's just an elevator ride away. There's no time to waste."

The elevator doors opened, Mr. Kitty meowed, and they both walked in for her fifteen minutes.

ۏ   ✕   ҩ

XV. Haley

Did she want to know the answers to Mr. Douglas's questions? She wanted to know the answers to her questions. She could hardly remember his questions, and his rushing away without waiting for her response didn't help the situation.

What did she know now? She knew that Mr. Douglas and Rosalind were both suddenly interested in Lord Walker. Of course they would be, he was the richest owner in all of Inland, the greatest producer of all time. Never before had anyone amassed as much wealth as Lord Walker and to want to know everything about him and how he got to be where he was seemed only natural. So that was a dead end.

What else did she learn from the meeting? That she was right about Rosalind's attempts at manipulation. Mr. Douglas had admitted to as much. He didn't care about her answers to his questions, he only wanted to ask them. She knew they were manipulating her, but for what? She hadn't told them anything. She didn't answer any questions about Lord Walker or their business. They didn't even care if she did. If anything, everything was making less and less sense.

She looked up from her thoughts, and she was at the front of the kitchen. She had passed by all the secretaries who she thought were so nosy before, but not one as much as glanced at her—or she hadn't noticed if they did. Her counter was covered in fresh-cooked turkeys, pots of potatoes, and three cheesecakes. The whipped cream was still in the bowl, so she could tell that Rosalind had whipped it by hand. Rosalind had even mixed six old fashioneds. Haley felt bad for doubting her and vowed to do something to make up for it as she stacked the food onto the cart. She looked around one more time to see if Rosalind was there so she could thank her but sighed when she wasn't and pushed the cart out into the Feast Hall.

The party was in full swing now. Third Feast was the halfway point, the hump they had to get over before they could start slowing down on alcohol and filling their stomachs with two more feasts to convince themselves they weren't drunk. She saw that the owner who had molested her was back to eating, though he was going slower than everyone else and looking around with a dazed—not drunk—look of terror on his face, like he was afraid he might get hit again at any second. She chuckled to herself at the sight of it.

Haley didn't notice Lord Walker's empty plates until she reached the head table. He had a bored look on his face as he stared into Mr. Loch's mouth. Mr. Loch talked and talked at him through the food he was eating with loud wet smacks. She thought Lord Walker was going to snatch the food right out of Mr. Loch's mouth to eat it himself, but the sound of three turkeys hitting the table at once made him jump and turn to Haley who kept piling more and more food in front of him.

"Haley, dear?" Lord Walker said. "I thought you were lost and gone forever. Don't you ever do that to me again, you hear! *Gimme*." He wrenched the gravy boat out of her hand and poured some directly down his throat before dumping the rest over his turkeys and potatoes and starting in on them with his bare hands, disregarding his platinumware. "*Ugh—ughm*—More—*Om—Nughm*—Gravy," he forced through the endless torrent of food.

"Yes, sir," Haley said. She set the rest of dessert and the old fashioneds on the table and couldn't help but wonder if it really made a difference whether the food was handmade or printed. The way Lord Walker poured it down into himself, it didn't seem like he could even taste it.

"Locky," Lord Walker said. "*Ughm—num*. You introduce—*ughm—nom—nughm*. The speaker. *Ughm—num*."

Mr. Loch scowled. He started to complain but thought better of it and stood to address the Hall. "Owners of Inland!" he called, and half the owners kept eating. "Owners of Inland!" he repeated, but it was no use, it was third feast, they were more intent on eating than they had been for the entire night so far.

Mr. Loch scowled and yelled, "Well here's the scientist, then! We all know what the technobabblers will say. Technology is advancing, but we need more money. *Ha*! And what do we say to that?"

He waited for a reply but there was none. Mr. Loch was third in line. He was nothing. If Lord Walker wasn't saying it, no other owner cared. Haley chuckled to herself again then glanced over at

Mr. Douglas. He sat, as always, statuesque and facing the symphony. She thought she saw a grin playing on his face as Mr. Loch continued.

"That's right!" Mr. Loch said. "That's right. You get what we give you, and you'll get nothing more. So work a bit faster, or get out the door! *Ha ha*!" One or two owners close to the head table laughed. Haley shrugged and pushed her cart on the way back to the kitchen.

"Well, here she is," Mr. Loch said. "Now get back to feasting. This food won't eat itself. *Ha ha*!"

Everyone was already eating, and Mr. Loch started in on his own food again. The symphony didn't even stop playing as the woman in the white coat climbed onto the hovering platform, and Haley didn't look up when it flew over her head toward the head table.

"Owners of Outland," the woman said. Haley heard it, but she knew none of the owners would, they didn't care, they had third feast to gorge on. Haley herself wouldn't have heard it if it didn't so strange. *Owners of Outland*. Didn't she mean owners of Inland? They were from Inland, not Outland.

"*Owners of Outland*," the woman repeated. This time her voice boomed so loud the entire Hall dropped their platinumwear and looked up at her. The symphony stopped playing, and Haley stopped in her tracks close to the back of the Hall to turn and listen.

"*Ah*," the woman in the white coat said with less volume. "Do you see that? If you speak loud enough, everyone has to listen. Now. You brought me here, like you do every year, to give you the scientific facts behind what keeps your society running, and every year you let the symphony play over my presentation, and you go on eating, drinking, and generally ignoring me."

A few pockets of laughter broke out in the crowd. Not at the head table, though. They were all staring in awe or ire, and Mr. Douglas was smiling.

"Yes, it's quite amusing," the scientist said with a smile. "Isn't it? I see how it gives you joy. BUT DO YOU GET JOY OUT OF THIS?"

The last sentence was so loud Haley put her hands to her ears to block it out. The scientist didn't yell, she used a machine to amplify her speaking voice. The owners must have been deafened by it, and the scientist waited a moment for them to regain their hearing before going on again at a reasonable volume.

"No," she said. "I didn't think you would. But that's exactly what you've brought it to. I come here every year, and every year I tell you that the system is in crisis, it needs restructuring. And every year you eat, and drink, and laugh, and kick the can down the road again. You leave me to deal with it, and I always have. I put my nose to the grindstone, and I invent the schemes, and band aids, and whatever you want to call them that get us over every hurdle in your way so far, but *still*, you ignore the source of the crises. Still you let your music play, and you eat your feast and drink your drinks, but you ignore where it all comes from. You ignore the contradictions in the system, and every year they get worse and the next hurdle gets bigger because of it."

Haley looked around the room. Everyone was still staring up at the scientist in awe. They didn't dare look away after she had deafened them once already.

"But, owners," the scientist went on. "The hurdles *are* catching up to you. They always do. The next one always comes. Reality won't give up on destroying your idealism, and science is only concerned with reality. My voice amplifier here is a metaphor for that. Do you realize that, or are you so drenched in your own propaganda that not even you can think straight?"

The scientist waited for a response, as if she actually wanted an answer. No one gave one. "No?" she said. "You have nothing to say now? You laughed about your ignorance before, but now you have no response to it? That's exactly what I expected from you. That's exactly what I knew would happen when I came here tonight. I examined the historical record, and that has allowed me to predict all of this. Yet still, every time I tell you the system is broken, you ignore me. What does that say about the sustainability of your empire?"

Haley realized she had been staring at the speaker for a long time now and remembered how she had left Lord Walker's plates empty before. She looked around the hall one more time and everyone—even the secretaries who were supposed to be serving food—was staring up at the scientist as she spoke. Haley almost got caught up with them again, but she broke away and pushed her cart out into the kitchen.

She was well underway with preparing four new turkeys when the sound of echoing footsteps alerted her to the fact that the kitchen was empty except for her and now Rosalind who was jogging toward her with an urgent look. "Haley," Rosalind said. "You shouldn't be here."

"But I have to prepare fourth feast," Haley said, still cooking.

"Fourth feast?" Rosalind scoffed. "Weren't you out there when the Scientist started her speech?"

"I—uh—yes. But what does that matter?"

"And you're still in here now?"

"You're talking to me aren't you?" Haley said, shrugging. What was Rosalind getting on about?

"Yes. I—well...Yes," Rosalind said. "You are. But y—we shouldn't be here right now. Come on."

"Here is exactly where I should be." Haley went on cooking.

"No, Haley," Rosalind said, grabbing her arm. "You don't understand. You can't be here. You need to be out there listening to the Scientist with everyone else. Now come on." She pulled Haley toward the door.

Haley pulled her arm away and stopped. "No," she said "I have to do this. I was late for third feast already because of that useless meeting with your Mr. Douglas, and I'm not going to waste any more time."

"You don't understand," Rosalind said. "The world's about to end and this is ground zero. Look around you. Why do you think there's no one else here?"

Haley looked around at the emptiness again and realized the oddity of it. She had ignored it in her zeal to be the first secretary out with fourth feast. "They're all probably out there listening to that scientist," she said with a shrug. "She's really loud if you hadn't heard."

"I didn't hear. Why do you think I'm back here? But you heard and here you are."

"And still you're amazed by it."

"Not amazed," Rosalind said, shaking her head. "Comforted. It is as it's supposed to be. Now please. Let me get some old fashioneds for you, and let's get out of here. Lord Walker'll thank you for as much." Rosalind ordered the drinks from Haley's printer.

Haley didn't trust her still. As usual, Rosalind was telling her less than she knew. She was somehow behind the emptiness of the kitchen, and Haley wouldn't be manipulated by her anymore. Rosalind picked up the drinks and started on her way out to the Feast Hall, saying, "C'mon."

"No." Haley didn't move.

Rosalind stopped. "Haley. You have to."

"I don't have to do anything I don't want to do. I'm not moving until you tell me why it's so important that I leave."

"*Ugh*. Haley. Now is not the time to assert your independence. I mean, *yay*—that's exactly what we were going for—but if you don't leave this kitchen right now, you'll never have another choice to make in your life."

"That's just another way to manipulate me. That's all you've done this entire time."

"No, Haley," Rosalind said, coming closer to her. "I haven't. Lord Walker has. I'm not the one who's doing it, I've been showing you how the manipulation works."

"And there you go again," Haley said, stepping away. "Driving me away from my duties. Driving me away from Lord Walker. Further proving that you're trying to manipulate me."

"No," Rosalind pled. "You don't understand. We want to help you. We want to free you."

"I *am* free. You want to take me away from Lord Walker."

"You're not free, though. You only think you are because you don't know any better. But you won't be alive to figure that out unless we get out of here soon, so it doesn't matter either way."

"You keep saying that, but I have no reason to believe you."

"Look," Rosalind said. "In a matter of moments, all the printers in here are going to explode. That's a fact. That's why we cleared the kitchen, and that's why I stayed behind, to get you out. Whether you think I'm manipulating you or not, you've seen me do some extreme things, and I hope that's led you to believe that I *will* continue to do them. So, please. Come with me."

"Go on then if you're telling the truth," Haley said. "You don't want to be here when the kitchen *explodes*, do you? I'm getting back to work."

"No, Haley." Rosalind shook her head. "I can't. It's my duty to protect you, and I won't leave this kitchen unless you leave with me. If you die here, I die here."

"Right." Haley gave her a thumbs up, nodding. "As if you'd die for me."

"I would, Haley," Rosalind said. "I will if you don't come with me right now. I'd rather not, and we don't have to, you just have to come with me until the end of the scientist's speech. Can you do this one last thing for me? Then I won't ever ask you for anything else."

Haley wanted to protest, but she remembered how Rosalind had handmade all of third feast and that she still owed her for that. She sighed and said, "Alright. But when the kitchen doesn't explode, we're even, and I'd rather not speak to you ever again."

"Fine," Rosalind said, smiling. "Whatever." She shook her head. "As long as you get out of here, I don't care. Here." She handed Haley the old fashioneds. "Take these and bring them to Lord Walker. The Scientist should be done after that, then you can come back to the kitchen—if you still want to."

"Fine," Haley said. "Whatever." She took the drinks. "Let's go."

Rosalind pushed her out of the kitchen and up toward the head table. She almost spilled the drinks because of it. The scientist had just finished her speech, and the room watched as her platform flew over their heads and disappeared behind the symphony. Haley thought she saw a little black fur ball run by the Scientist's ankles, but Rosalind shoved her again and Haley had to focus instead on keeping the drinks full and her clothes dry.

Then the explosion came. The entire Hall rocked with the force of it as Rosalind pushed Haley down under the head table. Gasps and screams echoed through the Hall, and the sound of footsteps shuffling toward the front of the room was made louder by Haley's proximity to the floor and the acoustic characteristics of the table above them.

"Do you trust me yet?" Rosalind said, smiling.

Haley struggled out from under the table and away from her. "Trust you? How?"

"Haley!" Lord Walker said from behind her. She turned to see his arms outstretched for an embrace. "Oh, dear," he said, smelling her hair as he hugged her close. "You're here! *Thank the Hand.* I thought I had lost you."

"No, sir," Haley said with a curtsy. "I'm fine, sir." She

handed him the drinks, still full even with her dive under the table.

"Sweet, beautiful dear," Lord Walker said, wiping a tear from his eye. "You see to everything, don't you. You're my savior. *My savior*." He downed one of the old fashioneds in one gulp then threw the glass to shatter on the floor.

Haley looked around. Rosalind was nowhere in sight, Mr. Douglas wasn't at his seat, all the owners were pushing closer and closer to the head table, and the remaining four of the Fortune 5 backed slowly away from the encroaching mass. She couldn't believe that Mr. Douglas and Rosalind had actually done it, but how could it be anyone else? Neither of them were there, and Rosalind all but told her that it was them. But then why did she save Haley? And clear out the rest of the secretaries? And how? It was all too much to process with the action going on around her.

"Woah *ho ho ho*!" Lord Walker boomed over the crowd, almost as loud as the scientist with her voice amplifier. All the owners stopped in place at the sound of his voice. The fighting and shoving died down. "Look at yourselves owners," he said. "Look at yourselves!"

They all looked back and forth at each other, and down at themselves. They would do anything he told them to do.

"Now," Lord Walker said, twirling his cane. "Who here's been hurt by what happened? Anyone?"

They looked at each other again. None of them were hurt personally—maybe their eardrums—but they weren't about to bring that up to Lord Walker.

"Our printers are hurt!" a brave voice called from the back of the crowd. Haley couldn't make out who it was. "Our property!"

"*Oh ho ho*! Property *schmoperty*," Lord Walker bellowed. "Those are Feast Hall printers. They're common property. We'll all share in the costs of repairing whatever damage was done, so what damage could there really be said to have been done?"

This time there was no brave soul to answer.

"No, my friends," Lord Walker boomed. "This is the work of *terrorists*. They seek to strike fear in your hearts. They want you to be afraid. Don't you understand that? And you..." Lord Walker chuckled. "You're fighting one another, pushing your way towards us—the Fortune 5—when we had nothing to do with it. No one was injured, owners. Or are you court jesters? Your actions peg you as such. You've let them win already. Do you see that? You've let them win!"

Still no one answered. But a good lot of them looked embarrassed and made their way back toward their seats.

"Now," Lord Walker said. "If you'll all just wait until the pro—"

The entryway doors burst open, and rows of pounding white boots came marching in to circle the room. The owners cowered into the center of the hall, and the protectors—in their screaming, unnatural face masks and white plate armor—formed a ring around them, in between the Fortune 5 and the rest of the owners. It was an awe inspiring display of discipline. Haley had never seen a protector in real life—much less an entire platoon of them in one room—but she was somehow happy for being caught on the side with the Fortune 5, or at least the four of them who were still there.

"As I was saying," Lord Walker went on when the protectors had all gotten into place, their guns pointed in at the owners who they were surrounding. "If you'll all settle down and wait until the protectors get here, we'll get this sorted out in no time. Is everyone okay with that?"

The owners in the ring were cowering as close together as they could, their bulbous stomachs touching one another. Haley pitied them a little bit.

"Now," Lord Walker said, looking up and down the line of protectors. "Is the Chief here with you, or are we going to have to find a new one?"

"Sir, no, sir," the nearest protector said, turning to address Lord Walker and putting a gun over her shoulder. She took off her helmet—which, unlike the other protectors', had a mustache and goatee—to reveal the same dark face as Mr. Douglas. She looked eerily like him. "Chief Baron, sir," the protector said, saluting. "Awaiting your orders, sir. We wanted to secure your safety and let you control the situation first, sir."

"Good," Lord Walker said, smiling wide. "Very good, Baron. Leave the decision making to your employer. That's the proper way to handle things. Now. You have the situation secured. Proceed with your investigation. I don't want anyone leaving this Hall until we find out who's responsible for this heinous action. Do you understand me? We *will* get to the bottom of this terrorist attack!"

"Sir, yes, sir." The Chief slipped her helmet back on, shouted out orders in a distorted voice which was lit in green, red, and yellow by her screaming face mask, then marched back into the kitchen with a group of protectors, leaving the owners cowering in their ring of guns.

"Do you see that owners?" Lord Walker called over them. "That's why we have these protectors. To *protect* us. Now they have the opportunity to show us firsthand their gratuity at the living we allow them. Isn't that right, protectors?"

"Hoo-ra!" the ring sang in unison.

The owners all cowered closer together. Haley thought she saw some of them starting to cry. She wouldn't be surprised if the whole lot of them had peed themselves at the sound of it, but the pneumatic pants took care of that, too.

"Hoo-ra," Lord Walker repeated. "Did you hear that owners? Hoo-rah. Can you do it again for me, protectors?"

"*Hoo-ra!*" This time it was louder and more fearsome.

"And this, my friends," Lord Walker said, "is only a small section of a behemoth machine. Back there, studying the evidence left by the explosion, we have the best forensic minds money can buy. I assure you." He winked. "I paid for them myself."

Mr. Loch and Mr. Smörgåsbord chuckled, but the owners in the ring were still having a hard time seeing the humor in the situation.

"That's right," Lord Walker went on. "*I* paid for most of this protector force, and I own more than that. That means they'll do exactly what I tell them to do. Doesn't it protectors?"

"*Hoo-ra!*"

"What are your vows, protectors?"

"Property! Liberty! Life!" they sang back. The precision of their chorus was inspiring, though it was made eerie and unnatural by the modulation of their voices.

"Property, liberty, life," Lord Walker repeated. "Their vows coincide with our ideals, they reinforce each other. We are nothing without them. They are nothing without us. Or, more precisely, they are nothing without me. *I* give them the property they need to exist. They depend on *me*. And they *will* have justice!"

The Chief burst out of the kitchen with her menagerie in tow. The owners in the ring went between watching her march up to the head table and staring in fear at the protectors who still surrounded them with drawn guns.

"Look here now," Lord Walker said, grinning. "Already they come with information. We'll have this straightened out in no time, no doubt."

The Chief marched all the way up to Lord Walker, taking her helmet off, and whispered in his ear. "It looks like it came from the other side," she said, but only Lord Walker and Haley could hear.

Lord Walker shook his head. "No. I don't think so. Not possible. If so, you're in deeper trouble than if it came from this side. I'll have you look again, please."

"But, sir—"

"*No buts.* You heard me. Don't make me say it again."

"Sir, yes, sir." The Chief turned and shepherded the crew back into the kitchen, mumbling under her breath.

"Now now," Lord Walker addressed the owners again. "We'll get to the bottom of this yet. A minor complication, that's all. We'll find a way over this hurdle, no doubt. In the mean ti—"

"In the mean time you have another complication to deal with." The voice came from on the stage. The orchestra was long gone, and a lone protector, wearing an older model helmet—with a dark visor instead of a facemask—stood pointing a gun—but a smaller version than the one the other protectors were holding—at the Fortune 5. The owners all pushed away from the stage, and the larger guns, held by the protectors in the ring, pointed at the lone protector on stage.

"*Ho ho ho!*" Lord Walker laughed. "Woah now, son. You do understand what you're doing, don't you? Threatening the life of an owner, threatening the life of *the* richest owner in all of Inland, the owner who also happens to hold a majority share in the protector force that surrounds you now. I see you're wearing the protector's pure white. Do you want to mar that any more than you already have, son? A retainer threatening his master. *Tsk tsk tsk.*" He shook his head. "Just don't do anything dumber than you've already done, son."

"The only dumb thing I've ever done was put on this uniform and pick up a gun for you," the protector onstage said. "I know what dumb is. Believe me. This here. This is the exact opposite of dumb. I'm protecting people. Just like I took this job to do. And who else do they need protecting from but you?"

"Now, now, son," Lord Walker said, pointing his cane at the protector. "At my word, every one of these protectors will fire on you. Do you think you can kill all of them before they kill you?"

"I don't want to kill them, sir. I don't have to. I only have to kill one of you, and—I'm sorry to say—I think you've just elected yourself. Sir."

"Fire!"

The room erupted in a torrent of gunfire. The sound was louder than the scientist's amplified voice. It went on and on and on, and when it eventually ended, the protector was still standing unscathed on the stage. One of the protectors in the ring closest to the rogue protector ran to tackle him but disappeared as he climbed onto the stage. Two more followed right after and disappeared just the same.

"I told you, owner," the protector on the stage said. "I don't have to worry about them. This is between you and me."

"Alright, now," Lord Walker said, waving his plump hands. "Alright. I get your point." His voice was starting to falter. He was taking on the voice he used when he wasn't confident in his power. "I get your point. But I don't see why we have to bring guns into this. Why don't you just put that down so we can talk about it like civilized men."

"*Ha ha!*" the rogue protector laughed. "Me put the gun down? After you had your entire army unload their guns onto me? The only reason you're asking me to put my gun down now is because your guns didn't work on me. Welcome to the Hell we live in everyday, owner. How does it feel?"

"Now, now," Lord Walker said, his voice cracking. "Don't get angry with me," he added in a deeper voice, overcompensating. "I'm sure there's a reasonable middle ground compromise we can find here."

"No compromises," the protector said. "This isn't for me. I'm doing this for her. I have to. I have no choice. I'm sorry."

Haley saw a childlike form appear from backstage, running toward the protector and yelling, "Don't!" She knew she had to act but didn't know what to do. Her legs did, though. They sprung her into action before the gunshots rang out. One, two. Just like that. She was in the air between Lord Walker and the bullets when she felt the malfunctioning in her chest. Her fluids weren't flowing right, and her electrical system was shorting out. She thought she heard Lord Walker call her name before her auditory sensors ceased to function and her memories stopped writing themselves.

                         ও   ✷   ৶

XVI. Ansel

"I never should have trusted you, Pidgeon! I knew it." Ansel wanted to hit him, but he was too far away.

"No, Ansel," Pidgeon said, shaking his head. "That's not true. I helped you!"

"Helped me? You think knocking my friend out and kidnapping me is helping me?"

"No." Pidgeon shook his head. "We didn't kidnap you. We rescued you. And he's not your friend. He's a protector."

"He was a better friend than you ever were. He gave me jerky, and *he* didn't run away at the first sign of danger."

"He *was* the first sign of danger!"

"He wasn't dangerous! He said he could find my dad. He was trying to help me!"

"*Ha*! Yeah right." Pidgeon scoffed. "More like he was lying to you so he could arrest you."

"Arrest me for what? You saw that gun he had. You said they kill whoever they want, whenever they want. If I was in danger, I would have been dead already. And now I'm never going to meet anyone with a better chance of getting my dad back. You took that away from me, Pidgeon. You and your stupid friends."

"I—I didn—I'm sorry," Pidgeon said, almost too low for Ansel to hear. "I was trying to help."

Rosa came out of the room where they were holding Tom. She had a big smile on her face. "Whatever you said to him did the trick," she said. "He's actually listening to what we have to say, at least. He may end up doing what's best for you after all."

"What are you making him do?" Ansel asked. "He should be getting my dad back!"

"We told you, girl," Rosa said. "It's not in his power to do that. He can aim a gun, though. And thanks to you, we might be able convince him that doing just that is his best way of protecting you. So you did well, child. I appreciate that. Now you and little Richie here are going to have to leave until we're done with him. Come back tomorrow morning, and he'll be waiting for you. You got it?"

"But, she doesn—" Pidgeon protested.

"I'm not going anywhere!" Ansel stomped her foot.

"Now I mean it!" Rosa stomped hers back. "You have no investment in that protector, girl. He's no use to you. We thank you both for leading him our way, and you have our food in your stomachs to show that gratitude, but we'll be doing business with Mr. Pardy overnight. He'll be in one piece tomorrow morning if you still want him, but until then, I'm going to have to ask you to leave. Thank you."

"No, but you sai—" Pidgeon was going to go on, but Ansel grabbed his arm.

"You won't get away with this," she said, looking Rosa in the eyes.

"Oh, *ho ho*, girl." Rosa laughed. "Get away with what?"

"Whatever you're making him do. Whoever you're trying to kill."

"That, *girl*, is far enough," Rosa said. "I'll have you leave now, and I hope not to see your face again. If you do decide to come collect your *friend* tomorrow, make sure I don't see you when you do it. Do you understand me?"

"I understand better than you might think, ma'am," Ansel said, nodding. "Thank you for the soup. Let's go Pidgeon."

Pidgeon tried to protest, but Ansel dragged him out under the stern gaze of Rosa. Neither of them said a word until they had burst out into the open air.

"What was that Ansel?" Pidgeon said, tearing away from her grip. "You can't treat them like that."

"And why not?" Ansel asked, grabbing him again and dragging him into the first alley they passed. She let go of his arm and peeked around the corner.

"Because they're—they're—*old*," Pidgeon said, scrunching up his nose. "And they gave us food, they helped us. And they're my—my fri—"

"Helped us?" Ansel snapped. "You mean kidnapped."

"I told you. That was—"

"*To protect me.* Yeah. I know. But did you ever stop to think that maybe I don't need protecting?"

"I didn't—I wasn't—I just wanted to help," Pidgeon said,

lowering his eyes. "We do nothing alone. Remember."

"*Shhhh*. Of course I remember," Ansel whispered. "But shut up." She pulled him behind a dumpster and sat on the dirty ground, leaning her back against the cold metal trash can.

"Wh—What are y—" Pidgeon tried to say.

"*Shhhhh!*" Ansel put her finger to her mouth.

"What are—"

"*Shhh.*"

She waited a few more heartbeats then started to breath.

"What are you doing?" Pidgeon whispered.

"I'm finding out what they're making him do."

"But how?" Pidgeon said, shaking his head. "And why? They told you to—"

"Whatever they want him to do, they can't do it from in there, right? So I'm gonna wait until they come out then follow them to wherever it is they are going do it. That's how."

"No. But Ansel. You don't understand—"

"Pidgeon. If you don't shut up right now—you know—I'm glad you ditched me. You would suck at hunting. You'd scare all the prey away."

"But—"

"*No buts.* Okay. That protector was my last chance, Pidgeon. Even if he couldn't get my dad out, he might be able to get me in. Or—I don't know—get a message in or something. I have to try. You know that don't you? You would do the same thing if you were in my situation."

"Of course I would. That's why—"

"That's why I need you to shut up. So we can follow them without being noticed. That's how hunting works, Pidgeon. Or I guess you already said you didn't know anything about hunting. Well this is lesson one. Shut up so the prey doesn't run away."

"If *you* would just shut u—"

"Wait." Ansel held up a hand. "Look," she said, pointing down the alley. "It's the cat!"

Back toward Anna and Rosa's place was the black cat licking itself on the sidewalk.

"No way," Pidgeon said.

"Let's get it," Ansel said.

"But what abou—"

She was already gone, and he had to sprint to catch up. The cat bounded down the street straight toward the building they had just come out of. Ansel thought she had it when it stopped right in front of Anna and Rosa's apartment, but it jumped into the door and disappeared. Ansel stomped to a stop, and Pidgeon ran into the back of her.

"Where'd he go?" he said.

"Did you see that?"

"What?" Pidgeon said, looking around for the cat. "What happened?"

"It went through the door."

"Did they see you?"

"No. I mean it went *through* the door. The door wasn't open. The cat just disappeared."

"Like in the alley?"

"*When you ditched me.*"

"He disappeared then, too," Pidgeon said, ignoring her.

"I'm going in."

She had already reached out to touch the doorknob, but her hand disappeared before she felt it, cut off in a straight line along her wrist like the clouds behind the invisibility screen in the sky. She pulled her hand out and laughed when it reappeared.

"Ansel," Pidgeon said, taking a step back. "I don't think you should do that. You don't know how it's going to—I don't know—affect you."

"Pidgeon," Ansel said with a grin. "The Curious Cat just jumped through there. You know what that means."

"No, Ansel. I don't think that's the Curious Cat. I think—"

She didn't hear the rest of what he had to say, because she jumped through the door into a big, dark closet with clothes piled up all around her. The cat sat on a particularly high mound of clothes in front of her, licking itself.

"I found you," she said.

The cat meowed.

She took it as a challenge. "Oh, yeah? Well I will then." She pounced toward it, but it ran out of the open door which provided the only source of light in the room. She chased it and lost all her senses in the blinding white lights that she ran into. She was defenseless, and the cat was gone for sure. When her eyes finally adjusted, she saw a giant in a white uniform, pointing a gun at someone behind the lights. Her first instinct was to flee, but then she heard what the giant was yelling, she recognized the voice. He was telling them that he was doing this for her. She never asked him to do that.

"Don't!" she screamed as the gun went off. She tackled him to try to stop him before he fired again, and they landed in a tangle on the floor.

"What are you doing?" Tom pushed her up off of him and pointed his gun at her, the gun he had just used to shoot someone in what he claimed was protection of her. She had never seen a gun until she met him, and she had certainly never had one pointed at her. She put her trembling hands in the air and saw his finger flinch, but he didn't pull the trigger. Instead he pulled off his helmet and looked at her wide-eyed. "Ansel," he said. "I..."

She didn't want to hear it. She didn't care anymore. She squirmed away and ran toward the costume closet in the hope that it would let her pass back through the other way.

"Ansel!" Pidgeon grabbed her and hugged her on the other side. She broke away from him and ran down the alley to sit behind a dumpster and cry into her hands.

"Ansel!" Tom called.

When she heard his bootsteps getting closer, she swung her fists towards his face, but only got high enough to hit him in his padded stomach. "Get away from me!" she cried as she swung at him again.

"No, Ansel," Tom said, holding her at arm's length. "You don't understand."

"*You* don't understand! You pointed a gun at me. A *gun!*"

"I didn't know it was you. Why'd you stop me? How'd you even get there?"

"You said you were doing it for me."

"I was doing what you asked me to do."

"I never asked you to shoot anyone." Ansel scoffed. "Who'd you kill anyway? You fired *two* shots."

"I don't—"

"You don't even know?" Ansel shook her head. "Then how could you know you were doing it for me?"

"I don't know if I hit him, because *you* interrupted me. I was shooting at the person who owns the protectors. They have to do what he says, so ultimately, he's responsible. Right?"

"*You* have to do what he says," Ansel reminded him. "He owns *you*."

"I—No." Tom shook his head. "I tried to kill him, to free us."

"Like you *freed* my mother"

"No. I didn—"

"But you did. You did, and nothing you can do will ever change that!"

"No. But I—"

"No!" Ansel stomped her foot. "Leave me alone!"

She sprinted out of the alley and down the street, grabbing Pidgeon along the way. He protested a little, but not much, and soon they were running as fast as their feet could take them down the Green Belt. Pidgeon begged to stop not far along, but Haley wasn't going to stop ever. She didn't care if he did. She didn't care if he left her like everyone else. He had already done it once, and he would probably do it again: lie to her just like Tom did and disappear when she needed him the most. She was stupid to trust either of them in the first place. She would get to the end of the Belt by herself if that was what it took.

She heard his footsteps drop out from behind her, but she kept on running anyway. She would run far and fast enough to leave it all behind, Pidgeon and the stupid Concierges that he said were after her, Anna and Rosa and whatever plans they had to kill more people, and especially Tom with his attempts to put responsibility for murders he had committed on her. There was no one left in the world who cared about her. No one at all except for her...dad.

She slowed to a jog, then a walk, then fell to her knees in the middle of the sidewalk. Her dad was the only thing she had left in the world, but how was she supposed to get him back? How could she do it when she was all alone? *We do nothing alone.*

She caught her breath and wiped her eyes, then turned to see if Pidgeon was still chasing after her. Her heart dropped into her stomach when he wasn't there. She had run too fast. She had gotten too far ahead of him. He hadn't ditched her this time, she had ditched him.

The tears came back at the thought of it. Now she really was alone. Before, with him chasing after her, there was still someone driving her on, there was still someone who would be there if she tripped up or lagged behind. But now she had gotten so far ahead that he had given up on her. Now she had less hope than ever of finding her dad. She didn't even know where to go anymore. She didn't know where she was. She found herself turning this way and that with tears in her eyes, and the people walking around her couldn't even spare a second glance.

Then she thought she heard her name. She wiped her nose—and sniffled and coughed—and it came again. It *was* her name. It was Pidgeon's voice. He hadn't given up yet!

"Ansel!" he called. "Ansel, wait up!" He was jogging and out of breath when he finally caught up to her to sit on the ground in a huff. "I thought—I lost you," he said through deep breaths.

Ansel chuckled a little, her eyes watering again, and said, "*You* lost *me*?"

"Yeah." Pidgeon shrugged, still breathing heavily. "You're fast."

"Pidgeon," Ansel said, working hard to keep her voice from breaking. "Why'd you keep chasing after me?"

"Well." Pidgeon shrugged. "*Because.* Besides...You needed me, right? I mean, you need me." He nodded hopefully at her.

"But you don't need me, Pidgeon," Ansel said, scrunching up her eyebrows and wrinkling her forehead.

Pidgeon looked hurt, sitting on the sidewalk, searching for a piece of grass to tear to pieces. "I do though," he said. "Unless you don't want to take me along anymore."

"Take you along?" Ansel frowned.

"Yeah, well." Pidgeon stood up and brushed himself off. "I guess that was a prank or something. I'll—uh—I'll just get back to the orphanage then."

"No!" Ansel cried a little too desperately. She composed herself and went on. "I mean, you still want to do that? You still want to come with me?"

"Of course I do. I wasn't lying when I told you what they did to me. I have to get out of there, and I need your help to do it."

"But Pidgeon," Ansel said, crossing her arms and looking away from him. "I can't leave yet. I have to try to get my dad back. Tom may not be able to get him, but I believe him when he says my dad's still alive."

"Tom?"

"The protector."

"*Ansel*. He killed your mom. He admitted to that. How could you trust him?"

"I don't trust him," Ansel said, turning back to Pidgeon and shaking her head. "I believe what he's saying. There's a difference."

"How can you believe him, then?"

"Because he wouldn't admit to killing my mom and lie to me about my dad being alive."

"Unless he wanted to arrest you."

"*Then he would have already*." Ansel sighed. "You saw how big he was. He could have picked me up with one hand and carried me away. Haven't we been through this already?"

"Yeah, well…"

"Well I'm not negotiating. I'm gonna get my dad back whether you help me or not."

"But how?"

"I don't know."

"So what are you going to do next?"

"I don't know."

"So you want me to agree to nothing, then." Pidgeon scoffed. "What's the point?"

"I just want you to know that's what my goal is, that's all I care about. I'm getting my dad back and nothing else matters."

"Well, let's do it, then," Pidgeon said, finally standing from the sidewalk and looking ready to go.

Ansel rubbed her forehead. "Pidgeon," she said. "You do understand what this means, don't you."

He didn't answer. Ansel could tell he wanted another blade of grass to tear apart.

"He was taken by the protectors, he's being held by them, so we have to go to them to figure out how to get him back."

"Ansel, we can't," Pidgeon said. "You don't—"

"You don't have to come with me. That's why I'm telling you now."

"But how are you going to get to him? Anna and Rosa. They can—"

"I'm not asking them for help," Ansel said, crossing her arms. "You weren't there, Pidgeon. There were people there that were bigger than the protectors, but they were a different kind of big, wide, too. And Tom tried to kill one of them, but I stopped him."

"What are you talking about Ansel?" Pidgeon shook his head, confused.

"I'm saying Anna and Rosa aren't my friends. You can go back to them if you want, and I'll just find my own way to get my dad back."

"But they can get him. When you disappeared I tried to tell you. That was them. They transported you. They can get your dad the same way."

"I don't care, Pidgeon." Ansel shook her head. "I can't work with them. It may be asking too much, but I'm asking it. Like I said, you don't have to come with me."

"I just don't know how you're going to get him without them."

"I don't either, Richard. But I will."

"Well…" Pidgeon thought about it for a second. "If you'll take me with you, I'll still come, then."

"You don't have to."

"Then if you'll take me with you, I still want to come. I can't go back to the orphanage. I won't."

She realized how selfish she had been. She realized that they were standing in the middle of the street with people walking all around them. She realized how vulnerable they were. "You're right, Pidgeon," she said. "I'm sorry."

"You don—"

"We need to get out of here, though. We're not hunters anymore, we're prey. What road are we on?"

"I don't know," Pidgeon said, looking around for any indication. "Roman or something."

"Roman and what?"

"*I don't know*," he repeated. "I was trying to keep up with you, I wasn't taking the time to read every sign I passed."

"Fine," Ansel said. "Okay. Just follow me." She went down the closest alley she could find in an attempt to set her bearings. She could almost see the street sign across the way when it disappeared along with Pidgeon and the rest of the city around him. She turned and made to go back to find him when someone grabbed her from behind, lifted her off her feet, and carried her back the other way. "Put me down!" she demanded, kicking and struggling to get away, but whoever it was didn't respond.

They carried her through a short hall into a big room that had a lot of metal tables covered with glass tubes and jars which were filled with different colored chemicals. There were little flames coming out of metal tubes, heating some of the glasses of color, and the chemicals were bubbling and boiling with their essences all mixing together. It was the most interesting thing Ansel had ever seen. She stopped struggling, too busy gawking at the place to fight. She was still staring in awe at her surroundings when the person dropped her on the floor in front of a tall chair which was turned with its back facing her.

"Let me go," Ansel said, standing and turning to find a big mechanical arm with its hand open and waving. "Who—What are you?"

It kept waving.

"You won't get anything out of that one," a voice said behind her.

She turned to see a woman sitting in the chair which was now facing her. "Who are you?" Ansel said. "Let me go."

"Settle down, girl," the woman said.

"I'm not a girl!" Ansel said, crossing her arms.

"We're here to help you," the woman said.

"Who are you?"

"I'm someone trying to get back what they took from me. Just like you."

"You don't know anything about me," Ansel said.

"I know more than you think, girl. I know you were there at the Feast with that protector. I know you're running away from home. I know you're looking for something and we can give it to you."

"You would have started with that if it was true." Ansel scoffed.

The woman laughed. "You're a sly little one, aren't you? It's partially true. We can get it for you, but we don't know what it is."

"Then how do you know you can get it?"

"We can get it," the woman said with a grin. "Don't you worry about that. Whatever it is, we can get it."

"I want Pidgeon to be here, first," Ansel said. "Can you get that?"

"You want a pigeon?"

"No." Ansel sighed. "*Pidgeon*. Richard. He was following me, but he won't come through the portal or whatever. He never does."

"You've been through one before?" The woman raised an eyebrow.

"*Pidgeon*," Ansel said. "Bring him here. Prove you can get what I want when it's simple, then I'll bargain with you."

"I swear," the woman said. "You Sixers are more miserly than the owners. Fine. Popeye, you heard the *girl*. Go get Pidgeon and bring him in. What does he look like?"

"I don't know," Ansel said, shrugging. "A kid. Dirty clothes. Dark hair. Pimply face. He'll probably be standing exactly where I disappeared, wondering if he should follow me or not. That is if he hasn't run off already. You're losing time."

"Go on Popeye," the woman said. The metal arm rolled out through the door they had come in. "There. Popeye's fetching your pigeon. Now how *did* you get into the Feast?"

"How did you know I was there?"

"I'm not here to play games with you, girl. You interrupted an important operation. Tell me how you got there."

"I don't know what you're talking about. I just saw a bunch of really fat people acting like babies. I don't know how that could be important."

The woman laughed again. "No," she said, shaking her head and trying to suppress a grin. "That wasn't the important part, you're right about that, but I still need to know how you got there."

"I'm not saying anything until I see—"

"Hey! Let me down!" Pidgeon's voice cut her off. The big metal arm dropped him on the floor next to her. "Ansel," he said. "How did you get here?"

"Alright," the woman said. "Your boyfriend's here. How did you get to the Feast?"

"*I don't know*," Ansel said. "I tried to open a door, and I ended up in a costume closet."

"The closet," the woman said, more to herself than to Ansel. "Of course. I should have known."

"So you already know about the closet," Ansel said.

"Ansel," Pidgeon said. "Anna and Ro—"

"*Shhhh!*" Ansel elbowed him.

"Girl," the woman said. "We're going to find out one way or another. You might as well let your boyfriend tell us now. We'll be more likely to help you if you cooperate."

"I'm not her boyfriend," Pidgeon said, crossing his arms.

"That doesn't matter, boy," the woman said. "Shut up. Now, your Pidgeon is here. I held up my end of the bargain. So tell me, how *did* you get into the feast?"

"I told you!" Ansel stomped her foot.

"Where did it happen?"

"I don't know," Ansel said. "Pidgeon?"

"St. Roch and St. Claude," he said. "That's where it—"

"You heard him," Ansel said. "Now how are you going to get my dad for me?"

"And you say you tried to open the door, but you went through into a costume closet?" the woman asked.

"Am I here all alone?" Ansel said. "Yes. Then I heard the protector say he was doing what he was doing for me, so I tried to stop him. I never asked him to shoot anyone. He was supposed to help me get my dad back just like you are now. Right?"

"Right," the woman said. "But you'll have to wait for the Scientist for that."

"Wait for the what?" Ansel said, losing her temper. "Listen lady. Tell me how you plan on getting my dad back, or we're leaving."

Pidgeon didn't look as sure of himself as Ansel was. He was still staring at the mechanical arm, afraid it might grab him again. The arm didn't seem to be paying any attention to him, though. It was sweeping up something on the floor. The woman laughed and turned her chair around so Ansel could only see the back of it. "Well leave then, girl," she said. "See if I care. We already have what we want. You should have held your cards closer to your chest if you wanted to negotiate."

"You're lying!" Ansel rushed at her, but Pidgeon grabbed her arm and turned her around.

"*Uh*...Ansel," he said, staring at the door they had come in.

A dark-faced man that was even taller than Tom walked into the room. He was wearing a black suit, with a black piece of cloth tied in a bow around his neck, and a tall, black hat on his head. He looked down at them, took the single gold-rimmed lens out of his eye, and said, "*Ahem*. Rosalind. You didn't tell me our visitor—or should I say visitors—were here. Hello, ma'am. Sir." He took off his hat and did a little bow. "My name's Huey. It's so nice to finally meet you." He held out his hand and bent over at the waist so Ansel could shake it.

She looked at it, not sure what to do. She didn't know what to think of this giant. Why was he being so nice? And was that woman in the chair as big as he was? It was probably a good thing that Pidgeon had stopped her before she could hit the jerk.

"Go ahead," the giant said. "I won't bite."

She put her hand in his, and when he closed it around hers, her hand disappeared. She drew it away as soon as she could, and he extended his hand to Pidgeon.

"You, too, sir," he said. "Even though I know less about you than I do about our mutual acquaintance whose name I don't even know."

Pidgeon took his hand. "Hi, sir," he said. "I'm Pidg—er—Richard. And this here's Ansel—*Ow!*"

Ansel elbowed him. "I can speak for myself."

"Well." The giant looked between the two of them, studying their appearance. It made Ansel feel self-conscious so she started kicking at nothing. "Ansel and Richard. As I said, I'm Huey. And you've already met my sister, Rosalind."

"Sister?" Pidgeon said.

"She said you could get my dad back," Ansel said.

"Rosalind," Huey said. "The lab? Really. We couldn't find a more comfortable place for our guests to wait?"

"I'm plenty comfortable here, Mr. Douglas," the woman in the chair said. "Thank you."

"I'm sure you are," Huey said. "But I imagine our guests would prefer a soft seat and a nice view."

"Then why don't you take them to a more comfortable location," the woman said. "Popeye and I here need to get some work done anyway."

"Work?" Huey scoffed. "If ever there was a time to take a break, it was now."

"A break?" The woman scoffed back. "You always want to take a break, brother. And, like always, you will. So go ahead. I'll get my break when my work's done."

Huey sighed and shook his head. He turned back to Ansel and Pidgeon. "Her position is so much more difficult than mine," he whispered to them. "It's a shame she can't enjoy these small victories like I do. Anyway. Let's go then. The Scientist has a little more business to tend to, but she'll be right with you. Let's go somewhere more comfortable to wait. Shall we?"

He led them to a door, opened it, and showed them through. They walked out into the little hall she had come in through, and Pidgeon kept walking for a bit, but Huey said, "Uh—*ahh*—Richard. This way, please." He reopened the door they had just come out of, but the lab was gone, and in its place was a room with a big desk and a table surrounded by several tall, puffy chairs which Ansel forgot all about when she saw the view out the window making up the opposite wall. Pidgeon ran up to it and put his face against the glass to get a closer look. Ansel looked up at Huey first.

He nodded. "Go ahead."

She ran after Pidgeon and put her face on the glass, too. There was more green grass and blue skies than could be found in the entire Belt. There were hills, and trees she had never seen before, and she couldn't count the number of animals that were standing out in the open for anyone's taking.

"What is that?" Pidgeon asked.

"How do we get there?" Ansel asked.

Huey sat on one of the puffy chairs, putting his hat and lens on the side table. "That's a wilderness reserve," he said. "And getting there isn't hard, if that's what you decide you want."

Pidgeon kept staring. Ansel took her attention away from the view and sat in the chair across from Huey. She had to jump and struggle to climb up into it. Huey smiled as he watched her. When she was comfortable, she said, "That woman said you could get my dad. Can you?"

"Oh *ho*. No, Ansel," Huey said, shaking his head. "Not me. But the Scientist can. I have no doubt about that."

"The Scientist?"

"Yes," he said with a smile. "You'll meet her soon. She...She can give you anything you desire. Or at least she can tell you how to get it yourself."

"Whatever I want?"

"Within the bounds of reality, of course," Huey said with a nod.

"And you're sure she'll help?"

"Certainly, child. Just you wait and see."

XVII. Russ

Russ's heart wanted to jump out of his chest and flop on the floor. His lungs wanted to push all the air out and never suck in anymore. His brain wanted to close all channels and end any synapse firing for all of eternity. *He did it*!

Well. He did *something* at least. He had been told what to say when he was elected. He was supposed to be humble and show his gratitude at the owners' charity in providing for him to make the movies he made. That's what the speech director had told him to do. The writer had given him the same in the script. He didn't have much time to practice it, but he was used to that. He *was* an actor after all. It was his job to be ready to take on any role at a moment's notice. And this role—the role of the voice of the entire creative community—this was a role he had practiced—and fulfilled—for many years already. But he was too prepared, he could act too well. He had acted so well, in fact, that he had fooled them into believing that he was going to read their script and play their part, but that wasn't his intention from the opening credits.

He followed his own script. He said what *he* wanted to say. At least he thought he did. He did, right? They had to know his words meant more than what they said. Didn't they?

The elevator door slid open and Wes was in the hall, waiting for his own elevator.

"Russ!" he said. "Russ, Russ, *Rrrruuussssss*. Just the star I wanted to see. How'd it go, Russ, baby? You did great, huh? I mean, who am I kidding? I know ya did!"

"I did what I had to do," Russ said, hoping Wes caught the undertones. He was such a subpar director, he probably didn't.

"Oh. *Ho ho*. Russ, my boy. I know you did. You always do. Right?"

Russ didn't answer. He wanted Wes to get out of his way and let him through to his dressing room. It was as if the idiot didn't know that he couldn't get into his elevator until Russ left his own and sent it away. He grit his teeth and tried not to let his adrenaline drive him to punch Wes in the face.

"That's right," Wes said. "It is. I know it. Now. About that documentary, Russ. The slip, snap, clicking. You know. I—"

"Don't you talk to me about slip, snap, clicking!" Russ snapped.

"Wh—What?" Wes shook his head. "No," he said. "I—"

"No. *You* have no idea. *I* know what slip, snap, clicking is really like. I've seen a real assembly line. You have no place to tell *me* how they would act when you yourself have never stepped foot on a line in your life. I'd say it's safe for you to take my advice as the most viewed actor in the history of actors when I say an assembly line worker might act a little differently than you think they would. You got that!?"

"I—No," Wes said, waving his hands and shaking his head. "Woah *ho ho*. I—I have to follow the script, you know. And the producer tells me what to do. I didn't have a choice, Russ. It wasn't my decision."

"Yeah yeah," Russ said, shaking his head. "You do have a choice, though, Wes. Everyone has a choice. You have the same choice I'm making right now when I tell you to fuck off. Now, if you'll excuse me." He stepped out of the elevator and let the doors close behind him. "I'll be heading back to my room to get some rest." He opened the door to his dressing room and stepped in before Wes could respond.

There went his heart again, trying to escape from its rib cage. His legs wouldn't let him sit down, they paced back and forth between his couch and mirror.

As he walked toward the mirror, he marveled at how great he looked. Not just his hair, clothes, and makeup, though, it was something altogether more than that. His face seemed resolute and somehow more confident—if that was even possible.

As he walked toward the couch, he thought about what he could do next to keep this energy flowing. He wanted to go out and yell at Wes again, but Wes was probably long gone by now.

Ugh. But it felt so good. It felt so right. He went back in his head through all the times he should have done the same thing in the past, starting with those two stupid pieces he was forced to put together for the last documentary shoot. He should have said no then. He should have stopped working when the bell rang. He should have dashed off home where he really wanted to be.

He slumped down on the couch, angry at himself for going along with everything he was ever told for so long. He was out of breath and his heart rate was finally dying down. He rubbed his palms on his thighs and took a few deep breaths.

No.

He stood up and walked over to the window. He put his arm up on the glass and rested his forehead on it, looking out on the scene below.

His dressing room was at the top of the tallest building around. Well, not *the* top, but it was higher than any of the surrounding buildings. It was so high he couldn't even see the ground without sticking his head out the window, but the window didn't open so that wasn't an option anyway. He looked up at the fluffy white clouds, floating through the blue skies, then down at the windows below him. He wondered if the buildings were all windows with no walls. It looked like it from where he stood. He wondered what it would be like to live in a glass building, who would live there.

Now that he thought about it, he had never seen those buildings other than from his window. He had asked them to keep the real view, but he had never stepped outside to experience the view in person. How many years had it been? Well, what better time to finally do it than when he was doing what he never would have done before?

His stomach growled in response.

"Not now," he said to it. "*Not now, you*! Why do you have such poor timing?"

He opened the door to the hall and looked up and down it, hoping to see Wes, or a writer, or—even better—a producer to yell at, but the place was empty. They didn't have a speech to give, so they were probably all out eating a Christmas feast at some fancy restaurant. Too bad.

He pressed the button to the elevator, and the doors opened almost instantly. There, sitting cross-legged in a big velvet couch, dressed in red with fluffy white trim and wearing—as always—stark red lips was Jorah. He smiled and bounced his foot like he had been waiting in that pose for Russ to call the elevator.

"Jorah," Russ said, taken off guard.

"Russy, dear," Jorah said with a smile. "Don't look so surprised. I can visit my besty on Christmas, can't I? You know you're like family to me."

"Right," Russ said. "But I—"

"How did the speech go, darling?" Jorah said, ignoring him. "You wowed them, I'm sure, but what'd you say to do it?"

"I—uh—well..."

Jorah stood from the velvet couch and embraced Russ. "Where are you going, dear? Don't you have some time to tell your Jorah about it?"

"No. I was—" Russ remembered the speech he had just given and the people he had seen, he remembered yelling at Wes and the feeling it had given him. He decided to be direct instead of regretting this instance like he regretted so many others. "I was going to take a walk," he said.

"Take a walk?" Jorah frowned.

"A walk."

"Where?"

"Outside."

"*Oooh*. The park!" Jorah clapped his hands. "Let's go to Central Park. I love that one."

"No." Russ shook his head. "I—"

"You're so right," Jorah said, frowning. "It's too cliché, isn't it? *Hmmm*." He tapped his chin. "I know, *the Garden of Fortuna*. Have you ever seen it?"

"I've never seen my front steps," Russ insisted.

"*The Myfront Steppes*?" Jorah said, grimacing. "I've never heard of them. *Oooh*. Is it something new?" He grinned. "Who told you? Tell me all about it."

"No, Jorah." Russ sighed. "It's not a place. I mean *here*, the bottom floor of this building. Where does the door go out to? Those are my front steps!"

"Oh...*Ooohhhhh*! *Ugh*." Jorah put a face on like he smelled something terrible. "Really? That?"

"Well, I've never seen it, Jorah. I mean, I look at it through my window, you know, but I'm so high up I can't *see* it. Have you ever been down there?"

"*Psssh*." Jorah scoffed. "No, sweetheart." He shook his head. "And there's a good reason for that. There's nothing out there. All the good places to go are somewhere else, and that's why Fortuna invented elevators."

"No, Jorah," Russ said. "But there is something—" His stomach growled so loud it interrupted him.

"Oh, dear," Jorah said, putting a hand to his mouth. "Did you hear that? Your stomach says food, not walking."

"My stomach doesn't control me!" Russ stomped a foot, half-jokingly.

His stomach growled again.

"*It* begs to differ," Jorah said with a smile.

"*I* beg to differ!" Russ flared his nostrils, made his breath heavier, and scrunched his brows into the perfect "I'm in charge here" pose.

Jorah clapped and laughed. "Good show, Russ. Good show! Now. Do you have any reservations, or should we go back to your place?"

"No, Jorah," Russ said, crossing his arms to keep in character but slowly losing his resolve. "I'm going downstairs for a walk. I want to do this, and you can't stop me."

"Oh. No no, dear," Jorah said, shaking his head. "Don't you worry. I won't stop you. But I must tell you that I'm not going down there with you, and *you're* not going to make *me*."

Russ lost character at that. "Um," he said. "Wha—No. I wouldn't. I wasn't—"

"Okay, then." Jorah nodded. "Do you have time to tell me about your speech and eat a little Christmas feast, or is your walk too urgent for that?"

"No. I—" Russ *could* just go down there after he visited with Jorah. And his stomach *did* keep growling. There was really no reason to say no. "Of course I have time for you," he said. "But reservations are another story."

"That's perfect, dear." Jorah touched Russ's chest. "To be honest, I wasn't up to facing the public anyway. My makeup is just hideous today. I couldn't bear the stress." He looked away and covered his face.

Russ shook his head. He couldn't believe that Jorah actually meant what he was saying. His makeup was perfect, as always. "Oh no, dear," Russ said. "Your face looks like a painting. I wish I looked half as good as you, and *I* just came from in front of an audience."

"Oh, please, sweetheart," Jorah said, waving a hand at him. "You're just being kind. Your face is twice as beautiful as mine. It always is. You have the newer battle station model, dear. It's inevitable. But forget that. I want to hear about the speech. Come come." He grabbed Russ's arm and directed him back into the dressing room, closing the door behind them.

Jorah plopped Russ down onto the couch and went back to the printer. "So, dear," he said. "What do you want? Christmas ham and turkey. *Oooh*. And we have got to get potatoes. And stuffing. And deviled eggs. Fortuna, I love Christmas! *Thank you owners*. What do you want, Russ?"

Russ wanted to get up, but the couch was so soft it took too much effort to struggle out of. "I don't want—" he said.

"Pie!" Jorah cheered. "*Apple* pie." He clapped his hands. "That's what we need. *À la mode*. What did you say, dear?" He went on ordering food and stacking it on the serving cart.

"Jorah," Russ said as he did. "Do you ever wonder where all that stuff comes from?"

"Where it comes from?" Jorah pushed a full cart over to the couch and started putting everything on the coffee table in front of Russ. "It comes from the printer, silly. Where else would it come from?"

"No," Russ said, shaking his head. "I mean, where does the printer get it?"

"It makes it." Jorah shrugged.

"Out of thin air? Just pressing a few buttons is all it takes to create anything?"

Jorah sat on the couch next to Russ and started scooping food onto a plate. "I don't know, Russ," he said. "I'm not a scientist. I'm an actor. We have mechanic bots and engineers to take care of all that. What does it matter?"

"What does it matter?" Russ scoffed. "*What does it matter*? That's where we get everything we need to live, Jorah. You have one, too."

"*Duh*. I'm a pretty big star myself, Russ. In case you've forgotten."

"No. I haven't forgotten. That's the point. *We're both big stars*. We have the privilege of owning our own printers. But what about the community actors? What about the camera operators, and set builders, and extras?"

"What about them, Russ? They go to a store with a printer, and they buy what they need. No one ever starves. No one sleeps in the streets. What's the problem?" Jorah forced the plate—piled with food—into Russ's hands and started filling another plate for himself.

"Well," Russ said, ignoring the food. "Why do they have to buy anything if all it takes to make it is to press a few buttons on a printer?"

"Because they don't own printers. Why else would they be in the store?"

"Exactly," Russ said. "I mean, how do we get printers anyway? Does it just take a few button taps to make one of those, too?"

"I don't know." Jorah chuckled. "I've never ordered a printer from a printer. Maybe you should try it."

"That's—that's the point, though, Jorah! The point is that if it doesn't take anything to create anything, then why are we selling everything in the first place?"

"*Fortuna!*" Jorah sat back in the couch and started in on his food. "I don't care, Russ," he said with a full mouth. "I don't even know what you're talking about anymore. I just want to hear about the Feast and the speech. What were the owners wearing? Are they all still stuck in retro tuxedo land? Have they gotten fatter? Have their hats gotten taller? What did you say? And why don't you eat something to shut your stupid stomach up already?"

Russ looked down at the piles of food sitting on his plate. He picked up his fork and poked at the ham and turkey, all slopped in gravy. It reminded him of the food on the tables of the owners he had just ranted at. He pictured their fat fingers, stuffing their fat faces with equally gravy-slopped food, and their flabby cheeks chugging drinks until they couldn't speak straight or listen to a stupid short speech.

"Oh. I forgot the drinks," Jorah said, setting his plate on the table and standing to order some. "How does a mimosa sound? I know, I know, it's Christmas, we should be drinking eggnog, but *ugh*. I hate that stuff. Don't you?"

Russ poked at his food some more as Jorah got the drinks. He didn't want to eat anything, or drink mimosas, but he *was* hungry, and the food did look good. He poked at some turkey then scooped up some potatoes and took a big bite. The gravy felt warm and comforting as it slid down his throat and into his stomach. Why had he been fighting the food for so long? He squirmed back further into the soft couch and dug in.

"There you are, dear," Jorah said, setting a drink on the table in front of him and sitting back to his own plate. "Now that's the Christmas spirit. It's delicious isn't it?"

"*Ughm.* Yes. *Om nom.*" Russ didn't stop eating to talk. He couldn't stop eating.

"Now, dear," Jorah said. "Why don't you tell me, how was the big Christmas Feast? Were they still listening to the same old carols played by an old-timey symphony?"

"*Ugh.* If I ever have to hear an entire orchestra play *This Land is My Land* one more time, I think my head will explode."

"*Ah ha.* Oh, and what about *Hand Bless America*?" Jorah said. "The worst." He sang a line of the song in a nasally voice.

"*Fortuna.* Stop!" Russ almost spit out his food with laughter.

"I know it. And were they wearing those hats, too?" Jorah held his hand high over his head, puffing out his cheeks and crossing his eyes to illustrate the point.

"Fortuna, yes," Russ said, covering his mouth to hold back the laughter. "And *tuxedos.*"

"*Ugh.* Really?" Jorah frowned. "They are *so* conservative. Haven't they ever heard of fashion? Turns out trends change."

Russ laughed. He took a sip of his drink and set it back on the table. "At least I was there to brighten up the scenery. What do you think?" He struck a pose with his fork and knife in hand and plate on his lap.

"Oh. Just beautiful, dear," Jorah said, clapping. "*Be—e—au—ti—ful.* You always did know how to dress the best."

"Oh, you're too kind," Russ said, blushing.

"No, dear. I'm honest. It's not kind when it's honest. It's just true."

"Thank you for your honesty, then." Russ winked.

"Of course, dear. What else would you expect from your besty? Now. Tell me. What *did* you say to those fat fatties?"

"Well…" Russ poked at his food with his fork. "They gave me a script, you know, like they always do, and I did my job." He stuffed a few big bites into his mouth so he couldn't talk anymore.

"Yeah," Jorah said, nodding. "So. Did you read it? What did you say?"

"*Muhhm*," Russ replied, stuffing more turkey into his mouth.

"Russy, dear," Jorah said, tapping him on the arm with the back of his hand. "*Manners*! Now tell me. I want to hear *all* about it. It's the biggest, most exclusive event for the entire year. So drop the gossip."

"Oh...well..." Russ had to say something. He was going to have to say something on his show, too. But would they understand? Would they hold it against him? What if he started spreading what he had said and the protectors came back? What if he didn't spread what he said and all those people kept getting forced to work on the assembly lines? There wasn't any right course of action. "I don't know," he said, stalling for time. "I just crammed. Short term memory, you know. I can't remember."

Jorah put down his plate. "*Russ*," he said. "C'mon. I'm going to watch your show. You don't have to advertise to me. Just tell me what you said."

"Well, I...You know—I told them that we were thankful and all that. I don't know." Russ shrugged, eating some more.

"That's it? Just like that? *We're thankful. Bye!*" He said it in a monotone voice and waved his fork and knife around with jerky, robotic movements. "No more showmanship than that?"

"No," Russ said, shaking his head. "Of course not. I mean, I—well...I kind of went off script."

"*No*." Jorah gasped. Russ couldn't tell if he was acting or not, Jorah was one of the best. "Off script. You don't say?"

"Yeah. Well, you know...They had the usual patriotic, *Christmasy* thank you letter, filled with historical quotes, and I didn't want to give them another rerun."

"Oh no," Jorah said with a shrug. "How cliché. So what *did* you say?"

"I don't know." Russ shrugged. "That Christmas wasn't enough, you know. That we have to work our whole life to give them what they deserve." He stuffed some more food into his mouth.

Jorah looked him in the eyes. "*Give them what they deserve?* Did you say it just like that?"

Russ shrugged, stuffing his face some more.

"You know...they might have taken that the wrong way," Jorah said.

"What do you mean?"

"*Ha*! What do I mean?" Jorah laughed. "I think you know what I mean. *You badass you.*"

Russ spit some food out onto his plate. "Badass? No. I'm no—"

"Yes you are," Jorah said. "You said it exactly like that, didn't you? *We'll give you what you deserve.* I know you, Russ. Better than anyone. You can't help but act the part. You gave them a lecture. You want a feast as big as theirs, don't you?"

"I—*Wha*—No!" Russ shook his head. "That's not what I want at all."

"*Uh huh.* Sure, buddy." Jorah rolled his eyes. "I believe you. But I'm right there with you, too. They eat while we work. Who asked them to take it all, right?" He stuffed the last bite on his plate into his mouth and set to piling it with food again.

"What do we need more for, though?" Russ asked.

"What?" Jorah said, giving him a look. "You've got to be kidding me."

"I'm serious. Look at all this." Russ dropped his plate on the table, and it made a loud clatter, sending food everywhere.

"Russ!" Jorah snapped. "What are you doing?"

"Look at all this," Russ repeated, waving his hands as if he were displaying a prize on a game show. "We have more than we'll ever eat, we'll throw more than half of it down the trash chute, and you're talking about a bigger feast?" He stood up, red-faced and breathing hard.

"Now now, Russ," Jorah said. "Settle down." He set his own plate on the coffee table and guided Russ back to the couch.

Russ hesitated but gave in. He took a few deep breaths to calm himself. This was Jorah he was talking to. Jorah who he loved and who had no more idea of where the food he ate came from than Russ himself did only yesterday. It wasn't Jorah he was mad at, it was the people who kept Jorah ignorant of what the world was really like. "*I'm sorry,*" Russ said under his breath.

"Excuse me, dear," Jorah said, cupping his ear.

"I said I'm sorry," Russ repeated a little louder.

"Sorry, dear," Jorah said, nodding. "That's right. Now eat

your food so you'll feel better. You've barely touched it." He forced the plate back into Russ's hands.

"I don't wan—" Russ complained.

"I don't want to hear it," Jorah said. "*Eat!*"

Russ took a bite. Then another and another. His anger and frustration seemed to drift away. He forgot what he was even talking about in the first place.

"By the way, dear," Jorah said after some time of silence. "Did you get a chance to see the Christmas Award Ceremony pre-show? I mean, I know you had work to do, but they have a pretty nice green room over there, right? I'd imagine they'd have to. Wouldn't they? One day I hope to see it."

"Not if I can help it." Russ smiled and sipped his mimosa.

"Oh, you can't, dear," Jorah said. "Don't worry." He winked.

Russ flicked a glob of potatoes in his direction but missed by a long shot.

"*Ooh*, girl," Jorah said. "You're lucky you didn't hit me."

"Or what?"

"Nothing." Jorah shook his head. "Just don't. Now you got me all off script. Look at you. What was I talking about?"

"The red carpet show," Russ reminded him.

"Oh. *Ooohh whee*. Yeah, girl." Jorah put his plate down and took a quick sip of his mimosa. "You didn't see it, did you?"

Russ shook his head.

"No? Good. Well, you'll never believe this. Okay. So Paige. You know her, right? Cute little girl. Well she was wearing the most sheer, see-through dress you have ever seen. I swear, Russ, it was made out of saran wrap or something."

"*Ugh.*" Russ sighed. "She didn't."

"*She did.* And—*predictably*—the papos ate it up. I swear to you, I've seen more angles of her vagina today than my battle station back home gives me angles of my face."

Russ spit out some mimosa, and this time, he managed to hit Jorah square in the face. "*Ha!*" he laughed.

"*Ugh.* Sweetheart," Jorah said, wiping his face and standing up. "Well, now the jokes not even true, because your battle station is gonna give me more views of my face than I've ever seen of her anything." He swept over to Russ's battle station to redo his makeup.

"I'm sorry, dear," Russ said. "But that was funny. And oh so typical. I mean, if I went out in saran wrap, I bet you'd be saying the same thing about me."

Jorah sat back on the couch, his face in perfect condition. "I don't know, Russ," he said, shaking his head. "Is there something you're not telling me?"

"What?"

"I was under the impression you didn't have a vagina to see." Jorah grinned. "Silly me. In the future I won't assume. After all, ass out of you and me and all."

"No, Jorah. *Ugh*. I would tell you if I did that! We'd have a party. You know me." He slapped Jorah on the arm. "You know what I mean."

"Yes, dear," Jorah said, smiling wider and chuckling. "I *do* know what you mean." He grinned. "And I agree. That's why I wanted to get your opinion on my New Year's Eve outfit decision."

"You can't be serious." Russ shook his head, matching Jorah's grin.

"Well," Jorah said. "It's not going to be saran wrap *exactly*. I was thinking of going for more of a silhouette, you know. Leave a little to the imagination. There's this LED fabric. Have you heard of it?"

"That stuff from Tesla?"

"Yeah, girl," Jorah said, reaching over to touch Russ's arm. "The best new designer in the business. She says I can make it so the lights turn the dress into a shadow play screen. You'll be able to see every little movement underneath." He stood and did a little dance with a lot of hip gyration to illustrate his point. "What do you think?"

"It *is* interesting," Russ said, putting his plate down to think about it. "Definitely more subtle than the saran wrap, full see-through dress. And I really like the shadow play imagery."

"I know, right?" Jorah said, smiling and full of himself. "I've been practicing getting it to move like a puppet, too." He danced some more.

"Well," Russ said, tapping his chin. "I'd say as long as you incorporate some of the history of shadow puppetry into the design of the dress—and your makeup and accessories, of course—you'd attract more attention and be less gratuitous about it."

"*Ooh, dear*. I love it!" Jorah's voice got so high it sounded like he was going to scream. "We'll make the rest of the dress the scenery for my little actor. You see, that's why I always come to you for fashion advice, sweetheart. You never fail me." He hugged Russ, spilling food off his plate.

Russ blushed. "I just helped you edit, dear. It was your idea."

"And humble, too," Jorah said, smiling. "No wonder you're the most viewed actor in all of history. Who wouldn't want to watch the perfect human being?"

"Oh, now," Russ waved a hand. "That's going a little too far."

Jorah put his plate down and stood up. He pulled Russ up, too. "Let's go to Tesla now," he said. "Tell her the idea. She can get started on it right away."

"Don't you think she's at a feast, though," Russ said. "It *is* Christmas."

"No, dear," Jorah said, shaking his head. "*Uh uh.* She's a designer, and a new one at that. *For us*, she's free. It'll be like a Christmas present for her."

"Yeah. I guess, but—"

"And we can take a walk after that," Jorah said. "We'll go out to the Garden of Fortuna. You'll love it."

"I did want to go for a walk..."

"It's settled then." Jorah smiled. "Let's go."

੬ ✂ ੭

XVIII. Mr. Kitty

Tillie was all packed up. She peeked her head out of the bedroom door and sighed. Mr. Kitty could tell she was upset when she opened the front door and called back, "I'm leaving, dad!" There was no answer, so she added, "Don't even try to stop me!" and slammed the door.

Mr. Kitty had to react fast to prevent his tail from being crushed. "Hey," he hissed.

"Sorry, Kitty. I—I didn't see you," Tillie said through her sobbing.

Mr. Kitty tried to rub up against her leg as she tried to walk, but he ended up tripping her. She landed with a thud in the grass, her backpack narrowly missing him.

"Sorry," Mr. Kitty meowed.

Tillie stayed face down in the grass, sobbing. Mr. Kitty climbed up onto her butt and kneaded it. She sobbed a little more, then turned over and scooped him up onto her lap. "Mr. Kitty," she said. "No one will ever believe me. Shelley didn't, Dad didn't and he should know already, who else would when I can barely believe myself?"

"I do," Mr. Kitty meowed.

"Oh, I bet you'd believe me if you understood what was going on," Tillie said.

"I do," Mr. Kitty repeated.

"Mr. Kitty, you're so talkative," Tillie said, pinching his cheek with a smile. "It's like you know what I'm saying. Do you understand me?"

"I do!" Mr. Kitty said one more time.

"Oh. I know you don't," Tillie said. "No one here does." She sighed and put him on the grass, then stood and hoisted her backpack up onto her back with a groan. "But there's still hope, Mr. Kitty. There's always hope. I'll go back to my dorm and ask some of my friends there, and if they don't believe me, then I'll just have to find that woman again. That's all I can do, right?"

Mr. Kitty didn't answer. He thought it sounded like an okay plan, if that was what she wanted to do. She could get more evidence from her dad's computer before she left, that way people would be more easily convinced, but even if she could understand his advice, she probably wouldn't break her dad's trust like that, so there was no point in suggesting the idea. Instead, he ran ahead through the yard toward the public elevator.

"I guess you approve," Tillie said, lugging her backpack along to catch up. "Just wait until you see my dorm, Mr. Kitty. You're gonna love it. There are no pets allowed, but you can keep quiet about it, can't you?"

"I'm a ninja," Mr. Kitty meowed, letting her pass him then bounding out in front of her again.

"You're gonna love my roommate, too," Tillie said with a smile and a new bounce in her step. "I can't wait. I'm so glad you're coming with me, Mr. Kitty!"

There was no line at the elevator—there usually wasn't in this neighborhood. Tillie called it, they stepped in, and she said, "Parade grounds." She took a deep breath. Mr. Kitty knew she was nervous about being called crazy again, so he rubbed his head on her ankles and purred. She smiled down on him as the doors slid open.

Here there was a line, a young, loud, raucous one. Mr. Kitty jumped, and hissed, and puffed up his fur at the sound of it. The line laughed at him, and Tillie said, "C'mon Kitty. It's alright."

She forced her way through the crowd which was trying to push their way onto the elevator before Tillie and Mr. Kitty could get off. Mr. Kitty slipped through the wake she made, out into a big, open, grassy circle that was lined all around with oak trees. There was a tall flagpole in the center of the field, surrounded by short walls with writing on them, and scattered around that were groups of humans playing frisbee, dogs running free without leashes, and other groups of people running around with brooms between their knees, throwing balls at each other. Tillie was right, Mr. Kitty did love this place. Why had he never been here with her before?

"Mr. Kitty," Tillie called, walking away from the green field. "My dorm's this way."

Mr. Kitty tore his attention away from all the new and interesting things to follow Tillie between gravel covered buildings and oak trees, past two big hills, down through a shady cypress swamp, to a patch of three-story buildings in the shade of a tall, ugly cement building. Tillie went up to the door of one of the shorter buildings and scanned a keycard. The door unlocked, and they went up a flight of stairs into a small apartment with three doors and a kitchen. Tillie tossed her backpack on the floor in front of the TV and walked around the kitchen with a sigh, checking the fridge and cupboards while Mr. Kitty crept around the place, sniffing everything and rubbing his scent on whatever called for it—most every surface.

"*Ugh*. There's nothing to eat!" she said.

Mr. Kitty jumped up onto the counter to rub his face on the sink and smell all the corners of the kitchen when the door opened and a human came in to throw her bag on the couch.

"There's nothing in this kitchen," Tillie said. "Do you have any paw points left this week?"

"No, girl," the human said. "We spent it all before you left. I thought you were supposed to be staying at your dad's anyway."

"Yeah, well…" Tillie shrugged.

"And is that a cat in the kitchen? *On the counter*."

"Oh. Yeah," Tillie said. "Well..." She scooped Mr. Kitty up and held him over her shoulder, patting his back. "This is Mr. Kitty. He's my cat. He's just visiting though."

"I like cats," the human said. "Just not on the counter."

"You hear that, Mr. Kitty?" Tillie said, patting him a few more times and kissing him on the head. "No counter." She put him on the floor, and he went over to jump on the coffee table and lick his coat clean, paying special attention to the spot she had kissed.

"What are you doing back anyway?" the human asked. "It's Christmas."

"Yeah, well…" Tillie said. "*That*. I don't know. I got into an argument with my dad. I thought you were supposed to be at your parents' house, too. What happened to your Christmas tradition?"

"Plans changed. I got the perfect Christmas gift—which I have to be here for."

"You have to be here?" Tillie raised an eyebrow.

"Enough about me. Why are *you* back?"

They both sat on the couch. The human reached out and pet Mr. Kitty. He let her go ahead for a few pats then jumped onto Tillie's lap.

"Well...Like I said," Tillie said. "I got into an argument with my dad."

"He's a manager, isn't he?" the human said. "I mean, I *know* your last name's Manager and all, but that's his job, too. Right?"

"Right," Tillie said, rolling her eyes. "That's kind of what we were arguing about."

"Yeah. It's tough dealing with managers," the human said. "No offense," she added hastily.

"Oh. No," Tillie said, shaking her head and waving a hand. "No n—n—no no. None taken. Believe me. I know better than anyone. He is my dad after all." She chuckled. "I guess you don't have the same problems, though. *Huh*? Your parents are lobbyists, aren't they?"

"Yeah, well," her roommate said. "I'm lucky enough to agree with their analysis of the economy, but there are some lobbyists out there who might be harder to live with than a manager."

"*Ugh*. Yes," Tillie said with a big sigh. "Have you heard Lobbyist Peterson's latest proposal?"

"Let me guess," her roommate said. "Take more resources from higher education and healthcare to funnel them into administration where they're *really working*."

"Pretty much exactly that," Tillie said, grimacing. "Disgusting, am I right?"

"Disgusting is exactly right," her roommate said, nodding. "That's why I'm lucky. My parents are doing everything they can to fight against jerks like that. Me, too. Soon."

"I wish my dad understood." Tillie shook her head. "I tried to tell him, but he didn't even believe me."

"You tried to tell him what?"

"I—*uh*—I don't know…" Tillie said. "I don't think I should be talking about it."

"Is it classified?"

Mr. Kitty felt Tillie tense up under him. "How did you know?"

"Tillie. I know we haven't been roommates for long, but I want you to know that you can trust me."

"What are you talking about?" It felt like Tillie was about to jump out from underneath Mr. Kitty. He prepared himself to leap off in case she did.

"What did you argue with your dad about?" her roommate asked.

"I...I can't."

"You can, Tillie. I already know. Was it about the 3D printers?"

"I—uh—How did you know?"

"Because I *know*."

Tillie's eyes grew wide. Her mouth fell open. Her roommate stood up before she could say anything. "Wait." She closed the blinds and turned on the TV at full blast, then added some loud music on top of that before sitting back on the couch and scooting extra close to Tillie. "Okay. Go ahead," she said

"I don't—What was that?" Tillie asked. "Why'd you do that?"

"If you're going to say what I hope you're going to say, then we don't want to be recorded. This way all they hear is white noise."

"I—*uh*..." Tillie frowned. "I never would have thought of that in my life. I've been telling people, though. Do you think they recorded me already?"

"I don't know," her roommate said with a shrug. "Maybe. I don't know if they're doing it now. I haven't heard what you have to say."

"Oh. Yeah," Tillie said, hitting herself in the head. "Right...Well, you know the printers, right. What am I saying? Of course you do. You just said that. Well you know that they don't rearrange matter or whatever, right?"

Her roommate nodded.

"Yeah, well, my dad did, too. Apparently. But I—Well, I...Do you ever watch Logo's Show?"

"Sometimes, yes, but I try to stay away from gossip news."

"Yeah, well, did you see his latest episode?"

Her roommate shook her head. "No. But I saw the emergency broadcast after."

"Yeah, well, okay. So you know then. Well, you know what he was talking about at least. You heard about the woman who tried to talk to him on the streets, that is."

"I have."

"Yeah, well," Tillie said, nodding. "Do you know what she said?"

"That humans work on the assembly lines."

"And that's true, Emma," Tillie said, looking her roommate in the eyes and nodding.

"I know, Tillie," Emma said.

"I know it sounds hard to—*What*?"

"I know that humans work on the assembly lines," Emma said. "I know that the assembly lines actually exist and not just in Russ Logo's world. That's why I'm not home with my parents. That's what my Christmas gift is all about."

"Your gift is about the humans on the assembly lines?" Tillie looked confused.

"No." Emma shook her head. "Not exactly. But yes. My gift is that I finally get to do something about it."

"But—I—How could you know? What could you do?"

"I've known for a long time," Emma said. "My parents have taught me the truth since I was a child. That's why I'm not surprised."

"But how? My dad didn't even know and he's a manager. They're supposed to know the economy like the back of their credit cards. How could he miss something as big as humans on the assembly lines?"

"You said you argued with him?"

"He said I was mistaken." Tillie scoffed. "As if I didn't know what I had seen with my own two eyes. He said I was being *emotional*."

"*Ugh*. You see, Tillie. It's not that he missed it, or that no one ever told him. He chooses not to know. They all choose to ignore it. I mean, how did you find out?"

"I saw a picture on his computer," Tillie said. "I knew they weren't robots." She shook her head, looking away from Emma for a moment. Mr. Kitty purred and rubbed his head on her hands.

"A picture?" Emma asked.

"Of a factory accident."

Emma looked away now. Mr. Kitty climbed over to her lap and rubbed his face on her arm.

"So how could he not figure out if I did, right?" Tillie said.

Emma still didn't answer. She didn't look at Tillie. She just pet Mr. Kitty's head while he purred.

"You said you were going to do something about it," Tillie

said. "But how?"

"You know the answer to this one, Tillie."

"The woman in the alley?"

"The Scientist."

"No." Tillie shook her head. "Who's that?"

Emma shrugged. "No one's entirely sure. She's the Scientist."

"And she wanted you to help her, too?"

"I've never met her in person. She offered my parents an opportunity, and now that opportunity extends to me. On Christmas Feast day nonetheless. Perfect timing."

"Christmas Feast?" Tillie said, frowning. "You mean Christmas?"

"Christmas Feast is what they call it in Inland."

"Inland?"

"So you don't know everything then," Emma said. "But I can tell you. As long as you don't tell anyone else. No one."

"You can trust me," Tillie said, zipping her lips and crossing her heart.

"First," Emma said. "Have you ever seen an assembly line worker in real life?"

Tillie shook her head. "Not besides the one I talked to."

"What about an actor, or camera operator, or scientist?"

"I thought robots—"

"Robots don't do much," Emma said. "Have you ever seen one?"

"No, but they—"

"And you watch Logo's Show. Don't you ever wonder why the restaurants he talks about don't exist?"

"Because it's just a TV show," Tillie said. "It's not real."

"But it's not just a TV show. What about the assembly line workers? You know that they're real. Where are they? Logo's Show takes place in another world, Tillie. The restaurants do exist, but we have no way to access them. They're in Outland 3 and we're in Outland 2. There's no way through except the elevators, and our elevators don't go that way."

"And that's how I ended up meeting with that woman," Tillie said, shaking her head.

"And that's how I knew what you would tell me," Emma

said. "Look, I can't stand this blaring noise anymore. Let's go for a walk. Your cat might enjoy it, anyway." She pet Mr. Kitty who had all but fallen asleep in her lap. He yawned and stretched his paws out in front of him.

"Yeah. I—*uh*—Sure," Tillie said. "Let's go." She stood up, and Mr. Kitty jumped onto the coffee table to stretch some more.

Emma stood and said, "One second." then went back to her room and came out wearing a big hooded sweatshirt. "Alright. Let's go," she said, and they went downstairs and out of the dorm.

Emma was right, too. Mr. Kitty did need a walk. He was too cooped up in their small dorm room. He ran through the grass, ate a few leaves of it in the falling sun, and almost lost Tillie and Emma in his excitement. He smelled another tree and clawed it a few times before running to catch up with them.

"I don't know," Tillie said. "I couldn't do anything alone, but it might be different with you there."

"You *can* do it," Emma said. She looked around to see if anyone was watching. "You don't even have to do anything. Just come with me. Look." She pulled a pouch out of her sweater pocket and handed a little disc to Tillie.

"What is this?" Tillie asked, turning it over in her hands.

"*A bomb*," Emma whispered to her.

Tillie stopped in her tracks. Mr. Kitty saw a bug and jumped on it. How would Tillie respond to this? She had finally found someone who believes her, but it had to be someone who might be a little crazy herself. He let the bug fly away and caught up with them again. Emma had scooted Tillie along so she didn't make a scene.

"Of course I wouldn't have done it if it was dangerous," Emma said. "Well, needlessly dangerous." She winked.

"I would call handing me…" Tillie leaned in and lowered her voice. "*A bomb* needlessly dangerous."

"I told you it can't go off yet," Emma said. "They have to be activated, and they're on a timer."

"And how exactly are...*they* supposed to help anything?"

"It all goes back to the division between the worlds," Emma said. "There are these machines that bend space and—"

"*Woah ho ho*. Wait a minute there," Tillie said, stopping again. "Bend space? What are you talking about? You can't bend space."

"No," Emma said, shaking her head. "*I* can't. But they can. The Scientist can. That's how the printers work. And the Scientist can get us to some of the Walker-Haley field generators which are used to do just that. All we have to do is rip, stick, and press then get out of there."

"Walker-Haley field whats? Bending space?" Tillie shook her head. "I don't know, Emma. It all sounds a little crazy. I don't—"

"Look," Emma said, cutting her off. "Come here." She dragged Tillie by the arm to sit down on the concrete steps under the flagpole. They had walked all the way out to the center of the parade grounds, far enough away from everyone so that no one could hear their talking. The field was clearing out the darker it got, anyway, and the sun was all but gone. "Have you taken any science classes in college yet?" Emma asked.

Tillie shook her head. "I took AP science senior year."

"Well, you might be able to understand," Emma said. "Do you remember…"

Mr. Kitty didn't care to hear the explanation. He didn't care how things worked. He only wanted to know what they did and how that would affect him. And since he already knew the gist of what Emma was going to say, he had no reason to sit there and listen to the lecture. He knew it would be a long one, too, explaining how to bend space. Humans never could just walk to get from here to there. No, that was just too much work. But bending space so here *is* there, now *that* was less effort. Right? Mr. Kitty would never understand.

He went off to chew the grass and sharpen his claws on a tree, then chase some squirrels—who were so much harder to catch than those pigeons. He climbed up a tree after one, to show it that he could, and licked himself on a branch while the squirrel cowered at the top of the tree. He climbed back down, and Tillie and Emma were standing from their lesson, intent on doing something.

"Come on, Mr. Kitty," Tillie called, motioning with her hand as they walked toward the elevator.

Mr. Kitty sprinted to catch up with them, dodging through the legs of passing students. The door to the elevator slid shut behind him, almost clamping on his tail. He licked it and sat down.

"Where to?" Tillie asked. "I mean, how do we get there?"

"The Scientist takes us," Emma said.

"But what do we tell the elevator?"

"The struggle itself is enough to fill one's heart."

The elevator fell into motion, and almost as soon as it did, the doors opened. There was nothing to see but a cement wall, but Mr. Kitty recognized the stale oil smell. Tillie and Emma's feet clanged on the metal floor as they stepped out of the elevator.

"I've been here before," Tillie said. "Well, not *here* but here. A place just like this. I got lost when I tried to go back and talk to the assembly line worker again. Mr. Kitty found me."

"I hate this place," Mr. Kitty meowed, looking at the wall where the door they had just come from used to be.

"This is one way through the fields to the other worlds," Emma said. "There are usually security and mechanic bots patrolling. Today, however, this bay has no one, courtesy of the Scientist. Now come on."

She jogged down the tunnel with her footsteps echoing back behind her. Tillie took off after her. Mr. Kitty rubbed his face on the wall where the door was, giving it one last smell, then tore apart his claws trying to catch up with them.

They went through the curving tunnel, down a few flights of stairs, then through another long tunnel to a big metal door that was painted with yellow and black stripes. They stopped to catch their breath, and Mr. Kitty licked his paws to rid them of the pain from running on the metal grating.

"*Ugh.* Unseen Hand," Tillie said through gasping breaths. "I'm *so* out of shape." She hunched over, resting her hands on her knees and her back on the wall. "I haven't exercised like that in...well...let's just say a long time."

Emma was barely out of breath. "Physical training is important if you want to help free the assembly line workers," she said. "If someone sees us, we'll have to run all the way back. And this time we would be going *up*stairs."

Tillie took a few more deep breaths. "You're really serious about this, aren't you?"

"This *is* serious," Emma said solemnly. "If you're here, you should be serious, too. If we were found...Well, just know that we don't want to be found."

"No," Tillie said, shaking her head and waving her hands. "No no. I—No, I know. That's why I've been freaking out. Because

I know how serious it is, you know. But that's the point, isn't it? This is so real and big, how can we do anything about it?"

"That's what I'm supposed to show you."

"So she asked you to do this then? The woman who asked me to—to do something for her."

"Not for her, Tillie," Emma said, shaking her head. "For *us*. For the assembly line workers. For the betterment of humanity. This is bigger than the Scientist. She only helps. We do the real work to tear down the system." She pressed a few buttons on the keypad next to the door, and the doors slid open with a hiss. Mr. Kitty jumped back and puffed up his tail at the sound of it.

"How'd you do that?" Tillie asked.

"That's another way that having the Scientist on our side helps," Emma said. "And in getting these." She pulled out the pouch of discs. "Now, come on."

Inside was a squat room with lights and buttons flashing all over the ceiling. The ground was smooth and hard. It beat the metal grating but was worse than vinyl in Mr. Kitty's opinion. Tillie and Emma had to duck to walk around. Emma watched Tillie marvel at the size of the place and the flashing lights.

"What is this?" Tillie asked, still walking in circles and staring up at the flashing ceiling which almost seemed to go on forever.

"This is the Outland 6 central hub," Emma said. "Every single Walker-Haley field generator that separates Outland 6 from Outland 5 converges right here in this room. This is the only thing keeping the two worlds apart."

"All of it in one room?" Tillie scoffed.

"Only for Outland 6. Outland 6 only has connections to Outland 5, so the owners don't really care if there's a little crossover. Not as much as they care about crossover in the other worlds, at least."

"So that's what you're going to do with the—*uh*—discs," Tillie said. "Destroy this?"

"That's what *we're* going to do. We're merging 5 and 6, transforming them into a whole new world. We'll be creating just as much as we destroy."

"And so what?" Tillie said. "We blow this room up to connect the two worlds, then what happens? They come back and separate them again? What about us? What about the actors? What about everyone else in the world—or, *er*—worlds?"

"This is the grand finale," Emma said. "The big bang. So much more is happening across the worlds as we speak, but you and I get to end the festivities with a fireworks show."

Tillie looked around at everything one more time. Mr. Kitty rubbed his face on her ankles. "So you're really going to do something to stop them," she said.

"It's wrong, Tillie. We reap the benefits from their exploitation. We can try to stop it, or we might as well be exploiting them ourselves. We're complicit."

"*Nous devons craindre le mal,*" Mr. Kitty meowed. "*Mais il ya quelque chose que nous devons craindre plus que le mal. C'est l'indifférence de la bonne.*"

Tillie scooped him up. "It sounds like Mr. Kitty agrees," she said.

"Do *you* agree?" Emma asked.

Tillie put Mr. Kitty back on the ground and he licked himself. "I want to," she said. "But it sounds too good to be true."

"It's not, though," Emma said, scoffing. "We're not even doing that much. Not by ourselves at least. We're a distraction. And there will be a lot more to do after this. Then you'll get to see that it's just shitty enough to be true."

Their laughs echoed through the squat room.

"So that scientist," Tillie said. "She really could use those pictures to do good."

"What pictures?" Emma asked.

"She didn't tell you?"

Emma shook her head.

Tillie took a deep breath, stomped her foot, and said, "Yes. I do. I *do* want to help. What do we do?"

Emma smiled wide. "Good," she said. "Great. Take some of these." She got a handful of discs out of the pouch and handed half to Tillie. "Start here with the red light. See it?" She pointed one out and waited for a response.

"Yeah. Right," Tillie said, nodding.

"Peel the paper backing off, stick the disc on the light, press the button, then go five red lights down and do it again," Emma told her, pointing out where each step would take place as she spoke.

"Got it?"

"Got it," Tillie said.

"When you get to the end, go five across and come back," Emma said, pointing some more. "I'll get the rest, then we get out of here. Ready?"

Tillie nodded.

"Then let's have some fun!"

They sprinted into action. Mr. Kitty rolled on his back and kicked at the air, then chased them around as they did their rip, stick, pressing. Emma finished a few discs before Tillie, even though she went further into the room and placed more of them, and when they were both done, they sprinted out of the tunnel, up the stairs, and to the elevator with Mr. Kitty close behind them. They all three collapsed laughing, coughing, and breathing heavily onto the floor of the elevator.

"I can't believe we just did that," Tillie said.

"I can't believe I finally got to," Emma said.

"What do we do next?" Tillie asked.

"We go back home like nothing happened," Emma said. "We keep our ears open for any news of the rest of the operation. And mostly we wait."

"*Ugh.* Wait?" Tillie frowned.

"It shouldn't be long now," Emma said. "The gears are in motion."

"I can get those pictures while we wait," Tillie said.

"Does that mean you want to join us?" Emma asked with a smile.

"I'm not stopping here," Tillie said, laughing again. "Parade grounds."

The elevator fell into motion, and the doors opened onto the big empty field. Tillie and Emma left, and they didn't notice when Mr. Kitty didn't follow them. Tillie didn't need him anymore, they had each other. The doors closed, and he let the elevator take him to wherever it would.

ᖷ   ✂   ᖶ

XIX. Ellie

She pounded her fists against the cold metal until her knuckles were bloody and numb. She flung her body at the door in vain and slouched down sobbing uncontrollably with her cheek on the rubber conveyor belt.

The door was closed. Her chance was gone. She had waited too long to bring her son to the beach, then she waited too long to live the experience for him. She failed again and again. He wasn't even alive, and she continued to fail him.

She wept and wept with her cheeks on the belt before she remembered that she had already set some of the discs. She picked one out of the pouch and pressed the little red button to see how long she had left. Five minutes. *Five minutes.* Was it worth it to try to leave? What did she have to live for anymore? If she stayed here and held the disc tight, they would all think that she decided to stay on the beach. She would disappear from existence just like that, erased from memory. She almost felt calmed at the thought of it.

But she didn't. She still hadn't kept her promises. She could probably set more of the discs before she left. And if they could get her to the beach once, they could do it again. Couldn't they? By that time she could do enough to pay for the privilege and not have to worry about making the same stupid mistake and missing her chance again. She had to do something. She couldn't give up and wait for the explosion to erase her responsibility. That would be doing even more of a disservice to her son.

She opened her eyes and picked herself up to jump down off the conveyor belt. The disc said three minutes now. She peeled off the paper backing, stuck it to the screen which told her what particular piece of crap was supposed to come down the conveyor belt every day, the machine that guided her work, the robot who used her, and she sprinted out of the hall, down the stairs, and out of the building entirely, not stopping until she left the front door, and then only slowing to a fast walk—she didn't really have time to act nonchalant. She was only half a block away from the building when she heard the explosion.

Her heart pounded at the sound, and her feet tingled. She could feel the ground moving beneath her, as if the whole world was shaking. She felt like she wanted to run, but she stopped herself. Then she wanted to look back. She stopped herself from looking at first, then thought it might be more suspicious not to look and decided to turn and see what she had done. An entire floor of the building—not as high as she thought it would be—was blown out, but the rest of it was still standing. There was a blasted-out gash, bleeding rubble, water, and electricity. Not as much damage as she had expected, she thought the whole building would come down, but she had left a mark at least.

She turned and hurried on her way toward the elevator to ride it to her bar. What else was there for her to do? She had just laid bombs in her workplace and blown it to smithereens. She had been to the beach and back in less than fifteen minutes. She had kept all her promises and broken all of them all at the same time. What was she to do but get a drink and enjoy the rest of Christmas?

The public elevator had no one. The street to the bar was empty. The bar was dark when she got there. It was closed. Of course it was closed. Even the bartender had a family to spend Christmas with. Even Gertrude. Everyone did. She kicked the door.

Stupid stupid stupid. She had drank her last beer and eaten her last egg before she went on her mission. She wasn't supposed to be coming back. She should have been on the beach, figuring out how to make a fishing rod or a spear, but instead, she was standing in front of a closed bar with nowhere left to go.

Her hand flicked over the address card in her pocket. Well, almost nowhere. Gertrude had invited her over. She wanted to know all the details, Ellie was sure. She'd probably have a drink to share, and some food. It *was* Christmas after all. And it would be nice to tell someone about what had happened, to unburden some of it somehow. Though she wasn't quite sure how much of it she wanted to tell. She pulled out the card and made her way to the nearest public elevator.

Gertrude's street looked just like Ellie's, though the buildings were different colors and in slightly different degrees of dilapidation. She held her breath as she pressed the buzzer next to Gertrude's name: Trudy Weaver. It took a minute for a response to come, and

Ellie was on the verge of leaving when a staticy voice said, "Yes? Um—*ahem*—Excuse me. Hello?"

"Um...Yeah," Ellie said, leaning close to the intercom and talking too loudly. "I was looking for Gertrude."

"Oh, Trudy, dear," the voice said, apparently Gertrude's. "Please. And this is she. May I ask who's speaking? You sound like a robot."

Ellie heard laughter from the background. "Oh—It's uh...It's Ellie," she said. "Ellie McCannik. From QA."

"Oh. Ellie, dear. Come on up. *Up up up.* Have a drink and tell us all about your day."

Ellie felt like she was intruding on something. "No—I, uh," she said. "I don't want to be any trouble." But it was no use because the door had already buzzed open and the intercom link had popped shut.

The inside of Gertrude's building looked exactly the same as the inside of Ellie's building. Her room was at the top floor, much like Ellie's was. When Ellie got there, she noted it was in the exact same place, too, though it was a different number, even instead of odd. She didn't know if she should knock or walk in, and she still hadn't decided when the door opened and Gertrude handed her a full glass of eggnog. "Merry Christmas, dear," Getrude said, hugging her. "Drink this and have a seat. I'll introduce you to everyone."

The room was full of people, but Ellie could tell it was emptied of things to make space for them. There was no bed in sight, and from the looks of it, this was the only room there was. Instead of a bed, there was a foldable table in the middle of the room with three people sitting around it. Ellie didn't recognize any of them, and she could tell by the arrangement that she was taking Gertrude's seat. She couldn't see any more chairs, either. She felt even more like she was intruding despite the full drink in her hand.

"Oh, no," Ellie said. "I couldn't. I just wanted to come—"

"Oh, no," Gertrude said, guiding Ellie to the seat. "Nonsense, dear. Sit down. Drink." She tilted Ellie's glass to give her a good long swig. Ellie did feel better for it. "Now. This here pretty, young face you see is Aldo," Gertrude said, pointing to a kid with disheveled hair sitting in the back corner of the small room. "Aldo, say hello to Ellie."

He smiled, and blushed, and took a big drink out of his glass.

"Aldo's shy but he has deft hands," Gertrude said. "Nimble little fingers. He works on the discs for us."

"Trudy!" Aldo gasped. "You're not supposed to tell."

"Quiet, dear," Gertrude said, waving his concerns away. "Please. Ellie here just placed some of your discs in her QA hall. Didn't you, Ellie?"

Ellie blushed, too. She agreed with Aldo. She didn't really want Gertrude talking about what she had done in front of a bunch of strangers. "Uh…" she said. "Yeah, well—"

"She knows what discs are," Gertrude went on, ignoring Ellie. "And she doesn't know anything about you besides how cute you are. So what's the harm?"

"Still," Aldo huffed. "It's not right."

"Oh, lighten up, dear," Gertrude said, smiling. "It's Christmas, a time for *celebration*. Your discs went off with a bang." She laughed.

One of the others at the table leaned in toward Ellie and said, "So you've joined the cause."

Ellie didn't know how to answer. She took a long sip of eggnog to buy time. Technically she didn't choose to join the cause. It was just the only option she had left. So maybe she *had* joined the cause after all. Whatever. It was easier to nod along either way.

"Welcome," the woman said without waiting for further answer. "I'm Vicki. This is Alena." She pointed to the fourth person sitting at the table. "We've known Trudy since before she got promoted and moved to this high class place." She smiled and winked at Gertrude who laughed.

"*Oooh*, dear," Gertrude said. "A long time ago that was, too. These are my best friends, Ellie. They're family. Vicki and Alena work down at a coal plant. They had a shift today, too. And they set their own discs."

"Trudy!" Aldo complained again.

"*Aldo!*" Gertrude replied in a high-pitched, mocking tone. "I want Ellie to know that she's one of us, that she's put herself on the line but she's not alone. You don't expect her to tell us what she did without a little leverage of her own, do you? It's four against one."

"Yeah, well." Aldo huffed. "She better not tell."

"Of course she won't," Gertrude said, turning to Ellie. "Will you dear?"

Ellie shook her head. She didn't know who she would tell.

"You see," Gertrude said. "You have nothing to worry about, boy. No one does. It's Christmas. The operation is underway. Our glasses are full, and we have good company. Now, where were we? Vic, you were telling us about how your shift went. Why don't you go back a little in the story for Ellie's sake."

"Oh, no," Ellie said, taking the drink she was sipping away from her mouth. "Don't mind—"

"Oh, no," Vicki said. "It's no problem. So, like Trudy said, Alena and I work in the coal plants. Well, that used to mean shoveling and all that, but they mostly replaced shovelers with robots so we just stand around in the fumes in case anything goes wrong these days. Then maybe a bot malfunctions, you know, and we take over the shoveling until a new one gets there or whatever. That's abou—"

"Is all that necessary?" Alena interrupted her.

"Uh, well. I don't know," Vicki said, shrugging. "I don't know how much she wants to know. Anyway. We worked our shift, right. And at the end of it—just like the Scientist said—the bots all turned off at once." She snapped her fingers. "Just like that. And we...Well, we were free to do what we had to do without interference.

"So we set the discs, and we got out of there, and we were waiting for the elevator to come when we heard them go off. And did they ever go of? *Whoooeeee*. I mean, we couldn't stop to see the damage, you know, but from the sound of it, they won't have any power from that plant anytime soon."

Aldo smiled and sipped his beer.

"Brilliant," Gertrude said, beaming. "Wonderful. Amazing." She sounded tipsy. "You fill my heart with joy. Tis the best Christmas gift a girl could ever ask for." She walked over and planted a big kiss on Aldo's forehead.

"C'mon man," he said, wiping it away in disgust.

"You blew up a power plant?" Ellie said. Everyone in the room looked at her, and she regretted opening her mouth.

"See!" Aldo said, as if she had already told someone about his involvement.

"Quiet, Aldo." Gertrude said.

"Yes," Vickie said. "We did. This particular plant powers

most of Outland 1's communication capabilities. Without it, their response to the rest of the operation will be crippled."

"But can't they just—I'm sorry." Ellie shook her head. She had almost let her mouth run off on its own again.

"No," Vickie said. "Go ahead. Your opinion's valid."

Ellie looked around at everyone else in the room. They all seemed to agree with Vickie, even Aldo, so she went on. "Well, I was just thinking...I mean, couldn't they just reroute the power from somewhere else?"

"I...uh..." Vickie looked to Gertrude for an answer.

"Yes," Gertrude said, frowning. "They could. And they will, dear." She smiled. "Probably they already have. *Ha ha*! But it's still not fast enough to catch us." She laughed. "It's not about shutting down their communications forever, you see. We only had to do it for long enough to get what we needed on the other side."

"So what was it that I was doing then?" Ellie asked. "Blowing up the conveyor belts to their homes? What good is that?"

"No, dear. *No*." Gertrude set her glass on the table and took Ellie's face between both hands. "You were a redundancy," she said, talking too close and jiggling Ellie's face as she did. "Quality assurance. Each of your discs went out to a different part of the operation. You played an important role."

"I—I didn't set them all," Ellie blurted out, pulling away from Gertrude's embrace. She took a big swig of eggnog.

"Where are the rest?" Aldo said.

"Right here." She tossed the pouch on the table and Aldo snatched it up. "I'm sorry."

"No no, dear," Gertrude said, shaking her head and waving it away. "No need to apologize. At least you came back. And you set some. There'll be plenty more for you to do, if you're up to it."

"But I didn't..." She shook her head.

"You did what any human would," Alena said. "You did what you could. There's no changing that now. All you can change is what you do in the future."

"I did the same thing on my first go," Vicki said. "She sent me undercover to a plant I had never been to and expected *me* to download files from the mainframe. *Me*. I asked her why she didn't just do it herself. She's connected to everything. She can change our elevator paths and our shifts and turn off the robots, why couldn't she do something so simple as downloading a little bit of data for herself? But she just said she couldn't do it, that I had to. So I went all the way into the control center of the plant, and I was going to download everything, but a cat jumped out—I shit you not, *a cat*—and it spooked me so much I had to get out of there."

Alena laughed. "Scaredy cat," she said.

"Hey," Vicki said, raising her hands in defense. "If you were there, you would have run, too."

"*I* downloaded my files," Alena said with a grin.

"Yeah, well," Vicki said, shaking her head and chuckling. "*You* didn't get chased out before you could."

"By a cat!" Alena laughed.

"You placed some, dear," Gertrude said to Ellie. "That's all that matters. You did your best and you're back to try again. You did more than just set discs, though. Didn't you? Tell us about that."

"Oh, yeah. Well…" Ellie sipped her drink.

"Ellie works in QA," Gertrude said to the group. They all looked at her like that meant something to them.

"Well, I got to see the beach," Ellie said when the attention had grown to be too much.

"The beach?" Aldo said.

"*The beach*," Alena said.

"Tell us, dear," Gertrude said.

"I don't know," Ellie said. "It was—It was like nothing I've ever experienced before. Have you ever gargled with salt water for a sore throat?"

Aldo cringed.

"Imagine that smell all around you," Ellie said, smiling at the memory. "*Everywhere*. And the faint hint of tuna dinner fresh out of the can. And that was just the smell!"

"I hate fish," Alena said, crinkling up her nose like she could smell it then and there.

"But it wasn't just that." Ellie shook her head. "The sky was this endless deep blue with no clouds in sight. And it butted up against the endless deep blue of the ocean water. And while the sky seemed so far out of reach and aloof, the ocean just wanted to reach out at you again and again until you finally agreed to meet its wet touch."

"Beautiful, dear." Gertrude smiled.

"And the sand," Ellie went on, unable to stop reminiscing. "*Oh*, the sand. It was amazing. I just want to bury my feet in it right now and feel the ocean breeze. It was like the biggest sandbox you had ever seen. I don't know." She shook her head. "I was a child again for fifteen minutes." She remembered Levi and finished her drink.

"Would you like some more eggnog, dear?" Gertrude said, already getting a pitcher out of the fridge. "In the Christmas spirit." She poured some into Ellie's glass.

"I went to the mountains," Alena said. "I always thought they were the prettiest thing ever. I don't know why."

"Because they're so big," Vicki said. "And old. Bigger and older than anything we've ever built."

"And they'll be there longer, too," Aldo added.

"Oh. Now, Aldo," Gertrude said. "Don't be so cynical at your young age." She tossed a piece of ice at him. "We'll be here for a good long time yet. Not *us* but us. You know what I mean."

"You'll be here longer than any of us," Vicki said, laughing.

Aldo and Alena joined in, too. Ellie gave a little chuckle herself.

"I can only hope so, dears." Trudy smiled. "I can only hope so."

Ellie sipped the eggnog and it felt warm throughout her body. She looked around the room and actually enjoyed the faces she was surrounded by. It was a feeling she missed. She didn't know these people, but she felt like she did. She felt like they knew her, too. Though not even Trudy did. But did any of that matter anymore? Did anyone know anyone? No. And these people were welcoming her into their family.

"You didn't choose to stay in the mountains?" Ellie asked, a little embarrassed by the question. Of course Alena didn't choose to stay in the mountains, otherwise she wouldn't be there to answer the question.

Alena chuckled.

"*I* wanted to stay," Vicki said. "I had studied up on how to build shelter and hunt in the cold, and I knew we could make it out there on that beautiful mountainside. *Alena*, here, convinced me otherwise."

"Just in time, too," Alena said with a smile.

"Well, I couldn't live without you," Vicki said, shaking her head and trying to suppress a grin. "Could I? Not even out there."

Alena blushed.

"How'd you convince her?" Aldo asked. "I think I'd stay if I ever got the chance to leave this shit hole."

"Aldo!" Gertrude said, spitting up some eggnog.

"It's true!" Aldo said.

"Honestly," Alena said. "I'm not sure I have convinced her still to this day."

"She stepped through the door," Vicki said. "That's all it took. All the freedom in the worlds wasn't enough if she wasn't there to share it with me."

"And she still tries to convince me to go back every day." Alena laughed.

"Well why don't you want to leave?" Ellie asked.

"That's a good question," Alena said, looking into her drink and really thinking about what she wanted to say before answering. "And a difficult one to answer, I'd say. I know Trudy talks about morality and all that, but it's something different for me. I would—I don't know how to say this better—but I would feel guilty if I left, you know. Like I was taking advantage of others because they had been taken advantage of with me. If that makes any sense at all. I don't know." She shook her head. "Besides, if we all leave when we get the chance to leave, then who's going to fight for the people that never get a chance to? You know. I don't know. I just—I would feel too guilty if I didn't do everything I could to help. I don't know. I feel like I've been talking forever." She shook her head and chuckled. "Someone else say something."

Aldo scoffed. "They can fight for themselves," he said. "We are."

"*Ha*, child." Trudy laughed. "What exactly do you think you'd be doing if we hadn't come along and let you into the family, huh?"

Aldo sipped his drink. "Yeah," he said. "Well, something. That's for sure."

"Something, dear?" Trudy laughed again. "You wouldn't even know who to fight or that the other worlds existed. You'd be just as ignorant and helpless as everyone else."

"I'm not ignorant!" Aldo slammed his glass on the table,

spilling some eggnog. "Don't call me that."

"Now now, dear," Trudy said, cleaning up the mess he had made. "We all are. It's not an insult. It just means that you don't know something. And none of us would know any of this if no one ever told us. That's exactly why I choose to stay, Ellie, dear. I plan to tell as many people as I can before I die and get more people to stand up and fight with us."

"Stand up and fight?" Aldo scoffed. "I've never heard of you doing any fighting."

"Nor me you, dear," Trudy said, smiling and whipping the wet rag playfully towards him. "But we all contribute to the struggle in the best way we can. For me it's recruiting and communications, for you it's tinkering with technology. They're both as necessary as the other. They're both vital to the struggle. You and I fight just the same as our friends here who go on the front lines and place your discs."

"Well said." Vickie raised her glass. "Well said. You do have a great gift for communication, Trudy."

Everyone laughed. Ellie, too. She was feeling more comfortable the more eggnog she drank.

"We all know that," Vickie went on. "But how great is Aldo's gift at tinkering? Ellie, tell us, did you get to see the outcome of your disc placement?"

"Oh, well..." Ellie sipped her drink.

"You don't have to tell us, dear," Trudy said. "But it would be a Christmas gift to have some news of the operation."

"Well..." Ellie said. "I didn't place all of them, you know."

Aldo scoffed.

"Yes," Trudy said, ignoring him. "That's fine, dear. But how close were you when the ones you did set went off? Did you hear them? Did you see any of the damage they created?"

"Oh. Well..." Ellie looked around the table at expectant eyes. "Yeah," she said. "I mean, it was kind of hard not to. The ground shook underneath me. It was like a small earthquake. And it was so loud I couldn't hear for a minute afterward."

Aldo grinned.

"How close were you?" Vicki asked, leaning in closer.

"Maybe a block away," Ellie said. "My ears are still ringing." She stuck a finger in one ear and wiggled it around to drive the point home.

"Did you see the damage?" Vicki asked.

"Yeah, well..." Ellie took a sip of her eggnog and glanced over at Aldo who seemed to tense up in anticipation of her answer. "There was a whole floor of the building gone, but the rest of it was still standing. It was like it had a huge wound on its side."

"Is that right?" Vicki looked at Aldo.

"Don't look at me," he said. "Where were you? The QA hall?"

Ellie nodded.

"Well those were direct charges. Back up. Meant to take out specific targets and cause minimal collateral damage. If the building's still standing, then it's meant to be standing. Even if she set only one of those discs. I *guarantee* it."

"That *is* right," Vicki said. "Well done then." She raised her glass. "To a successful operation."

Everyone clanged their glasses over the table and took a big swig of whatever they were drinking.

"Now." Vickie put an empty glass on the table. "If y'all don't mind, I can't speak for Alena here, but I'd like to get some rest after that long day of work—*with overtime*—so I'm going to bid my *adieus*."

"*Ugh*." Alena stood from her seat. "Me, too, Trudy," she said. "But you know we love the drinks and company as always."

"And you know you two are always welcome, dear," Trudy said with a smile, setting her own glass on the table. "Just come ringing, and if I'm here, there's something to drink." She winked.

"Well, we'll be here tomorrow afternoon to get some more news," Alena said. "Right?" She raised her eyebrows.

"I'm hoping as much as y'all are, dear," Trudy said.

"Alright, girl," Alena said. "See you then." She hugged Trudy and waved to Aldo then turned to Ellie and said, "Nice to meet you. I hope to see you again soon."

"You, too." Ellie said, holding out her hand, but Alena came in for a hug instead.

Vicki shook hands with Aldo and hugged Trudy then stopped in front of Ellie. "You did good today," she said.

"I could have done better," Ellie said, shaking her head.

"No." Vicki shook her head. "You can always do better. But

you did good. That's what's important. You got that?"

Ellie didn't know how to respond.

"I look forward to working with you in the future," Vicki said. She shook Ellie's hand. "Bye y'all. See you tomorrow." She waved to everyone as they left.

The door closed behind them, and Trudy finally took a seat. Ellie felt bad for forgetting that she was standing for all that time. She wanted to say something to make up for it, but nothing was sufficient.

"Well, dears," Trudy said. "Another round of nog?"

"Nah," Aldo said, standing. "I should get going, too. I have some more *tinkering* to do."

"Good luck with that, dear," Trudy said. "You're one of the best."

Aldo looked at her like he didn't believe what she was saying. "Uh...thanks," he said. "And nice to meet you." He nodded at Ellie and slipped through the door.

Ellie sipped the last dregs of her eggnog. She set the empty glass on the table.

"Well, dear," Trudy said, finishing her own glass and setting it on the table. "I guess you've got something important to get to yourself. Don't let old Gertrude keep you from it. I understand."

Ellie shook her head. "Nope," she said. "I've got nothing."

"Now now, dear," Trudy said, shaking her head. "Honestly. I'm fine. I have plenty to keep me busy. I don't need your pity."

"It's not pity."

"Oh. Sure..." Trudy gave a thumbs up, smiling and nodding. "Okay."

"Trudy," Ellie said, looking her in the eyes. "I honestly have nowhere else to be."

"How kind." Trudy winked.

"No. I mean...I tried to go to my bar before I came here. It was closed. That's when I realized that the bar was all I had. But that's not enough anymore. That's why I came here in the first place."

"So I was your second choice," Trudy said with a smile as she went to the fridge to pour two new glasses of eggnog.

"Honestly." Ellie sighed. "This entire place was my second choice."

"I knew it!" Trudy said, almost spilling the drink she was pouring. "*I knew it.*

"You knew what?" Ellie asked, frowning.

"I knew something had to happen to keep you from placing all those discs. You had plenty of time if you *chose* to come back."

"Yeah." Ellie shook her head. "Well, maybe I didn't *choose* to come back."

"Maybe you did," Trudy said, sipping her drink. "Maybe it was your subconscious choosing for you."

"Maybe it was just a stupid mistake that I regret."

"You know," Trudy said. "I did the same thing."

"What?"

"I wanted to stay over there, but I didn't make it back."

"I thought you had never been across," Ellie said.

"I thought you wanted to join the struggle." Trudy smiled and sipped her drink.

Maybe Ellie didn't know as much about Trudy as she thought she did. "So?" she said.

"So I didn't make it back either," Trudy said. "But when I started working with the struggle, I knew it was what was best for me. It was difficult, yes. It *is* still difficult. But I wouldn't have it any other way."

Ellie hated her and loved her all at the same time for that. Trudy represented everything Ellie could become. She set a bar for Ellie to reach merely by existing. "You know, Trudy," she said. "I think this is the start of a beautiful relationship."

"Me, too, dear." Trudy smiled and nodded. "Me, too."

ଓ ✳ ଛ

XX. Tom

"Ansel, wait!" Tom called as the children ran away. They were so small he only had to jog to keep up, but he knew it was no use. "Pidgeon!" he called, sprinting to catch up with the boy—who was lagging behind—and grabbing him by the shoulder to stop him.

"Please don't hurt me," the boy said, holding his hands up in front of his face. A little puddle formed at the front of his pants.

"I'm not—I won't—" Tom said. "You're Pidgeon, right."

The kid was shaking still, but he dropped his hands. "R— Richard, sir." He nodded.

"But they call you Pidgeon, right? She does, *Ansel* does." The name tasted like guilt in his mouth.

"Yes, sir," Pidgeon said, nodding. "All the kids at school do."

"I don't care about the kids at school, son. I care about Ansel. Now I need you to catch up to her and protect her with everything you've got. You understand me?"

"I—uh—I was, sir," Pidgeon said, shaking more violently. "But you stopped me."

"No, kid," Tom said, stepping closer and looking him in the eyes. "I mean you stick by her side *no matter what*. I'm coming back here, and I *will* find her. If you're not there with her when I do, then I'll find you next, and it won't be to protect you. You got that?"

"No. I—But—Why me?"

"Someone has to protect her while I'm not there." Tom shook his head. "You're the only one who's left, so you'll have to do."

"But what am I supposed to do?"

"I said you'll do. You'll do whatever it takes. And don't let me find out that you didn't."

"But, I—"

"Go!" Tom stomped his foot to scare the kid away. Pidgeon's eyes grew wide as he fled clumsily away. He looked like he probably pissed himself again.

Tom took off the old model helmet that Rosa and Anna had given him and carried it by his side, roaming the streets of 6. What good was the helmet to him now? If anyone wanted to shoot him, they could go right ahead and do it. He didn't care. He had failed and failed and failed, and he was on his way to face the consequences of that failure. At least if someone shot him now, they would keep him from that experience. In fact, he didn't know why he was still carrying the stupid thing at all. He tossed it at the building closest to him and felt better for having the weight lifted.

Why did he need any of it? He unbuckled his plated vest as he walked and tossed that on the ground, too. Now they would have an even bigger target to put him out of his misery.

He didn't know where he was, but he kept walking. Without his helmet and vest, people didn't recognize him as a protector. The streets filled up as he wandered through them.

Maybe he didn't have to go back and face the consequences after all. Maybe he could stay here in Outland 6 and blend in as one of them. He was a lot taller than they were, sure, but they didn't seem to notice or care. No one even glanced at him twice now that he was out of his protector uniform.

He plopped down on the sidewalk with his back leaning on a rough brick building and untied his heavy white boots, throwing them on the ground next to him with a thud. Why not? He didn't need any of it anymore. And maybe if they found him shoeless and half-naked they'd be easier on his punishment. Probably not, but he was beyond caring.

He got up and tried out his socked feet. The ground was rough, and every few steps he'd hit a pebble, or a shard of glass, and feel a shock of pain shoot up through his foot, but he almost liked it. It was freeing. Or, no, that wasn't right. It was grounding. He could feel the ground underneath his feet, and he finally knew where he stood. He tore his undershirt off, too, and walked on with nothing but his white protector cargo pants and white cotton socks.

People did start to look at him then. He had gone over that line of blending in right back to standing out more than ever. Now, though, instead of running away at first sight of him, people either pointed and stared, or tried to avoid eye contact as they scurried by. The crowd parted in front of him however they reacted. He felt as if he were afflicted with some contagious disease. They all steered clear of him until a little boy ran out and offered him a bright red poinsettia.

Tom looked down at the kid's dirty, smiling face and the flower in his hand. He extended his own hand to reach for the flower and it shook with the effort. He put the poinsettia to his nose and smelled it. Tears welled up behind his eyes and something caught in his stomach. "Thank you," he whispered. The kid smiled wider then ran back into the crowd of people.

He *did* still care. Of course he did. He cared about his son back home, he cared about setting a good example for him. That's why he had done all of this in the first place, to protect his son, not to protect Ansel. She was collateral assistance. He was supposed to be setting an example for his son, building a world that was safe for him to live in, but what was he doing instead? He was half-naked in the streets of Outland 6, giving up on his life. What kind of an example was that?

He put the flower in his pocket then tried to find some landmark to show him where he was. So few of the intersections had signs, it was impossible to find out that way. He didn't recognize anything. He tried the next street, and the next, then turned a corner and went down another street or two.

He was starting to regret taking off his shoes. His feet burned. Every step now was like walking on glass, whether he actually stepped on a piece or not. At the next intersection there were still no signs in sight. He checked the bottom of one foot, and as suspected, his sock was soaked in blood. *Great*. Exactly what he needed, open wounds on the bottom of his feet so he could catch whatever diseases the streets of Outland 6 carried. Still, he had no choice but to carry on. Going back to find his shoes now would only open him to more risk.

It was three more blocks before he found a sign, and he didn't recognize the street name. Still, it was a sign. He followed the street he had a name for until he came to the next named street a few blocks away. This one he did recognize. He knew where he was, and he knew where he had left to go. He sighed in relief and his feet ached less because of it. It was four blocks to the Neutral Grounds, then there was a transport bay every fifteen blocks along that. This street was right in the middle of two transport bays—of course—but it was somewhere, which was a lot better than nowhere.

He had hoped to see a protector and be able to hail them before he got to the Grounds, but he didn't see anyone between where he was and the closest transport bay, a transport bay which wouldn't open without his comm link. He sat down with his back on the bay doors and checked his feet again. The entire bottom of both socks were soaked in blood, so he had no way to tell how bad the injuries were. For all he knew he could be soleless. He wanted to peel his socks off to get a closer look, but he thought that would only make things worse, especially if he ended up having to walk some more.

What to do now? He could sit there and wait for someone to come out of the bay, giving his feet a rest in the process, but there was no telling how long that would take. He looked at his feet one more time and tried blowing on them to ease the pain, but it didn't help, the socks were in the way. It did stretch his already worked muscles, though, so he went on for a while anyway to give them a cool down. Then he leaned back and looked at the trees in the Grounds.

What was he going to tell the Captain when he finally got back? How could he explain this? His nakedness? How could he explain being ambushed by tiny troll ladies?

Okay. He got hit in the back of the neck and knocked out. That was a fact. He wouldn't be lying if he said it. And there was physical evidence to back that up. Then they took his gun, comm link, and all his gear, and they sent him off to fend for himself. He walked for blocks and blocks, until his feet were bloody, and he finally found a transport bay. They had to believe him. Look at his feet.

Or they knew it was him at the Feast. Then what would they do? He didn't want to think about that. He was lucky he didn't have to, because the transport bay doors opened behind him, and he fell backwards at the feet of three protectors.

"Well, well, well," one of the protectors said through bright, shining teeth.

"Pardy. You make our job easy," another said in the same modulated voice.

"Home base, we have the golden egg. Be back in five," the third added.

"Already?" came a voice over their comm links.

"Congratulations, Officers. Bring him in."

"Tom Pardy, you are under arrest for attempted assassination and dereliction of duty. Surrender now or face justice."

Tom stood and backed away from them, wincing at the pain. "I—what?" he said, holding his hands up. "No. I didn't—"

One of them took out their stun gun. "Just come quietly, or we'll do this the hard way. You were a protector once, Pardy. You know how this goes."

"No. You can't," Tom said. "You don't understand. I can explai—"

Tom felt the pinch of taser darts sticking like tiny fishhooks into his bare chest, a shock of electricity surging throughout his body, and the hot pressure of a deafening explosion behind him which flung his body into the back wall of the transport bay where the three protectors broke his fall before he blacked out into nothingness.

ʚ ✳ ʚ

Tom awoke for the second time in his life bound to a chair and gnashing at his restraints. A bright white light blinded him. It was much whiter than the yellow light Anna and Rosa had used to blind him. This wasn't their dump hideout in Outland 6. The seat here was harder and colder, though it was about the same height. The air smelled antiseptic, sterile, overcleaned. This time it wasn't Sixer scum who held him in captivity, it was his fellow protectors.

He heard the door open and close, but here it didn't affect the brightness of the light that blinded him. Here a camera digitally tracked his pupils to ensure maximum light exposure with a light that was bright enough to penetrate eyelids. The protectors had blinding down to a science.

Whoever opened the door walked in and sat at the chair across from him. That's all he could tell by the sound. All protectors wore the same boots, so all their footsteps sounded the same. The person didn't say anything for a good long time. They let Tom struggle in vain until he gave up, clenching his eyes tight against the rays which he couldn't stop.

"*Pardy, Pardy, Pardy*," the voice finally came, Captain Mondragon's voice. "You should know by now that this struggling is useless. You *are* a protector after all. Aren't you?"

"You killed Rabbit," Tom said, his eyes still clenched against the hot lights.

"Watch your mouth, Pardy," the Captain snapped. "That's a heavy accusation to be lobbing at a superior officer. Now, we can chalk that one up to duress and move on. But before we do anything, can we turn these lights off, please? I think he's had enough. Thank you."

Tom's eyelids turned from red to black. He opened his eyes slowly, and it was still blackness until they adjusted to the room. It was an interrogation room. There was a metal table, big black two way mirror, and the Captain sitting across from him, raised up a little to look down on him in his too short seat.

"There, Pardy," the Captain said, grinning. "That's better. Isn't it?"

"Why are you holding me?" Tom demanded. "I've done nothing wrong."

"*Pfft*, Pardy." The Captain laughed. "Please. Give us some credit. You know our capabilities."

"I know you're capable of killing an officer on duty."

"Then you should know what will happen to you if you try to get in the way." The Captain smiled. "Pardy," she said, shaking her head. "Come on. I tried to help you. I'm *trying* to help you. I gave you the world on a platinum platter. You simply have to work with me, Pardy. You can do that, can't you?"

"Work with you?" Tom scoffed. "After you sent me into that shit shift?"

"You asked for Outland 6, Pardy."

"Not the solo Street beat right after my initiation."

The Captain laughed. "No, Pardy. You didn't ask for that. But when you asked for 6, you showed me that you weren't willing to cooperate. I made it clear which precincts I thought would be most profitable for both of us."

Tom shook his head. He struggled against his cuffs again then slammed his fists on the table. "I have my reasons! I had no choice!"

"Yes, Pardy." The Captain smiled. "Good. You had no choice. That's what I told them. Everyone else thought you were a rebel mole, or you went insane after killing your first Sixer, or something. But not me. No. I told them, *Not Pardy. Pardy goes by the books, that one. He's got his reasons and they support Property, Liberty, Life or I've never done an honest day of protector work in my life.* That's what I said, Pardy."

"You're mocking me." Tom sneered.

"No, Pardy." The Captain looked offended. "No. Well..." She chuckled. "Maybe a little. But I did say that. And that *is* what they think."

"That's why they think I came back without my gear?"

"Oh. Sweetheart." The Captain gave him a wry grin, shaking her head. "That's precious. But no. That's why they think you tried to assassinate Lord Walker. They think you had a hand in all that other stuff, too—and Amaru are they looking for a head to take over that one—but I know you better than that, Pardy. Don't I?"

"Lord Walker?"

"*Ugh.* Pardy." The Captain frowned. "You're not helping my case here. You're not helping *your* case. If you don't know the name of the man you tried to kill, how could you have a legitimate reason to kill him?"

"That's—No. *I didn't*—"

"We know it was you, Pardy. Our tracking capabilities don't end at guns and comm links. You might as well come clean now. We know where you were during your entire shift—*ahem*—and beyond. And we know your boots and armor were in the Feast Hall when the assassination attempt occurred. Taking into account the size of the shooter and your absence from duty, it was obviously you. Now that we have that out of the way, why'd you do it, Pardy? And make it good this time."

"I don't even have my boots. I didn—"

"You did it because..."

"*Why'd you kill Rabbit?*" Tom demanded.

"Pardy." The Captain shook her head. "I told you. Watch your mouth. Now I'm the only one on your side here. You'd do better for yourself not to alienate me. Being honest with me is the only way that I can help you."

"Did you kill anyone else besides Rabbit?" Tom asked, gritting his teeth. He had never hated a fellow protector before. It seemed wrong to do it now, but he couldn't hold back his anger.

"I shot the scumbag trash, low-class Sixer that dared to draw a gun on a protector. I shot the wannabe person that shot your Rabbit. Do you have a problem with that?"

"Who was it?"

"I don't know, Pardy. Why do you care? They murdered an Officer of the Law and they're dead because of it. Case closed."

"No. But the woman—"

"So it *is* about her, then," the Captain said, shaking her head. "Pardy, we kill people in the line of duty. It happens. If you can't deal with that, then you're not cut out to be a protector. Maybe you'd feel more comfortable doing housework."

"She said she had a husband," Tom said, ignoring her. "Was he the one who you killed?"

The Captain smiled. She leaned closer over the table. "Why do you care so much, Pardy?"

"Just tell me!"

"This isn't a negotiation, son. It's an interrogation. Or did you not notice the shiny, new bracelets we gave you? Silver *is* your color, boy."

Tom swung his fist at her and moved his chair forward with the force of it against his handcuffs.

"Well, now you notice them for sure," the Captain said with a smile.

"What do you want?"

"I told you. I want to know why you did it. But make it good this time. You have an audience."

He looked over at the black mirror. "I was protecting a little girl," he said to it instead of the Captain.

"A little girl?" the Captain said. "By shooting Lord Walker?"

Tom looked back at the Captain. "Is her dad alive?"

"*Her dad.*" The Captain scoffed, shaking her head. "Of course. I should have known. *We* should have known. We do have a department for this type of thing, don't we?"

"Is. He. Alive?" Tom demanded.

"How old *is* your son now, Pardy? Ten, eleven years old. I must confess, I don't know much about your personal life."

"Leave him out of this."

"How can I?" the Captain said, shaking her head. "That's what this is all about, isn't it? I should have known when you started talking about that trash's daughter earlier. This is my fault really. I'll pull in the favors required to pay the consequences, but that's all I need to know from you, Pardy. I wish you had thought of a better story, though. I had a lot invested in you, son. Well, good luck anyway." She stood and made to walk away.

"Wait!" Tom called.

She stopped but didn't turn around.

"Her father. Tell me. Is he alive?"

The Captain took a few slow steps back to the table and leaned over it to get close to his face. "For now, Pardy," she said. He could feel the heat of her breath as she spoke and smell the liquor she must have drank before the interrogation. "But not for long. You get caught with that many printers in Outland 6 and there's nowhere left to go. I'll hurry it along now that I know he's so important to you, though. You can count on that." She pushed herself up off the table and walked out chuckling.

"I want to see him!" Tom yelled after her, but the door closed and she didn't respond.

He fought against his chains until he bled, then he gave up. There was no use. His life was in their hands. Whoever *they* were. The Captain and her superiors, whoever was listening behind the black mirror, they decided his fate now. Not him. The door opened, and a pair of Officers he didn't recognize marched in. One of them tossed the clothes out of Tom's locker onto the table while the other undid his cuffs.

"Change into your clothes, citizen."

Citizen? "The names Pardy," Tom said, rubbing his bloody wrists. "Officer Pardy."

"Not anymore, *citizen*. Dress yourself." They pointed their guns at him.

"Alright, alright." Tom slipped out of his white cargoes and into the jeans and t-shirt he had worn to his first day at the academy. They were fresh, and clean, and hadn't been worn since. They felt soft and comforting against his skin. He only regretted the circumstances under which he had to put them back on.

"So. What now?" he asked when he was dressed. "Is that it? No trial?"

"You've been tried, citizen. Come with us." One of them shoved Tom towards the door which the other had opened. They marched him at gunpoint through the halls to the transport bay where the Captain was waiting by the bay's open doors.

"Well, Pardy," she said. "This is the best I can do for you."

"What?" He said through gritted teeth, fighting the urge to punch her.

"You're clearly not stable enough to be a protector. Look at how worked up you are now. Dangerous, really." The Captain shook her head. "And even more clearly, you miss your darling son. So it's back to housework for you, Pardy. The only thing you're good enough for."

"I—but—"

The two officers pushed him through the bay doors into the elevator and got in with him. The doors closed, the floor fell out from beneath them, then the doors opened, and one of the protectors poked Tom in the back with a gun. "Out!"

He stepped out of the doors, and they slid closed behind him.

He looked up at the sky then down at the courtyard around him, spotting a tree that he wanted to climb. He ran over to it and sat at the bottom, taking off his shoes. He got one off and his sock was still bloody. It reminded him of everything he had just been through, everything he had just done.

What was he doing now? He felt like he had been here before but with less clothes. He remembered it like it was a bad decision made a long time ago. He thought it was probably still a bad idea. There was something—*something*—but he couldn't quite put his finger on it. A little black cat scampered across the sidewalk in front of him and disappeared on the other side.

His son.

He stood and limped—more from having only one shoe on than from having bloody feet—down the few blocks to his house. He checked his pockets but didn't have a key, and he had to knock on his own door to get in. He was banging excitedly when his wife yelled at him to shut up, she was coming, then opened the door. "Tommy," she said when she saw him. "I—"

"*Chels.*" Tom hugged her as she squirmed away, surprised.

"What are you doing here?"

"I—uh—" It wasn't the reaction he had expected. But what *did* he expect?

"And you only have one shoe on. Tom, what happened? Are you alright?"

"Chelsea," Tom said, grabbing her hands. "*Chels.* I—I'm fine now. Where's Jonah?"

"I don't know," she said, shaking her head, clearly still confused. "He's outside playing or something. Settle down and tell me what you're doing here."

"I—I don't know," Tom said, avoiding eye contact. "I did something. I—I'm not a protector anymore."

Chelsea crossed her arms and frowned. "Not a protector?"

"There was this girl, Chels. *This girl.*" He shook his head. "She reminded me so much of Jonah. I just had to see him. Where is he?"

"What girl, Tom? What are you talking about?"

"This—This girl." Tom sighed. Water welled up behind his eyes. "I...I killed her mom, and I had to—"

"You killed her mom?" Chelsea's arms uncrossed.

"I—I didn't mean to. I thought she had a gun."

"She had a gun!" She embraced him in a long hug. "Sweetheart."

Tom felt his heart drop to his stomach. The tears came. He had never cried in front of Chelsea before, but he couldn't stop himself now. "N—No...She didn't."

"Sweetheart," she whispered in his ear, patting his back. "It's okay. I'll get you back up and on your feet in no time. Then you can get back to protecting the worlds."

He pushed away from her, tears still in his eyes. "No. You don't understand. I can—I can't go back. They won't take me anymore."

"What?" She didn't sound as understanding as she did before. Her arms crossed again.

"They took my badge. I won't be a protector ever again."

"No." She backed away from him. "How? Why?"

"I had to," Tom said, shaking his head and looking at his feet. "The girl. If it was Jonah, we would have wanted someone to do the same for him."

"*If* it was Jonah, Tom. *If.* But it wasn't. It was some Sixer trash. Are you telling me you threw your life away for trash?"

"I—No—" Tom said, shaking his head. "I didn't throw my life away."

"Well, you're never going to be a protector again. Right?"

"I…" Tom shook his head again, eyes still glued to his feet.

"Then you threw your life away, Tom." She stomped into the house.

"Wait!" Tom called. She stopped herself halfway through closing the door. "Where are you going?"

"To submit my application to the Protector's Academy," she said. "You don't expect me to live in a two housekeeper family, do you?" She didn't wait for an answer and slammed the door behind her.

Tom turned around and slouched onto the stoop with his head in his hands. He *had* thrown his life away, hadn't he? Being a protector was the only way to build a respectable life in Outland 1. He knew that. It had been drilled into his head since before he understood words. What was he now? A housekeeper, the lowest of the low in 1. Better than any Sixer, sure, but that wasn't saying much. And all for what? A filthy, scrawny piece of trash from Outland 6.

"Dad?" a voice came, breaking him away from the world inside his head.

He looked up from his sorrow to see Jonah standing there in the yard with a friend who Tom didn't recognize. "Jonah?" he said.

"Dad, what are you doing here?"

"Jonah." Tom stood up, realizing how ridiculous he must look wearing only one shoe. "I, uh…"

"Hey, I'll see you later," Jonah said to his friend who scurried away, giggling. "Dad. What are you doing here?"

"Jonah," Tom said, trying not to cry. "I missed you so much." He picked Jonah up in a big hug, but Jonah squirmed away.

"Dad, shouldn't you be at work?"

"No, son," Tom said. "I shouldn't."

"But you told me—"

"Jonah. Listen to me. Everything I told you was wrong."

"What?"

"It was all based on bad information, son. Red herrings."

"Red herrings?" Jonah was obviously confused. Tom couldn't blame him.

"Yeah, you know, something that sounds like a clue but—"

"Yeah, dad." Jonah scoffed. "I know what a red herring is. I'm not stupid."

"Oh. Well..." Tom had to gather himself for a moment. He hadn't seen Jonah in so long he had forgotten how old he was now, how much he already knew about the worlds. "Of course, son. But school, and television...The news—Those are all red herrings," he said.

Jonah laughed. "You're kidding, right?"

"No, son. It's all wrong. You have to think for yourself. Pretty much do the opposite of whatever they say."

Jonah chuckled some more. "Alright, dad. Is this some sort of test or something?"

"No." Tom shook his head. "I'm serious. Red herrings."

"*Pffft*. Sure, dad." Jonah smiled. "That's why you're wearing one shoe, right?"

"I, well..."

"Alright, dad," Jonah said, skipping up the stairs and inside. "I'll keep that in mind. But come on inside. It's almost time for dinner."

Tom sighed. No one was ever going to believe him. Still, what was there left for him to do? He followed Jonah inside to see if he could help with dinner.

₨ ✳ ₰

XXI. The Scientist

The speech went well. The amplifiers deafened the owners and made them shut up for a little while, so she had that going for her. Which was nice. But there was also the obstacle she didn't foresee, there were always obstacles you couldn't foresee.

When she had finished her speech, she went backstage to count her fifteen minutes down as Rosalind fetched her daughter. Then the protector came from the dressing area. The Scientist hid behind some unused scenery as the protector went out to give a speech of his own and fire two shots, then a little girl came running out of nowhere to tackle him. They both disappeared back into the dressing area, then Huey came rushing backstage behind Rosalind who was carrying Haley's lifeless body over her shoulder.

"He's going to try to stop you," Huey pled, chasing her. "You can't just take her in front of everyone like that!"

"I'd like to see them try!" Rosalind said, laying Haley on the ground in front of the Scientist. "You have to help her."

Tears welled up behind the Scientist's eyes.

"*Hellooo*," Rosalind said, waving a hand in front of her face. "She needs help now. We don't have time for this." Owners had started crowding around the stage to see what was going on, and protectors would be on their way as soon as they were sure that Lord Walker was alright.

"I can't do anything here," the Scientist said. "I need—"

"Let's go, then." Rosalind lifted Haley's body and carried her toward the closet elevator. The Scientist and Huey followed, and they were gone through the hole and back to the lab before anyone could tell the difference.

"Alright, here?" Rosalind asked, laying Haley on the lab table.

"No," the Scientist said. "The engineering room. I'll meet you there."

Rosalind picked Haley up and disappeared out into the hall.

The Scientist searched frantically through the drawers to find the serum. "Is there anything I can do?" Huey asked.

"Wait," the Scientist said, grabbing what she needed. She ran out into the hall, closed the door, opened it again, and ran into the engineering room. Haley was sprawled out on the drafting table as Rosalind brushed the hair out of her face.

"She doesn't look good," Rosalind said.

"I'll fix that," the Scientist said, filling a syringe with serum and flicking the air bubbles out, always sure to do it, even when she was in a hurry.

"Are you sure?"

"I am. But I need you to leave so I can...I'm going to be using some..."

"You don't have to make excuses," Rosalind said, standing from Haley's side. "Just fix her. And get me when she's better."

The Scientist watched the door close behind Rosalind. She went back to filling the syringe and tapping out any air. Satisfied, she plunged it into Haley's thigh then set to extracting the bullet. The serum helped to push it out, and the process was easier than she expected it to be. This was a Sixer round, not a protector round. That was the first clue as to who was behind it.

The bullet out, and with less effort than she expected, the Scientist only had to pull up a stool and wait for the nanobots to take effect. With such quick application, there would be virtually no damage. The tears came back to the Scientist's eyes when Haley blinked herself awake.

"Wh—Where am I?" Haley asked, groggily.

"You're safe," the Scientist said in almost a whisper.

"Where's Lord Walker?" Haley asked, sitting up fast.

"He's safe, too," the Scientist said, reassuring her. "But he doesn't matter. You do."

"Wh—who are you?" Haley asked, frowning.

"I'm..." The Scientist shook her head. She couldn't answer that just yet.

Thankfully, Haley stalled a little longer for her. "Where *am* I?" she asked again, looking around the room.

"You're in my lab." The Scientist tried to blink away her tears. "One of them at least."

"And who are you?"

"I—I'm...a friend. I'm the Scientist."

Haley waited for her to go on, but when she didn't, she said, "But what's your name?"

Oof. The Scientist had given her name up when Lord Walker had taken her daughter from her. He had taken her name from her, too, and given it to her daughter instead. "I'm Dr. Haley," she said after a long silence.

"Haley? That's my name."

The Scientist tried not to cry. "Yes," she said, shaking her head. "Yes it is."

"Why am I here?"

"You were shot, saving Lord Walker."

"He is okay, though. Isn't he?"

"Yes, dear. He is."

"*I took a bullet for him.*" Haley shook her head.

"You did."

"*Ugh.* Why'd I do that?"

The Scientist laughed and cried at the same time. "I don't know, dear," she said, sniffling. "You tell me."

"I don't know, either," Haley said, shaking her head still. "I guess I was supposed to. Wait, *where am I?*" She looked around the room again.

"It's alright, dear," the Scientist said, chuckling so as not to cry. "You're safe."

"Why do you have to keep reassuring me I'm safe if I really am?"

"Well, you've been shot," the Scientist said. "Your system is going through shock. I injected you with nanobots, and they'll fix you right up, but it takes a little bit of time."

"Nanobots?"

"Yes." The Scientist nodded. "The main ingredient in the smoothies you eat. But an injection is the only thing that could work fast enough to heal a wound like yours."

"How do you know all this?"

"Well, I'm a scientist, dear. *The Scientist.* It's my job to know."

Haley shook her head and rubbed her eyes. She rolled her shoulders then put her hand on her chest. "My chest hurts," she said.

The Scientist chuckled. She started to cry again. "Yes. You were shot."

"But why?"

"That's a long story, dear. And one I don't know all of yet. But you don't have to worry about that now. We'll have plenty of time to figure it out."

"Do I know you from somewhere?" Haley asked, squinting to get a different perspective.

The Scientist nodded, trying to hold back full blown sobs, although she couldn't contain her tears. "Yes, dear," she said. "I—I'm your mother."

Haley shook her head. She looked confused. "No," she said. "I don't have a—a *mother*."

"Who told you that?" The Scientist frowned.

"I'm a robot," Haley said, nodding like it was obvious. "*I wasn't born.*"

"Have you always existed?"

"Well, no. Not always. But I wasn't born."

"You *were* born. You were born right here in this room. Right there on the table you're sitting on now."

Haley looked around the room. "No," she said, shaking her head. "I would have remembered that. I remember everything. I was turned on in Lord Walker's kitchen, and that's the first memory I have."

"It's not the first thing you remember, though," the Scientist said. "There are pieces left from before that. They tried to erase them, but they couldn't. That's why you recognize me."

Haley rubbed her eyes. "No," she said, shaking her head. "I mean—I thought I did, but it must be that you look like someone I've seen before. That's all."

"You, dear?" the Scientist asked, raising an eyebrow.

Haley shook her head. "No, of course not."

The Scientist chuckled, trying not to take offense. "You're my daughter. You were made to look like me."

"No." Haley shook her head. "I look nothing like you."

"Not anymore," the Scientist said. "No. I'll give you that. But you look like I did when I created you. That was a long time ago, dear. We humans change over that kind of time."

"Y—You're serious," Haley said, shaking her head in disbelief.

"I am, dear. I've never been more serious in my life. I've

waited all this time to see you again and here you are." The tears came back stronger than ever.

"No." Haley shook her head.

The Scientist knew it wouldn't be easy to convince her, but she had to keep trying. "Yes," she said. "I invented the technology that is you. I invented you. You were the first android I ever created, and I did it right here in this room. I turned you on while you were laying on that table, and this was the first sight you ever saw. Well, except try to picture your own face instead of mine." She smiled through her tears, though she knew it only accentuated her wrinkles and crow's feet.

"That's why I recognize this place?"

"And why you recognize me."

"You're...you're my mother?" She kind of frowned as she said it.

"And you're my daughter," the Scientist said, letting out a big sigh of relief at finally getting the message across.

"I didn't think I could be a daughter," Haley said. "Or—I mean—I didn't think I could have a mother."

"You can. And you are. And you do. I've been waiting your whole life to get back to you."

"Is that why Rosalind was asking all those weird questions?"

"Yes, dear. She's your sister. We want you to live here with us. We don't want to waste any more time without you, and you won't have to work for Lord Walker ever again."

Haley didn't seem convinced. "What? And work for Mr. Douglas instead?"

"No," the Scientist said, shaking her head. "Of course not. Come live with me, finally enjoy the childhood you never had. I'll cook *you* breakfast, and *you* can watch TV all day. You can do whatever you want. I just want you to do it here, near me, so I can share the experience with you."

"But what about Lord Walker?"

"Lord Walker will be fine," the Scientist said. "He'll get another secretary to replace you. He'll make sure she looks and sounds just like you, and he won't know the difference."

"No." Haley shook her head. "But I'm the best. He's always told me so. That's why we're number one in the Fortune 5."

"He's number one on the Fortune 5, because he started out as number one on the Fortune 5. No offense to your abilities, Haley, but the newer models trade just as efficiently as you do. That's why Mr. Douglas is catching up so quickly."

"No. But I—"

"No, Haley. Listen. We don't have much time. I'm offering you the opportunity to come live with me, your mother, and do anything you want while you're here, or you can go back to work for Lord Walker and do whatever he tells you to do. Those are your options."

"I don't even know you," Haley said, shaking her head. "How can I believe you?"

"I don't know. How can you believe anyone? You just have to trust me."

"*Trust who?*" Haley demanded. "You could be anyone telling me anything."

The Scientist was getting anxious. All her worst fears seemed to be coming true. Grasping at straws, she said, "What about Rosalind?"

"Rosalind?"

"You know her. You can trust her, can't you?"

"I—I don't know," Haley said. "Maybe."

"Well, I'll take you to her, and you can decide for yourself," the Scientist said, standing from her stool. "Come on."

It took a moment for Haley to trust her own legs even. They were fine, though—thanks to the nanobots—and she followed the Scientist out to the hall. The Scientist opened the door again, and there was Huey, a little girl, and a little boy, sitting on the puffy chairs, looking out on the wilderness scene and the mountains.

"What is that?" Haley asked.

"Who is that?" the girl asked, getting up from her seat to stare at them.

"Where's Rosalind?" the Scientist asked.

"Mr. Douglas," Haley said.

"Haley," Huey said.

"Are you the scientist?" the girl said, tugging at the Scientist's white coat.

"Yes, dear. Just a moment, please. Huey, where's Rosalind?"

"In the lab, ma'am." He bowed.

"*Ah*. Of course. Come with me." The Scientist pulled Haley

back into the hall.

"But, Mr. Douglas..." Haley said as the door closed.

"Yes, dear. How do you think Roz could work for me if he didn't? She's actually been at it longer than he has, you know." She opened the door, and Rosalind was playing cards with Popeye at a table in the lab. "There she is," the Scientist said. "Rosalind, dear. I have someone here who would like to talk to you."

Rosalind stood up fast and turned around, knocking cards onto the floor. Popeye waved then set to cleaning up the mess—and making more of one in the process.

"Haley," Rosalind said, crossing to her.

"Rosalind?" Haley said.

"You made it." Rosalind hugged her.

"I—uh. Yeah. I did."

"And the Scientist told you?" Rosalind looked between the two of them.

"That she's my mother? Yes. But I don't know if I—"

"That you're my sister, Haley. That *we're sisters*. She's my mom, too."

"No, but..." Haley shook her head. "We can't have a mother. We're robots."

"I'm not a robot," Rosalind said. "I'm a person. And I do have a mom. *She's our mom.*"

"Then why don't I remember her? I remember everything I've ever experienced."

"Because you don't remember everything you've ever experienced," Rosalind said. "They have access to your memory bank. They tried to erase your memories, but they couldn't do it. There are still pieces. I know there are."

"It's true, dear," the Scientist said, nodding. "We're working on repairing memories here in the lab. If you stay with us, we can work on repairing yours, too. If you want us to, that is."

"You haven't even decided to stay yet?" Rosalind said, looking at Haley in disbelief.

"I—Stay?" Haley scoffed. "This is just too weird." She stepped back from the both of them.

"It's strange, Haley," Rosalind said. "I know that. Believe me. I went through the exact process you're going through when mom explained to me where we came from, but you have to believe me when I say it's much better than being a slave to some owner."

"But you still work for Mr. Douglas," Haley said.

"*With* Huey, dear," the Scientist said. "They work together."

"*Um. Mom*," Rosalind said, giving the Scientist a look. "Do you mind if I talk to her alone for a minute? Would that be alright with you, Haley?"

Haley shrugged. She looked overwhelmed.

"*Hmmm.* I don't know, dear," the Scientist said. "We don't have much time. They'll be looking for—"

"They'll be looking for her either way," Rosalind said. "And it won't take long, just a few minutes between sisters. Please."

"But, dear—"

"Besides," Rosalind cut her off. "You have a little visitor to deal with, remember? She's been waiting a long time."

"I—Well...Okay," the Scientist said, shrugging. "I guess. A *few* minutes. But I want to talk to you before you leave, Haley. *If* that's what you decide to do."

"Of course," Rosalind said, shoving her out the door. "We'll be right out."

The hall door closed behind the Scientist. She sighed and wiped her eyes. Rosalind was right, she knew more than anyone what Haley was going through, and she would be the best person to help her through it. The Scientist had to accept that. She already had more than fifteen minutes with Haley, anyway. She had no room to complain. She only had room left to wait and hope that Rosalind could convince Haley to stay, hope one of her daughters could convince the other to rejoin the family. Her stomach gurgled thinking about what they were saying behind the closed door. She had to do something to get her mind off it.

The door opened and Huey almost ran into her. "Oh. I'm sorry, ma'am," he said, bowing low.

"No no, dear," the Scientist said, shaking her head and waving her hands. "I shouldn't have been standing in front of the door. What is it?"

"Our guests, ma'am," Huey said. "Well, the girl. She's...anxious to see you. She's losing what little patience she had."

"Well well," the Scientist said, walking into the office. "Let me meet this girl at once, then."

"I'm *not* a girl," she said, standing from a puffy chair to cross her arms and stare defiantly at the Scientist.

"Yes you are," a boy behind her said, peeling himself away from the view.

"No. I'm not," she said.

"I'm sorry, dear," the Scientist said. "I didn't know. How should I refer to you, then?"

"Ansel," she said. "My name's Ansel."

"And you're a girl," the boy said.

"*No, I'm not*. Stop saying that!"

"Well what are you then?" the boy prodded her on.

"I don't know," Ansel said. "Nothing. It doesn't matter. What matters is that you're the Scientist, right?"

"Yes, dear," the Scientist said with a smile. She liked this Ansel already. "That's me. What can I do for you?"

"Well, I gave you the information you wanted," Ansel said. "So you have to give me something now, right?"

The Scientist chuckled. "Now, I don't know what information you gave us," she said. "But I'd still be willing to offer you an opportunity. What opportunity is it that you want?"

"My dad," Ansel answered without hesitation. "I want my dad back."

"*Hmmm.*" The Scientist frowned. "Where is he?"

"The protectors took him. And they...they killed my mom."

"Oh, dear." The Scientist moved to comfort her, but she backed away.

"So, can you do it?"

"If the protectors have him, we can get him," the Scientist said. "*If* they have him. But I can't tell you for sure right now."

"But you'll do it for me," Ansel said. "You'll find him."

"Of course, dear," the Scientist said. "Anything for a determined little gi—er—child like yourself. Huey here tells me you demanded to see me."

"I've been jerked around before, ma'am."

"I understand, dear." The Scientist smiled. "I understand. You won't be getting that here, though. You can trust me."

"Good." Ansel uncrossed her arms, satisfied.

"And you, boy," the Scientist said. "You are a boy aren't you?"

"Yes, ma'am." He looked a little scared to be talking to her.

"And do you have a name?"

"Pidg—er—Richard, ma'am," he said.

"We call him Pidgeon," Ansel said.

"Well, Richard," the Scientist said. "Do you have any requests? You brought this information, too. Didn't you?"

Richard looked at Ansel as if he needed her permission to speak. Unsure of himself still when he didn't get it, he said, "Yeah, well...There is one thing." He tugged at a thread on the hem of his shirt.

"Go ahead, dear," the Scientist said.

"Well," he said. "It's just. We don't really have a place to stay, you know. And I'm a little hungry. And...*I could use a bath.*" He blushed and covered the stain on the front of his pants. "And with you getting Ansel's dad for us and all, I just thought that maybe...I don't know—never mind. It's stupid." He shook his head.

"*Oh.* Of course, dear," the Scientist said. "Of course. How could I neglect that? We could manage it, right Huey? We have a couple of free rooms, don't we?"

"Yes, ma'am," Huey said, bowing his head. "What would you like to eat, sir?" he asked Richard.

"Oh. *Um.*" Richard's face turned a deeper red. "Anything really. I don't know. It doesn't matter."

"I'll surprise you, sir," Huey said. "And Ansel?"

"I'm not hungry."

"Very well." Huey left the room.

"So," the Scientist said, sitting in one of the puffy chairs. Ansel sat in the chair across from her, and Richard went to look out the window. "You say the protectors took your father."

"That's right," Ansel said, all business.

"When did it happen?"

"One, two days ago." Ansel shrugged, shaking her head. "I've lost count."

"Good," the Scientist said, nodding. "Recently then. That's good."

"Tom was supposed to help me," Ansel said.

"The protector who you stopped at the Feast?"

"If that was a feast."

"Ansel, I know we'll be able to get your father."

The door opened, and Richard turned with an eager face, but

when it was Haley and Rosalind and not the food, he went back to staring out the window.

"You're back," the Scientist said, crossing the room to them. She couldn't tell whether Haley was staying or going. "Have you met our guests?"

"She's the one I gave the information to," Ansel said, walking over to them.

"We've met," Rosalind said.

"And this is my—this is Haley," the Scientist said.

"I'm Ansel."

"Hello, Ansel," Haley said, curtsying.

"So," the Scientist said. "How did your conversation go? Did you come to a decision?"

"I chose…" Haley stalled.

"Well, we—" Rosalind said, but Huey came in pushing a cart piled with food, trailed by Mr. Kitty in his red collar.

"Food!" Richard yelled, jumping up and down around the cart as Huey pushed it in. Mr. Kitty ran out of his way and jumped onto one of the puffy chairs to lick himself.

"The cat!" Ansel said.

"I didn't know what you wanted, sir," Huey said. "So I brought a little of a lot. I hope you approve."

"*Om*—thanks—*nom*," Richard said, stuffing his face with red beans, shrimp, and sausage from the cart.

"Mr. Douglas," Haley said.

"Please, Haley," Huey said, bowing. "My name's Huey. You can use it while we're here."

"Huey," Haley said, a little awkwardly, as if she still didn't feel comfortable calling him that. "Y—You actually work *with* them." She seemed more shocked than she had when the Scientist told her that she was her mom.

"I do what I can," Huey said, tipping his hat.

"And you're my sister," Haley said to Rosalind.

"That's what I've been trying to tell you," Rosalind said with a sigh.

"And that means…" Haley looked at the Scientist who thought she saw tears in Haley's eyes, but it must have been an illusion, Haley wasn't built to do that. "That you're my mother."

The Scientist was, though. And that she did. She didn't make a sound, but she couldn't hold the torrent of tears. "*I am*," she whispered.

"Mom." Haley embraced her as she cried.

"You're her mom?" Ansel said. "But you're so *old*."

Rosalind laughed. The Scientist did, too, while she cried. Then everyone joined in for a chuckle. Even Mr. Kitty meowed.

"Yes, dear," the Scientist said. "But families come in all shapes and sizes."

"*And ages*," Richard added, a hunk of bread stuffed in his mouth.

"And ages," the Scientist repeated, wiping her eyes.

"But you're still gonna get my dad, right?"

"Of course we are, dear," the Scientist said. She looked around. Huey, Rosalind, and even Haley nodded. Richard went on stuffing his face. Mr. Kitty licked himself. "We'll do it together."

Ansel smiled. "We do nothing alone."

ꝗ **End of Book One** ꝗ

Thanks for reading. If you enjoyed that please join us at

www.BryanPerkinsAuthor.com

to keep up to date on future releases in the Infinite Limits series.
And, if you're so inclined, don't forget to leave a review on Amazon,
Goodreads, or any other site you might frequent.
Thanks again, until next time.

-Bryan "with a Y" Perkins

Acknowledgements

First and foremost, I'd like to thank Sophie Kunen for being, if not the first to believe in my writing, the first to convince me she did. I still write between the leather you gave me. This one's for you, as they all are.

Next, I have to say thank you to David Garifo for keeping me sane when I first moved down to New Orleans—which happened to be at the same time I was doing the majority of the heavy lifting on this novel. David's once-every-week-or-two visits were about the only personal interaction I got while living in that attic on Elysian Fields, so thank you, sir, for all you did, and still do, to support my writing in your unique way.

And third, a special thanks goes out to Matt Maresh, the first person other than me to actually read this thing through all the way to the end. This version's a little different than the version you read, Matt, but I don't expect you to read it again. Save your eyes for volume two when I might need the same boost of confidence.

Almost last, but certainly not least, thanks to my parents, Mom and Dad, for teaching me that I can be anything in the world I want, and my brothers, Tor Tor and Rob, for believing in me when I thought I could be everything.

And finally, thank you readers. I hope you enjoyed reading this as much as I did writing it, and I hope you'll join me again in volume two. Always remember:

We do nothing alone.